THE WARRIORS OF WIWO'OLE

The Fourth Book
of Dubious Magic

For Roland and Rosco – mahalo

and for Meredith – my pomaikai

With thanks to all my supporters at www.Patreon.com/Renoir
- especially Tegan McKechnie

THE WARRIORS OF WIWO'OLE
Copyright © 2017 Renoir
All rights reserved.

ISBN: 978-0-9946175-0-7

Published by *Meredian Pictures & Words 2017*
Angels Beach, Australia

CONTENTS

CONTENTS (CONTINUED)

1 PATIENCE

It was a young land, as lands go. Its history of human habitation was brief by the standards of much of the world. The people who lived there now were of a variety of races from around the globe. Those who considered themselves the original inhabitants had perhaps a scant few hundred years start on the most recent arrivals.

Compared with much of the Earth, the footprint of man still rested quite lightly on the land. It hadn't been mined, and it still possessed a greater percentage of its scant natural resources than many other places.

There were still those who loved and respected the land, and who took from it only what they thought the land could sustain. In return, the land, while it wore several faces, remained beautiful and welcoming.

This land still had patience.

*

Patience. It required patience to train young minds. Even more to find the right ones – ones that could be guided into paths less travelled.

Some seemed promising. Some were malleable, but lacked the drive to sustain their own momentum. Some had fire, but perhaps too much. Their passion obscured their focus.

Professor Ritter looked at the meticulous card index of past students. The lecturer would not trust his private observations to a computer system. He was well aware of how secure even the best of those systems weren't.

With a fingertip he delicately raised one card partially out of the index. He pondered the name.

"A prospect," he mused aloud.

Of course, they were all prospects to a greater or lesser extent. But he was quietly confident that this one would make a difference. If not, there would be others. Unlike some of his colleagues, the man called Ritter was patient.

*

Patience. The gradual assemblage of materials and equipment as opportunity and discretion would permit took time. Move too fast, do too much all at once, and there was too great a risk of being noticed. Flying under the radar required a knack.

The careful extraction of volatile chemicals from otherwise harmless sources could not be rushed either. The mind, the eyes and the hands were steady.

Getting some proportions wrong could mean a finished product with little or no effect, and that would mean time and resources wasted. Getting other proportions wrong, or handling them carelessly, might have more catastrophic effects. That would also be a waste, in so many ways.

Better to be as careful as possible. The cause was just. It had history, tradition and faith behind it. It was worth being patient.

*

Patience. Harlan B. Hunter was used to waiting. It routinely took months to gain official permission to access archaeological sites across the world. His next project, in the far south of the Pacific Ocean, would be no different. Even politically stable governments could be beset by bureaucratic red tape – sometimes even more so than those with a revolving door of revolutionary rulers.

In the meantime, he was content to wait at home. He was especially content now that a new beloved enriched his life. This too was a benefit of patience, he reflected.

As much as he had enjoyed previous relationships, he could see now that the best of them had in truth been friendships. Albeit with very pleasant benefits in some cases.

Even the less successful relationships had taught lessons about trust and self-awareness. He had learned about recognizing his own and others' values.

Quite recently time had brought him to the woman who, they both quickly realised, was his true soulmate.

When time brings you a gift like that, he reasoned, that was evidence of the value of patience.

Patience. The esteemed businessman sighed. It was another of the inter-
minable social events that he was obliged to attend.

"Yes, Tanabe-*san*. No Tanabe-*san*. As you say, Tanabe-*san*. If I may
make a small request, Tanabe-*san*…?" All very respectful, and as shallow
as a puddle, he knew.

Being owner of the company should mean being able to avoid such
events he thought, but that was not the way of the strict Japanese society.
Although it would never be said aloud, as long as he was in the country
Hiro Tanabe would be expected to represent the business at the functions
that were where the real deals were done.

He smiled as he accepted a glass of wine – a delicate elderberry ice wine,
a local product he was both proud and fond of. The woman who handed
him the drink was tall and graceful. In younger days she had been an out-
standingly beautiful model, more than deserving of the name she had adopted. Shareta, meaning 'stylish'. At a small margin over fifty (she didn't
identify the margin and nobody asked) she was still more than striking.

Nonetheless, as she had walked across the room to him she had attracted
many thinly veiled looks of disapproval. She seemed oblivious to them,
but inwardly he winced on his wife's behalf.

As if sensing his thoughts Shareta laid a gentle hand on his arm and
winked.

"Ignore them, as I do. We shall be away soon," she said softly.

"Indeed, *ma pomaikai*," Hiro replied. "Thanks to your talent. In the
meantime, I know – have patience."

*

Patience. Carlos Calvera was not particularly well-endowed with that
virtue, but he was managing to keep a tight reign on his feelings.

"You have done your part, *mi amigo*," he said warmly. "Now trust me to
do mine."

His companion Hector scowled over his beer and replied, "There is no
need for you to do anything. I have won the tournament. I will win the
next one. I will establish myself in the United States…"

"Exactly! And as you do so, I will ensure that our business grows and thrives."

Hector didn't answer. He cast a glowering look around the clubhouse. He sneered at the backs of the motley collection of ex-pats from around the world making up the regular clientele.

Carlos swallowed his irritation and was silent. He knew that while they were both ruthlessly ambitious men, the paths of their ambitions were not necessarily the same. But they were useful to each other, and when opportunity presented itself, well – Senora Calvera's youngest son was able to be a patient man.

*

Patience. Keep the head still. Check the alignments: feet, shoulders, and eyes. Don't bunch the muscles.

Make the movement slow and even – don't rush anything. Steady backswing but not too far! Gauge the distance, that's it. Now release the arms…

Good sound. Crisp.

The ball runs well. Has she read the green right? Yes!

Thirteen feet up a gentle slope, so shallow you wouldn't spot it if you didn't take the time to look closely. Then a sharp little bank left, accelerating the last two feet and cleanly into the cup.

Glexie Hill smiled. She knew her putting game was her biggest weakness, but she was confident it was getting better. An hour of concentrated practice after work every night was showing steady improvement. She could win the tournament next week – she knew it.

An escape from the New Hampshire routine to the delights of Hawaii beckoned. All it took was practice and patience.

*

Patience. There is an energy that moves in the world. All things are made of it and all things are moved by it. It has many names, such as qi and chi.

In Hawaii it is called *mana*.

There are those, it is said, who have the ability to control this energy. Perhaps it is this manipulation which some people call 'magic'.

The *mana* doesn't care what it's called. It is patient.

.o0o.

2 FAREWELL TO A FRIEND

It was an inappropriately sunny morning in the leafy Canberra suburb of Waramanga.

A shaggy haired man knelt by the low branches of the spreading bush and laid his hand on the bare, recently turned earth.

"Thanks old friend. For… well… lots of things. For saving my life – maybe – more than once, eh? For being my mate."

Another man and a woman stood watching in the doorway of the small cottage. The man looked up at his brunette companion and gave a little sigh.

"There was a time when I would have laughed at being upset about a cat dying. Well, not laughed. But I wouldn't have, you know, *got* it," he said.

She nodded. "And now you do," she replied.

"Not entirely. But I know enough to respect it. Kat was in Central Australia with us, when all that… weirdness happened. He was… good." His mind's eye replayed images of the cat attacking a rogue gun-toting American colonel, and later, in some way he really didn't understand, helping stop an insane homicidal archaeologist.

"What *did* happen on that trip?"

"A complicated story. A couple of complicated stories, actually. Strange, dangerous stuff."

The brunette raised her eyebrows. "Worse than what we've just been through on Mundara? Held as prisoners and nearly killed by crazy Russians?"

There was a shrug in response. "Maybe not worse."

A tall thin young man came out of the cottage kitchen to join the pair watching the kneeling figure.

"Kettle's boiled. Ready for coffee?" he asked.

"Thanks Darren," said the woman. "Come on, Wilko. Let's go in."

The young man quietly stepped out into the garden. "You want a coffee, John?" he asked softly.

The man who had called the cat his mate stood up and smiled. He grasped Darren's arm briefly and said, "You did well, old buddy, burying him there. Coffee sounds good, thanks."

Soon the four were sitting around the large dining table. Nobody had their legs actually under the table, due to a peculiar circumstance.

The table had for some months now been doing service as Darren's bedroom.

Darren Bond was the younger brother of an old University drinking buddy of John B. Stewart. When he had first arrived at the cottage his host assumed he was there temporarily, to attend a role-playing convention. It turned out though that the young man had travelled from Brisbane to Canberra in search of work, and hadn't realised that his old friend's abode only had one bedroom, that was not going to be shared. They were close, but not that close.

Rather than send Darren back north, or wish him luck with trying to find affordable rental accommodation in Canberra when he didn't have a job, John B. had found an unorthodox but effective solution.

A mattress went onto the floor under the fortunately big dining table. A couple of tablecloths draped down as 'walls', supplemented by piles of books and some boxes of the assorted weaponry Darren collected.

And so the four of them sat 'side-on' to the table, savouring their coffee.

Three of them had only just returned to Canberra from Melbourne. Wilko (christened Robert Wilkes, but even his parents in Tasmania rarely called him that any more) and Elizabeth Dance had rescued John B. from a secret laboratory on a tiny island off the south coast, without ever really understanding the whys and wherefores of the whole situation.

Stewart had tried to explain the little he knew himself but Wilko in particular didn't want to know. He'd shared many of the perils that had recently beset John B., understood none of them, and had had enough of what he called "dangerous bloody weirdness".

Darren hadn't had the chance to ask many questions since they'd arrived at the cottage. All of them had been preoccupied with Kat's passing. The big white Persian had been more than important to John B. – often described as 'his best mate'. It was a description neither Darren nor Wilko begrudged.

The young man continued to contain his curiosity. It was his research that had enabled Elizabeth and Wilko to find and rescue John B., but he was content that he could talk to his housemate later when the others left.

After draining his coffee and offering some sincere words of support to John B. Wilko announced he was off to the golf club.

"There's a special tournament on today. A Strokeplay Challenge, but only open to those of us with handicaps of ten or up. Trying to give the mugs a go at something I suppose," the Tasmanian explained. "You ought to come, John. Take your mind off things. Some travel company is sponsoring it and they've put up some good prizes apparently. Probably a tax dodge."

Sometimes the man couldn't help being cynical. That didn't mean he wasn't right, which is one of the worst things about being cynical. Or one of the best things if you really enjoy your cynicism.

Stewart smiled and declined the suggestion.

"My handicap's certainly high enough, but there's a good reason for that.

My golf is rubbish at the best of times, mate, even when I *am* feeling competitive," he said, and Wilko nodded. "And I don't reckon I'm any chance of concentrating today. You go have fun. I wish you the best of luck for the tournament!"

Darren grinned and said, "That ought to make you a winner, mate!"

"You know what I reckon about 'magic'," replied Wilko sternly, but he smiled as he continued, "Thanks for the thought though, both of you."

Ever since John B. hit his head on a poker machine months earlier his wishes had been coming true. Not always in a way that he'd had in mind, but he was sure that he was a wizard. There weren't many other people who agreed. Darren was one who did. Wilko emphatically was not.

As Wilko made for the door Elizabeth also finished her coffee and stood up.

"I'd better make tracks too," she said. "I just dropped my bag off at the unit and came straight over here without unpacking. I'd really better go and do something about that."

"How's the single life coming along, Q?" John B. enquired politely.

'Q' was the nickname the wizard had coined for Elizabeth some time earlier. It was something only the two of them shared. In recent weeks Q had left her unsupportive controlling husband Sonny and moved into a small unit not far from the Waramanga cottage.

"I'm getting used to it. It's nice to be able to make decisions for myself – what to wear, what to eat, what to watch on TV. I'd forgotten how good English crime dramas are."

"What were Sonny's viewing tastes?"

"Sport on weekends. So-called 'reality' bloody television."

"Plenty of sport on the TV here," Darren said mildly. If he objected he wasn't going to make it obvious.

Stewart winced. "Not that other rubbish though. I've got enough weirdness in my own reality, never mind whatever it is some loon in a network office dreams up. I don't see the attraction."

"For Sonny it's the women. The less they wear the better."

Darren shrugged at John B. who smiled sympathetically at Q and said, "Some people don't know how lucky they are, mate."

The wizard walked the green-eyed brunette to the cottage door.

"I'll see you at work on Monday, pretty lady," he said.

"You're coming in?" she asked in some surprise.

"Sure. Why not?"

"Well, after everything that happened on Mundara… I thought you might… or you might not…"

The wizard took her hand in both of his. "I'm feeling okay," he said. "Whatever that mad scientist Solovyev did to me – well – it's passed. All that's left is memory. What about you? That ugly goon of his had a go at you didn't he?"

Elizabeth's smile flickered for a moment. She was thinking of a vicious kick that had left no bruise but had hurt. Hurt a lot.

"Nothing permanent. Nothing like the bastard got in return." The Russian thug had been killed, if not deliberately then certainly without regret, then his body incinerated.

She laid her other hand on top of John B.'s and continued, "Like you – I'm okay. Just memories. See you in the office. So long Darren!"

"Bye Elizabeth!" was the reply called from the discreet distance of the lounge room.

There was a final mutual squeezing of hands before Q turned and walked away to her small car.

John B. watched the little vehicle depart up the tree-lined street, then turned and walked back inside.

Darren was already on the couch as the wizard sank into his favourite overstuffed armchair.

"So – 'Q'? Does she make dangerous exploding gadgets in her spare time?" enquired the young housemate.

Stewart smiled. "You know, that never occurred to me. It makes sense that you'd think of it though!"

Darren's full name was Darren James Bond. He sometimes regretted that he didn't look like a debonair master spy.

The wizard continued, "Elizabeth's maiden name is McKew. Q's just a contraction of that. I'm the only person who calls her it, I think. The only one allowed to, I suspect."

"That sounds good. So are you two…?" Darren sought a tactful term.

John B. shook his head. "She's only just gotten away from a relationship that was a whole lot messier than any of us realised, mate. We're just good friends."

Darren opened his mouth to reply, but closed it again. He'd seen first hand just how concerned Elizabeth had been when John B. had disappeared in Melbourne, and how she'd taken charge of finding him. If his old friend wasn't admitting to anything more than 'just friends' between them, well, that was his business. His and hers, perhaps.

"I think there's cricket on the telly. Mind if I watch?"

It was a measure of John B.'s respect that he asked, his young friend realised, given that the wizard owned the place.

"Of course not. Better that than a reality show, hey?"

 They shared a laugh. "Spare me from reality!" said Stewart. "It's far too dangerous!"

.o0o.

3 STARTERS CALL

It was some hours later – the sun was sliding down past the western horizon – when the phone in the cottage hallway rang.

Darren was closest, and got to the jangling instrument with a couple of strides of his long legs before it had time to frustratingly stop.

"Hello? Oh, hi Wilko! What? Hey, that's great! I told you didn't I? Okay, okay… Hang on, I'll go get him."

After resting the receiver across its cradle he returned to the lounge room. "It's Wilko calling from the golf club. He won the tournament! He's pretty excited – I don't think he's quite sober."

"I don't bloody blame him!" said John B., enthusiastically jumping up from his chair and going to the phone.

"Wilko! Well done old lad! I told you… yes, yes, all credit to you, mate. I just wished you well, you're the one playing the shots. Four birdies, no bogeys? Bravo mate, well done indeed. Outright winner! So what's the prize?"

Darren heard Stewart go suddenly quiet, and then whistle softly.

"Wow, that's impressive. Ten days in Hawaii. What? This was a qualifying tournament? Cool! When's the big… What? Jeez, they don't give you much time to get organized, do they? Alright, alright."

There was another spell of silence in the cottage as Wilko bounced between excited descriptions of the last few holes and fretting about the organization needed to get to the event in Hawaii.

When he stopped for breath John B. was able to say, "You should talk to Elizabeth when you get to work on Monday. She's brilliant at organizing stuff like that. And she'll be chuffed at your winning! Now listen, enjoy yourself there tonight, and don't drive home, okay? I'd come and pick you up, but well, you know…"

Wilko did indeed know that Stewart's faithful old Hillman Hunter had been mysteriously blown up some time earlier. He didn't know why, but the car's erstwhile owner had never completely understood either.

"Now, have a couple of drinks for me and… sorry, what? A trip for two? Who – no, don't be daft, mate. You don't owe me… Wilko, you did *not* abandon me in Melbourne. You weren't to know what had happened. And you came back looking for me, remember? I… okay, okay. Thank you. Seriously, thank you. We can talk about it on Monday. Go enjoy yourself now, hey? And remember, a taxi home! Great! Thanks, mate, you too. Have fun!"

John B.'s expression was slightly bemused as he sat back in his chair. "Wishing him luck worked, eh?" said Darren happily.

"I don't think it hurt. He'd never admit it, although there was a brief mention of a rebound off a tree and up onto a green. He wants me to go to Hawaii with him though."

"Cool! When?"

"In a bit over three weeks. Time enough to organize visas or whatever. Good thing I've got a passport. I presume Wilko has, too."

"What's your boss going to say?"

"Hmm… well, I reckon it's a good thing Ron's a golfer too. At least he'll get how big this is for Wilko. Just as long as he wasn't playing in the same tournament!" John B. smiled as he got up from the chair again.

"I reckon this calls for a drink," he said. "Rum and orange?"

"Great, thanks!" replied Darren.

Minutes later, glasses were raised – rum and orange in a tall glass, a hearty measure of good single malt whisky in a tumbler. Both men grinned as the wizard toasted, "To beautiful Hawaii!"

*

Eight thousand kilometres or so across the Pacific, another phone call was taking place.

"Excuse the lateness of the hour, please, Professor Ritter. I am – troubled – and need to talk with you."

"Ah! Good evening. I was only thinking about you recently. No apology is necessary. Have I not said that for you my door is always open, my telephone ever available? That is not idle politeness."

"I appreciate that sir – more than you can know."

'I doubt that', mused Ritter to himself before replying, "You said that you are troubled."

There was the sound of a deep breath being taken down the phone.

"You know I had plans, Professor. Not plans – intentions. I shouldn't call them plans if they aren't detailed, should I? But something's happened over here. Something I've got to do something about."

The professor winced at the sentence structure. It wasn't language that he taught, though.

"Do you wish to explain this 'thing' to me? It is evidently important."

"No. No need for you to know, sir. It's not important, not at all really, but it's what it represents… It's made me realize, it's time. Time I started taking action."

"So 'it' has given impetus to your intentions. That is a good thing, surely?"

The response was rushed, "Professor, people will die!"

"It is the nature of people that they die. No one can change that. The question is, what can that death achieve?"

There were other questions of course, but Ritter was not about to put them.

"Yes, yes," came his caller's voice. "What will be achieved. Thank you Professor. I wasn't having doubts, not really. But the step – from intention to action…"

"Requires courage in your convictions. I have never thought that you lacked that."

"Thank you, Professor. I…"

Ritter interrupted, "What I would counsel, as I have ever done, is caution. Beware of the lure of the grand gesture – too much too soon. A mountain is best conquered in careful stages, not at a run. The true grandeur is in that final conquest. Each milestone along the way is a little victory to be savoured but never mistaken for the ultimate objective."

There was a thoughtful silence.

"Yes sir. Thank you. I appreciate your… reassurance. Calm. Certain. And cautious – yes, Professor, I know how to be cautious."

There was a soft click. As the line went dead Professor Ritter leaned back and smiled.

Patience.

.oOo.

4 THAT'S A BIG CALL

Nearly two weeks had passed.

Wilko had managed to rein in his excitement, and done some 'due diligence' checking that his travel prize had been approved by the relevant golfing authorities and wouldn't affect his amateur status.

Even if he won the event in Hawaii, (unlikely as he thought it) it seemed that the promoters had somehow arranged it so that the value of the prize was technically not enough to get the winner into trouble. Accountancy was his long suit, not law, but the Tasmanian had made enough phone calls to be satisfied without needing to know the fine details.

John B. sat in his favourite armchair considering his options. It was a weekday morning, Darren had left for the early shift in a new coffee shop (the '*Has Beans*') and in theory he should be leaving for the office. But with his newfound financial security he certainly didn't need to be there. That was where his thoughts were going. In all honesty he knew he'd really only worked because he enjoyed the company, and didn't feel that he had anything better to do.

Even before his magical powers first manifested themselves he probably could have found other options had he been particularly inclined. But he'd managed to make it a low-pressure job.

A few drinks at lunch and after work, enjoy the company of some good people, some of whom he'd become close to – what more did he need?

But in that last two weeks he'd realised he felt a change. Not just the buzzing in his head that seemed to be a symptom of the magic – he'd become quite used to that. It was something more. He'd been turning up and doing his job, but with even less enthusiasm than ever.

The looming prospect of Hawaii was exciting. The golf he could take or leave, but he was looking forward to the place itself. The venue was to be the Big Island, the Hawaii that gave its name to the whole State.

Kat died curled up on an atlas open at a map of the world – was that a message?

His fingers traced a distracted pattern on the cover of the new mobile phone that sat on the arm of the chair.

Yes, John B. now had a mobile phone – at Elizabeth's insistence. "After your disappearing act in Melbourne," she'd said.

"That wasn't my fault. And I doubt Doctor Solo and his friends would have let me call anyone if I *had* had a phone!" he'd protested.

"No, but we could have tried calling you, and known something was wrong a lot sooner."

Her logic was reasonable, and her concern appreciated. And Stewart had recognised that it was simply a good idea to not argue with Q when she was determined.

Still, he didn't have to use it any more than necessary. He stood up and stretched. With something like a purposeful stride he went out into the hall to use the old-fashioned phone there. He dialed the number for his boss, Ron Kaiser.

Kaiser Ron, as he was popularly known among his staff, had in recent times been feeling that he was losing his grip on the team he managed. They'd always been an eccentric bunch admittedly, and perhaps there wasn't that much grip to lose. When nobody was listening he'd quietly concede that they were most efficient and productive without a tight rein.

John B. Stewart had always been one of the least disciplined of his staff. Capable enough, Ron thought – more than capable if a task piqued his interest. But otherwise he seemed to have the attention span of a small child. Not that Ron knew much about small children.

But since the unfortunate business in Melbourne that he'd never quite understood (although Elizabeth seemed to have sorted it out and he was happy to leave details to her) Stewart was even less focused than usual.

Now his 'loose cannon' was on the phone, asking for yet more time off.

"I appreciate your approving the two weeks off to go to Hawaii with Wilko, Ron…"

"Yes, well, I couldn't really stand in the way of an opportunity like that for him. Wish I'd have known about the tournament myself – I might have had a crack at it. Nuisance to be losing him again, but in fairness he's not taken much leave before, so he's entitled to it. He's a good work-er."

If John B. noticed that Kaiser Ron's observations were all about his old friend he gave no indication of it.

Instead he continued, "I'd like to take off the next week-and-a-bit before we go. Use the time to arrange stuff so Wilko can stay at work without fretting. It's what a good caddy should do, eh?"

In truth, there was little to arrange. The company sponsoring the event seemed to have organized most everything. But it was a convenient ex-cuse.

Ron raised his eyebrows. The caddying angle was an interesting way of considering it. Still, if it meant not losing the productive Tasmanian…

"Alright, John, you do that. Ah – it might have to be leave without pay."

"Okay. Fair enough," replied Stewart with absolutely no demur.

Now the boss looked concerned. That was far too casual a response to the prospect of losing ten days' income. He certainly wouldn't have ac-cepted it so readily himself. "John, is everything… all right?"

There was a brief silence as his errant employee evidently wrestled with some deep thought before saying, "Yeah… yes, thanks Ron. Sorry I hav-en't been quite with it since I got back from Melbourne."

"Yes, well, I don't know exactly what went on there, but I do realise I owe you a bit of an apology. I gather you weren't well, and I'm afraid I – er – assumed the worst." By which he meant, like others he'd assumed Stewart had gone on a bit of a binge and had passed out in a pool of Scotch somewhere.

  John B. smiled. It would be difficult to explain exactly what had gone on in the laboratory of the mad Russian scientist Konstantin Solovyov.

"Not to worry. As you say, I wasn't well. Not quite myself, as the saying goes. Apology accepted, and appreciated, though. But frankly the whole thing has left me wondering about my future. I'm not sure I'm cut out to be a career Public Servant, are you?"

"Ah, well… actually, probably not," said Kaiser Ron with an awkward faint attempt at diplomacy.

  They both grinned, and even down the phone probably each knew the other's expression.

"Anyway," said John B., "I think a couple of weeks of peace and quiet in beautiful Hawaii should give me the chance to think everything through. I reckon when I get back you'll get me back to my best…"

  Kaiser Ron suppressed a waspish reply.

"…or I'll drop in to pack up my desk."

.o0o.

5 AND THEY'RE OFF

Q had offered to drive both John B. and Wilko to the airport. Wilko had declined the offer, suspecting (rightly) that three people, two lots of luggage, and a large loaded golf bag would be too much for her little two-door car.

"I'll get a taxi," the Tasmanian had said. "Anyway, you'd be going in the wrong direction to pick me up."

So the brunette had only the wizard to chauffer, and with her usual organizational efficiency had arrived at the airport half an hour before check-in had opened.

"Better that than arriving late," she said as she pulled up outside the terminal. "Should I park and wait with you?"

John B. smiled. "It's a nice idea," he said, "But parking here's not cheap. Wilko won't be long. As much as I'd enjoy your company, pretty lady…"

They sat there, each returning the other's smile. The moment was shattered by the shrill blare of a car horn. The driver of a shiny new red Alfa-Romeo was demanding that Q's car move along and make more room for him.

Stewart sighed. "Time I was off," he said.

He grabbed her hand and squeezed it, then pressed her fingers to his lips. "Thank ya, ma'am," he drawled.

"Y'all are welcome, kind sir," she replied in kind.

Pointedly ignoring the Alfa driver, John B. took his trusty kit bag from the boot of the small car. "I'll ring you," he called through to Q, patting the new mobile phone in his pocket.

"International roaming is expensive," she shouted back.

"I reckon you're worth it. But I got one of those SIM cards that claim to work anywhere in the world."

"My, haven't we gone technological all of a sudden?" she laughed.

"Don't tell anyone. I asked the girl at the phone shop!"

The Alfa horn blared – a long blast as the driver leaned on it.

"Better go," said the wizard. "I wish this clown would get lost."

John B. and Q waved their farewells. As her car pulled away he blew a kiss after her, not knowing she'd seen him in the mirror and returned the gesture. The wizard strolled into the terminal grinning broadly, taking absolutely no notice of the angry Lothario who kangaroo-hopped his Alfa into the space vacated by Q's car.

An expensively dressed girl emerged from the passenger's seat, unimpressed by her soon-to-be-ex-boyfriend's petulance. She fetched her own luggage from the back of the flashy red car, which quickly sped away. No exchange of fond parting gestures there.

The Alfa driver stomped his foot on the accelerator and the car lurched forward. For reasons known only to the makers of the complex circuitry, the onboard computer gave the electronic equivalent of a violent sneeze.

The satellite navigation system reconfigured itself. Instead of racing off to a dirty little rendezvous in Sydney the driver, automatically following the instructions of the mechanical voice as usual, eventually arrived, confused and angrier than ever, in a paddock somewhere north of Gundegai.

Meanwhile, John B. sat in the airport bar, looking into a shot of single malt and pondering his future. He wished for things and they happened. Not always predictably, or in the way he might have had in mind, but they happened.

When his magical powers first manifested, after he'd drunkenly run his head into a poker machine, he'd tried telling his friends and workmates that he'd developed a magical gift. Almost all of them offered responses in the range between 'amusement' and 'derision'.

That was one reason that he'd stopped talking about it.

The other was that since his powers had appeared, he'd found himself in a succession of weird and dangerous situations. He'd come into conflict with a deranged sorceress, a rogue Army colonel, a professor who used human sacrifice to invoke an ancient sea god, and a Russian scientist who kept himself alive with machines that drained the life energies of other people.

He'd been shot at, drugged, almost blown up, tied down, knocked around, injected with snake venom... He'd survived it all, obviously, and maybe that was to do with the magic. But would he have been in those situations without it?

John B. gazed into the depths of the whisky. He wasn't a man often given to introspection, although he enjoyed his own company. He'd quite enjoyed the relatively simple life of a Canberra Public Servant before he'd "hit his head", but notwithstanding his conversation with Kaiser Ron, somehow he knew he wouldn't be going back to it for long, if he went back at all.

He certainly didn't need the income. The experience with the Russian had left him with exclusive access to a more than substantial Swiss account containing enough funds for a long and comfortable lifestyle.

He'd often said that he only went to work for the company, but he was realising that friends were friends, whether you saw them regularly or not. The ones worth preserving, anyway. His best mates would remain his best mates regardless of if he sat at a desk near theirs or not. And the one who might be more than that - well, time would tell, wouldn't it?

He replayed their little farewell. He could wish… No. That was too unpredictable, too dangerous. And somehow, he sensed, not right. He couldn't say how, but instinctively he knew that the magic shouldn't be used for his own gain. Not a significant emotional or financial gain, at least. That might fall out of what he did, but it shouldn't be a deliberate ploy.

The scotch was finished in a mouthful. John B. looked around the airport bar. Still no sign of the man he was looking for, so he ordered another drink.

“I wish Wilko would hurry up and get here,” he said to himself, knowing as he did that his Tasmanian mate would soon arrive. After all, he was the

one who’d won the chance to live out a dream and play in a golf tournament in Hawaii. ‘Mind you’, mused the wizard, ‘I don’t think that this wish will hurt...’

.o0o.

6 NOW ARRIVING

The Hawaiian Islands sit in splendid isolation in the middle of the Pacific Ocean, over 2000 miles from the nearest continent.

Hundreds of individual islands make up the 50th State of the USA, although only seven of these are regarded as significantly inhabited.

The most populous of them is Oahu. That's where the State capital Honolulu is. Waikiki. The legendary surf at Waimea Bay. Setting for film and television: Elvis to Steve McGarrett, *Jurassic Park* to *Gilligan's Island*.

It's also where Honolulu International Airport is the hub of flights to and from all over the world: Asia, Europe, Australia and of course North America.

Hiro Tanabe could have easily afforded to upgrade the seats that Shareta had been allocated as part of the prize for winning the tournament in Kobe. The couple had agreed not to, though. Neither liked ostentation or fuss. By avoiding First Class, or worse – Business Class, they felt there was less chance of Tanabe-san being recognised and pestered by the type of people he longed to be away from.

Shareta of course still attracted second looks, wherever on the plane she travelled. Many were admiring, drawn to her height and grace. A few were looks of uncertain recognition from her modeling past. And still some were disapproving – a small number even contemptuous. There were still those who thought that Koreans should be kept segregated from proper Japanese society, as indeed should all those of inferior race. Old prejudices still persisted.

Two who tried not to let their reactions show on their faces were another pair on the same flight to attend the same golf tournament. Seated well away from the Tanabes they said little to each other or anyone else, evidently content to pore through a succession of golf magazines and business journals, and watch finance programs on the in-flight service.

Dark haired Takafumi Makkuro had won a qualifying tournament at a club just outside Tokyo. He wore a black and grey polo shirt and slacks. His silver haired companion Shigekiyo Yuki wore an outfit of similar design, but in tones of white and cream. It was an odd habit that the two men had fallen into over several years of friendship. They had been business associates even longer.

Yuki's silver hair was misleading – he was the younger of the two, and neither was remotely elderly. His hair had simply changed colour quite early in life, rather to his chagrin.

Other flights, other competitors, arrived throughout the day. From England came a gentleman and the man he worked for. Two girls flew in from the north east coast of the USA, and a couple who'd endured a journey from Texas that they were sure had been made as complicated as possible just to spite them.

All had made their way through International Arrivals, gone on to the Domestic terminal and caught their inter-island flights to the real destination – the airport at Kona. That was on Hawaii itself – the Big Island that gave the State its name, and which was the venue for the golf tournament they were all attending.

The flight from Madrid had been stuck circling in a holding pattern.

Carlos Calvera was actually quite pleased at this turn of events. He'd been enjoying an in-flight movie and had thought he'd be missing the ending. Another example of things working out right for him!

His companion Hector Fernandez, winner of the Malaga tournament on the Spanish tourist coast, was irritated at the delay. It didn't take a lot to irritate Hector. So his mood wasn't helped after landing in Honolulu when a Customs officer approached him and said, "You've got balls, sir?"

"*Que?*"

"You are Mr. Fernandez? Hector Fernandez?"

"*Si*. What of it?"

"Just a question, sir. Something a little odd in the routine check of your inbound baggage."

Hector looked peeved. Carlos, close at hand, kept his face neutral. He was a very good poker player.

"Odd, *senor*?" asked the expressionless man.

The officer continued to address Fernandez. "You're bringing golf equipment into the country, correct?"

"*Si*. Of course. I am here to play in a tournament on your Big Island."

"Ah, a tournament. Lots of practice, I suppose. That explains it."

The Spanish golfer scowled. "Explains what?"

"We had thought that there was an unusually high number of golf balls in your bag. But if you're here as a tournament player… Still, you could have bought some here."

Hector looked haughty. It came naturally to him. But it was Carlos who answered. "*Senor* Fernandez prefers to practice using the same equipment that he uses in competition, *si*? And he is kind enough to bring plenty so his poor caddy is not running back and forth returning the balls he has struck. I gather all of them up at the end of a practice session."

The Customs officer looked thoughtful. "I guess that makes sense. I don't play the game myself."   He looked down at the document he held. "Your bag is checked through to Kona. Good luck in the tournament, Mr. Fernandez. Sorry sir, I'm afraid I didn't recognise your name."

"It is our hope that soon you will, *senor*. *Gracias*!" Carlos smiled genially at the officer.

Hector managed a polite nod before the Spaniards turned to go and catch their inter-island flight. The Customs man didn't see the baleful glare the golfer gave his companion, who only shrugged in response.

The last to get to Honolulu was the plane from Australia bearing Wilko and John B. The flight from Canberra to Sydney had been on time, but departure on the big international leg of the journey had been delayed, for reasons that were never clearly explained. Stewart considered wishing he knew why, but then decided he might sleep better if he didn't know.

The two Australians' luggage was among the first to appear on the airport carousel, which Wilko took as reasonable recompense for the aggravation of the delayed departure.

He was disappointed though when they walked out into the Customs area to find they'd got there just after a sizeable crowd of Asian tourists. Wilko couldn't tell what country they were from, and frankly didn't care. All he knew was that they would slow the process of getting through to catch the connecting flight to the Big Island.

John B. heard his companion's impatient muttering and sympathized. "I wish this crowd weren't in our way," he said.

There were signs on all the walls of the Customs Hall instructing 'No photographs!', not just in English but also in four other languages. For emphasis, each sign had the large distinctive picture of a camera behind the red circle and diagonal line that should be universally understood in any language.

One woman in the group was either ignoring or oblivious to the signs, and was taking lots of pictures on her mobile phone. Perhaps it was be-cause the image on the sign was of a real camera, not a phone, she thought there was a difference. Or perhaps she was one of those people who think such instructions don't apply to them.

Either way, a uniformed Customs officer made several attempts to reason with the woman in English, Japanese and sign language to no avail. She went so far as to reach around him and take more photos, apparently be-rating him for being in her way.

That was the last straw for the officer who seized her phone and took it from her hand with just enough force to still be considered 'reasonable'.

"Madam, you have been warned! I am hereby confiscating this device!" he bellowed in a voice that echoed around the hall even above the babble of tourist voices.

The woman started to beat ineffectually at the Customs man's chest, shrieking at him so shrilly that it was hard to determine her language, never mind what she was actually saying.

"I think it's something like: 'Don't you know who I am?' – that's pretty standard for things like this," observed Wilko, annoyed at the impending further delay.

"Indeed," nodded John B. sagely. "It's terrible when people forget themselves like that. I do hope someone recognizes her."

Evidently many people did. It seemed that she was some sort of celebrity in her own country, and almost the entire crowd were either the woman's entourage or her fans. Suddenly the Customs officer was swamped as the crowd swarmed around him, protesting loudly at the affront to their heroine. Whistles blew and other officials rushed to the aid of their beleaguered colleague. They really only added to the small riot.

Walking calmly and deliberately around the melee, Wilko and John B. lined up politely behind the three other people left in the queue. The Tasmanian steadfastly refused to look at the expression on his companion's face. He was sure it would be a smug smile.

The wizard's little smile wasn't quite smug, but he was clearly pleased at how the magic had worked out this time.

"Next stop, Kona," he said happily.

"Look out, the Big Island," added Wilko.

.o0o.

33

7 WELCOME TO HAWAII

The inter-island flight was quick and quite comfortable. John B. had discovered that his favourite form of in-flight entertainment was to plug a decent set of earphones into the plane's music system, close his eyes, and lose himself in rock star fantasies.

Wilko preferred to read. The airline magazine was giving him some appreciation of the scenic beauty of their destination. That was good. He didn't really think he had a big chance of winning the tournament – he was surprised enough to have won the qualifier – so he was looking forward to taking a lot of photos.

The Tasmanian was a good photographer, even though he was his own harshest critic. At times when either his swing or his putter (or both) were especially errant he'd consider giving up golf and spending his weekends travelling around taking pictures he might be able to sell.

Of course, then he'd have a good day out on the fairway and The Addiction as he sometimes called it would kick back in. There were times when he envied John's ability to walk away from the game and not miss it. Golf was routinely frustrating, aggravating and demanding. Even the best professional players would say that. It was a constant war against the elements, the course and yourself. But more than a couple of weeks without a club in his hand would set Wilko to pining for the smell of a freshly cut green.

He looked over at his travelling companion, eyes closed and apparently lost in a reverie of playing keyboards and singing for the band Supertramp. Wilko chuckled quietly to himself, amused by the sight of John B.'s fingers playing air piano and his lips moving soundlessly like a mime doing karaoke.

'He does live in his own little world,' mused Wilko to himself, not begrudgingly but with a smile. 'I'm sure he really has got himself convinced about this whole 'magic' nonsense, even.'

John B.'s eyes didn't open but he quite audibly sang the words, "Right, you're bloody well right."

Wilko started – was he reading minds now? No, it was the song. Another bloody coincidence!

*

It wasn't long after that they'd landed and disembarked in Kona.

"There should be someone here to meet us," said Wilko.

"Well, it'll be you they're after, so while you're keeping an eye out for whoever it is, I'll make a phone call," replied John B.

"What time is it in Australia?" asked the Tasmanian in some surprise.

"No idea – I'll have to figure that out later. No, this is a local call."

In response to Wilko's puzzled expression Stewart continued, "I brought Harlan's number with me. I thought it'd be nice to catch up if he's on the island, since he's the only local we know."

Harlan Hunter was an archaeologist who they'd met while on a holiday in Central Australia. The Hawaiian had been the first intended victim of an insane professor who'd tried to turn himself into an ancient Phoenician god. Harlan had been abandoned and left to die of thirst or hunger in an isolated part of the desert.

It was while helping Harlan's pretty English girlfriend Jazz that John B., Wilko and a couple of other friends had gotten caught up in the weird but deadly Phoenician plot. Wilko had taken a particular shine to Jazz, which seemed to be reciprocated. Nor was that apparently diminished when Jazz and Harlan were reunited. The relationship between the English girl and the American man appeared affectionate but casual, all of which left Wilko feeling somewhat uncomfortable.

35

Still, he knew that Stewart and Hunter had seemed to strike up a particular friendship. He was starting to discover that his old friend had studied a

range of subjects over the years, including ancient history. He also knew that he'd been very interested in some meditation techniques the Hawaiian used.

What Wilko didn't realise was that those techniques had been key to Harlan's survival when stranded in the desert, and had also been a great help to John B. when he was held prisoner by the Russian scientist.

"Okay. Yeah. Always good to get tips on what to see from a local, I guess," said Wilko, trying hard to keep any sign of hesitancy out of his voice. Harlan was a nice guy, and he really didn't entertain any serious expectations about Jazz. Happy imaginings maybe, but they could be easily put away. Well, maybe not 'easily', but it could be done.

"Good thought," agreed the wizard. "So you look for our reception committee and I'll ring and see if he's in."

He was.

"Hi John B.!" came the cheery voice down the line. "Really good to hear from you! How're things?"

Stewart briefly explained where he and Wilko were, and why, and then asked if the archaeologist was anywhere nearby.

"We're over in Hilo, on the other side of the island. It's a few hours drive but that's no big deal. Why don't you give me a call when you guys know what your program is? We can arrange a time to come over – maybe dinner after one of the games? Or are you getting some days off?"

"No idea yet, but I'll let you know, mate. You said 'we' – is Jazz here with you?"

"Oh, of course – you wouldn't know! Sorry! No, we went our separate ways not long after that business when we first met you."

"Sorry mate – didn't mean to put my foot in it…"

"Not at all, my friend. We just realised we weren't all that close, after all.
It was very amicable."

John B. smiled. He couldn't imagine Harlan being anything but amicable with anyone – it was a word that fitted him perfectly. And in truth, the relationship between he and Jazz *had* seemed a little lacking in passion. He reframed his question.

"So the 'we' you'll be coming over with is… ?"

"A lovely lady named Haveta. We met at the University when I got back from Australia. She'd joined the staff while I was away. We realised pretty quickly that there was a mutual interest, and well…"

"Life's good?"

"Life is excellent, John B."

"Delighted to hear it! I'm looking forward to meeting her! Ah, Wilko's waving – he must have found our transport. I'll give you a call as soon as I know what we're doing over the next few days."

"I've got your number on my phone now," observed the archaeologist. "I can call you if Haveta or I come up with any ideas of things to see and do."

"Sounds brilliant, mate. Talk soon!"

John B. ended the call, and started pushing the precariously laden luggage trolley over to where Wilko was signaling. Golf clubs, he thought to himself, are bloody awkward things to travel by plane with!

Wilko was standing beside a powerfully built Polynesian woman, wearing a beret knitted in Rastafarian colours. She was taller than the Tasmanian but had to look up slightly to meet John B.'s gaze. That seemed to irk her.

"This is Namakaeha. She'll be our driver while we're here," said Wilko.

"G'day. Nice to meet you," said John B. and extended a hand.

"Yeah, thanks. I'll take the bags. Follow me." So saying, Namakaeha ignored the proffered gesture, stepped between the wizard and the trolley, and set off across the forecourt of the terminal.

Wilko shrugged at his friend and very quietly said as they followed, "Don't take it personally mate.   I got the same sort of warm welcome."

Namakaeha slid open the side door of an 18-seater bus and briskly unloaded the luggage into the rear seats. She started to wheel the trolley away and jerked a thumb at the bus.

"In you get," she said.

"Anyone else we have to make room for, or wait for?" asked Wilko.

"The rest are already here. You're it," replied the driver.

John B. tried another smile and said, "Saved the best till last, eh?"

"Whatever."

"Welcome to the friendly isles," muttered the wizard under his breath as the bus pulled out of the car park.

.oOo.

8 WHO'S WHO

It wasn't a long trip from the airport to the hotel on the outskirts of Kona, but even so the absence of cheerful conversation, or indeed any conversation, from their driver didn't seem to John B. and Wilko to augur well for her company for the next two weeks.

"Still, as long as she keeps us safe I suppose," said Wilko quietly to his companion.

"True enough. You just worry about the driver in your golf bag, eh?"

Wilko groaned mildly at the pun. But things in that department rapidly got worse when they arrived at the *Sun Spot* Motel and met their host and tournament organizer.

He had a perm that failed to disguise the thinning of his brown hair. A smile that was as broad as it was insincere. White pants and shoes, and a shirt that was covered with black outlines of palm trees and volcanoes set against an explosion of reds and yellows.

"Guh-day, as you guys say down your way! Harry Barber. 'Hands On Harry' they call me. Welcome to Kona, it's gonna be a great couple of weeks. A pleasure to have you here. You must be Bobby Wilkes."

The man fairly bounced with energy. John B. managed to liberate his hand that had been grasped and pumped violently.

He used it to point to his left and said, "Wrong bloke."

The tournament-winning golfer held out his hand, arm already tensed to control the vigour of the greeting.

"Robert Wilkes," he said before Harry could finish drawing breath. "Call me Wilko."

"Wilko? Shouldn't your name be Roger, then? Eh, eh? Never mind, pleasure to meet you. Welcome aboard! Get yourselves settled in. Key's at Reception, playing schedule's in your room. Drinks at six – we've got the Function Room to ourselves, dinner at seven. Feel free to mingle, make yourself at home – assuming your home's got a poolside bar, eh?"

Hands On Harry turned on a white rubber heel and strode away to dazzle someone else – preferably female John B. guessed.

Exchanging shrugs the two Australians set off to introduce themselves at the Reception desk and thereafter hopefully catch an hour or two's post-flight snooze before drinks.

It was only a little more than a half hour after collecting the room key that John B. was back at Reception, while Wilko slept soundly upstairs.

The girl at the desk looked puzzled.

"But sir – your room has already been paid for by Mr. Barber," she said.

"Yes, I know, and I appreciate that, but I'd like another room please," repeated John B. patiently.

"Oh! You've got a twin room, and you want a double," she said, dropping her voice discreetly.

John B. shut his eyes and smiled ironically at the picture in his imagination. "No," he replied emphatically. "I'd like my own room. Separate from Mr. Wilkes."

"You don't get on?"

"We get on very well. He's one of the best friends I've ever had. I just don't want to try to sleep in the same room as him, that's all. Do you have any others available?"

"Um…" The girl checked the register. "We've got a nice double room still available for tonight. I don't think Mr. Barber will pay for an extra room though."

Between the lines John B. heard a hint that getting payment from Mr. Barber for the room he already *had* booked would be a challenge.

"That's okay. I'm happy to pay – right now even." He took out the credit card he now kept topped up with funds from the Swiss bank account he'd 'inherited'. "Tell you what, I'll stay in the twin room. Move Mr. Wilkes into the double room – he'll be more comfortable, and that might help his golf game!"

The girl smiled. "That's nice of you, sir," she said.

John B. spent the next half hour on the phone to the various motels listed on their itinerary, trying to make similar arrangements. He was successful in all but two of them.

'Right – Plan B,' he thought to himself. He'd managed to buy a set of the dense earplugs used in especially noisy factories. If he could find a decent bottle of single malt whisky at a convenient liquor store that might provide the necessary adjunct to the ear protectors.

The issue was Wilko's snoring. It was a phenomenon that had attained something like legendary status amongst his friends.

It wasn't the volume that was the most troublesome characteristic, although there was no lack of that. It was the range of sounds produced. Grunts, gurgles, whistles, sighs, squeaks and snorts to name a few – varying wildly in pitch and duration.

"You lie there all night wondering what'll come next," John B. had explained after an early attempt to share a room while travelling with his Tasmanian buddy.

Another colleague who'd tried to sleep in an adjoining room had described it as "almost musical", but then this was a woman who had an album of *Songs Of The Humpback Whales* in her classical CD collection.

The only person known to have been quite undisturbed by Wilko's nocturnal sound effects was the pretty blonde English girl Jazz. She'd spent a night sleeping peacefully in a holding cell adjoining Wilko's in an Alice Springs police station after they'd been falsely accused of drug running. She was unique in quite a few ways, both John B. and Wilko had privately mused, each with their own meanings in mind.

When he was advised of the new arrangement soon after Wilko was quietly delighted at the prospect of a double bed to himself, even if he resolutely refused to acknowledge his snoring. 'Exaggeration' and 'imagination' were the words he usually used in response to anyone else's complaints. He didn't envisage sharing the double bed with anyone – he

was just looking forward to the extra space. Even for a man of his stature, most single beds feel constricted.

*

Shortly after six the two Aussies strolled into the *Sun Spot*'s Function Room. It wasn't big or grand. The walls were decorated with papered-on palm trees and cartoonish hula girls. A table in the middle of the room held some empty glasses, an almost-empty carafe of white wine, a half full jug of something orange that may have some real juice in it, and two more jugs each with a small amount of beer remaining in them.

Eighteen chairs had been placed around the perimeter of the room, thirteen of them already occupied. Hands On Harry Barber was seated in the centre position of the far wall, clearly ready to hold court.

Standing just inside the doorway and smiling through clenched teeth John B. whispered to his friend, "Oh no – it's a circle party!"

Just as they started to step forward two new arrivals shouldered their way between them and strode across to occupy the two empty chairs to the left of the doorway.

"*Buenos dios!*" called Harry with not even a hint of a Spanish accent. He got nods in response.

John B. and Wilko grabbed a glass each and drained the beer jugs. The three remaining vacant chairs were side by side. Wilko chose the middle one. With a grin Stewart sat beside the elegant Asian woman who greeted him with a gracious smile.

As they took their seats, Harry stood and gave the room his best smile. It didn't look truly sincere, but it was his best. He launched into his welcoming speech that, to his credit, he did with no reference to notes.

"Ladies and gentlemen, welcome to Hawaii! I won't wait for Namakaeha to join us – you've all met her anyway and you'll see plenty of her as she drives us around the beautiful Big Island.

Firstly, I'd like to congratulate the great winners of the different tournaments around the world. It's given you the opportunity to play on six of the best golf courses in the world – all here on the wonderful west coast. What's more, it's given you the chance to win your very own great property here in this slice of paradise. I guess I shouldn't use the word 'slice' in front of you golfers, eh, eh?"

  He looked around the room to a mixed reaction. Some polite laughter, some groans (not all of them playful) and a few looks that made it clear that the joke was either unappreciated or unnoticed. He carried on regardless.

"When we get to Keelakekua on Day 3 we'll stop into the great Royal Green Estate so you can get to see just what it is you're playing for. I'm sure you're going to be impressed!

Now I think it's time for some introductions. You all know me – 'Hands On' Harry – I'm here on behalf of the company behind Royal Green. I suppose I'm the boss, but you certainly don't have to call me that! I'll be your tournament organizer and referee, though I'm sure I won't be needed in that capacity. We're all friends here, or at least I'm absolutely sure we all will be by the end of the week. I hail from beautiful downtown Venice Beach, just out of Los Angeles. But these days I make my home here in beautiful Hawaii, and that should tell you how beautiful it is here – to leave behind the great Venice Beach, well you know it must be special here!

That's enough about me. I'll go around the room and introduce our various winners. If you could stand up, say a few words about yourself, and perhaps your travelling companion if you see fit, well that'd be just great."

  Just as Harry began to wave a hand to his left, their bus driver walked into the room.

The smile slipped fractionally as the 'boss' acknowledged her. "Great of you to join us. Everyone's just about to introduce themselves."

The Polynesian woman managed a diplomatic smile as she sat in the last remaining chair, between Wilko and two Japanese men. They'd ignored her as she'd approached, but the Tasmanian ventured a polite nod that he was surprised to have returned. Namakaeha sniffed doubtfully at the glass of orange drink she'd poured. She opened her mouth to introduce herself but Harry didn't give her the opportunity.

"Like I said, you all know Namakaeha already," he said. "She'll be our driver. She's a local so she can help you out if you've got any questions about the islands."

"You really local?" asked a tall brown-skinned man on the opposite side of the room. He was obviously an islander himself.

Namakaeha met the man's direct gaze. "Born Haleiwa. Lived here for years."

"Haleiwa. Oahu. Not really local then."

"It's all Hawaii isn't it? All great!" interjected Harry with a forced laugh. "Well my friend, I guess you're a good place to start. Ladies and gen-tlemen, the winner of the Kapolei Country Club tournament – our local winner, Keeaumoku Papipi."

As the tall man stood Namakaeha muttered audibly, "Kapolei, on Oahu."

Papipi drew himself to his full, considerable height. "Yes, on Oahu. I travel across the islands frequently and I happened to be working in Ka-polei when the tournament took place. In fact I am truly local, although from outside Hilo on the other side of this island. This is my friend and caddy, Kahekili Mehameha."

Kahekili nodded and rose slightly from his seat. He wasn't as tall as Keeaumoku, but was broader across the shoulder. What was most distinc-tive about him though was his tattooing. His right arm was adorned with a dark 'sleeve' of close hatched lines that extended all the way to the back of his hands The entire right side of his face and neck were black except for the eyelid, but even that had a black circle resembling a pupil at its centre.

The tall Hawaiian sat down, making it clear his introduction was over. With a sideways glance Kahekili did the same.

Harry bounced back up out of his chair. "Great! Now let's welcome, all the way from Rutland Waters in the United Kingdom, Mr. Armitage Shanks!"

A ripple of subdued polite applause greeted the small man next to Mehameha as he stood, rather stiffly.

"Good evening. My name is Armitage Shanks the Third. I own an estate in the smallest county in England, my family has been involved in the production of world class porcelain ware for several generations and now breeds racehorses."

He turned a nervous smile on the two young ladies sitting near him and continued, "My hobbies include hunting, shooting, fishing and of course, golf. This is my man Hoadley, who shall be acting as my caddy during the tournament."

The older fellow beside him, the only man in the room wearing a suit, inclined his head politely. He was sitting compactly beside Barber, his hands folded neatly on his lap and arms tucked in. If he was avoiding physical contact with the 'tournament organizer' he was doing so discreetly.

The English golfer was about to continue. "My…"

Whatever else Shanks was about to reveal about himself was lost as Harry again jumped up from his chair and said, "That's great, isn't it? Horse breeding and your own estate, wow! Guess you don't really need to own a piece of Royal Green, but I guess it'd be really appropriate if you did, hey?"

It seemed that Harry was one of those people who believed that anyone British with any evidence of breeding was only two steps removed from royalty. It probably explained why he resisted the urge to make a joke about Armitage's surname – an unfortunate one for a golfer. As the Englishman sat down awkwardly Barber indicated the young woman two seats away from himself.

"This lovely lady is the winner of the tournament at Portsmouth Links in New Hampshire, Miss Glexandria Hill."

The young lady with the odd name smiled and stood. She had long wavy brown hair, and wore a brightly coloured dress, the sleeveless cut of which showed off to best advantage the tattoo covering much of her left arm. It was a complex but beautiful design of tropical flowers surrounding a seascape with stylized rolling waves and crashing surf.

"Hi everyone. Call me Glexie. Um, let me see… I'm a CPA but I work as an insurance assessor, my favourite drink is bourbon and soda, I live and work in New England but I don't like the cold so I'm going to do my damnedest to claim Mr. Barber's slice of paradise. And I know that means avoiding my slice. And this is my best friend Ariane."

Glexie sat and Ariane stood in perfect synchronization, the dark-haired friend speaking as she rose to prevent Harry, beside her, cutting her off.

"Hi. I'm Ariane Cook. I work with Glexie, looking after legal stuff. I play some golf too. Mostly I like to watch."

With that somewhat cryptic comment she sat back down to a round of applause for her and her best friend.

Where Glexie's outfit was all colour and light, Ariane wore a black sleeveless top, a black and white striped mid-length skirt, and long black boots. Not severe, but not frivolous either.

'She's a game player,' thought John B. to himself, smiling. Others in the room looked less impressed. One of those was the dark-haired Japanese man sitting alongside Glexie, the next to be introduced by a slightly flustered Harry Barber.

"Please welcome the winner of the Subarashii tournament, from Tokyo, that's in Japan – Mr. Takafumi Makkuro."

Makkuro stood and gave a small formal bow. He was dressed in black slacks and a deep blue shirt. He neither smiled nor scowled, looking like he was fulfilling a necessary but tedious social obligation and avoiding eye contact with everyone in the room.

In a carefully modulated voice he said, "*Arigatoo, Barber-san. Hajime-mashite. Doozo yoroshiku...*"

"*Eego, arigatoo*," said John B. in a low voice, three seats away from the Japanese golfer. "English, please," he translated in an even lower voice to Wilko.

The look that Makkuro gave Stewart in response was about as dark as his outfit.

"Of course. My – what word? *Tomodachi.* Colleague. Caddy. Shigeki-yo Yuki."

The golfer sat quickly. His caddy rose without meeting his gaze. As usual, his clothing was the pale image of Takafumi's – beige slacks and a white shirt. Unlike the man he caddied for he cast a piercing gaze around the room.

"Thank you for the welcome, Mr. Barber. It is good to meet you. May our future relationship be a pleasant one. Takafumi and I are *tantoo* – man-aging directors – for modest companies in Tokyo. *Gorufu* - golf, is very popular. You may not know that Tokyo has more than 2,300 clubs. So we are very honoured to have won at Subarashii and to be here. We will see you on the tees."

Applause went around the room.

"He's the diplomat of the pair," observed Wilko. John B. nodded.

As Shigekiyo bowed and resumed his seat, 'Hands On' Harry again jumped up.

"That's great, guys, thank you. Next up, our Aussie winner, from Canberra – Roger Wilko! Ha ha – sorry, Robert Wilkes."

With a smile that was part grimace the Tasmanian got to his feet.

"Um, thanks mate. G'day everyone. I'm Wilko. Um… I work for the government, nothing interesting there I'm afraid. For fun I take photos and play golf. This is my mate John. Like, um, Shigeyo said, see you on the tees."

The silver-haired Japanese smiled and gave a gracious nod to the awkward attempt to get his name right.

John B. stood and smiled around the room.

"G'day. I'm John B. Stewart. Like Harvey said, we're from Canberra, the capital of Australia."

Harry Barber's fixed smile twitched at the riposte to his playfulness with Wilko's name, but before he could cut Stewart off the Australian continued.

"I'm not going to caddy for Wilko on the sound principle that even if I accidentally gave him any good advice he wouldn't take it. He'd have worked it out for himself anyway. I'll just pat him on the back at the 19th hole. Cheers!"

As John B. sat Harry stood, giving the wizard a glare that was quickly masked by what Wilko in his head was already calling The Public Relations Smile.

"Heh heh, yeah, cheers mate." Barber's attempt to sound Australian meant the word came out as '*moyt*'. "Now, please welcome the lovely Shareta Tanabe, winner of the Mt. Maya Country Club event at Kobe in Japan."

At Barber's introduction Makkuro and Yuki exchanged condescending looks that seemed to say, "Oh, Kobe. That explains everything."

The Korean-born former model ignored them. She'd had plenty of experience of that sort of behaviour. She gave a gracious bow to their host.

"Thank you, Barber-*san*. Mister Barber," she corrected, with a little smile to John B., beside her. "For my dear husband Hiro, who is also my caddy, it is our pleasure to be with you all. Hawaii is close to both our hearts. As you have been told, there are many golf clubs in our country. Perhaps you did not know the oldest of these is our neighbouring club in Kobe which opened in…" She looked down at her husband, whose lips soundlessly framed the answer she sought. "1903. Thank you, my love."

Makkuro looked sour. Shigekiyo Yuki at least managed an acknowledging nod.

Shareta continued. "Hiro owns a cosmetics company in Japan, which is how we met. I do my best to assist him, but in recent years as we make more time for ourselves we are able to spend more of that time on the golf course. Hiro, do you wish to say…?"

Her husband smiled and shook his head.

"In that case, I will wish those of you who are here to compete your fair share of success, and to all of us a most pleasant visit to this beautiful place."

The applause that swept around the room even included grudging contributions from the Tokyo pair.

'Hands On' Harry was still offering his approving applause as he stood. "That was a great little speech, Shareta – thanks! It's great that we've got a couple of lovely ladies adding some glamour to the competition." Possibly feeling the glare he got from Ariane right beside him, he added, "As well as the talent they've obviously got, of course! Now, speaking of talent, it's time for me to introduce our Spanish winner, *Senor* Hector Fernandez from Malaga's *Casa Torremolinos*."

The Spaniard rolled his eyes at Barber's dreadful attempt at a Spanish accent. He looked reluctant to get up from his chair so his compatriot stood instead.

"*Hola, senors* and *senoritas*! I am Carlos Calvera, and I have the privilege to be here with my friend Hector. He is a well known figure on the

Costa del Sol." Carlos grinned and shrugged. "I suppose I am too in my own way. Many thanks to *Senor* Barber for this opportunity to win some Hawaii. I would wish you all luck but – this is business, *si*?"

The Spaniard's grin took some of the heat from what might have been considered a graceless statement. There was a ripple of uncertain applause around the room.

From a few seats away Wilko watched Hector, the surly half of the Malaga twosome, and thought, 'I don't think he's a bloke I'd want to cross.' He probably wasn't the only one to be making a similar mental note.

Even Harry looked slightly concerned as he rose to make the final introduction. "Last but certainly not least…" he began.

The large man beside Carlos didn't quite leap to his feet, but he moved as fast as he could. His 'Hawaiian' shirt was a mash-up of light blue and orange sprinkled with ukuleles and coconuts. It would have seemed garish except that it paled alongside Harry's ensemble.

"Damned right about that, fella! Mah name is Buck Wilmington. Folks call me Big Buck. This here's mah prize filly Wilma."

The 'prize filly' didn't turn a hair at Big Buck's description of her. There was so much product in the hair it probably wouldn't have turned in a Texas twister.

"Ah hail from Beaumont in the great state of Texas. Ah'm here as the winner of the J. E. Broussard Memorial Club tournament. Mah Pappy taught me the value of a dollar, so even though he left me a damned fine pile of them Ah'm damned sure Ah intend to win this here event and relieve Mister Barber of his property. So you all enjoy yourselves, y'hear? But remember that the luck runs with Big Buck."

Wilma burst into enthusiastic applause. There was a moment of stunned silence from the rest of the room as the paunchy Texan dropped back onto his chair. Was he serious? Apparently so – he didn't seem like a man given to joking, especially about himself. Harry attempted to lead a round of applause for Wilmington that gathered brief, desultory support.

"Well, that's the introductions out of the way," said the host, rubbing his hands together. "Great! Everyone feel free to mingle, hey? There'll be a great dinner served in a little while."

He spotted several Significant Looks directed at the empty drinks table. Realising it was early days yet and he had to keep the punters happy, he spread his arms expansively and said, "I'll just go and arrange another round of drinks!"

'Hands On' Harry's jovial demeanour masked his irritation. He'd make the best of it. There was clearly some money in the room, but it wasn't quite the line-up he'd wanted.

He'd organised the tournament in the way he had because as he'd circulated in the local social scene he'd formed the view that it was a good place to find his target market - retirees with time and more importantly money on their hands. (This says something about what a deep thinker he wasn't.) The various 'qualifying' golf clubs around the world had been chosen because he'd known that there was money in the region. Plenty of other clubs had been approached and wanted nothing to do with 'Royal Green' - a credit to their perspicacity.

He slipped out of the Function Room and into the adjoining bar. The guests and their driver sat in their circle awkwardly for a few moments, some looking around, others resolutely avoiding eye contact.

'I suppose someone's got to be the first to move,' thought John B., and he stood.

Evidently Carlos had a similar idea as he also got to his feet. Both men made their way to the middle of the room, arms extended ready to shake hands. As if that was a signal, others started getting up from their chairs, or turning to chat to the person beside them.

"G'day," said John B. with a smile.

"*Buenos dias*," replied the Spaniard. He returned the smile but Stewart noticed that he didn't quite meet his eyes. Carlos appeared to be running his eyes up and down John B. as they shook hands.

'Appraising? Looking for something?' mused the wizard to himself.

"So, *senor*, you are Civil Service, yes?"

"Public Service it's called down our way, but yes. For now."

"Aah – you have plans? Business perhaps?"

John B. chuckled. "I think 'plans' is too strong a word. More like a vague intention to move on, but I haven't worked out where to. And yourself – you're in business on the Costa? Doing what?"

"Oh, a little of this, a little of that. There are many English tourists around Malaga, with many different needs, yes?"

"Yeah, it's the nature of tourists everywhere. Fortune favours the person who finds a need and fills it."

"*Si, senor* – a wise saying."

One of the hotel staff entered, struggling with a tray of jugs full of beer and juice. Harry followed, making no effort to get hands on and help.

John B. and Carlos poured beers for themselves as Wilko joined them. The Spaniard and the Tasmanian shook hands.

"Your mate isn't joining us?" asked Wilko.

They looked over to where Hector was still sitting, arms folded, and looking straight ahead.

Carlos shrugged. "Hector is very – ah, focused, yes? He is not so good with people."

"Especially if he's competing with them?" John B. hazarded a guess.

The Spanish caddy smiled. "Especially – yes."

Elsewhere around the room people made an effort to mingle, with varying degrees of sincerity.

Wilma led Buck on a beeline for Shanks. Aristocracy, of whatever country, should stick together as far as she was concerned. Buck was less enthused about the Englishman's pedigree, but at least he was white.

For his part, Armitage found the Wilmingtons' attentions irritating. There were two young, attractive women in the room – only two in his opinion – and they were where his interest lay. He was sufficiently well bred to make (barely) polite conversation with the loud Texan and his wife. But while his right hand held a beer he hardly sipped, he had his left hand behind his back signaling to his valet.

Hoadley dutifully arrived at his master's side and deftly took over answering the Americans' questions. While he engrossed them in a description of the antique furniture in the manor drawing room, Shanks slipped quietly away.

"Of course, mah family had a piece lahk that in our house in the Hamptons," was the last thing he heard Wilma say before he scurried to the other side of the room.

Glexie and Ariane were enjoying the company of the Tanabes. Shareta and Hiro were both easy and charming conversationalists. Hiro was especially enjoying the New England ladies' lack of deference.

"I am surprised that neither of you girls have visited Hawaii before," he remarked, then gave a small apologetic bow. "I am sorry – that is not a respectful term. You young ladies are hardly girls, but I'm afraid you rather seem such at my age!"

Glexie laughed, "No offence taken. Especially if you're not offended if I automatically call you 'sir', okay?"

Hiro smiled and gave a deeper bow. "Okay."

His wife gave her husband a wry look and said, "You overstate your age, dear heart."

"They say a man is only as old as he feels," said Glexie.

"Or the woman he feels," added Armitage Shanks III, arriving just in time to interject himself into the conversation.

Ariane winced on Shareta's behalf but the Korean woman's smile never slipped.

Hiro squeezed his wife's hand. "Then I have discovered the secret of travelling back in time, my friend," he said.

It took a moment for Shanks to process Tanabe's chivalry. Then he turned a gap-toothed grin onto Glexie and said, "I think that's a journey I'd like to take." Seeing the girl's puzzled expression he hastily added, "Not that I'm very much older than you! In my prime you know!"

"Oh, I'm sure," replied Ariane drily.

"Oh yes, absolutely. The Shanks family has been famous for their breeding stock for generations."

"Uh-huh," said Glexie uncertainly.

As Armitage prattled about his favourite topic of conversation – himself – he was quite oblivious to the fixed smiles and glazed expressions settling on his audience.

In different parts of the room both the Hawaiian and the other Japanese twosomes talked amongst themselves.

The Polynesians conspicuously turned their backs on everyone.

Makkuro and Shigekiyo however had occupied a corner from where they could watch the whole room. In quiet tones they were discussing their assessments of various personalities. Their deliberations were interrupted by Harry Barber, brimming with bonhomie and extolling the virtues of Big Island real estate. Makkuro responded in monosyllables, if at all. Yuki carried their part of the conversation whenever Harry actually stopped long enough for him to speak. That seemed to be how the pair operated.

Anchored to his chair, arms folded, Hector Fernandez was watching the room in a manner very similar to that of the Japanese partnership. His analytical gaze, though, was reserved only for the golfers. The non-competitors were of no interest to him.

He watched the players' movements, the way they walked, the way they stood. The Japanese woman – did she favour one knee slightly? The American girl had strong shoulders, perhaps an athlete. Her long game was probably her strength.

The loud American appeared to do everything in big movements. His arms swung like an ape's. Tricky putts and precise chip shots would be his undoing. The Australian was solid, not tall. His proportions were such that the extra inches of height and arm length that Hector had over him should mean a more effective swing.

He mentally catalogued all of his observations, ready for when the tournament was under way. He was absolutely determined to get out of Spain. He knew Carlos' "business" aspirations, but he had some dealings in his own past that provided powerful motivation to move on and set up elsewhere. If golf provided a means of doing so he would seize the opportunity, and woe betide anyone in his way.

Wilko was quizzing Carlos about the Costa del Sol. The trip to Hawaii was already getting him thinking about travelling and seeing more of the planet. ("The travel bug's bitten!" John B. would later remark.) It hadn't been high on the Tasmanian's agenda before. He hadn't been averse to the idea, just hadn't pursued the thought very far. But seeing the beaches of the world was appealing.

Smiling, John B. left his friend to his discussions of the beauties of the Spanish coast and strolled away. His beer glass empty, he quietly slipped out into the adjoining bar and bought himself a measure of a good whisky. Beer was fine in moderate quantity, and the local brew was very tasty, but his drink of preference was always a fine single malt.

The wizard went back to the 'Welcome Reception'. Nobody seemed to notice his departure or return. He ambled across the room.

He stopped by Namakaeha who was sitting alone and looking bored.

"Tell me about Haleiwa," he invited, hoping to establish some sort of rapport or at least casual chat.

The driver looked up with a start, clearly not expecting to be spoken to by any of the visitors. "Eh? Why?" she asked sharply. Rapport was not going to come easily.

"Just curious. It's not a place name I've heard of before."

"Mmph. Not a place for tourists. Not enough bright lights and glamour."

"There's more to Hawaii than that, though, isn't there?" asked the wizard genially.

"Damn right there is!" She looked away from him, sharply and deliberately. The conversation was clearly closed.

Stewart shrugged, raised his glass politely, and moved on.

He found Hoadley, who had managed to extricate himself from the Wilmingtons when Hands On Harry had come to woo them with his sales pitch for Royal Green Estate. The two men shook hands. The manservant didn't bow, to John B.'s quiet relief. The wizard also noticed that Hoadley, too, had managed to get to the bar and replace his drink with a glass of – he sniffed discreetly – decent quality cognac. Nice.

As they made small talk they looked around the room at the company –

not critically like Hector Fernandez or Takafumi Makkuro, but curiously and with some amusement.

"Pardon my asking," said Hoadley. "But how did you know that the dark haired Japanese fellow spoke English? He seemed a little put out at your revelation."

"Yeah, I suspect he's the type to listen in on conversations people think he doesn't understand. For one thing, he knew when Harry was introducing him. For another, more importantly, I saw his reactions when Ariane was talking."

"Very astute, sir."

"Not sir. John B. Save 'sir' for your boss, okay?"

"I shall try, s… John B. A deeply ingrained habit, though, I'm afraid."

"No worries. Appreciate the effort, mate. Speaking of your boss, he doesn't appear to be winning the hearts of the ladies over there."

Shanks was still expounding on his own manly virtues, oblivious to the fact that by now both Glexie and Ariane were looking anywhere but at him. When either or both had tried to walk away the Englishman had simply stood in the way, continuing to talk. He wasn't being consciously rude – just, in his own mind, winningly persistent.

Hoadley sipped at his brandy and shook his head. He sighed and said quietly, "I fear that when it comes to the language of love, Mr. Shanks is illiterate."

Trying to respect the manservant's tact, John B. barely suppressed a guffaw. He kept his reaction to a broad grin and replied, "He just likes looking at the pictures, eh?"

For a moment the older man looked like he may have taken offence on his master's behalf, but a small smile betrayed him. The brandy glass and the whisky glass were clinked together.

As if drawn by the sound of conviviality, Hands On Harry suddenly appeared beside them.

"Great to see you guys are getting along!" he said. "Always glad to see a cross-cultural exchange happening. Got your own drinks I see. Not keen on the Hawaiian beer? I'm surprised – I thought the Aussies and the Brits were great beer drinkers."

"Actually, it's…" John B.'s effort to defend the honour of the local brewery was wasted, or indeed not even noticed by their host.

"I'm a Bud man, myself. Great, dependable stuff. But you'll get a taste for the local beer. I sure have. That's the way of this island, it's so great you can't help falling in love with it. That's what I found." He slapped the Australian's arm with forced jollity. "You'll be the same soon, trust me! Wait till you see the Estate. Hey Hoads, I think your boss should really look at expanding his property holdings out here. There's a Union Jack on the Hawaiian flag you know, so it'd be appropriate, hey?"

John B. tried again to ford the torrent of Barber's babble. "The story of the flag is an interesting one, I've read. It's…"

"Hey, there's just so much about this place that's interesting isn't there? It's what makes it so great. You should have a word with your feller, Hoads. Win him over on the idea of buying here. Be a great place for you to work. Might even get you out of that suit, hey? Dress like a local!"

Grinning his salesman's grin, Harry smoothed an imaginary crease on his eye-splitting shirt. "I think I'll go and talk to his Lordship myself!" he said and walked away to double the delight of Ariane and Glexie.

"Mr. Barber is a rather dull fellow, with a sense of self-importance which is inflated beyond both politeness and accuracy."

"A pompous ass," agreed John B. "A type you're familiar with?" he ventured.

The manservant pursed his lips and said, "Sadly, such chaps are all too common in the circles in which Mr. Shanks likes to move. I cannot, of course, include him in that broad assessment."

"Because he's *not* a pompous ass? Really?"

"Professional courtesy. I have been with the family since my youth, and watched Mr. Shanks from childhood grow to be the man he is today. Alas, Mr. Stewart, he is *my* pompous ass."

The wizard smiled sympathetically and raised his glass. The gesture was returned with silent appreciation.

One of the *Sun Spot*'s dining room staff appeared in the doorway of the Function Room to announce that their meal was ready. A haphazard exodus began, Big Buck at its head. He was clearly a man who, as he put it, "liked to get his muzzle in the feedbag".

It would be nice to report that over dinner later the air of amiability had spread to everyone in the group. But it wouldn't be true. The aloof stayed aloof. The surly stayed surly. And the insensitive and unaware continued to blunder across other people's feelings and opinions.

John B. swirled the Scotch in his glass and looked up and down the long table they all shared. At least there were a few people whose company he figured to enjoy. The rest – well, it was only for a couple of weeks. Just relax and enjoy the experience, he thought.

.o0o.

9 TEEING OFF

Nobody had overindulged at the dinner or afterwards, so there was a bus full of clear heads for Namakaeha to deliver to the golf course at Wawaloli after breakfast.

Actually, not quite full, as there were two unexpected vacant seats. Over wheat cakes, bacon and thin maple syrup, Wilma Wilmington had announced to all and sundry that Big Buck had decided that he was "more comfortable" doing his own driving and had gone off to hire a car to convey them both around the next two weeks of competition.

No one particularly minded. The Wilmingtons had already managed to not endear themselves to many of the group – particularly the non-Caucasians. Even Wilma's attempts at politeness (to Keeaumoku: "It's nice to see you people making an effort to make something of yourselves") came across as condescending. Not least because they were.

The bus had not long arrived at the Wawaloli course when Buck and his 'filly' arrived in their new wheels. For all his claims of wealth, Big Buck clearly wasn't about to lash out on anything extravagant. It was a big old Buick Regal sedan, a six-cylinder automatic. It was certainly roomy, but didn't have a lot else to recommend it. The fake wood trim was showing its age, and the two hundred horsepower engine sounded like quite a few of the horses were dead or dying.

Wilma had pursed her lips at the sight of it - surely something better could have been managed. Even one of those 'Hummer' things would have been preferable. But Buck had been in a particularly parsimonious mood. His grumpy thrift even overcame his natural desire to show off.

The car loving Wilko shook his head and quietly said, "If you had to hire a car you could do a lot better than that, surely!"

John B. patted his friend's shoulder and said, "To do better, old mate, you'd have to know better."

The company separated into three smaller groups: the two competition foursomes (Wilko, Hector, Glexie and Takafumi; Armitage, Shareta, Buck and Keeaumoku, together with their caddies), and the four companions for whom 'Hands On' Harry had booked a tee time for their own game – John B., Ariane, Carlos and Wilma. He'd decided before meeting them all to do that, hoping to ingratiate himself further to potential investors. He wouldn't be making *that* mistake again.

It was a glorious day for golf, as if the Hawaiian weather gods had decided to co-operate with Harry Barber in promoting the island as a place to live and play.

Notwithstanding the weather, though, it proved a long day for the Tanabes. Not because of any issues with Shareta's standard of play, but their playing partners were not good company.

Buck, the only one of the four without a caddy, had hired himself a golf buggy. Between shots he parked his ample frame on the cart some distance from the others, mopping sweat from his face with a large handkerchief. Halfway through the round, as it became clear he was already trailing the others, he started making 'accidental' noises at key moments. He would cough or flap at a "pesky fly" just as a tee shot was played. On the downswing of one of Shareta's putts he dropped his hat. At a similar moment for Shanks he 'inadvertently' bumped the accelerator of his buggy causing it to jerk forward distractingly.

He knew that if he tried such ploys 'at home' in Beaumont he'd have been drummed out of the Club long ago. His behaviour was frankly a measure of his disrespect for his opponents, a fact not lost on any of them.

"You *are* having a great deal of misfortune today, aren't you, Mr. Wilmington?" observed Hoadley evenly as his employer ground his teeth after missing yet another putt. "I do trust it won't escalate into something more serious."

There was a sharp edge under the velvet of Hoadley's voice. Even the insensitive Big Buck caught it, and his behaviour improved thereafter.

Shanks himself said little to anyone during the entire round, keeping very focused on his game. Hoadley was smoothly and, it seemed, genuinely polite to the Tanabes over eighteen holes, but his attention was very much directed at his employer. Armitage needed all the help he could get, and it was noticeable that he was far more successful when he took his man's advice on shot and club selection.

The Hawaiian pair was hardly more sociable. Keeaumoku, like the English golfer, seemed totally absorbed in his own game. The strangely tattooed Kahekili Mehameha made some desultory small talk with the others but mostly conversed with Papipi in Hawaiian. This didn't greatly bother Mr. and Mrs. Tanabe until Hiro overheard an indelicate comment about the view from behind as his wife bent over a tricky shot.

When he next stood beside the black-sleeved caddy he leant over and quietly said, "I was born and schooled in Waikiki, *kane'oplo*."

Mehameha's eyes widened (the effect of which was made more peculiar by the black tattoo on the right of his face). Hiro had been polite, simply addressing Kahekili as 'young man' in Hawaiian, but the impact was con-siderable. After a whispered exchange, both Polynesians became rather more diplomatic. Hardly friendly, but more diplomatic.

After they checked scorecards at the end of play, Mehameha, who had clearly been mulling things over for the past couple of hours, took Hiro aside for a moment and said, "There is more to being truly Hawaiian than the hospital you were born in."

"Agreed," said Hiro mildly. "It is a matter of heart…"

"It is a matter of history! There is only one true Hawaiian race!"

"That is certainly true!" said Keeaumoku arriving unexpectedly behind his caddy. Something in his voice indicated that the detail of this was, in fact, a matter of some division between the two islanders.

Tanabe looked up at the broad blue sky. "Gentlemen, it is too beautiful a day, and too beautiful a place, for any harsh words. Let us simply enjoy

Wawaloli. There are some lovely tidal pools near here for us to enjoy.
May their cooling waters settle any heated feelings."

It was a difficult response to argue with, even for the truculent Mehameha. Hiro smiled, offered a small bow, and walked away to rejoin his wife.

In the end, Shareta's good if unspectacular round was enough to edge
Keeaumoku by a single shot, with the Englishman a further shot behind,and the Texan last by another stroke.

The other foursome competing for Harry Barber's piece of prime real
estate were doing so for the most part in a friendlier manner.

Both Wilko and Glexie took their golf seriously, but both were sociable
souls who didn't let the game get in the way of trying to enjoy the company of whoever they were sharing the course with. Hector and Takafumi
were far more focused on their own play, but the Japanese caddy Shigekiyo Yuki was reasonable company. The Spaniard, while he could politely be called competitive, kept himself to himself unlike, say, Big Buck
Wilmington.

The fabric of the shirt Glexie had chosen for the day was co-incidentally
similar to the one Buck wore. It looked a lot better on her. There was
considerably less of it to catch the eye, for one thing.

After a few holes of 'getting to know you' type small talk, Wilko finally broached the question that had been at the back of his mind since the
'Welcome Social' the night before. They kept their voices respectfully
low, and were silent when Takafumi then Hector launched their drives.

"Umm… your name. Glexie. It's – unusual, isn't it?"

The American girl grinned. "Yeah, I know. I've been hearing that – only
not always so politely, thank you – since I was a kid. Bit of a funny story.
I was named after my grandmother… hang on, sorry, your shot."

Wilko's tee shot got plenty of air, and that was its undoing. The extra
height took the ball up into a crosswind that swung it out to the left. The

ball landed two yards into the rough grass.

Glexie stepped up to the tee and hit a crisp clean drive that landed on the left side of the fairway, a respectable distance, but it was the position of the ball that gave her a contented smile. It opened up the green nicely, so she could avoid the bunkers guarding the right hand approach.

As they walked up the fairway, she continued her explanation.

"So, *my* grandmother was named after *her* grandmother."

"And they were both named Glexie?"

"Not quite," she replied with a laugh. "My Great-Great-Gran was Alexandria. She died fairly young – the family pretty much just knew her as 'Granny'. When it came to naming my Gran, they looked at some old handwritten document, couldn't read her signature, thought the A was a G, so my Gran got stuck with Glexandria. And that got passed down to me. Simple, eh?"

"It is when you explain it all," said Wilko with a smile.

They returned to a companionable silence while Makkuro addressed the ball with the iron his white-shirted caddy had selected for him. All four of those watching could tell by the sound of the contact how well the shot was struck. It flew low and straight, well and truly making up for the rather underhit drive.

Glexie and Wilko both applauded quietly. Even Hector Fernandez gave a nod of approval.

Takafumi returned the respectful nod. *"Arigatoo.* Thank you," he corrected before his caddy did it for him.

As they worked their way around the Wawaloli course the tricky wind conditions started to play on the minds of the golfers. Too much elevation meant suffering the fate of Wilko's earlier tee shot, as all of them discovered at least once. But the wind at lower heights had stiffened up, too.

The second shot on the tenth hole was a good example. After the cross-breeze had taken him to a point of the dogleg he'd wanted to avoid, Hector took a long time choosing a club – long enough for Wilko, Glexie and Takafumi to start getting antsy. The wind was now coming straight at him and he didn't want to be short. He had 153 yards to the hole. He pulled out a six-iron and sucked in a deep breath.

The swing was clean. The ball had plenty of distance. It flew right at the pin. Over it, landing safely ten feet behind.

"Too much to hope it might roll back," the Spaniard muttered.

Glexie shrugged. "You can't complain about the shot, though."

The game stayed close. Wilko's play improved over the back nine. His putting especially, not always his strength, actually saved him on a few holes.

On the sixteenth Hector saw a chance to get a break on the others. He was playing downwind this time, 174 yards to the pin.

He looked at the flag, then down at his clubs. His brow creased, then he clamped his jaw tightly before saying, "Worked last time. The wind should make up the difference."

He went with the six-iron again. And just like on the tenth hole the swing was clean and the strike was pure. Too pure. The ball flew right over the pin, landed twenty feet long, and slammed to a halt.

"How the hell did the damn ball go so far?!?" cried Fernandez in anguish.

"Don't know your own strength?" asked Wilko solicitously. He hoped that light-hearted banter might defuse the Spaniard's tension. He got a glare in reply.

By the time they finished at the eighteenth, Glexie and Takafumi tied one shot ahead of Wilko and Hector.

“If all the games are like this it’s going to be a nice close tournament. Well played everyone!” said the Tasmanian.

Hector’s response was a grunt. A close tournament was not what he wanted.

.o0o.

10 FEATHERS FLY

The last group to tee off was the four companions who Hands On Harry had vaguely organized to play amongst themselves – John B., Ariane, Carlos and Wilma.

Probably because there was no competitive edge to the game, theirs was the most relaxed and amiable of the combinations on the Wawaloli course. Wilma and Ariane were clearly determined to win, but neither was aggressive about it. The two men were both sanguine about the quality of their play, or lack thereof.

Only Wilma had her own equipment – all conspicuously monogrammed with a florid W. The others had clubs and bags rented from the Wawaloli pro shop. That was at their own expense – Harry Barber's largesse had extended only as far as their green fees. Even that was a reluctant expense only agreed to because it meant the Club would substantially reduce the fees charged to the competition players whose tab Harry *was* obliged to meet.

Curiously, unlike several of those playing in the tournament all four of them wore shirts from golf clubs in their home countries. Carlos wore the bright red colours of the Casa Torremolinos, Wilma the lollipop pink of the Beaumont Ladies, Ariane a white shirt with black sleeves bearing a Newburyport club logo, and John B. wore his characteristic purple (uncharacteristically collared) – a club shirt from Hideaway Bay, a little course in Queensland he'd visited.

Watching the cross-breeze take his second shot away into the distance John B. leaned on his club and casually remarked, "I liked the definition of golf I heard in a bar a while back: an endless series of tragedies obscured by the occasional miracle, made tolerable by the drinks afterwards."

Carlos had to hold up play briefly, waiting until he stopped laughing before he could play his own shot.

By the fifth hole it was clear that Ariane would only be beaten by an unexpected lightning strike. Wilma was just as assuredly going to be runner-up. She was more gracious about the prospect than Big Buck would have been, and she quietly admitted as much to Ariane as they strolled along.

"Buck has never ever settled for being second best. Ah realised before we got married that Ah'd just have to make allowances for that. So Ah've never talked about our families, before or after the reception – and wasn't *that* a difficult day!"

"Your families don't get on?" asked Ariane, trying to move discreetly to put a little more distance between them. Wilma's breath was not pleasant to be close to.

"The families are fine. Especially mine. Diplomatic to their core. It comes with the breeding, of course. We're the *Hampton* Whittlehamptons you know. The Whittlehamptons have been pillars of the Virginia establishment for hundreds of years. Of course, that's Buck's problem. His family isn't Old Money."

"Is there much Old Money in Texas?" mused the legal officer.

"Oh, Ah doubt it. Buck doesn't talk about where his family wealth came from, although his grandfather did let slip at our wedding that it may have had something to do with trading in illicit whiskey."

"He said that?"

"Not as such," Wilma admitted. "But he did mention that the whiskey being served at the reception wasn't as good as his family's moonshine."

John B. and Carlos had just caught up with them at that point. Stewart grinned at Wilma's last remark. "Whisky's a very subjective topic," he said. "I know Scotch drinkers who won't touch bourbon, or even the Irish stuff. Personally, I'd much rather a single malt than a blend any day. Even within single malts, there's Highland, Islands, Speyside and Lowlands, all with their own fans."

"Speyside," said Ariane, earning the raise of an approving eyebrow from John B. Not so much for her choice as for the knowledge she indicated.

The Spaniard shrugged. "At home we get the John Walker. Not for me. *Cerveza* or *vino*. Beer or wine, for me."

"JW's a respectable blend," John B. said. "I've drunk enough of it to know, I must admit!"

"Wine is the only alcohol Ah will touch," said Wilma, slightly sniffily. "Drinking less whisky might improve your golf game, you know, Mistah Stewart."

They'd reached the patch of low rough where his last errant shot had landed. Everyone maintained a polite quiet while he cracked a shot that did at least fly in the general direction he'd intended.

Millions of dollars get spent every year around the world on golf tuition, training videos and clever mechanical 'teaching aids'. Millions of words have been written about the golf swing. But when it comes right down to it, there are three basics to master – grip, stance and weight transfer. If you get any of them badly wrong you've not got much chance of playing the game well.

Almost everything else is about 'feel', and things that might be described as 'technical flaws' don't necessarily matter that much. Jack Nicklaus was said to have a 'flying elbow'. Purists said Tom Watson's swing was too long. Arnold Palmer could sometimes look comically like a corkscrew at the end of his follow through. All three did pretty well out of the game – they got their grip and their stance right, and knew how to transfer their weight properly.

John B. knew that. He knew he had a 'lazy' stance, especially when he wasn't putting. That was his killer, he knew.

"Maybe it is the Scotch," the wizard admitted, "but it's not a sacrifice I'm prepared to make."

Several holes later, Wilma was again expounding on the virtues of Hampton, Virginia, as oblivious to her companions' lack of continued interest as she was to their efforts to stay clear of her exhalations.

"It's the oldest continuously occupied settlement in America you know. Since 1610," she said.

"Settled by white Americans, you mean, I presume?" asked John B. as mildly as he could.

"Of course. What else?"

The wizard took a deep breath. "Well, I'd have thought some of the older tribes had been in the same place for a long time. Even if the place is now a reservation – they didn't all get relocated."

Wilma looked at him blankly. "Tribes? Oh – Indians. Ah suppose so. Ah mean *civilized* settlement."

John B. gave a thin smile and said nothing. 'Let's keep it civil and friendly,' he thought to himself. 'It's not like I'll ever change her mind, though I might wish she'd stop thinking that way.'

"Pardon?" said Wilma.

"Sorry – I didn't realise I'd said anything," Stewart apologized, instantly concerned at his louder-than-intended mutter.

Ariane had her own way of responding to Wilma's attitude though. "I do know one thing about Hampton," she said. "It was the first place in the States to have slavery."

It had been meant to be scathing, but the former Miss Whittlehampton actually smiled proudly and replied, "Yes. Right back in 1619. New York tries to take the credit but you're quite correct."

"I don't know that the auctions in New Amsterdam are something most New Yorkers take much pride in…" Ariane's voice trailed off. Like John

B. she realised that there was no point in trying to argue with Wilma. The woman clearly had a hide like a rhino.

They played on. Ariane's lead over Wilma increased. Carlos' and John B.'s scores trailed further behind. None of the foursome seemed much concerned.

After struggling to finish off the seventeenth hole, Carlos held up the putter he was using and sighted along the shaft. There was nothing wrong with it, but nonetheless he said with a smile, "I think maybe she is a little bent, *si*? Maybe the clubhouse hire us not so good equipment?"

"Maybe. Hire gear in other sports tends to have a hard life. You'd expect a good Club like this to provide top notch gear though," admitted John B. "I'm not going to blame my clubs, *amigo*. I'm the problem, not them. Golf is the only sport where your most feared opponent is yourself."

Again Carlos laughed heartily. He slapped a jovial hand on the other man's shoulder. "*Senor*, you have the good attitude!"

As they all approached the tee of the final hole Ariane smiled at the Australian and said, "Well, at least you recognise your own limitations."

"It would be difficult not to," observed Wilma, rather less sympathetically than the other playing companions.

John B. was unperturbed. He was under no illusions about the quality of his game. "No matter how badly you're playing, it's always possible to get worse," he said. "Still, I do wish I could hit one birdie before we finish!"

His tee shot was one of his best of the day, and was the longest of the four, albeit not by much. He watched the others take their second shots, selected his club, and gave himself a quick mental gee-up.

The wizard stretched and flexed his back. He set himself, checked where his feet were planted, consciously aligned his shoulders, and hit with a smooth swing. The ball flew fast and true straight down the fairway.

Something flew out from the trees at the left of the fairway. Flew directly into the path of John B.'s well-struck drive. From as far away as the tee the four golfers could hear the *whup* sound as the ball struck and looped high before landing perfectly down the fairway – the impact had actually improved the direction of the ball's flight.

The bird's flight was another matter, as it fell to earth in a flurry of feathers. The foursome rushed down the course to where it had landed.

It was a modestly sized bird – perhaps twelve inches long. Judging by the left wing it was agitatedly extending, its wingspan would have been maybe three times that. It was predominantly brown – the colour reminded the approaching John B. of good quality milk chocolate. The breast was much paler, a whiter shade of beige, and as he got near the bird the wizard could see brown spots mottling the lighter feathers.

"It's a hawk," he said as he slowly walked towards it.

"Well, at least it's still alive," said Ariane, stopping a cautious distance away from the flapping wing and snapping beak.

Wilma brandished a three-iron. "That's easily fixed!" she said.

John B. quickly grasped the shaft of the monogrammed club. "Don't!" he said sharply.

Carlos looked pensive. "It might be better – for the bird, *si*? It has a broken wing, I think…"

The bird screeched and snapped in the direction of the Spaniard as he tentatively moved towards it. Ariane also tried to approach but was greeted with snapping and agitated flapping of the undamaged wing.

"I don't know if it's broken, not from here," said John B. "Just stand here, alright?" he said to Wilma, letting go of the three-iron.

Cautiously he walked over to the hawk and knelt by it. It glared at him, but was quiet. Talking very softly to the bird – the others couldn't hear

him but he was actually apologizing – he reached out and with his fingertips carefully moved some feathers on the damaged right wing. For
a moment it looked like the raptor would lunge and remove one or more
of those fingers, but it stopped its movement and sat quietly on the grass,
evidently allowing the examination.

"I've hit the… um… shoulder I guess. The point where the wing joins the
body. It's swollen, but the skin's not broken, and the actual wing doesn't
seem to be damaged."

The wizard went to stand up, but as he began to move away the bird
flapped its good wing. The noise it made was not so much a screech as
a keening whistle. *Eee-ooh!* It quietened only when John B. knelt back
down to it. The hawk struggled to its feet and hopped towards the Australian on quite long yellowish legs.

The man reached out a tentative hand, and held his arm steady when the
bird jumped onto it. He winced as the talons dug in, first into his forearm,
then as the hawk sidled its way up to perch on his shoulder. A couple of
blood spots appeared on the purple fabric of Stewart's shirt.

Slowly and cautiously the wizard stood up.

"How did you do that?" asked Ariane quietly.

"I honestly haven't a clue. It wasn't my idea." John B. walked slowly
towards the others, watching the hawk's reaction. The bird stretched its
good wing, drawing a flinch from Wilma especially, but made no move to
shift from its perch.

"I guess we play on," said Ariane uncertainly.

John B. turned his head to look at the bird on his shoulder. It swiveled
its head and looked back at him. "Um… not sure if that's going to happen
for me…" said the wizard.

The distraction of Stewart's feathered passenger affected the women and
Carlos. All of them sprayed their approach shots, Ariane and Wilma both

finding sand traps to the left and right respectively, the Spaniard's mishit shot bouncing once on its way into a thick rough.

Despite clipping the hawk, John B.'s second shot had still been the best of the four. He approached where his ball had finally landed, and again turned to face the bird.

"Well, Hawthorn? Am I allowed to play?" he asked.

"Hawthorn?" repeated Ariane, standing nearby.

"Australian football team. Nicknamed the Hawks – they play in brown and gold," Stewart explained.

After seemingly giving the question some thought, the bird jumped down onto the wizard's rented equipment, clinging slightly precariously to the leather lip of the bag. John B. selected what he thought was an appropriate club and carefully extracted it without disturbing his new feathered friend.

A few moments were spent flexing shoulders – Hawthorn wasn't a heavy load but the talons were uncomfortable. Stewart then proceeded to play his best shot of the day – possibly, as he reflected later, the best shot of his inauspicious golfing career. The ball sailed majestically onto the green, bounced twice and rolled to rest seven feet from the hole.

Even Wilma was moved to applaud.

A tidy putt gave him the one-under-par result he'd wished for, that still wasn't enough to prevent him from finishing bottom of the group. He actually won the final hole, but the end result was as had been clear for much of the game: Ariane, Wilma, Carlos then John B.

As they entered the clubhouse the new adornment on Stewart's shoulder attracted plenty of responses, not all of them positive.

"You can't bring that in here!" exclaimed the bar manager, even as the Club Secretary was rushing over to say the same thing.

"I assumed the bird was a local member. She was a hazard on the eighteenth hole." That stopped both men in their tracks, at least long enough to hear the explanation of what had happened.

"Is there a vet nearby?" John B. asked at the end of his account.

The locals didn't know of any. The bar manager offered up a beer carton with the top removed and the sides taped up for reinforcement. The Club Secretary provided one of the Club towels to line the box. Stewart carefully transferred the bird into her new makeshift nest (he was guessing at the hawk's gender based on no evidence that he could identify). Ariane wondered to herself about how the Australian managed to change their attitudes and win their assistance with no apparent effort.

The four golfers were seated around a table, on the centre of which rested the cardboard 'nest'. Hawthorn's head was raised up over the edge of the box, dark eyes sweeping the room, alert to any movement. John B. from time to time cautiously held small chunks of smoked meat that the bar manager had provided. The hawk nipped the morsels from his fingertips with a curved beak that was fairly small, but looked extremely sharp.

Both Ariane and Carlos tried their hands (as it were) at feeding the bird – Wilma kept her hands a very safe distance away. Hawthorn didn't behave aggressively, but showed no interest in accepting their offerings either. She (or he) keened as they reached out, perhaps in warning, perhaps in rejection.

"A good day out, even with the, er, unexpected finish. Here's cheers!" said John B. raising his glass of single malt. Around the table, another scotch, a beer and a glass of white wine were raised in acknowledgement.

When Namakaeha arrived soon after to make her last pickup of the day her brow creased as she saw the contents of the box cradled in the Australian's arms as he stood up to leave.

"That's an *'io*," she said. Stewart heard disapproval in her voice. That's what her voice routinely sounded like, to be honest, but this time there seemed a little more edge to it.

"It had a run-in with a golf ball I'm afraid. Have you any idea if there's a vet around here?" the wizard asked as they all made their way out to the bus.

The driver barely shrugged as she replied, "Never noticed one."

"I take it the hawk's not a totem for you, Namakaeha," said John B.

She stopped, spun and glared at him. "There is *no* animal that's sacred to me! I am…"

The Australian raised a curious eyebrow but said nothing.

After a deep breath the surly woman growled, "Never mind."

The other three, a few paces behind, missed the exchange and climbed onto the bus chatting casually about the game, the locale, and of course the bird in the box.

Hardly surprisingly, Hawthorn remained a hot topic of conversation that evening, even when the whole group was reassembled after dinner.

"Well everyone, it's been a great start to the tournament, hasn't it?" enthused Hands On Harry.

He brandished a clipboard. "We've got an early leader – the lovely Mrs. Tanabe."

There was a round of applause, more enthusiastic than polite. Many of the group found it hard not to like Shareta, who bowed graciously at the acclamation.

Harry continued. "After that it gets a little crowded, which is great for competition, isn't it? In equal second, Mr. Makkuro, Mr. Papipi and the lovely Miss Hill. Only a point further back we have Mr. Fernandez and – roger wilko! Mr. Wilkes."

The Tasmanian winced but joined in the round of applause that carried on as Barber finished his wrap-up.

"And just behind them, Mr. Shanks and Mr. Wilmington, both of whom have plenty of time to make the lost ground. In about a half hour's time we'll be heading up the road to the *A List* Resort Hotel at 'Anaeho'omalu Bay. Don't worry about how to pronounce it…" (It was clear from the looks on a few Hawaiian faces that Harry hadn't been close to getting it right.) "… I know everyone just calls it 'A Bay. The hotel is going to lay on a great breakfast I'm sure."

"Wanna bet the dinner there is more expensive than here, that's why the late departure?" John B. whispered to Wilko.

"I reckon your money's safe, mate," was the equally quiet reply.

Harry ground on. "Just to remind you, the first group to tee off tomorrow is Hill, Papipi, Tanabe and Wilkes; followed by Fernandez, Makkuro, Shanks and Wilmington. I, ah, understand the rest of you – non-competitors – aren't keen for another game. Don't worry, there are some great ways to spend the day around beautiful 'A Bay."

As the group started to break up and head back to their rooms to finish packing, Harry quietly took John B. aside. "I gather you've picked up a pet?" the tournament boss asked disapprovingly.

"No. I've picked up an invalid, at least until such time as I can find a helpful vet. You're a local, Harry – do you know of anyone?"

Barber looked disconcerted – he wasn't used to being taken so casually when he was trying to express his authority. "Um, no… I'm not really an animal kind of guy." He tried to sound stern again. "But the hotel management…"

"Nah, I've spoken to them, they don't know anyone either. I'll ask at the new place." The wizard patted Harry on the shoulder. "Don't worry mate. Hawthorn isn't getting out of the box, the room's not suffering and neither is the bird as far as I can tell. There's nothing for anyone to worry about."

.o0o.

11 TAKING THE FAIR WAY

The players in the first tee-off group of the day were at breakfast in their new hotel with their travelling companions and their driver, who would shortly be taking them to the course at 'Anaeho'omalu. Keeaumoku and Kahekili were at least attempting to be sociable, although it was clear that small talk didn't come easily to either of them. Perhaps the revelation of Hiro Tanabe's Hawaiian birth had prompted their efforts, although Shareta was barely acknowledged once it was established that she didn't share her husband's origins.

That didn't bother the former model, for a number of reasons. For one, she had plenty of practice at putting up with being rudely excluded from conversations. Not everyone in Japan treated those of Korean origin as pariahs, but there were still many who did. Further, and more importantly as far as Shareta was concerned, she much preferred to chat with Wilko, Glexie and Ariane anyway. The two Polynesians' conversation mostly seemed to revolve around golf and island politics. The latter made her uncomfortable, and golf was to be enjoyed, not over-analysed, in her opinion.

In any case, she'd started the morning with a run (or a moderate jog, at least) to get her body and mind clear, and that had given her an appetite. A good breakfast was Shareta's number one concern.

John B. had just returned from the kitchen, where he'd talked the cook into giving him a few pieces of raw beef that was otherwise destined for that night's stroganoff.

"To feed Hawthorn," he explained.

"You keeping that bird in your room?" asked Namakaeha.

"I haven't found a vet, and I'm not about to abandon the poor bugger."

The driver shrugged. "I suppose that's good. Probably better Har… Mister Barber doesn't hear about it."

The wizard smiled. "Mister Barber's opinion means less to me than a pushbike to a puffer fish. I'm paying for my own room."

That prompted a raise of the native woman's eyebrows. A man of surprises, she thought, but said nothing as she turned away apparently to concentrate on her own breakfast.

Reaching for a piece of toast from the little rack in the centre of their shared table John B. happened to notice the brand of marmalade laid out for their use.

"Hey – I recognise this!" he said enthusiastically. "This is the brand that used to give out free Golly badges when you sent in the tokens off the label. I had a few of them when I was younger – Golly dressed up in different costumes."

Glexie looked at him blankly. "Who's Golly?" she asked.

"A golliwog," he explained. "You know – the kid's toy? Black face, red coat? You don't see them much any more."

Keeaumoku's brow creased over his coffee. "Good thing too," he said.

John B. was genuinely puzzled, and looked it.

The Polynesian continued, "Sort of thing that teaches kids a bad attitude to coloured people. Demeans them."

In his mind's eye Stewart saw some of his old collection of badges. "By dressing them up as racing drivers, footballers, doctors and nurses – that sort of thing? I don't get you."

"By making a toy out of them. Takes away their status as real people," Keeaumoku explained in a low voice.

"No more so than any other doll, surely?" asked Glexie.

Ariane gave a wry smile and said, "You and I both know there are some pretty unrealistic dolls out there, hon."

Shareta was smiling a little wistfully at Ariane's comment. "When I first began modeling there was a particular doll I very much wanted to look like."

Glexie grinned in response. "I bet I know which one!"

"It would have been a white doll," said Keeaumoku grumpily.

"I never played with dolls!" said Kahekili, adding a defensive note to the conversation.

"I was young," said Shareta. "I don't think I especially noticed or cared what colour she was. Although, looking back, I think she may have been the colour of that artificial tan that nobody naturally is. A strange sort of orange."

Hiro looked at his wife with the benign fondness that he usually did. "It is interesting, yes, that children seem not to distinguish people by colour until they are taught to?"

"That's what I'm getting at," said Keeaumoku. "It's subliminal. Those golliwog things turned black men into clowns. That's why they ought to be gotten rid of."

The wizard shook his head. "Sorry mate, but to me that's like saying we should get rid of teddy bears 'cos they give kids an unrealistic attitude to grizzlies."

Ariane looked at him thoughtfully. "I've known children to do quite silly things around bears in Alaska. Adults too, mind you."

Keeaumoku ignored her comment. "Well, they offend me," he said decisively.

"I don't like them either," declared Kahekili. "What about you, Namakaeha?"

The driver shrugged. "I think there are more important things in the world to get upset about," she replied.

There was a sudden commotion as Wilma Wilmington stormed through the dining room, so angry that she'd left Big Buck trailing in her wake. She slammed the door open on her way out to the car park, her husband fishing the Buick keys from his pocket as he followed.

"Hey! You want…?"

Namakaeha's question, or possible offer of help (unlikely, but possible) was cut off sharply by Big Buck.

"You just know yer place, girlie!" he snapped as he barreled out.

The driver opened her mouth to reply, but the burly Texan was already out the door.

"I wish I knew what was all about," mused John B.

Armitage Shanks and Hoadley walked into the room, tears of mirth still glistening in Shanks' eyes. Even his manservant's air of imperturbability was close to cracking. They came to the table where the others were sitting.

"Oh, that was priceless!" exclaimed the wealthy Englishman. "We were stuck in the elevator with the two of them. Bloody terrible experience, that. They never stop talking. Especially her! And her breath! My Lord, have you smelled it?"

"I'm afraid so," replied Ariane.

"It could stop a truck," agreed John B.

Namakaeha rolled her eyes. "Had her sitting right behind me when I got them from the airport. Glad they've got their own car now."

Shanks nodded vigorously. "Well, as we stood in the elevator, Hoadley –

dear, dear Hoadley – offered her a breath mint…"

Several of his audience thought they knew why Hoadley carried them – in regard to bad breath, Armitage was a man throwing stones in a glass house.

"… And he said to her, politely as ever of course, 'I wonder if you have a touch of gingivitis, madam?'"

"It did seem a plausible diagnosis," Hoadley observed.

"But the funny bit… the funny bit… ha ha, was her reaction." Shanks started to crack up again. "She said… ha, she said… 'I have not got, and have never had, red hair!' Ha ha – she thought 'gingivitis' meant she had ginger hair!"

"We get it, Shanksy – no need to labour the point," said Glexie, smiling nonetheless.

Even the grumpy Keeaumoku and Kahekili saw the funny side of the exchange and relaxed into smiles.

"Oh dear, Mister Shanks," said Hiro solicitously. "And now you have to share the golf course with her. I gather she will now be caddying for her husband."

"Eh? Oh! Oh, that's right! Uh-oh. You think she'll try to put me off my game? I mean, *he* was bad enough yesterday!"

"When we played Wilma did seem to know the etiquette of golf," observed John B.

"Knowing it and observing it might be different, especially if she feels provoked," said Ariane, mischievously.

Now Shanks look worried. "Oh dear. Oh dear."

Hoadley tried to look solicitous. "I'm sure there is nothing she can do which might detract from your game, sir.”

Shareta hid her smile. She’d seen Shanks play.

Armitage looked worriedly at his man. “You look out for me, right, old chap?”

“Of course sir. Shall I fetch your breakfast now?”

“Good idea,” Shanks said, sinking into a chair. The others at the table exchanged looks.

Namakaeha stood up. “Time I got you all to the course.”

“Not me,” said John B. “I had enough yesterday to last me a long while. I gather this A’ Bay is pretty impressive. I might find my way there and just hang out on the beach, maybe take Hawthorn out for some fresh air.”

Keeaumoku nodded approvingly. “The *‘io* shouldn’t be kept inside.”

The bus driver glanced over at Stewart and said, “Suit yourself. I’ll come back for the Spaniard and the other Japs later.”

“That will give them time for breakfast, assuming they want any. They’re evidently aware of their later tee-off time,” said Shareta.

“I will await your return, too, Nama… Nama… Miss. I haven’t had the chance to break my fast yet either, y’know,” said Shanks.

The driver ignored him, only possibly because of his inability to pro-nounce (or perhaps remember) her name. She jammed her colourful beret on her head and strode out to the car park, closely followed by the other two Polynesians.

“Actually, the beach sounds like a great idea, John. Mind if I join you?” asked Ariane.

The wizard grinned and said, “I’d be delighted.”

Wilko shook his head almost imperceptibly. 'How does he do it?' the Tasmanian wondered. His bemusement only increased with the response of Ariane's best friend.

"Hey, I'd be right there too if I didn't have a game to play!" enthused Glexie. "How about I join you after I'm done?"

"It's a big beach. Love to see you there," replied John B.

"Big enough for a little Tasmanian bloke?" asked Wilko.

Stewart smiled happily at his old friend. "Of course."

The sound of the bus horn came from the car park.

"I believe we're wanted," said Shareta.

Her husband shook his head. "I'm not sure that is the word I'd use, *ma pomaikai*. But come, my friends, we should go. Enjoy your game, Mister Shanks."

With smiles and waves Glexie and Wilko accompanied the former model and her caddy out to the bus.

Hoadley returned with Shanks' breakfast on a tray just as Ariane and John B. were vacating the table.

"We'll leave you to some peace and quiet before your opponents arrive," said Ariane.

"And the lovely 'Hands On' Harry," added John B.

Hoadley looked at Stewart balefully. "Thank you for that thought," he said, and pushed away the small plate of toast he'd prepared for himself.

Clearly the prospect of Barber's company at the table affected Armitage's appetite less than that of his manservant. Shanks nodded vaguely at the departing pair as he stuffed more bacon into his mouth.

"Join us at the beach later, mate?" invited John B., addressing the staff, not the employer.

"A tempting invitation, si… John. Thank you, for all that it is not perhaps my natural environment. Let us see what the day brings."

Shanks' fixed attention on his plateful of food allowed Ariane to signal over his head to Hoadley, indicating by sign language that, as far as she was concerned, the invitation did not extend to the landed gentry. Hoadley smiled and gave a small nod of acknowledgement.

*

It's a truism in many endeavours, not just sport, that we tend to play to the level of our opposition. It's how 'underdogs' pull off unexpected upsets as often as they do, and why anticipated walkovers sometimes finish as close contests. Maybe the better player or team 'takes it easy' – consciously or otherwise. Maybe the lesser competitors are inspired to try harder, or they actively learn from their opposition.

On the previous day's form, a bookmaker might have installed Shareta as favourite to win her group, but results were proving tight.

Papipi was even more grittily determined to eliminate mistakes from his game, although perhaps he was overdoing it. There was a stiffness to his game that hadn't been evident the day before.

It reached the point where on the seventh fairway the tension in Keeaumoku's neck and shoulders was pulling his head down – he stood fractionally too close to the ball and the long shot he attempted was ruined when it was the heel of his club that struck the ball instead of its face. The ball careened off, almost at ninety degrees to the intended flight path. The other three players all winced on his behalf. No one likes to see the dreaded shank shot.

Kahekili took him aside and said quietly, "You're trying too hard, man. Too tense – you're losing your rhythm."

The advice didn't seem to help, and the frustration quickly began to show in the manner of the heavily tattooed caddy, even more than in Papi-pi himself.

By midway through the game the Hawaiian was trailing the field, albeit not by much. It seemed the 'A Bay course rewarded the relaxed. Glexie and Wilko were competitive, but not aggressive. Neither was Share-ta who, with Hiro, gave every sign of simply enjoying a day out on the green. A welcome improvement on the previous outing.

Wilko couldn't help but admire Shareta's long, languid swing as she drove her tee shot straight down the fairway. He also couldn't help but notice how much the Korean towered over both him and Glexie. She probably even had a small edge over Keeaumoku and his caddy.

As if reading his thoughts, Glexie approached the former model as she stepped off the tee and politely asked, "Excuse my asking, Shareta, but just how tall *are* you?"

"Six foot one, in your measurements," was the smiling reply.

Glexie nodded. "Same height as Greg Norman. Until he and Nick Faldo came along most of the game's best were average height or under."

'Jeez – she really does know this game,' thought Wilko admiringly. "Big Jack Nicklaus?" he wondered aloud.

"Under six foot," Glexie replied. "I think the nickname was more about the way he dominated the game than his actual size."

"Are you gonna play or chat?" grumbled Kahekili. Even Keeaumoku had the decency to look uncomfortable at his caddy's churlishness.

Strangely, that moment seemed to help the Hawaiian's game. As if, in response to the tattooed Maui man's rudeness, the Big Island native made a decision to 'switch off' and not be so wound up. 'Feel' his swing, not 'think' it. With that, his swing improved, and so did his scoring.

The foursome came to the final hole with scores level. None of them managed to stay on the fairway. Shareta and Wilko both hooked their tee shots into the rough. Keeaumoku's second shot had too much carry and skipped into a bunker. The second shot also betrayed Glexie who, while the Hawaiian had simply used too much power, chose a 6-iron instead of a 7 and over-clubbed into loose rough on the far side of the fairway.

Their respective attempts at recoveries varied in success, but in the end it was Glexie who made it to the final green first, albeit with the ball twenty feet short of the flag.

'Putting. Not my strength. No! Not true, I *know* my short game is better!' The New England golfer gave herself a good talking to as she stepped up onto the green. She paced the distance from ball to hole, and then returned, assessing the slope. Finally she squatted, satisfied herself that there were no bumps or ridges to negotiate. 'I don't need to nail this in one. Get it close, girl, that's all.'

Instead of trying to focus too tightly on the hole, she visualized a circle with a three feet diameter around the hole. 'Get it into that target area – that would be enough.'

It was a perfect putt. She found the bulls-eye of her target, the ball dropping into the cup with a satisfying *clunk*. It was enough for Glexie to finish the round three shots clear of her three playing partners. All three applauded, as her finish merited. Only Kahekili Mehameha lacked the sportsmanship or courtesy to acknowledge the shot.

The black tattoo on his face emphasized the hostile glare he turned on both his playing partner and the young woman who'd defeated him. Winning and losing clearly mattered deeply to the Maui native. Glexie didn't even try to disarm him with a smile.

*

The players in the second group were not quite so evenly matched. Takafumi Makkuro and Hector Fernandez dominated their rivals from very early in their game.

Despite his caddy's best efforts, Armitage Shanks III could not match the Japanese and Spanish golfers.

Even less successful was Big Buck Wilmington. 'Caddying' for her husband, Wilma's role was driving the golf buggy hired for the day. Her advice was not required, and this did nothing to improve her mood after the earlier perceived affront from the Englishmen. Her peevishness in turn seemed to be reflected in Buck's play which deteriorated from the standard of the day before.

At best, the American's shots were falling shorter than expected. At worst, on more than one occasion he 'topped' the ball, pushing it into the ground momentarily, before it popped out and flew a disappointingly short way forward.

Shigekiyo and Hoadley both saw Wilmington's problem, but neither felt any inclination to try to discreetly offer the Texan any assistance. If Wilma recognised his error she made no indication of it. Perhaps she knew from experience how much attention her husband would pay to her.

Big Buck was hitting the ball off his back foot, not the front, so consistently got only thin contact. No matter how much he tried to bring his weight to bear on his shots, he kept getting the transfer of that weight wrong. Some days are like that. An error creeps into your game, a quirk or something you don't normally do – it may never strike again but the day becomes an exercise in frustration.

It does help if you get some good advice, especially if you listen to it.

"The 3-wood, Hoadley."

The man's hand hesitated over the cluster of club heads. "Are you sure, sir?"

"Of course I… wait… what are you thinking?"

"Might I suggest that the 5-wood may give you more elevation over those trees? You would achieve a comparable distance, sir." The manservant tactfully didn't say that was because his employer simply didn't hit the ball with enough power for the other club to make a difference.

It worked. Armitage's ball cleared the line of foliage by a narrow margin and landed neatly on the fairway on the other side of the dogleg.

Meanwhile Takafumi and Hector each maintained a strict focus on their own game.

'The key is to compete against yourself, no-one else,' the Spaniard reminded himself as he strode down the fairway alongside the black and white-clad Japanese pair.

All three had to stop sharply as Wilma cut across their path in the golf buggy. Makkuro was about to shout something at the Americans, but Shigekiyo laid a hand on his arm and shook his head. "Not worth it. Concentrate on your game."

Fernandez didn't have anyone to restrain him, but managed to steel himself to stay silent. But if looks could kill the Wilmingtons would both be piles of smouldering ash.

When they caught up further along the fairway Yuki approached the cart while the Spanish golfer was preparing his approach shot.

"I think that you would be well advised not to take a golfing holiday in Japan," he said quietly.

"Ah don't think that would be very likely," sniffed Wilma.

"Ah'll play where Ah damn well please!" Hector turned and glared with such venom that even Big Buck had the sense to lower his voice as he continued. "Was that some kinda threat, mistah?"

"Not at all, Buck-*san*," replied the caddy evenly. "I merely observe that you require the vehicle to get about the course comfortably, and such conveyances are not permitted on some courses in my home."

"Conv…? You mean the buggy? Ah can't take a golf cart out on a Japanese golf course? That's damned ridiculous!"

Shigekiyo spread his hands in a gesture of helpless apology. Totally insincere, but the Wilmingtons didn't pick it. He paused while Hector played his shot, and then said, "Take the course where the Korean woman plays – Mount Maya. I have been there. To protect the… what is the word? …*pristine* condition of the course carts are prohibited and players may only use eight clubs in a game."

"It must be a flat layout to get around without a cart," said Wilma, intrigued in spite of herself.

"Oh no – the course has been carved from the side of a mountain. It is most challenging. In many parts it is narrow and impossible to avoid walking on the fairway or green. Caddies are required to carry the eight clubs in a canvas bag, with no wheels to damage the playing surface."

"Damnedest thing Ah ever heard!" exclaimed the Texan. "Now, where's mah ball?"

Shigekiyo politely pointed ahead, twenty yards in front of where Fernandez had just played his shot. Unfortunately for Big Buck it had taken him an additional stroke to reach that point.

That was the way the day went. With each hole it seemed the American slipped a little further behind his playing partners. Even Armitage Shanks III had a better round, thanks in no small measure to Hoadley's shrewd advice.

By the day's end Hector had held his nerve for a two stroke victory over Takafumi, with the Englishman four shots in arrears. As for Big Buck – let us say he did not hold the 'A Bay course in high regard. That was evident by the squeal of tyres as he sped the Buick out of the car park after the game. It took a bit of deft driving on Namakaeha's part to avoid losing the front of the bus to the big Regal sedan.

As Hoadley later quietly remarked to John B., while he spoke no Hawaiian himself, he was confident that if you left all the swear words out of the bus driver's shout at the departing Wilmingtons, she wouldn't have said anything at all.

.o0o.

12 BEACH BUNNIES

Ariane and John B. made a somewhat mismatched pair as they arrived at the A' Bay beach in the complimentary shuttle laid on by the *A List*. The dark-eyed legal officer looked quite elegant in a white straw hat, long white cotton shirt worn over her swimming costume, with a black waterproof canvas bag full of books and a towel hanging from her shoulder.

The Australian was characteristically scruffy. The purple t-shirt was a new one, adorned with a turtle depicted in traditional local style, but his bush hat was old and battered, and his black-and-blue board shorts had faded to shades of grey. His towel was draped over his shoulders, and he carried a cardboard box in his arms.

The box contained a small cloth shoulder bag with sunscreen, wallet and room key, and a remarkably docile brown bird of prey.

"I thought it'd do her good to get out in the fresh air," Stewart explained. "If her wing's healed up she can just fly away."

"You think it's healed already?" asked Ariane.

"No idea. I'm no vet, I'm afraid."

The young woman smiled. "You seem to be doing alright with the hawk."

"A wing and a prayer?" suggested the wizard.

"Mm," said Ariane in a low hum. She wasn't fond of puns.

Fringing the sand where it met the car park were a number of mobile vendors' stands. They sold hot dogs, shaved ice and a range of drinks, none of which were alcoholic. There was even a trailer-mounted rack of surfboards for hire, even though the gentle conditions of the sheltered beach didn't lend themselves to board riding. The surf kayaks advertised on the sign hanging from the trailer had evidently already been rented by the time John B. and Ariane strolled past.

A very large islander in a loud shirt apparently slumbered in a canvas chair beside the trailer. He had big hands, clasped across a substantial belly that rose and fell in a slow rhythm. An outsized panama hat covered his face.

"Tough job, but someone's got to do it," said John B. with a smile to his companion. The apparently sleeping figure raised one meaty thumb in acknowledgement, broadening the grins of both of the pair walking by.

At the end of the line of vendors was a large tree, under the branches of which were clustered several of the Big Island's homeless population. The 'trolley people', so called because many of them keep all their worldly goods in bags and boxes crammed into shopping trolleys that they wheel from place to place.

There are maybe four thousand homeless people in Hawaii's population of 1.5 million. Like the vast majority of people in that situation across the Western world, most are victims of circumstance – bad luck, bad health, and/or a lack of crucial support when it was required. Many are solitary by nature, or have become so over time, but a primal need for companionship creates communities of the dispossessed. The 'membership' may be transient but the fabric of the community helps sustain the people who pass through it.

The group under the tree was one such community. The individuals themselves would drift up and down along the Kona coastline, pushing their trollies or toting their packs, walking or cadging lifts where possible. Some worked where and when they could, some begged, some busked (for a loose definition of 'busking' – sometimes street entertainers make their money from people who want them to *stop* performing), and others scavenged.

'Income producing' activities tended to happen in town, or when and where there was a plentiful supply of tourists. A quiet midweek day in 'A

Bay was simply a time for gathering, swapping stories, or just silently being in the company of other human beings who didn't judge or condemn or pity.

Some of the visitors to the beach would deliberately look away from the trolley people. Others looked at them disapprovingly, openly wondering why the police didn't "move them on" (without considering where they could be moved on to). John B. and Ariane were among those who looked at the group with sympathy, but a sense of helplessness.

Perhaps the wizard might have 'wished' to help, but he feared that the size of the problem was beyond him. How could he pick and choose which one or two to help? And he was afraid that the seemingly fickle nature of his magic could mean doing more harm than good. An ethical dilemma he couldn't resolve.

The beach wasn't empty but certainly wasn't crowded either, so Ariane and John B. were able to choose a comfortable patch of sand on which to spread their towels. Hawthorn peeped out over the edge of the box and looked around. The good wing stretched and the small sharp beak opened in what looked remarkably like a yawn, then the *'io* settled comfortably down onto the bottom of the towel-lined box and promptly fell asleep.

"Well, if she *can* fly she's obviously in no hurry to do so," observed Ariane.

She and the Australian took turns applying sunscreen lotion to each other's backs. Each evidently enjoyed the experience, both the giving and the receiving.

Gently rubbing the cream in between Ariane's shoulder blades Stewart noted the whiteness of her skin. "You look as much like a regular on the beach as I do," he said.

"Actually, there are a few nice spots around our way. Nothing like this, I admit, but good places to spend a day relaxing. I'll show you if you ever come over. But no, I don't tan. I'm lucky though, I don't burn easily either."

"Ah. Whereas I just go from white to red without the 'tan' bit happening in between." They both laughed. "It's a Celtic thing, I think," the wizard suggested.

"So that's your background. You didn't strike me as the Bronzed Aussie type."

"Australia's a nation of immigrants. Always has been."

"Except for the Aboriginals."

John B. wondered if Ariane was trying to be provocative, or somehow testing him. The thought was underscored when she turned to face him, rather than let him continue talking to the back of her head.

He played the comment with a straight bat. "Not necessarily," he replied. "There's not one single Aboriginal 'race' – there are several, all of which presumably arrived on the land one after another. I don't think anyone knows which was first, or even if there was someone else here they were all 'invading'. I think we're all immigrants if you look hard enough."

Ariane looked thoughtful. "When you called Wilma about non-white settlement yesterday I figured you were a bit more culturally aware than most."

"Is it an issue up your part of the country? Or a personal interest?"

"A bit of both, maybe. A terrible number of the Algonquin native Americans died off in the early days of white settlement. A plague in 1617 killed a lot. The tribe that was actually called the Massachusetts shrank from three thousand to five hundred people in less than a year."

"Sounds nasty," the Australian said, taking the sunscreen from her as she finished applying it to her face and smearing some onto his own features.

"It was. No-one's sure how the epidemic started, but almost certainly the disease came from one of the traders or pirate ships along the coast."

"I know the story – European disease hits local population with no resistance: wipeout. The same thing happened right across the Pacific, including here."

Ariane nodded. "Then there was a war in 1675 and '76. There were maybe a dozen British townships wiped out, but there were over five thousand native casualties. A lot of the survivors fled. Up to Canada or down to the New York area. Those that were left died out or got assimilated over the generations into the various New England settlements that grew up. There are still some people that call themselves Algonquin, but honestly, I think some of them are just trading on the name – more's the pity."

"That's a shame," said John B., genuinely sympathetic.

"Mm. Sadly, we're several generations too late to do anything effective about it," she replied, laying back on her towel and closing her eyes.

"No. It's not like we can rewrite history. Not the facts of it, anyway."

A small murmur in response indicated that Ariane was drifting off into a light slumber. 'Not a bad idea,' mused the wizard to himself, and attempted to do the same. He was drowsy, not having slept well, but found after some minutes that it just wasn't going to happen.

'Ah well,' he thought, 'I haven't got much to complain about. Beautiful day, beautiful beach, an attractive bird on either side of me, both of whom are sleeping peacefully, half their luck, but all things considered you couldn't wish for a whole lot better.'

He ran a careful fingertip along the crown of Hawthorn's feathered skull. Whatever strange attachment the 'io had apparently made to him, the sentiment was becoming mutual. Impractical of course – it wasn't like he could take the bird back to Canberra with him. Think of it as a holiday romance. Well, not a romance, obviously. No more than the friendship that was growing with Ariane.

As she dozed, John B. studied the young woman on the towel beside him. Her features might be called 'elfin' if the elf ate a little better than most. Her pale skin was offset by jet black hair in a loose curly bob. Cupid's bow lips and a nose that turned up ever so very slightly at the tip made for a look that reminded him of some glamorous film stars of the 1930's.

It wasn't obvious at that moment, but he knew that what separated Ariane from being "pretty" were her eyes. Dark and penetrating, they certainly added to the 'other-worldliness' of her appearance, but their intense analytical gaze was more disturbing than attractive.

He could readily understand how she so disconcerted 'Hands On' Harry Barber, a man who evidenced as much depth as a custard skin.

At rest though, the wizard considered to himself, with the gimlet gaze shuttered away, she was striking.

She wore a strapless one piece costume – the geometric black and white print was well chosen to highlight the best of her figure and draw the eye away from the fact that she had a little more waist measurement than she wanted. If asked (which he wasn't) John B. would have said that there was absolutely nothing wrong with her figure. A little more voluptuous than Q maybe. He couldn't be totally sure, having never seen Elizabeth in a swimsuit, or anything else that particularly showed off her figure.

He realised, rather to his own surprise that he was, unconsciously or otherwise, using Q as a benchmark of sorts – largely 'sight unseen' as it were. His imagination was filling in the blanks in his experience.

The wizard didn't quite know what to do with that little moment of self-awareness. He really didn't think it was right or fair to *wish* for a progression of their relationship. Hope, however, was quite a different thing, and he was surprised to realise the depth of the hope that he felt.

"You look a million miles away," said Ariane, awake and watching John B.'s face.

"Sorry," he said. "Exploring the inside of my own head."

"Don't apologise. It's something more people should do."

She sat up, took a book from her bag, and proceeded to immerse herself in a classic old doorstopper sized fantasy novel.

Stewart adopted a comfortable lotus position and settled himself into one of the meditation exercises Harlan had taught him. If sleep were to be elusive, this would be a good alternative.

Time passed gently, Ariane in a world of dragon riders and John B. in a place of quiet that still seemed new to him.

They made a few forays into the warm water of 'A Bay, both avoiding proximity to loud splashing children. There was a smiling recognition that aversion to shrill kiddies, over-boisterous and under-disciplined, was another shared attitude. Occasionally one or other would amble up to the vendors' stalls to fetch drinks.

Neither was much impressed with the hot dogs that were their lunch. John B. had yet to develop a taste for cheese that was poured on (although he worried that he could get used to it if he wasn't careful) while Ariane was disappointed in the quality of the frankfurter. Hawthorn didn't share her misgivings and happily scoffed the leftover that was offered. It had to come from the Australian's fingers though – the original offer from Ariane was ignored.

"At least she's not snapping at me. I guess that's an improvement."

It was still fairly early in the afternoon when Glexie and Wilko arrived at the beach in the resort shuttle.

"None of the others wanted to come with you?" enquired John B.

It was Glexie who explained. "Shareta and Hiro have taken a taxi and gone shopping, I think. The two local boys have taken themselves off to that little practice putting green at the hotel."

"Keeaumoku looking for an edge, is he?" asked her best friend.

"You wouldn't blame him," said Wilko. He jerked a thumb at the New England golfer. "This shark cleaned all of us up with a cracker of a putt on the last. Winner by three."

Ariane laughed and hugged her friend. "Well done, girlfriend!" she enthused.

"Sounds like it," agreed John B. "Sorry mate," he said sympathetically to his old pal.

Wilko shook his head. "I played alright. I'm happy enough with my day. Glexie just nailed a twenty-footer like a pro."

"Whoo – that should change the betting order for the tournament," said the wizard.

Glexie laughed. "It might if I could play shots like that all the time! I'll just enjoy the memory, and use it to gee myself up any time I lose a bit of confidence. It might just make the difference!"

"If it helps – no harm to Wilko's prospects intended – then I wish you some difference, the good kind, my friend," exclaimed John B., thinking just in time (he hoped) to temper his enthusiasm with careful choice of words.

The Tasmanian glanced sharply at his friend. 'Prospects? Of course, golf, the tournament. Right.' The litany of improbable coincidences and strange happenings that surrounded Stewart was starting to make an impression on even his no-frills straightforward mind.

As Glexie spread a towel on the sand beside Ariane, they all looked around at the sudden sound of a flute being played moderately well, nearby.

"Am I seeing things?" wondered Wilko aloud.

A giant rabbit was dancing across the sand, doing a Pied Piper impression.

"That's different," agreed Glexie.

It was a man in an Easter Bunny costume, gamboling his way between people on the sand as he tootled on a wooden flute. Most of the laughing beach crowd happily tossed money into the leather bag slung around the unlikely minstrel's hips.

He danced his way over to the golfers and their companions. It would be nice to say the dance was the Bunny Hop, but soft sand made it more of a hop, skip and a jump. They all reached to donate. John B. laid a hand on the fur-clad leg.

"Brother, that is a tough way to earn a living in this climate!" he said sympathetically.

The faux-fur rabbit's shoulders slumped. "Pal, you ain't kiddin'!" said a voice inside the big white head. "But hey, it's workin'!"

"The money is that good?" asked Ariane in some surprise.

"The money's a bonus, ma'am. Main reason I started doin' this was to lose weight."

Wilko, mindful perhaps of his own occasional efforts to lose a couple of inches around his waist, stared. "You're kidding?"

"No sir. I sweat off pounds every time I wear this suit. Like I said, the money is sure a nice thing, but I'm just right glad I've dropped best part of eighty pounds since I started doin' this."

Glexie was wide-eyed. "Eighty…? Wow! That's… um… dedicated!" She couldn't help wondering just how big the anonymous man in the white fur must have been, or was now. The baggy suit gave no real clue to his shape. With an appreciative smile she stuffed another couple of notes into the pouch. The bunny played a little trill on his flute, bowed to the foursome, and danced away.

Wilko offered, "A round of drinks to toast the winner?"

The gracious offer was duly accepted, and John B. got up to help.

As they made their way up towards the car park Wilko quietly said, "Not like you to be so keen on anything non-alcoholic. I take it you've got a bottle of Scotch in your bag to give it a kick?"

"Oddly enough, no. Never even thought of it. I think I'm just enjoying feeling relaxed. No stress of work, or any other weird stuff threatening me."

"It's no bad thing you know, cutting down," said the Tasmanian solicitously.

The wizard took the advice in the generous spirit in which it was offered. "I know. Thanks, old buddy. It's nice to have a drink just because I enjoy it, rather than feeling like I need it."

Looking at his companion as they spoke, John B. inadvertently collided with one of the trolley people. He was about to apologise, but found himself having to dodge a roundhouse blow from a powerful arm.

His would-be assailant snarled – something about "all alike" – and drew his fist back to try again. He was a big man, wearing only faded camouflage pants torn to board short length and a grubby blue baseball cap embroidered with the words 'Vietnam vet'.

John B. dodged another swinging blow, this time giving the elbow a sharp shove as it went past to upset the big man's balance. Now shouting incomprehensibly the man stumbled but quickly regained his footing. He set himself in a crouch, tensing to jump at his opponent. Stewart planted his feet firmly, bending his knees a little, ready to either dodge or strike at the man while he wasn't grounded.

Wilko took a step back. He didn't like violence, and he'd seen Stewart fight before. He didn't know where in his old friend's past it came from – a street fighter's blend of fists, feet, even forehead. Barely-controlled mayhem. It wasn't pretty. "John, please don't…"

"I wish I didn't have to!" Stewart replied as the other man stopped shouting and began to snarl before he pounced.

But before the trolley man could spring a booming voice rang out: "Easy!!"

The homeless man uncoiled from his crouch and looked at the ground. Beside him stood the surfboard vendor. Wilko blinked – he hadn't even noticed the newcomer move, but there he was, and was clearly the source of the bellow that had stopped the impending fight cold.

The trolley man was big, but the figure beside him was bigger. Both stood over six feet tall, but the man in the brightly coloured shirt was at least sixty pounds heavier.

John B. straightened his stance uncertainly. "Hey!" he called to the homeless guy. "Sorry I bumped into you, man – no offence meant."

The man barely looked up as he shuffled back behind his homeless companions under the tree. Most of them took a step away from him, one or two mumbled tentative words of support.

Stewart looked at the outsized islander and held out a grateful hand. "Thanks."

The response was surprising – a massive arm was thrown around his shoulders in a genial hug. For a moment the big fellow looked at him as if expecting recognition, then his expression changed into an open, welcoming grin.

"My apologies for that unpleasantness, my friend. Ese is not the man he used to be, I fear, but for the most part he means no harm."

"Are you sure about that?" asked Wilko uncertainly.

"Not entirely," admitted the big Hawaiian, his grin not slipping at all.

"Ese? I thought you'd said 'easy'. Well, either way, I'm glad it worked," observed John B.

The large arm hadn't moved from his shoulders. "Ese is sometimes known as 'Big Easy' to his friends. And yes…" the islander said with a look to Wilko, "…he does have friends."

The wizard shifted slightly under the weight. "I really would like to chat – seriously – but first we promised drinks to a couple of young ladies. Would you like to join us, or should we not take you away from your boards?"

"The company of young ladies, as well as your good selves? I would be delighted! My wares shall be perfectly safe."

Together the three made their way to a canvas-roofed table behind which stood a skinny blonde man selling cans of soda from a big polystyrene icebox.

Having made their selections Wilko started to open his wallet, but was stopped by the wave of a massive hand. "They're with me, Weed," boomed the distinctive voice.

'Weed' handed over the drinks with a smile. "Sure thing, Courtesy," he said.

The two Australians introduced themselves to their new friend. As they walked back past the trolley people John B. looked for his recent adversary.

"Is 'Big Easy' okay, do you think?" he asked.

Courtesy shook his head. "I do not think Ese is ever quite okay. He has lucid moments – he's an intelligent man. He went to Vietnam as an engineer, but something happened to him there."

"That's an all too common story," said John B. "Any idea what?"

"Regrettably no. I have heard him lament of destroying things he was trained to build, but no specific incident. He did return to University when he came back to Hawaii, but I fear the pressure of study was beyond

him. He works a day here, a day there, odd jobs or laboring, but he is –
unpredictable.”

The wizard nodded sadly. “Damaged goods. Here we are – Courtesy,
meet Glexie Hill and Ariane Cook.”

The big man bowed extravagantly as the drinks were handed over. “A
pleasure, fair ladies. Welcome to ‘Anaeho’omalu Bay!” He doffed the
panama, revealing a long mane of black hair, shot with silver and thinning
on top. The same black-and-silver characterized his goatee beard. Ariane
tried to guess at his age and realised that between his appearance and his
larger-than-life persona she had no idea.

The massive body showed surprising suppleness as he lowered himself
to the sand beside the group. If he thought there was anything unusual
about Hawthorn’s presence he gave no hint of it. It might have been every
day that he met a bird in a box on the beach. The ‘io hopped onto the
edge of the box, looked curiously at Courtesy, then jumped up onto the
knee of John B., who was sitting cross-legged.

Stewart winced momentarily as the talons dug in, but then the hawk
balanced and released its tight grip. The girls, and for that matter Wilko,
looked at the raptor with a degree of nervousness, but both John B. and
Courtesy continued to talk so casually that they were soon drawn back
into friendly chatter.

The Falstaffian figure didn’t try to dominate the conversation: he listened
as much as he spoke, but the sheer force of his personality was obvious.

Courtesy reminded Wilko of an old black jaguar he’d once seen in a zoo.
Age and comparative inactivity had let the muscle development soften,
but there was no mistaking the power the big frame still held. But the
voice was the real reminder: sometimes a roar, but at other times a soft
growl that could still be heard at a remarkable distance. Perhaps ‘heard’
was the wrong word – it was more like the voice could be felt, at some
deep primal level.

The Hawaiian asked the foursome about their travels. The girls knew their way around the north-east of the US but admitted to not having ventured much beyond there. Wilko confessed to being in a similar situation.

"The big one for me really was moving from Tasmania up to Canberra. Beyond that I haven't travelled much," he said.   "A couple of weeks in the Outback…" (At a secret underground military base, then confronting a reincarnated Phoenician god in the Central Australian desert, not events that he'd ever acknowledge publicly) "… a couple of days here and there mostly for work. This is my first real trip overseas – it's proving interesting."

John B. nodded vaguely and said, "Yeah, I've seen a lot of Australia. I remember talking to a bloke in a bar in Brisbane, telling me how embarrassed he was when he went to London. People were asking him about Ayers Rock, the Barrier Reef, even the Opera House in Sydney, and he'd never been to any of them. Knew as much about them as the Brits he was talking to, and in exactly the same way – he'd seen them on TV. So I figured it was best to know your own country before being any sort of roving representative."

Courtesy gave the man in the purple t-shirt an odd look. Amused? Quizzical? "Your own country?" he asked in a quiet rumble.

The question set the wizard to pondering before he replied, "Well, that's what it used to feel like, or so I thought. Now I'm away from it the feeling's quite different. Here just feels so right. I'm not quite sure where I belong…"

"Tassie's always going to be home for me," said Wilko.

His old friend smiled at him. "That's a nice thing to be able to say."

Wilko gave Stewart a long, thoughtful look. Ariane fancied she could hear little wheels turning in his head before the smaller man said, "You never talk much about your family."

"They never talked much about themselves," came the dismissive response. "What about you, Courtesy? Are you much of a traveller?"

There was another moment of what might have been uncertainty as the big man looked like he was sizing up the shaggy-haired Canberran. Then a huge grin split his face. "Indeed I am! Indeed I am!" he answered in a jovial roar. With only a little prompting from the ladies he spent the rest of the afternoon regaling his audience with tales of "sights he'd seen across the seven seas".

It was with genuine reluctance that Wilko eventually pointed out that the shuttle back to the *A List* was almost due, and they should pack up and head for the car park.

The Tasmanian's proffered hand was engulfed in Courtesy's massive paw. "I'm afraid it's good-bye, mate," said Wilko. "We're off to Keea… Kee-oo… Kee-somewhere tomorrow."

"Keauhou is the course, and we're staying at Kealakekua," advised Ariane.

Courtesy raised a dark eyebrow. "I hope none of you are the type to be bothered by history."

"What do you mean?" asked Glexie.

"The first white man to die on these islands met his end at Kealakekua. A man named William Watman died of some sort of seizure – a stroke, modern doctors say. He was a sailor on the *Resolution*."

"I think the only strokes any of us are worried about are the strokes these two take out on the golf course," quipped John B. as he tucked Hawthorn's box under his arm, the bird again resting quietly. "But thanks for the concern, mate. Good to meet you, my friend," he concluded with a wave as the foursome made their way out to the car park.

"Be seeing you!" boomed the big Hawaiian in reply.

The wizard glanced back. Somehow he didn't doubt him.

.o0o.

13 THE STUFF OF LEGENDS

John B. stretched and rolled his shoulders. He'd enjoyed the shower, taken to wash the combination of sunscreen, sand and sea salt from his skin and hair. He selected a clean purple t-shirt from the pile of clothes spilling from his kit bag and pulled it over his head. He was just tucking it into his jeans when the phone rang.

Puzzled, he picked up the receiver.

"Mr. Stewart? It's Sandy at Reception. You have visitors – shall I send them up to your room?"

It took John B. a moment to recall – Harlan. The wizard had phoned on the evening that they'd been given their itineraries and arranged that the archaeologist and his new lady-love join them on a night that suited them, which happened to be this particular evening.

"Thanks Sandy. I'll come down. Er, no offence, but this room isn't really big enough for entertaining." 'Or tidy enough,' he confessed to himself with a rueful look at the open plan wardrobe he'd made of the floor.

Rapping on Wilko's door and calling through news of the visitors as he went, the wizard trotted down the internal stairs to the Reception desk. A slim man, dark haired and bearded, stood waiting alongside a similarly slight woman with long blonde hair and ivory skin. She might have been an undersized Valkyrie.

John B. strode up to Harlan and the two men embraced warmly. The Australian stood back and observed his friend. "You look well, mate – you've put on weight," he said.

"Really? He must have been a rail the last time you saw him!" was the comment from the blonde woman standing beside the archaeologist.

"Well, I wasn't at my best. I'd been on… um… an enforced diet," admitted Harlan. He took the woman's hand. "John B., this is my dear one, Haveta."

"Pleased to meet you," said the wizard taking her other hand and giving his usual gallant bow.

"Likewise. I gather I have you to thank for this guy coming back to Hawaii alive."

The Australian gently tried to shrug off the credit. "I had help," he said.

"How is the noble Kat?" asked Harlan. "He was the one who really sorted out the fish-god drama. I don't imagine you could bring him to the islands – I presume Darren is looking after him."

Stewart's smile slipped. "Kat's no longer with us. Passed away quietly a few weeks ago."

"Oh, John! I'm so sorry." The American was genuinely contrite. The big white Persian had left a lasting impression. "Was it at least a peaceful passing?"

"I reckon so. Thanks mate. I think he was helping me out one last time, in a strange sort of way," said the wizard.

Before Harlan could question that remark Wilko arrived at the foot of the stairwell and gave a cheery wave.

"Hello Wilko!" called the archaeologist. He and the Tasmanian shook hands.

If their exchanged greeting was less effusive than that shared by Harlan and Stewart, it may be regarded as a measure of the smaller man's comparative reserve. Any awkwardness about Hunter's previous girlfriend Jazz was felt only on the Australian's part and he was determined not to let it show, especially in front of the new girl!

After Haveta and Wilko were introduced to each other, John B. suggested they move to the bar adjoining the resort's restaurant. On the way he chatted to the maître d' and arranged for the visitors to be seated with him at dinner.

"Put their meals on my room tab, please," he directed. "Can't expect 'Hands On' Harry to pay for extra mouths to feed."

The maître d', experienced enough at his job to be tactful, nodded and refrained from expressing his relief that this meant at least two of the night's meals would be paid for promptly.

Over mai tais the two Australians got acquainted with the new love of Harlan's life. The Nordic looks weren't deceptive: Haveta was second-generation Scandinavian. While Harlan had been working on the Central Australian expedition that had almost claimed his life, she had joined the University of Hawaii as a lecturer in marine biology. They met at a staff meeting after the archaeologist's return, and as Harlan described it, looked into each other's eyes and found exactly what they didn't know they'd been looking for.

"After all, you did wish me the best, John B.," said the Hawaiian.

Wilko rolled his eyes. "Don't encourage him, Harlan." He looked at Haveta. "You're not another believer in this 'magic' nonsense are you?" he asked, forgetting his diplomacy for a moment.

The blonde laughed. "I'm a bit more skeptical than my dear man here," she said. "But I am willing to concede there are plenty of things in the world that we don't understand."

"Yeah, well, that's true. I've seen a few of those," Wilko admitted.

John B. was looking thoughtful. "Haveta, I know you're a *marine* biologist, but does your zoological knowledge extend to birds at all?"

She laughed again. "Not much beyond the basics that apply to bones and muscles across the animal kingdom. Why, have you got a sick seagull in your room?"

"No. A hawk," Stewart answered straight-faced.

The laughter stopped suddenly. "Seriously?" she asked.

The wizard nodded. "An *'io*, I've been told."

"Well… er… I can look. But a vet might be better, if you can find one who specialises in birds."

"I haven't been able to find one at all. None of the places we've stayed in have a clue – do you know anyone?"

Harlan shook his head. "This isn't our side of the island I'm afraid, my friend."

The marine biologist accompanied Stewart up to his room, leaving Wilko and Harlan at the bar.

"I'm sorry about that," said Wilko, musing to himself that Harlan was a trusting soul. Not that he thought John B. had any designs on Haveta, but he was conservative at heart and thought it looked – well – a bit odd.

"No worries, I believe the expression is," Hunter smiled. "John B. is an unusual man."

"Ain't that the truth?"

For a while they chatted about the coming days' itinerary, and the beauties of Hawaii. Wilko had taken less photographs than he'd intended, distracted by the golf, but the archaeologist gave him some useful tips on places to visit near the courses they'd be playing on.

"We're both free on the day you're in Waikoloa. We could drive over, meet you after you've played and show you some sights," Harlan suggested – an offer Wilko enthusiastically accepted.

They'd finished making arrangements by the time Haveta and John B. returned.

"How's the patient?" asked Harlan.

"Improving, I think," answered his 'dear one'. "Wouldn't let me near at first, but once John B. picked her up she was quite docile. I think it's just

a bad bruise and some lost feathers. When the swelling goes down she should fly again."

"It is a 'she' then?" asked Wilko, more interested than he'd let on.

Haveta looked a little sheepish. "I really don't know. My specialty is sea life, remember. I seem to remember the '*io* is supposed to be bigger than Hawthorn, but that may just mean it's a juvenile. That would probably be good. She, or he, will heal quicker. But John seems to be taking the right sort of care – the bird doesn't seem stressed."

The four friends were still chatting when the others in the tournament party started to trickle in for pre-dinner drinks. Appropriate introductions were made (or in some cases, attempted – Big Buck's bad day on the course had made him even less pleasant than usual).

'Hands On' Harry was about to complain about the extra diners, but John B. quickly pointed out that it had all been arranged, extra chairs had been added to one of the tables, and the cost of the visitors' meals was already taken care of. That last item, especially, seemed to soothe Barber.

After fifteen minutes or so of milling around the bar, at a signal from the maître d' everyone moved into the dining room, where they found two long tables laid out. Small hand-written place cards showed that Harry had made a quick 'hands on' decision about seating arrangements while the group was in the other room.

At the extended table, joining Stewart, Wilko and the visitors, were all of the Hawaiians including Namakaeha and Hiro. Shareta of course was there with her husband. And, perhaps as a gesture of irritation with the

Australians (one of them at least) the last two seats at the table were given to Wilma and Big Buck.

Or maybe it was just that Barber didn't want to share his own table with the Wilmingtons himself. The other four competitors and their travelling companions were placed with the Royal Green boss. This delighted Armitage Shanks III, and did nothing to brighten the evening of Glexie and Ariane.

*

Over dinner, in response to a polite question from Hiro Tanabe Haveta mentioned that her name was Swedish, meaning 'daughter of the sea'.

"Maybe that's why I feel so at home here," she said.

"Despite your Northern European origins, eh my dear?" smiled Harlan.

"That's right," she averred. "The place is so clearly dominated by what I've always thought of as 'my' element."

Namakaeha looked up suddenly from her meal. "That's bull! The dominant element of Hawaii is fire – the fire of the goddess Pele!"

Keeaumoku poked the air with a chicken leg. "She's quite right. Even being from Oahu she understands the truth of it."

The driver turned on him angrily. "What do you mean 'even from Oahu'?"

Papipi waved the drumstick airily and replied, "Those of us from the Big Island know we have a greater affinity with Pele. This is where She is still active, after all."

"But Oahu is the seat of her legends!"

Harlan stroked his beard thoughtfully. "Pele's legend extends across all of the islands – indeed, according to legend she is the source of those islands. Which of course reflects the volcanic origins of the whole chain."

"It makes sense that the islands have more in common than they have differences, surely?" suggested Shareta.

Harlan nodded. "Culturally, yes. Although it *is* only in the last two hundred years or so that they were unified as one country. More recently, a state."

"One country. Damned nonsense. Course it's a damned state," snorted Big Buck through a mouthful of food.

He got dark looks from everyone at the table except Wilma, though even she looked uncomfortable at her husband's tactlessness.

"But it *was* an independent nation prior to statehood, Mister Wilmington. Just like California, Vermont, and your own Texas," observed Hiro.

That last observation might have mollified another Texan – indeed, on a good day it may even have worked on the parochial Big Buck, but this was *not* one of his good days. 'Hands On' Harry's pre-dinner report on the tournament standings after the second round had only stoked the fire of his temper.

"How the hell does a damned Jap come to know so much about American history?" he demanded.

Hiro didn't even sigh. He put a calming hand on the arm of his wife who'd been about to respond sharply to the question, and in a very even voice replied, "I was born and raised in Hawaii. My father and his two brothers served in the American armed forces in World War 2."

"Ah didn't even know that was allowed!" said Wilma in genuine surprise.

"Oh yes. My father was a pilot. My Uncle Horoko was a sailor who, alas, never saw active duty…"

"Ah-ha!" Big Buck was about to seize on that remark but swallowing a mouthful of potato delayed him long enough for Tanabe to finish.

"… as he was one of the many killed at Pearl Harbour in 1940. The uncle for whom I was named also did not survive the war. He was in the Army."

Wilko, a keen student of military history, cautiously said, "The 442nd?"

Hiro nodded, his face betraying a mix of sadness and perhaps embarrassment at what he feared might be seen as 'showing off'.

"What was, or is, the 442nd?" asked Haveta.

Wilko looked to the Japanese Hawaiian, who politely gestured that the Australian should explain.

"The 442nd Regimental Combat Team was, I think, the most decorated unit for its size and length of service in the history of American warfare. Correct me if I'm wrong please, Hiro, but I think they were all American-Japanese, or of Japanese descent at least, three quarters of them from Hawaii, the rest from the internment camps on the mainland. Started out with about 4,000 men, and over the few years they were together there were so many casualties there were about 14,000 blokes in the Unit. And they won about 10,000 Purple Hearts between them."

"You know your stuff, brother," John B. said quietly and proudly.

"Thanks mate. You studied ancient history, I studied the War. Well, not studied, but I've read a lot," Wilko answered, equally quietly.

Big Buck gave a grumpy grunt into his dinner. He was acutely aware that his own family had no particular military pedigree.

"Well," said Harlan, obviously impressed. "They certainly continued the great tradition of Hawaiian warriors. Like the *pahupu* our friend here resembles," he said, indicating Kahekili.

Mehameha's chest swelled. "The tattoo is symbolic. The right side is the strong, male side. Where the weapons were carried. The *pahupu* are the protectors of Maui."

Namakaeha gave him a sour smile. "Your memory's selective, isn't it?"

Several at the table looked at her curiously.

She continued, "Remember the Professor telling us where the design came from? From the chieftain who took over Maui, who wore it first? The one from Oahu?"

Keeaumoku laughed. "He could hardly forget – he's named after him, aren't you Kahekili?"

The caddy didn't flinch. "Under Kahekili Maui didn't fall to Kamehameha like all the other islands did. The *pahupu* saw to that. Do you remember Professor Ritter telling us *that*?"

Harlan and Haveta both looked thoughtful. They each had at least had some dealings with the professor at University staff meetings. It was she who spoke: "I'm a little surprised Ritter would provoke the old rivalries."

"Not provoke, educate," corrected Keeaumoku.

"Ensuring the old traditions aren't lost," said Namakaeha, agreeing with Keeaumoku for the first time any of them had noticed.

John B. wondered to himself about how charismatic a character this academic must be. It was the only time he'd seen any of the three islanders seem at all deferential to anybody.

"Is this Professor Ritter Polynesian?" he asked.

"No," said Harlan. "He came to the University from one of the Institutes in Europe, I believe. He's an ethnographer, seems very much a specialist in traditional cultures. We work in similar fields – my job entails more field work, his is more historical research. And I avoid lecturing as much as possible. Professor Ritter is much more student-focused, I must admit."

"He's passionate about ensuring Hawaiian tradition and history are passed on, not lost," declared Keeaumoku.

Hiro nodded. "There is much to be said for honouring history."

His wife continued the diplomacy, she hoped, asking Kahekili, "So your tattoo copies the traditional markings of these *pahupu*?"

The Maui native smiled proudly. "Pretty much. I did decide against having my eyelid turned inside out and propped open."

"I don't blame you!" said Wilko, shuddering.

Kahekili's proud smile took on a condescending edge. "Sorry if that disturbs you, *menehune*," he said with doubtful sincerity.

"The eyelid tattoo is an effective substitute," said Haveta, quickly.

"They were famous, feared across the islands as ruthless killing machines," said Kahekili proudly.

There was a brief silence as everyone in the group digested not just the statement, but also the way in which it was said. Kahekili seemed oblivious.

He continued, "According to legend their spirits still protect the islands. Only family is truly safe."

Namakaeha looked at him coldly, Keeaumoku in something more like condescending amusement as he pointed out, "The '*aumakua* legends are not confined to the *pahupu*, my friend. All the families have them."

"The true families," the driver corrected.

Wilko looked lost. "Sorry, what's an amooka?"

It was Harlan who answered. "The '*aumakuas* are ancestor spirits, said to walk the old trails at night, guarding the land."

"I wonder if the old rivalries persist among the ghosts?" mused John B.

"No such thing as damned ghosts," announced Big Buck, who had all the imagination of a concrete slab.

There was a distant look on Hiro's face as he said, "I remember a story of the night walkers that my father told me."

"It was in the years before the War came to Hawaii, but was underway in Europe. A German officer had come to the islands, attempting to recruit support from people of Japanese origin. Tokyo had not declared her intentions, but there were those in the German High Command who evidently knew something of what was to come. This man had come to visit my grandfather, claiming knowledge of relatives back in Hokkaido. The rules of politeness obliged my family to make him welcome and offer food and lodging for the night. No more than that, I hasten to add," he said with a look at the Wilmingtons.

"As I said, my father and his brothers fought proudly as Americans when the time came. This particular German officer was an arrogant and un-pleasant man, according to my father. He accepted my family's hospital-ity as no less than he deserved. That evening, over the drinks and cigars that were the end to dinner that was expected of his hosts, my grandfather told stories of the history and traditions of Hawaii – the land he had come to call home. Among them was the story of the night-walkers, who were said to pass along a trail not far from my family's home."

"Not in town, then," observed Harlan with a smile.

"No. My grandparents had come here to work in the plantations, as many poor Japanese did at the time. When they saved enough to buy some land and build a home, it was on an unproductive part of the plantation which was being sold off. The German openly laughed at the native traditions. Perhaps as a result of too freely availing himself of my grandfather's wine and spirits, or his arrogance – for whatever reason, the officer went out late at night to defy the '*aumakua* and walk the old trail."

John B. looked over at Buck. "To prove there were no such things as ghosts?"

"That may have been so. My grandmother later suggested that their visitor had wanted to prove that native superstition was no much for modern German intellect."

"Let me guess," said Wilko. "The German was never seen again, right?"

Hiro smiled. "Oh no, my friend. When he did not appear at the breakfast table, the family went to look for him. He was found no more than ten minutes walk from the house, lying cold and dead on the trail. My uncle Horoko found him, and said that the man had died with a look of terror on his face."

"An excellent story, Mister Tanabe," said Keeaumoku approvingly, "And not the only one of its kind."

"It's like I said, only members of the family are safe. Those who aren't *kama'aina* risk death at night in the old country," said Kahekili with some satisfaction, and a significant look at the non-Polynesians at the table.

Harlan was probably the most amiable man John B. could remember meeting, but there was a definite edge to the archaeologist's voice as he said, "For those of you who don't share our local language, *kama'aina* means a 'native' Hawaiian. It's a rather vague term though. Even Max Ritter is circumspect about its use. Tell me, Kahekili - how would you define 'native'? The people of Polynesia migrated to these islands from across the Pacific too. So what if they got here before the Caucasians? Or the Japanese? How long do people have to live here to become *kahiko*? Sorry everyone, that means 'traditional'."

Keeaumoku looked uncomfortable on his friend's behalf as the tattooed man struggled for a response. Namakaeha gritted her teeth and said nothing.

Hiro again tried to play the diplomat. "I think the true test of *kama'aina* is in one's relationship to the land. There are those born here, like their father's fathers before them, who have no regard for the islands. They would rather leave for more exciting places, or perhaps they stay only to exploit the land. Such people are not true Hawaiians. There are others who arrive here from across the seas and straight away feel the islands speak to them. Instinctively they belong, and love the land.”

“Well, there’s a lot to love about the place,” agreed Wilko, jumping in to support the peacekeeping effort. “It’s beautiful, the weather’s fabulous, you don’t have all the dangerous critters we’ve got in Australia…”

“There are sharks,” reminded Haveta the marine biologist.

“And the ‘*io* in the air,” said Hiro with a smile to John B. “But they are our only natural predators. There are none on the land.”

Keeaumoku waved an admonishing finger and said, “You forget Pele, and the ‘*aumakua*.”

Tanabe smiled and replied, “Then let us say, no predators of an earthly nature.”

“Not quite,” said John B. “There’s man.”

Just as that somber note had been struck, ‘Hands On’ Harry struck a ringing note at the other table, rapping a wine glass with his spoon.

Satisfied that he’d attracted everyone’s attention, the tournament organizer stood and said, “Okay everyone, remember , tomorrow morning we’re off to Wiwo’ole first thing after breakfast. I want to introduce you all to the great Royal Green Estate – let you see what you’re competing for. I think you’ll be impressed enough to want a piece of it whether you win or not. The afternoon’s tournament play is at the great Kamehameha III course by the sea at Keauhou.”

Wilma turned to Big Buck. “That’s on our map ain’t it, honey?”

“Reckon so. We’ll get ourselves there all right. Ah’m damned sure Ah ain’t gonna be puttin’ mahself in the hands of no-one that believes in *ghosts*.”

The Tanabes, Wilko, Harlan and Haveta winced. John B. and Kee-aumoku barely contained derisive laughs. Kahekili and Namakaeha glowered, a piece of cutlery bending in the driver's hand. Wilma looked around nervously, mumbled a "Goodnight, everybody," and scurried out.

Big Buck followed, with only a grunt as farewell. No one at the table minded.

"Well, he's a character, isn't he?" said Haveta.

"Yeah, the sort we'd be better off without," said Kahekili, getting to his feet.

The Wilmington's departure at the end of Barber's little speech seemed to be the trigger for a mass exodus from the dining room.

Keeaumoku gave Harlan and Haveta a polite farewell, apologizing for the rudeness of the other two Polynesians who'd stalked off without a word. The Tanabes were similarly courteous to the visitors.

"I hope that we may meet again," said Shareta warmly.

"I'd like that," agreed Haveta.

"At Waikoloa, then? I've promised to show Wilko some good spots for photography," said Harlan.

Hiro smiled. "A beautiful part of the country."

"And historically very interesting, as your colleagues would know. It's an area Max Ritter's students get well schooled in."

Wilko grumbled slightly. "I think those three could take the 'rest' out of a rest day, given the chance."

"An 'ar-rest day' might be more in order," suggested John B., to satisfactory groans.

The Australians walked their guests out to the car park. They were surprised to find Namakaeha out there staring up at the sky, apparently stargazing.

"Nice night for it," said Harlan genially.

"Not yet," replied the driver in a distracted voice. She shook herself, glared at the foursome, and stormed back into the building, evidently much annoyed at having been disturbed.

The four friends exchanged puzzled looks, then embraces before the Hunters got into their car.

"See you soon – look after that bird," said Haveta, with a wave.

"That's a promise. I'm not going to mess with a native Hawaiian!"

.oOo.

14 CALLING HOME

With a curse under her breath, the brunette closed the freezer door and went to pick up the ringing phone. Her expression changed, though, when she saw the caller ID on the screen. The smile was evident in her voice as she said, "Hi babe!"

John B. was likewise smiling. "Hey pretty lady, just thought I'd give you a call and see how things are going down there. What's the time – I didn't wake you, did I?"

"No babe, it's just gone six – I was just about to make dinner." Elizabeth's irritation at being taken away from the task of selecting the night's frozen meal had totally evaporated.

"Sorry – I lose track of the time difference."

"What time is it in Hawaii?"

"A bit after ten. Listen, I won't keep you from eating…"

"Don't you dare hang up! It's been a long day and I could seriously do with a friendly conversation!"

"What's wrong?" asked the wizard, concerned.

"Oh nothing major – the air conditioning in the office was playing up. By the end of the day it was really stuffy, and everyone was just being irritable. Me included. It's good to hear your voice."

"Mm, likewise, I'm sure. Kaiser Ron should have shut the place down for the day," said John B.

Q chuckled at the memory of the heat causing their boss's latest exotic hairdo (another experiment by his wife the stylist) to wilt. "He would have loved to! Oh, but there's a magic number the temperature has to get to for that to happen, and with you being away, well, we didn't have the magic. Never mind, tell me about your day."

"Well, I proved to myself yesterday, yet again, that I really should give up golf. I'm a danger to wildlife."

 He went on to explain the incident with the hawk.

"Oh, poor bird! So what did the vet say?"

"Would you believe I haven't found one yet? A biologist looked at her this evening and reckons she's doing okay, as long as I keep her warm, comfortable and fed."

"That's all any girl can ask for."

"Yes, ma'am. Truth to tell, she seems to be becoming a bit attached to me." John B. didn't mention as he said this that Hawthorn was at that moment perched on the end of the bed on which he was stretched out. The 'io was watching, as if listening in to the conversation.

"So, no golf for you today, I assume. What did you get up to?"

"Lazed on the sand, threw myself in the water a few times – oh! Thinking of overheated like the office was, you won't believe the guy we saw this afternoon! I was on the beach talking with Glexie and…"

"What's a Glexie?"

"Oh, sorry. She's one of the girls in the tournament. Good golfer."

"So you're hanging out with the girls on the beach, eh?" There was just a little edge to Elizabeth's voice. The day's irritation hadn't quite disappeared, it seemed.

"Q, I'll hang out with anybody who's worth talking to. Hey, you're not being – jealous – are you?"

There was a pause before she replied, "I'd just like to be there."

"Pretty lady, I'd like you to be here too, believe me."

There was another momentary pause. Q was a little surprised at just how pleased she was to hear those words, and to feel a little unwinding of tension in her shoulders – tension she hadn't even realised was there.

"Okay. Thank you. What's she like?"

"Long dark hair – similar colour to yours but a little straighter. Not very tall. Lots of tattoos including a surprisingly nice sleeve. I'm not usually impressed by them."

"Pretty?"

"The sleeve? Yeah, it is. Ocean theme. Lots of waves, coral, shells and fish. Very intricate."

"I meant the girl, wise guy."

"Not as pretty as you. She's nice, but not quite my type. She's an insurance assessor."

"I used to work for an insurance company, remember?"

"Yes, but you got better," he replied, and was pleased to hear a chuckle down the phone.

"Yeah, I joined the Department. Big step up!" Elizabeth said laughingly.

"Ah, but look at the company you get to keep. Other than the heat, how *are* Tinkerbell, Kaiser Ron and the crew?"

"Oh, much the same as always. Oswald's developed a taste for playing heavy metal music through his headphones."

"Oswald? You're kidding!"

"He's been getting a little weirder ever since that day he got taken to hospital while we were all out of the office. Just before you, er… went off into the desert."

Neither of them realised that the mild-mannered Oswald had been on the wrong end of a spell cast by a mad sorceress to scramble John B.'s mind. Since it had hit the wrong target, the effects were not quite what had been intended.

Elizabeth continued. "Anyway, he's playing it so loudly that it's been bugging Jeff Masterman. So Jeff's taken to playing his classical music right up loud through *his* headphones. Standing near them it sounds like dueling hornets' nests with a doof-doof rhythm."

"Sounds like fun."

"No, not really. The truth is that the place just isn't as much fun without you."

"Sweet of you to say so, pretty lady."

"You're welcome. Anyway, you were talking about what happened on the beach."

For a little while John B. told of the guy in the rabbit suit (which got incredulous laughter), the interaction with Big Easy (which got sympathy) and the meeting with Courtesy (which got intrigue). By the end of his descriptions he was yawning.

"Am I keeping you awake babe?" asked Q, in genuine concern.

"I'm keeping me awake, and I don't begrudge a moment of it. I am tired though – haven't slept well the last couple of nights."

She nodded. "Strange beds, probably. I get that sometimes when I travel for work."

"Maybe. Bad dreams are more to blame."

“Nightmares? What’s brought them on? Hawaii not agreeing with your subconscious?”

“I don’t think it’s that,” said John B. with a shake of the head. “I really, *really* like this place. I’m serious about wishing you were here to share it. They’re not quite nightmares, I think – I can’t remember any detail when I wake up. Just vague impressions – a really bad day at school, something about a fireplace.” He yawned again. “Nothing to worry about, sweetheart.”

There was another tiny pause before Q said, “You’ve never called me that before.”

“What? Oh! Sorry – no offense meant!”

“None taken, you silly bugger. It’s nice, thanks. Just caught off guard.”

‘Me too,’ John B. thought, although he didn’t say it. What he did say was, “I think I really *am* tired. Time for me to sign off, I reckon. Have a good evening, pretty lady. Enjoy your dinner. I hope tomorrow is less of a hassle.”

“Thanks, I will, and I’m sure it will be. You take care of yourself. No sunburn, and no more bad dreams, hey?”

“Sounds like a plan. Goodnight, pretty lady.”

“Goodnight babe.”

After they each put down their phones, both of them spent some time staring into space. The conversation had produced some unexpected moments, and both of them had some thinking to do.

Elsewhere.

“Professor Ritter?”

“Yes? Oh – it’s you. How are things progressing?”

"Steady, but sure. I'm sorry to call so late…"

The teacher smiled thinly. He slept little, but didn't care to publicise that fact. "Not at all. I've said before, I'm always happy to talk to you. But if things are moving along well, why do you feel the need to call?"

"Uuh… well… I feel I'm being distracted. One particular irritation…"

"Causing you to lose focus?"

"Yes! That's it. I feel like I'm losing sight of the bigger picture."

"Hmm," the professor hummed thoughtfully into the phone for a moment. He actually knew exactly what he wanted to say, but felt it may be more effective to sound like some consideration was required. Even the best of students shouldn't feel that they were taken for granted. "Tell me, my friend, are you familiar with the operation of an SLR camera?"

"SLR…?"

Ritter kept his sigh away from the phone. "Single lens reflex. A popular choice for photographers before digital cameras appeared, and the mobile phone started to replace *them*."

"Oh, yes sir, I know the things you mean. Just didn't recognise the term."

"And do you know anything about their operation?"

"A little, I think."

"How does the photographer focus?"

"By adjusting the… oh! Yes! I get it. By *doing* something."

"Focus requires action."

"Of course! Thank you Professor Ritter! What would I do without you?"

.o0o.

15 THE BUCK STOPS HERE

"It's come to a damned fine pass when a man can't enjoy a smoke in his own damned room!" growled Big Buck Wilmington.

"It surely is, Buck," agreed Wilma. "But you know they only do it so they can charge extra if they find you *have* broken the rules," she continued, tapping the small sign warning of a $200 cleaning fee if occupants smoked inside their accommodation.

"Of course! Any damned excuse to gouge more dollars out of us." Big Buck's brow furrowed as he thought for a moment. "How would they know if Ah'd been smoking in here?"

The truth, of course, was that a man with corks up his nose and cling-film over his nostrils would smell one of Buck's cheap cigars from three rooms away two days after it had been lit.

If Wilma was aware of this she didn't mention it, just replying, "Ah'm sure they have their ways, dear."

"Ah'm going to have a word with that hustler Barber tomorrow. His company's supposed to be paying our bills. They should be responsible if the damned hotel tries to charge me for having a cigar in my room."

"Yes Buck, they should. But you'd better check with him first – we do not want to be handed a $200 check by one of those native girls at Reception."

"Ha! Ah'd tell her what to do with her damned check! Still, you're right. Ah'll make sure Barber has it covered in future, but for tonight, well, a bit of fresh air before bed will do me good."

The intrinsic lack of logic in sucking on a cheap stogie in the 'fresh air' simply never occurred to the Texan. He snatched up a cigar and lighter, and stormed out of the unit. Big Buck seldom went anywhere without storming.

It happened that the Wilmingtons were in the last unit in their single storey block. It adjoined a substantial area of garden – an area mostly in darkness due to the foliage obscuring what would have been barely adequate lights even before the plants grew up.

Buck was engrossed in fiddling with his lighter as he paced around the garden. He'd accidentally jammed the safety switch on and couldn't get a flame out of "the damned useless damned thing". He was oblivious to the figure behind him – the figure that walked up quietly and swung a heavy metal bar forcefully into his right temple.

Big Buck was dead before he hit the ground. The shadowy figure quickly frisked the corpse and gave a small grunt of satisfaction at finding car keys in the trouser pocket. Buck's body was moved under a dense cover of bushes where it wouldn't be seen or stumbled over by anyone else entering the garden.

The dark shape made a rapid but silent exit in the direction of the car park.

If anyone ever checked the CCTV footage they'd see a roughly dressed unidentifiable figure, face masked by a baseball cap and a scarf, getting into the Wilmington's Buick and driving away casually. They wouldn't see the Buick turn down a small service road, because the cameras didn't cover that area. They wouldn't see the car being parked, and the driver making their way through a discreet gap they'd earlier made in a fence. It was the very fence that enclosed the garden where Buck's body lay.

While all of this was going on, Wilma had decided that it was time to raid the mini-bar for a soothing nightcap. Big Buck's behaviour over dinner had been provocative, she knew that, but some of the other white folks at the table should have helped him stand up to the natives, surely! She'd frowned at the plastic wine glass but at least it was clean. From the refrigerator she'd extracted a small bottle of Californian White Blend.

Not much, she thought, but it would do. And surely that Barber fellow's company would be meeting the cost of drinks, even if, as she suspected, fines for smoking in the room might be a bit more than could be expected.

To her great chagrin, though, when she went to open the screw cap on the little bottle it wouldn't budge.

She pursed her lips and glared at the offending item. It should *not* require Buck's help to open a simple bottle of wine. Seized by a flash of inspiration, she opened the closet door then shut it again on the top of the screw cap, using the edge of the door as a kind of vice.

Pushing on the door with her right hand she turned the bottle with her left. There! Movement! But not quite right. The whole cap was rotating around the top of the bottle, but not unscrewing. The little metal band that held the cap on hadn't broken off at its perforation as it was intended to.

Wilma glared at the little bottle, bereft of any further ideas but determined now that *this* was the bottle of wine that she wanted to drink. Californian White Blend clutched firmly in hand, she marched out to look for Buck. He would just have to sort it out.

She strode into the garden and saw in the gloom a dark figure near a shadowy bush. If the thought that the smell of cheap cigar should have been in the air entered her head, it didn't find anything to connect to.

"Buck! Ah want you to…" was as much as Wilma managed to say before the figure turned and cracked the metal bar across the side of her head. The proud daughter of the Hampton Whittlehamptons died as quickly as her husband had.

It was a busy night for the murderer. First Wilma's body, then Buck's, were carried out to the Buick and propped up in the back seat. Then all of their belongings were cleared out of the unit and packed into the car. The unit key was left neatly on the table, the lights turned off and the door closed.

The shadowy figure drove the Buick up, up into the high country inland of 'Anaeho'omalu. There were deep holes and fissures here in the old lava, many of them masked by foliage. It was into one such hole that the Wilmingtons and their luggage – even their matching monogrammed golf bags and clubs – were tossed. It would be a long time before they would be found. Even the archaeologists didn't explore much up here.

The few bloodstains on the upholstery had been carefully wiped up with one of the monogrammed hand towels that had then followed its luckless owner into the Earth. Then the Buick was driven down to the airport, and calmly parked where the rental vehicles are returned.

Leaving the keys on the front seat, the murderer made a casual exit from the car park. A little walk from the airport, another vehicle was waiting, parked in a little-used side road. It was a non-descript van, mostly still white except for where scratches and dents had left it discoloured by the rust that the salt sea air so swiftly engendered.

Another drive, and the van was parked near, but not too near, the motel at 'A Bay where the night's activities had begun. The shadowy figure's movements betrayed no hint of tiredness, but no suggestion of pleasure either.

Action had been taken, and it had been done well.

.oOo.

16 FINDING THE GREEN

The group's departure for Kealakekua was delayed by the fact that the Wilmingtons were nowhere to be found. They didn't appear at breakfast, or at the nine o'clock appointed 'meeting place' in the hotel foyer. A quick check revealed their room to be empty, the beds made and the key on the table.

It should be said that, beyond the show of concern that politeness required, the only person who seemed much disturbed by their absence was 'Hands On' Harry Barber. He'd earmarked the wealthy Texan as a potential property investor, and was loathe to lose a prospect.

The whole point of the tournament had been to attract buyers. Not a golfer himself, Barber had assumed it was a rich man's sport. The club fees seemed to support that theory, and most of the vacationing golfers he'd met in Hawaii were at least comfortably off. He'd done his research, and the golf clubs he'd targeted around the world were all in well-heeled locales.

Wilko walked in from the car park. "No sign of the Buick," he announced. "I guess that settles it. They've gone on to the hotel ahead of us."

"I suppose it is not surprising that *Senor* Wilmington would not wait for us all, *si*?" suggested Carlos.

"It would have been the polite thing to do," said Shareta.

"And thus exactly what he wouldn't bloody do," replied John B. "We might as well head for the *Resolution Inn*, hey Harry?"

Their destination had been named for the unfortunate William Watman, whose fate Courtesy had described. Perhaps not the memorial the sailor would have expected, but at least the little plaque on the hotel wall recognised his small place in history.

The *Resolution Inn* was one of the places where Stewart hadn't been able to secure a separate room, and the prospect of trying to sleep that night was perhaps already making him irritable.

Barber pursed his lips in annoyance at not being able to 'pitch' at the Wilmingtons en route to the hotel. 'They'd better show up at the Estate!' he thought. "I guess you're right. We might as well get a move on. Are the bags loaded, Namakaeha?"

"Of course," said the driver. She and several of the group had taken care of that task earlier with no sign of any Hands On assistance. She adjusted the tilt of her woolen hat. "Let's get going."

*

'Hands On Harry' was not impressed to find that there was no sign of Big Buck and his wife at the *Resolution Inn*. He was uncharacteristically quiet as he shepherded the group back onto the bus to visit the new estate. The golfers and their entourage were much less reluctant to talk about the absent pair.

"It would seem he has conceded defeat already," suggested Shigekiyo.

Wilko looked surprised. "I know he had a crook day yesterday, but that's golf! One day you can play rubbish, the next day you could be a world-beater!"

"Lost face," said Makkuro simply.

"I don't know that that's a Texan concept," said Ariane.

"But pride certainly is," said John B. "Big Buck's took a dent on day one, then from what I hear, got a real belting yesterday."

Glexie looked skeptical. "But to walk away from a free holiday? The Wilmingtons didn't strike me as the type to miss out on anything free."

"Never underestimate the male ego," pointed out her best friend.

The bus pulled in to a cul-de-sac, amid a sea of lush rolling grass. A few outcrops of hard black lava rock poked up here and there. Surveyors' pegs gave some indication of proposed allotments, and where some roads might go, but as yet the only structure visible was a demountable office, sitting on a concrete slab obviously intended for a much bigger building – presumably a house.

Namakaeha folded her arms and remained resolutely behind the wheel of the parked bus. Clearly she wanted no part of what was coming next.

A shriek from Hawthorn made it equally clear that the '*io* had no intention of staying in the bus with the driver. As John B. bent to pick up the nesting box the hawk jumped up onto his shoulder. The pair looked at each other and seemed to come to some mutual understanding. The wizard stepped out onto the estate content in his role as an ambulatory perch.

Barber led the way towards the prefab office. The others walked behind, with at best modest expressions of enthusiasm. For some at least, that improved as they crested a small rise and realised that Royal Green Estate really did open up directly onto the beach in a small sheltered cove.

Glexie stopped in her tracks, grabbed Ariane's hand and squeezed it for a moment. "Look at that, hon," she breathed.

Her friend returned the squeeze. "Impressive," she agreed.

'Hands On' Harry stood on the step leading to the office, turned and threw his arms wide. "Isn't it great?" he asked enthusiastically.

It must be said that there was nobody unimpressed with the appearance of the estate.

John B. spoke, with more than a hint of suspicion in his voice. "It looks beautiful, Harry, I've got to give you that. Which bit does the winner get?"

Harry slid open the glass door of the office. "At this point," he began, "I'm going to hand you to my office manager Nikki Martin…"

A sandy-haired girl seated behind the desk in the Spartan office waved her hand, trying not to look too irritated at Harry as she signaled that she was on the phone.

"Ah-hah… um… well, it's great to see Nikki's busy, so I guess I'd better show you around after all."

Things were not going to plan for Harry today. He'd intended to have his office manager look after the group as a whole, while he targeted those he perceived as the 'high wealth' individuals in more private conversation. Okay, so he hadn't landed the complete set of high rollers he'd anticipated when he devised the golf tournament plan, but there was money amongst them and he was determined that some of that would be invested in the Royal Green Estate. So he put a brave face on it as he led the little band to the top of the highest of the small rises.

He launched into his spiel about what a "great investment opportunity" he was offering, and the "great future" that lay ahead for the Royal Green Estate.

"What's with the name, anyway?" called Keeaumoku.

"Well, 'royal' because this stretch of the coast is often associated with, er, the famous king… er…"

"Kamehameha," said Hiro in cheery helpfulness.

"Yes – that's right – and the 'green' for the lushness of the lawns we've managed to develop."

Even the pickiest of his crowd had to recognize that the effort of turfing what had been a bare lava field was quite impressive.

Harry went on, "I think, too, that it adds a little extra appeal to the golfers among you for your address to include the name 'Royal Green', eh?"

"What was wrong with the real name – Wiwo'ole?" asked the Big Island native Keeaumoku tersely.

John B. couldn't resist adding to Barber's obvious discomfort. "That's got a nice ring to it, Harry. What does it mean?" he asked as innocently as he could.

"Ah… er…" Harry stammered. He found it hard enough to look the purple-garbed Australian in the eye. The addition of the predatory gaze of the hawk coming from the same eye-line only made matters worse.

"Fearlessness. Bravery," explained Kahekili.

"Wow – hard to go past that as a name, I'd have thought," observed the wizard.

"Well… ah… it's more of a regional name than this particular location. The local police district for instance, uses the name." 'Hands On' Harry didn't lack some ability to think on his feet.

"Is that true, Keeaumoku?" the Australian asked quietly.

The local shrugged. "Yeah, broadly, I suppose." To Harry he continued, more loudly, "I should point out that this is my land anyway, in a historical sense."

"But in a legal sense, it's not. It belongs to the Royal Green Estate Company. Do you understand property law, Mister Papipi?" asked Barber.

He was miffed. He'd expected the Kapolei Country Club tournament to be won by a wealthy tourist, not an uppity local. Well, at least if the Polynesian took out the tournament, there'd be one more competitor who might be convinced to buy what they hadn't won.

"Not especially," was Keeaumoku's answer. "Don't care."

Ariane, looking on quietly, showed no reaction but wrote a mental note to herself.

Feeling a little more composed, and determinedly not looking at the hawk or Stewart, Barber fielded a number of questions about proposed facilities, services, commercial developments – much more the sort of enquiries he was used to from prospective buyers than ones about the property's name. After a few minutes of this he held up his hands and again spread his arms expansively, like he was delivering the Sermon on the Mount.

"It's about time I let Royal Green speak for itself. I'll let you have a wander around – soak up the great atmosphere. And remember, while you're all here as our guests, you can buy your own piece of this paradise at a very special price," said Harry.

"Special for who?" wondered John B. aloud, to the amusement of those around him.

Royal Green's business principal and chief salesman managed to corral Armitage Shanks III and the black-and-white Japanese businessmen, then lead them away in earnest conversation. He'd worked out that they and the Tanabes were where the money was, and the latter couple was side-stepping him quite adroitly, so far. John B. had correctly read Barber's thinking, and privately wondered, with much amusement, how 'Hands On' Harry would react to knowing that the scruffy Australian had access to more financial reserves than almost all of the group. Much as he was coming to appreciate Hawaii, he wasn't about to invest in it just yet, and certainly not on the word of H. Barber.

The two Australians strolled over towards the beachfront, alongside Glexie and Ariane. Hiro and Shareta were a little ahead of them.

"You're asking a lot of questions, mate," said Wilko quietly.

"I just want to have some confidence around your potential winnings, old friend."

The Tasmanian laughed. "Hah – thanks for the thought mate, but I wouldn't be betting on me with *my* money."

The wizard smiled. "Well, somebody has to win it. I'd like it to be someone deserving, and I don't want that person to be disappointed. Let's just say I'm trying to keep Harry honest."

"You might be asking a lot of yourself," observed Ariane. "I hope you like a challenge."

John B. winked at her and said, "He's not the first rogue I've had to deal with."

The New England girl looked at Wilko to gauge his reaction. The Tasmanian didn't give much away beyond a little nod of the head. Life around John B. Stewart had become surprising (not to mention challenging) in recent times.

The office manager Nikki had finished her telephone conversation and emerged to circulate among the visitors. She made the mistake of walking over to the six now standing at the beachfront. She stared open-mouthed at the raptor perched on the shoulder of the man in the purple t-shirt. None of the others seemed bothered, so she steeled herself to act casual.

John B. repeated his earlier question about where the 'prize' allotment would be. The woman looked puzzled.

"Hasn't Har… Mister Barber said?" she asked.

"He referred us to you," explained Hiro.

"I did some checking while I was back in Oz. To keep the prize value under the 'amateur' threshold it's apparently a block designated as 'promotional' and so 'without significant retail value'. Not sure what that really means though. All we've ever been told is that the prize would be a 'major beachfront property', whatever that means," added Wilko.

"It sounds like he's leaving the decision up to you," said John B. with a grin.

Nikki looked thoughtful. Despite the nickname Harry had coined for himself, she was acutely aware that most of the work was left to her. Barber spent a lot of time on the phone trying to 'do deals' with potential investors and high profile government officials, but when it came to dealing with contractors and making day-to-day decisions on what bills could and would be paid it had been made clear that "that's the office manager's responsibility". Nikki Martin - office manager and company director – an appointment she suspected had been made so there'd be someone else to blame if, or rather when things went wrong. She looked around at where they stood.

"Well then – I'd say you're standing on it," she replied.

It almost certainly wasn't what Barber had in mind, but if he wasn't prepared to make a commitment and wanted to leave her to deal with the punters as best she could, well, he'd just have to put up with it. She gave a decisive nod, and walked off to talk to the two Hispanic-looking gentlemen who would hopefully not ask more awkward questions.

Ariane and Hiro in particular exchanged looks, as if to say, "You're a witness to that, aren't you?"

Wilko stood looking out over the ocean. His purple-shirted companion put a hand on his shoulder and said, "I know it's not Tasmania, mate, but there are a lot worse places to live."

"It's pretty good, isn't it? Hey! Don't you dare try to use your 'magic' to sway the result!" he said sharply.

"I would never do that old friend," said the wizard with total sincerity, oblivious to the puzzled look Glexie threw in their direction – neither Australian had realised she was standing quite so close. "All I'll do is wish that whoever wins it will treat the land with the respect it deserves."

"I can't argue with that, I suppose, can I?"

Hawthorn stretched. The damaged wing had a little more movement now.

*

The Kamehameha III course at Keauhou was modeled on a traditional links course, with several holes following the line of the beach in creative ways. That's where the term came from – old Scottish courses that linked the land and the sea.

More so than with any other course, the weather is as integral a part of a links game as the greens, the flags and the cups. Unlike Scotland, it wasn't sleeting, raining or even misting. But what the players did face this day was a swirling twisting wind that blew up off the ocean as the afternoon wore on. It was like the sea breeze's big brother with a bad attitude.

Shareta, Wilko, Armitage and Hector at least had the advantage of the slightly earlier hit-off and so managed four holes before conditions started to escalate through 'tricky' to 'bad' to 'diabolical'.

As Shareta hit an excellent drive on the third hole Shanks lamented that she had the added advantage of playing off the Ladies' Tees. "It's not like she needs the extra yardage!" he said plaintively.

Wilko, like Shanks a good head shorter than the former model, shrugged resignedly. "Rules is rules, old son. They're the same the world over."

After struggling with the wind on the first day of competition, Hector determinedly kept his shots low whenever possible. It was a sensible strategy that the others attempted to follow whenever possible. Unfortunately, it didn't always quite work out.

Witness the fourteenth hole. By this time the wind was playing fiendish tricks with lofted balls.

Pro golfers, and those who aspire to be, are sticklers for precision. Real sticklers. A caddy who wants to keep their job will never say to a player, "Oh, it's about 150 to that front bunker and I'd say maybe 175 or 180 to the hole."

Hoadley knew his job. After a few moments careful gaze he turned to Shanks and said, "It's 154 to the bunker, sir. 167 to the front of the green and 181 to the pin. The wind is across but helping you slightly. However if you get above the protection of the trees it may help you more than you expect."

"Righto old man," said Armitage, and proceeded to chop the face of his club under the ball. It flew high and was, as the caddy had warned, caught by the wind off the Pacific. In other circumstances, Shanks might have been well pleased with a shot that travelled 180 yards or more. Not this time though, as he watched his ball take one bounce off the little ridge behind the green and disappear into the world's biggest water hazard.

Shareta and Wilko looked sympathetic – they knew how vulnerable they were to the same outcome. Hector had no interest in *simpatico*.

"This is how the shot should be played," the Spaniard said as he lined up his shot.

Certainly he struck the ball at the right angle to keep the flight path much lower than Shanks' had been. Two days earlier that would have probably been enough. Today's fluky ocean wind was a different matter. The crosswind abruptly swirled and became a headwind. Fernandez' ball stopped so suddenly that it almost looked like it had flown into an airborne pillow, landing with a *plop* in an awkward lie in the bunker short of the green.

Hoadley leaned to his employer and said, just audibly to the others, "Don't believe him, sir."

It was all Shareta could do to suppress a giggle.

Given the conditions, nobody carded scores they were especially pleased with. Shareta and Hector edged Wilko by a single stroke, with Armitage two further behind.

"I hope we don't get too many more days like this," said Wilko as they waited in the clubhouse for the bus to collect them.

Hiro nodded sympathetically.

"They're the sort of conditions that take the fun out of the game," continued the Tasmanian as he sipped at a beer.

*

Not much fun was a good description of the afternoon Glexie was having out on the course, and the wind conditions were only a small part of that.

With no caddy (Harry wasn't going to pay for one, and she'd decided she couldn't afford the unnecessary luxury), she found herself having to play almost in silence – the Japanese and Hawaiian pairs both choosing to converse mostly in their own language. It unsettled her a bit, as she wasn't used to being conspicuously ignored by men. Rather the opposite, in truth. Not that she actively encouraged it – she didn't flirt, but she was a gregarious soul who liked to chat.

An early attempt to engage in small talk with Kahekili about the similarity between his surname and the name of the course only managed to cause tension between the two Hawaiians. It seemed they had a fundamental disagreement about whether the *first* King Kamehameha – unifier of the islands his namesake later ruled - should be regarded as a conquering hero or a villainous invader.

Their argument spelt the end of conversation with the girl from that quarter. It also signaled a worsening in Keeaumoku's play for several holes until he managed to bring his temper, and thus his concentration, back in check. His game had threatened to spiral out of control. The wind was playing enough havoc without rushed club selections and even more rushed shots adding to the trouble. And each poor result added heat to his aggravation. It was only when he took himself off to a spot directly overlooking the rolling waves and spent a short while gazing out across the ocean that he was able to rein in his emotions.

Briefly Glexie considered risking approaching him to see if he was alright. She took a few paces towards him and saw several dark triangular dorsal fins in the water that appeared to be the focus of the Hawaiians attention. Her momentary delight at the prospect of dolphins evaporated when a few of the swimming shapes became visible within a rising wave. Sharks. Swallowing hard, she turned away, resolving to mind her own business and concentrate on her own game.

She knew better than to try talking to Makkuro. He wouldn't even make eye contact with her. Shigekiyo Yuki was at least polite in the exchanges that circumstances obliged him to make with her, but it was very clear he had no interest in chat, about the course, the wind, the game, golf in general or anything else.

In the end, she reasoned, it probably helped her. Ignore any annoyance and make the most of the lack of distraction. Given how badly the conditions affected the approach games of all three golfers, she was especially glad of all the time she'd spent practicing her short game. It kept her competitive with the two strong-hitting males, whose power advantage was nullified by the unpredictable wind.

Takafumi won their game within a game, although his score was only one ahead of what Armitage Shanks had carded. It was a narrower win than he'd wanted though – only a stroke ahead of Glexie and two up on Keeaumoku.

The Hawaiian's seeming commune with the ocean, or perhaps its denizens, had achieved some damage limitation to his game. If it did more, he wasn't saying.

.o0o.

17 TROUBLE IN STORE

After waving farewell to Glexie as the bus took her off to her game, Ariane wandered around the hotel looking for some company. Harry had stayed on at the Estate office, doubtless to the dismay of Nikki. He really didn't count as company anyway. No more than Namakaeha would on her return. The driver spent her time between jobs reading. Any attempt at conversation by anyone was met with monosyllabic answers and a view of her beanie over the top of a book.

Carlos would have been an acceptable option, but he'd left shortly after Hector, calling a cab to take him on an expedition of bar-hopping. Ariane didn't mind a drink, but she thought there should be better things to do with a Hawaiian afternoon than spend it in a succession of hotels and sports clubs.

That left John B., and to be honest, he was the preferred option anyway. The Australian was scruffy, and in the most fundamental way not her type, but she didn't have to fancy the man to enjoy his company. And she was pretty sure he didn't have the wrong idea about any attentions she seemed to pay him. He seemed comfortable with platonic, and that suited her very well indeed.

It took some searching, but eventually she found Stewart at a small table by the pool, writing postcards with his back to her. Hawthorn was perched on the back of the chair beside him. The Australian was just finishing the last of his writing as she approached.

"Right – dear Scarlet in Alice Springs, Q of course, Tinkerbell and the gang in the office, and that's Darren's done. That's everyone," he said to the *'io*.

"Hi John. Sounds like I found you at just the right time," said Ariane.

He turned and smiled. "G'day mate. Yeah – all done with these. I'll buy some stamps at Reception and ask them to post 'em for me."

Returning the smile Ariane said, "I couldn't help overhear. 'Scarlet', as in O'Hara? Is she your girlfriend?"

Stewart threw his head back and laughed heartily. "Oh jeez, I'm so glad she can't hear you ask that! She'd be mortified! No, no. Scarlet – Charlotte O'Hara Burke is someone I used to work with. We got to be friends when we, ah, travelled together. She moved up to the Red Centre permanently after we'd visited there. No, Ariane – I don't really have a girlfriend. Friends who are female – one in particular, I must admit, but, um, not a girlfriend as such."

"Uh-huh." If the legal officer believed him she certainly didn't sound like it. She decided to let the matter rest. "Anyway, have you got any plans for the rest of the day?"

"I had thought about heading for the beach, but this wind that's picked up is putting me off the idea."

"Too cold for you?"

"Not that so much as not fancying getting sand blown into eyes and other places where sand doesn't belong," he replied.

Ariane nodded. He'd painted an unpleasant picture in her head.

John B. looked thoughtful. "If you feel like a stroll, we could do a bit of the King's Highway. Get a cab out a couple of miles and walk back."

Ariane smiled and said, "A walk sounds good. Let me go and put some decent shoes on."

"Ah – that's a good idea! I'll meet you at Reception in five minutes or so, hey?"

The King's Highway is a 175-mile long walking trail that, in pre-motorised Hawaiian history, was used for commerce, troop movements, carrying messages, collecting taxes, and other 'official' activities as well as simply travelling between settlements to visit friends and family. King

Kamehameha I had determined that he would no longer either commit or permit highway robbery on his island. To that end he made a law guaranteeing free safe passage to any and all who used the trail.

Originally the trail is thought to have gone right around the Big Island, but over the years much of it has disappeared under the rising tide of modernisation. Parts are still preserved though, especially along the western coast, where it's also known as the *Ala Kahakai* or 'shoreline trail'.

Ariane had expected the rescued hawk to be perched on John B.'s shoulder as they walked the trail. Talon holes in his purple t-shirt indicated that was where Hawthorn had taken to riding. But it turned out that when Stewart had gone back to his room for his shoes, the brown bird had jumped straight into the box that served as a nest and promptly gone to sleep.

"Still healing," he'd theorized.

Their walk was, as John B. had suggested, a leisurely stroll. Left to herself, Ariane might have made more of a brisk pace just out of habit, but her companion moved at a casual amble and there seemed no good reason to do otherwise.

Much of the *Ala Kahakai* took them across fields of the hard, sharp-edged lava stone called *a'a*, and it was here they really appreciated the ingenuity and efforts of the workforce Kamehameha had used to prepare the trail. Rocks that had been worn smooth by water had been brought from the seashore and laid as steppingstones. Elsewhere, flat lava slabs had been laid over rough areas of *a'a*. There were other paths simply made by laying more brittle clinkers across the hard lava. The impact of hundreds, or thousands of feet over generations had worn them down into a bed of pebbles that made a relatively comfortable walking surface.

There were places across flatter ancient lava flows where the trail could only be distinguished by a line of small chunks of white coral. John B. explained to Ariane that he'd read how these pebbles reflected moonlight and made the trail passable at night.

The pair stopped to look for small bright red shrimps in a couple of little ponds they passed. The *'opae'ula* were popular aquarium pets, but the travellers just enjoyed the simple pleasure of spotting the little critters in their native habitat.

At one point they came across a cluster of carvings that had been made in the black volcanic rock.

"I've read about these," said Stewart. "One theory is that they're just distance markers, but there's also some suggestion that they've got some ritual significance. Maybe memory markers or part of a story line."

"Hmm, that makes more sense," said Ariane as she knelt to examine them. "Carving into this rock would have been hard work – you'd think that whoever did it had a really good reason. It's funny – some of these symbols or whatever they are look a lot like ones I've seen in a museum back home. Old Algonquin carvings."

The wizard nodded. "That doesn't surprise me. There are similar carvings – very old – in parts of Scotland. From what I've read no-one knows what *they* really mean either, but the same patterns and symbols turn up in odd places all over the world."

"Racial memory?" the New Englander suggested.

"Could be. Wilko would shrug and call it coincidence but I can't help wonder. It's like a niggling feeling that I should – I don't know – recognise them somehow."

She looked at him, puzzled. "Is there any reason why you should?"

"No. Like I said, just an odd feeling."

Away from the ocean's edge the wind, while still fresh, was less aggravating. Certainly it wasn't enough to offset the warmth of the sun. Their comfortable perambulation whiled away the afternoon, just as they'd hoped.

On the outskirts of Kealakekua they spotted a shop at the side of the road, not far from the Trail.

"Fancy a drink?" asked John B.

Ariane shook the water bottle she'd been carrying. "Not much left in this, and what there is has gotten warm, so, yes. Good idea."

As they approached, they realised that there was a little group of 'trolley people' at the side of the store. Among them was the former Vietnam War engineer Ese. It was hard to tell if the big man recognised the Australian. The two men did make eye contact, at which the veteran quickly looked down and turned his back. Stewart was happy to not pursue the encounter.

"They get around, apparently. I wonder how?" the wizard quietly said to the young woman beside him.

"Same as we just did, I suppose. Walk. That's one advantage of the trolleys, though it's not my idea of a mobile home. Come on, let's get those drinks."

'Self-Service Supermarket' said the sign above the door.

"No good for people who can't help themselves," observed John B.

Ariane rolled her eyes. "Are you always like this?" she asked.

"Sometimes I can't help myself," Stewart replied.

The store was bigger than it had looked from outside, and stocked a wide range of items from camping equipment, like the gas bottles on racks out front, to a quite impressive variety of groceries.

The proprietor, Bill Fitzwilliam, was an overweight, rather florid man who was perched on a stool behind the shop counter. He called out as John B. and Ariane entered – the only two customers in the store, as it turned out, "Anything special you folks are lookin' for?"

"These will do for a start, then we'll have a look around. Thanks," said Stewart as he selected two cold bottles of soda squash from a small display unit on the counter. He paid for them with a handful of rather ratty dollar bills. They were lighter than coins but a lot less durable, the wizard reflected, not for the first time.

"Sure thing. You want somethin' stronger, it's in the cold cabinet along the side there," said Bill, waving in a generally 'over there' direction.

John B. grinned. "Not a bad idea. We'll take a look, thanks mate. Start with these to take the edge off the thirst, though."

"You do that. Anything you're lookin' for, I probably got it. And if I haven't got it, I can get it for you," said Fitzwilliam, who gave a conspiratorial wink that made the Australian surprisingly uncomfortable.

He took his change and delivered the squash to Ariane who was idly scanning the grocery shelves.

"Our host over there reckons he has some stronger options in his cold cabinet. Maybe a beer?"

"Tempting, after the walk," agreed Ariane. After a mouthful of her drink she indicated the shelves she'd been examining. "He's got some quite exotic stuff in here. Real Scottish shortbread, Argentinian cheese bread mix, tinned artichokes, even jars of truffles in oil!"

"Impressive. He did say he stocked anything we might want, and if he didn't he could find it."

"Well, that's good service," she said.

John B. looked uncertain. "Yeah, it sounds it. But something struck me as a bit creepy – hey! There's our bus!"

The eighteen seater had just pulled up outside the 'Self Service Supermarket'. Glexie and the two Japanese got out and headed into the store. Keeaumoku and Kahekili followed, evidently with less enthusiasm.

Namakaeha, who clearly hadn't wanted to stop but was prevailed upon by her insistent passengers, got out of the driver's seat and stood at the front of the vehicle, radiating grumpiness.

Glexie was delighted to find two friendly faces in the store, and greeted both Ariane and John B. with hugs.

"Wow! Fancy meeting you guys here! Oh, I am so glad to see you!" Trying to keep her voice diplomatically quiet, she launched into a description of her afternoon and its frustrations.

Looking over her shoulder John B. suddenly said, "Uh-oh, it looks like there might be more unpleasantness in the offing…"

Big Easy had shuffled over to the bus and started to climb on board. Whether he was looking for a ride, a place to sit down, or a chance to pilfer anything that might have been left lying around only he would know. And that, only maybe. But Namakaeha suddenly noticed and went after him.

She reached up, grabbed the hem of the greasy black hooded jacket he was wearing, and tugged hard. That pulled Ese off balance enough for the driver to grab his arm and drag him back off the bus. John B. couldn't hear their voices from inside the store but it was obvious that heated words were being exchanged. Namakaeha still had a hold of the big man's arm, while he'd balled his fists and was leaning threateningly towards her.

Her response was to plant an open palm squarely in the centre of his chest, a forceful shove that rocked the veteran onto his heels. He staggered back, hitting the side of the bus. By the look on his face he appeared to be growling. They squared off, looking like a pair of heavyweight prizefighters.

Suddenly Kahekili ran into the picture. Evidently he too had seen what was going on from inside the store. To the wizard's great surprise the man with the warrior tattoos rushed to put himself in between the two antagonists. Stewart still couldn't make out what was being said but it was clearly effective. The shoulders of both the would-be fighters slumped. Namakaeha turned away, muttering angrily. Ese withdrew, shuffling guilt- ily away. The big man didn't seem to shrink back into himself as he had when confronted by Courtesy, but his readiness to fight had certainly been defused.

Kahekili started to walk away. Keeaumoku had walked out of the store, belatedly, and had a quiet word with his caddy. The Maui native glowered at his golfing partner, gave a terse reply punctuated by a jabbing finger to the shoulder and stormed away. At first John B. thought he was following Big Easy – that was the direction he took – but instead he stopped and stood with arms folded at the other end of the bus from Namakaeha, who was in the same posture. They looked like a pair of belligerent bookends.

Makkuro and Yuki had been oblivious to the goings-on outside. They had quickly found their way to the cold cabinet and been pleased to find cans of a Japanese beer they were both fond of. As they were about to walk away though, Shigekiyo had noticed something else that gave them even greater delight. He grabbed his friend's shoulder and brandished a grey lump that was wrapped in plastic.

Takafumi looked mildly interested, then his caddy turned the package over and showed him the price ticket. Anyone watching would have thought they could have seen the wheels spinning and the numbers flash- ing behind the businessman's eyes. His silver haired companion had re- acted in exactly the same way. They grabbed several more of the shrink- wrapped packages and hurried to the counter.

Yuki engaged Bill Fitzwilliam in quiet but earnest conversation. The shopkeeper was no poker player. The expression on his face shifted rapidly from boredom to puzzlement to avarice to craftiness. Makkuro extended a hand. Fitzwilliam looked at it uncertainly, until Shigekiyo slid some large denomination notes across the counter. The proffered hand was grasped and shaken quickly before the grey packages were wrapped in white paper and stuffed into a bag. The store owner and the dark haired businessman exchanged curt nods. The two Japanese men walked briskly out to the bus.

Oblivious to the rather furtive transaction happening at the counter, John B. and the two girls had arrived at the cold cabinet. The wizard and Ariane were contemplating beer options when suddenly Glexie said, "Eeew! Gross!"

"What's the matter, hon?" asked the legal officer.

An edge of plastic gripped gingerly between thumb and forefinger, the accountant held up one of the grey packages. "It's a… it's a…"

"Shark fin." Stewart's voice dripped with displeasure.

"Why would anyone buy one of these? A weird souvenir?" asked Glexie.

Ariane shook her head. "They make soup out of them in Asia."

"Wow – some people will eat anything," her best friend replied. She flipped the package back on its shelf and they made their way to the counter, clutching three bottles of the local lager.

"That's not the worst of it," said Stewart grimly. "My problem is with how they're sourced. The sharks get netted, their fins hacked off, then get thrown back in the sea still alive. The ones that don't get torn apart by other sharks bleed to death, or drown because they can't swim properly without their fins." He gave Fitzwilliam a dark look as he handed over money for the beers. "It's a cruel bloody practice. If it isn't illegal it should be."

Bill laughed, immediately earning him the scorn of his three customers.

"It's supply and demand," the shopkeeper said. He didn't mention the two customers he'd just sold a parcel of fins to, but had them in mind as he continued, "There are plenty of people out there who want to buy them, and as long as they've got money to pay, I'll have product to sell. Like I told you – if you want it, I've got it, or I can get it. That's market forces, buddy."

"I wish *your* market would crash," John B. said bitterly.

Fitzwilliam wore a smug smile. "Not much chance of that, buddy. I've got this little part of the world all sewn up."

The three visitors didn't waste any more words on the venal trader. If he hadn't already paid for the drinks before the conversation happened, Stewart would have boycotted the store on principle. They made their way out to the bus.

"Room for two more," Ariane said to Namakaeha, more in statement than question. The driver shrugged and made no argument.

As they passed the seat Kahekili occupied – conspicuously a few rows away from Keeaumoku, the wizard bent and said to him quietly, "Well done breaking up Big Easy and Namakaeha."

The tattooed man gave a half smile. "Thanks. I knew the old guy at University. We all did. Some of the others used to give him a hard time." He was looking at the backs of both the driver and his golfing partner. "I always thought he should have some respect as a warrior though. Whether you agreed with the war or not, he got damaged fighting."

"Well said, mate," affirmed the Australian, and moved to sit down.

"Thanks," Mehameha called after him in a low voice.

Openly disagreeing with Keeaumoku evidently didn't sit well with the man. John B. wondered silently whether it was the actual disagreement that was the problem, or the fact of it being observed in public.

.oOo.

18 COLD BLOODED

Bill Fitzwilliam sat behind the desk in the little office at the rear of his shop. Ordinarily he'd be well home by now. The shelves had been restocked, the till counted, and the money secured in the safe. The combination of his comfortable armchair, a cold beer and a Hank Williams album was as appealing a prospect for the evening as ever, but there was money to be made. Who would have thought he could undercut the price of shark fins in Japan and still turn a good profit?

He drummed his heels on the wooden floor. At last, he saw a cab pull in to the parking area beside the store. He heard doors open and close, then the sound of the vehicle driving away. There was a discreet rap at the outside door. He stood up and opened the door the inches the security chain would allow.

Partially visible by the office light spilling through the crack, Takafumi Makkuro offered a scantly polite wordless bow.

"Your buddy there with you?" asked Fitzwilliam.

The dark-haired golfer nodded once.

"Talkative, ain'tcha?" muttered the shopkeeper as he unfastened the chain.

Makkuro stepped into the office, closely followed by his caddy Yuki, who was carrying two insulated shopping bags.

"You carrying 'em back to Japan in those?" asked the storeman, wondering at the inefficiency of the Japanese Customs service.

"No. We will make other arrangements. These are to remove the goods from your premises," answered Yuki.

"Ah. Right. Well, they're in the cool room. First though, I need payment."

Makkuro pulled a wallet from the pocket of his dark slacks and opened it. It was thick with $100 notes. Fitzwilliam reached, but the Japanese businessman snapped it shut and pulled it away sharply from the grasping hand.

"We will see the items first," said Yuki.

The shopkeeper looked from one 'customer' to the other and shrugged. 'I can play the 'no talkee' game too,' he thought to himself, and beckoned the two visitors to follow him to the cool room.

Once there he lifted several plastic bags down from a shelf. Their contents were obscured by condensation on the inside of the bags.

Briskly Fitzwilliam led the way back out of the refrigerated storeroom and towards the office. Makkuro laid a restraining hand on his shoulder, but it was the caddy who spoke.

"Wait," said Yuki. "Are these the same quality as those we purchased this afternoon?"

Fitzwilliam contrived to look affronted at the thought that he could be in any way dishonest. "All of my stock is top quality!" he lied sharply.

Neither of his customers was perturbed by his indignation.

"The fine item displayed in the shop window is not always that which is found in the warehouse," said Yuki impassively. "Let us see."

Had Fitzwilliam been aware of some of the dubious business practices both Japanese men routinely engaged in themselves he may have appreciated their caution more. As it was, it was with poor grace that he led them out into the shop.

"I'm not turning the main lights on," he warned. "Don't want no-one drivin' by thinkin' I've started opening late. You'll have to put up with the security lights."

They made their way to the cold cabinet. Makkuro selected two plump shark fins displayed prominently on a shelf. The cryovac packaging caught the red glow of the security lighting, emphasizing the curve of the meat.

Yuki reached deeply into one of the bags the shopkeeper held, and pulled out two more fins, similarly wrapped. He and Makkuro exchanged one fin each and started to compare.

Fitzwilliam muttered impatiently under his breath. The caddy nodded, apparently satisfied. Makkuro, however, walked away looking suspiciously at the shark pieces he held. He stalked to the front of the store, hoping that the light of the street lamp not far away may be more helpful than the dim glow above the cold cabinet.

He stopped suddenly. A movement outside? Had he glimpsed a dark face, or at least the whites of a pair of eyes in the shadows at the other end of the storefront? He felt a sudden unease.

"Shigekiyo!" he called to his companion.

Yuki caught the note of urgency in the way his friend had called his name. He ran to join him by the glass doors.

Shaking his head, now seriously wondering if this transaction was worth the trouble despite the attractive profit, Fitzwilliam started to trot after the caddy. Well, it was more of a wheezing stagger than a trot. He hadn't moved at much more than a ponderous stroll for several years.

"Now what's wrong?" he snapped when he'd caught up.

"Makkuro-san believes he saw a person moving suspiciously outside," explained Yuki.

"You're paranoid, both of you. You'd think you were buying crack co-caine, not a couple of bags of damned shark fins!"

The two Japanese turned to face him, Yuki spinning quickly on his toes,

Makkuro moving slower and more ominously. Wordlessly the golfer held the two fins out to the store owner. Clearly he was harbouring similar misgivings about the value of this deal.

"Now just a damned minute! I've gone to a lot of trouble tonight to have these ready for you," Fitzwilliam lied in protest.

The three men were standing right by the front window that looked out on the racks of LPG gas bottles. The rack of gas bottles beside which someone had placed a black rucksack. A black rucksack that contained some very potent explosive and a simple timing device. A device that ticked over the critical time at just that moment.

Bill Fitzwilliam, Takafumi Makkuro and Shigekiyo Yuki never knew what hit them. What did in fact hit them in rapid succession was the window glass, exploding LPG, shrapnel fragments of the gas bottles, the concussive force of the bomb itself, and the roof of the supermarket crashing down.

*

It gets called the cold light of day, even in somewhere as warm as Hawaii. Even when it's shining on a scene still further heated by the embers of a fire which had consumed all but a few scraps of building framework.

It gets called that because at times the light seems remorseless, shining no pity on what it illuminates. It's that kind of cold.

Sheriff Barrett Lawson stood surveying the ruin. The firemen had left. They hadn't been able to offer much information on what had happened beyond the obvious: something had caused the gas cylinders to explode.

The shop had burned briefly, brightly, intensely and thoroughly.

Lawson nudged at some embers with the toe of his shoe, causing them to glow red. He frowned. It was an expression that marred what was otherwise a handsome face. The son of an African-American father and a Polynesian mother, he had the best features of both, and skin the colour of good coffee.

He was Sheriff of the Wiwo'ole District. As the senior law enforcement officer he led a small team whose 'beat' extended along the northwest coast of the Big Island. Trouble was rare, which suited Barrett very nicely, thank you.

One of his privileges of rank was to be allowed to use his own private vehicle as the Official Police Car by the simple expedient of sticking a removable blue flashing dome light on the roof. It meant he could run his Pontiac Firebird up and down Highway 19 to his heart's content at taxpayer expense. As part of his routine travels he'd encountered Bill Fitzwilliam on a few occasions. He had a hunch Bill might be something of a rogue at heart, but there'd been no complaints so he'd turned a blind eye to anything a little suspect.

As far as Lawson knew there should have been no-one in the store overnight. If there had been, it would take a good forensic examination to find the evidence. He sighed. If it weren't for the fact that Fitzwilliam wasn't answering his phone at home the whole mess could have been left for the insurance company to clean up.

If the shopkeeper didn't turn up soon that forensic examination would have to happen, just in case. And that would be a nuisance.

*

"Bit of excitement last night, eh? Sirens and fire engines and what have you," said Shanks, dipping a toast finger into his fried egg.

"Didn't hear a thing," admitted Wilko.

John B. diplomatically refrained from saying that it would be a stretch to hear the Apocalypse over his friend's snoring. The Tasmanian had a lifetime's experience of sleeping through his own nocturnal noiseworks. He wasn't sure how Hawthorn had coped, although the bird seemed calm enough, so evidently had slept, and indeed still did. The wizard's industrial strength earplugs and a couple of sedative single malts meant that he too had missed the night's activities, as he explained. It had been

157

a dreamless sleep too, although that wasn't a piece of information he thought to share.

"An enviable situation, Mr. Stewart," observed Hoadley, carefully cutting another slice of toast into fingers for Armitage.

"You're right there, Hoads," said Glexie. "I'm glad this is meant to be a rest day. Nothing more stressful to do than be driven to - what is it – Spencer's Beach."

 Their rooms had been on either side of Wilko's.

"Sadly, I am a light sleeper and I find nocturnal sounds… intrusive," said the gentleman's gentleman as delicately as he could.

 Glexie nodded. "Normally I sleep pretty well, but last night, what with one thing and another…"

"Probably a bit nervous about the tournament, eh?" suggested John B., attempting to be diplomatic. Wilko was oblivious anyway.

 Harry Barber bounced over to their table and leaned in over Ariane's shoulder, ignoring both her and the dark look she turned on him.

"On the road by ten, okay folks? Bags at reception, Namakaeha and I will load them on the bus and we can be at the *Kawaihae Harbor Inn* in time for coffee and doughnuts." He turned and bounded to another table without waiting for a reply.

 Ariane's smouldering glare followed him. "When he says 'Namakaeha and I' of course he really means that Namakaeha will be expected to do it herself."

"Yeah, I think his 'Hands On' nickname is a bit delusional. I haven't seen much sign of him getting his hands dirty," agreed her roommate.

 Wilko swallowed the last of his breakfast cup of tea. "I'm already packed and ready to go," he said. "I'm going to grab my camera, have a bit of a walk and take some photos.”

“I’ll bring your bag down with mine,” offered John B.

“Thanks mate – that’d be good.”

The Tasmanian strolled away, fitting the action to the thought. He was quiet enough to retrieve his camera and slip away without disturbing the sleeping ‘io.

His departure was the cue for some diplomatic shackles to be released. The genial Australian had become popular enough to earn some polite tact, at least when he was within earshot. But once he’d left, some of the sleep-deprived felt free to express their frustrations.

“It sounded like someone was dragging a wooden table across a tiled floor,” complained Shanks.

Keeaumoku had been in the room across the corridor. “I’m sure I heard fingernails on a blackboard,” he said.

“How can a little *menehune* like that make so much noise?” wondered Kahekili.

Glexie looked at the tattooed man, frowning slightly. “I’ve heard you use that word before. What does it mean?” she asked, as evenly as she could muster. She liked Wilko and suspected the term was offensive.

When Kahekili looked like being evasive Hoadley provided reinforce-ment for the insurance assessor. “I wondered the same thing, Mister Mehameha, having heard you use the same expression for my esteemed employer.”

“Eh?” said Shanks through a mouthful of eggy toast, dimly aware he’d been spoken about.

“Um… legendary characters. Little men – a bit like Irish leprechauns, I suppose,” was Kahekili’s awkward explanation.

Keeaumoku couldn't seem to resist the urge to correct his companion. "More historical than legendary, perhaps. They're supposed to have been the original inhabitants of the islands, before our ancestors arrived from other parts of the Pacific. Small dark people, good builders according to the stories Professor Ritter told us. When the Polynesians came they retreated up into the high parts of the islands and eventually just disappeared."

John B. looked thoughtful. "Interesting story," he said. "One that's got parallels all over the world, funnily enough. Maybe even…" with a look to Kahekili, "I wonder if the origins of the leprechaun stories are based in a similar history? Ah well, a thought for another time. Listen everyone, I do apologise for my old mate's snoring. If I knew what could fix it I'd have done it a long time ago. I'd like to say you get used to it, but I haven't found that to be true, I'm afraid."

He got a sympathetic pat on the arm from Ariane. "I think the *Resolution Inn* has thinner walls than the other places we've stayed. It hasn't really been a problem anywhere else."

"Oh, I could hear him in Kona," said Shanks.

"Indeed sir, but I would point out that the sound did not keep you awake for long," observed Hoadley.

John B. gave the gentleman's gentleman a sympathetic smile. He'd caught the subtext – the valet had not been so well rested, quite likely caught in a crossfire of slumber land sound effects.

"I'd better go pack," said the wizard, rising from the table with a handful of bacon and sausage pieces for Hawthorn. "I'll see everyone at ten."

That seemed a reasonable assumption. After all, he didn't know the group had been reduced in number. Again.

.oOo.

19 CALLING TIME

John B. would be the first to say he was nothing like as neat as his travelling companion. Well, perhaps second, after Wilko. The nesting box had been the tidiest thing on Stewart's side of the room before he'd gone round gathering up the books and clothes that were scattered across the floor. It was his standard organizational system, he'd explain – the horizontal spread. The hawk perched on the bedhead watching him and digesting breakfast.

John B. was just zipping up the kitbag when the phone on Wilko's bedside table rang. The startled Hawthorn keened and flapped the undamaged wing.

"Sorry, mate," said Stewart soothingly. "I hadn't realised he didn't take the thing with him." He sat on the bed and stroked the ruffled head feathers of the *'io* as he picked up the mobile with his other hand, not looking at the caller ID.

"Hello, Wilko's phone. John B. Stewart speaking."

"John, hi! It's Jazz! Is my favourite little guy around?"

The wizard smiled. Evidently Jazz was the only person who could use a term like that for Wilko without upsetting him. Embarrassing him, probably, but not making him angry.

"No sorry – he's out taking a few photos before we head off to the beach."

"I didn't know Canberra had a beach."

"Oh, sorry – didn't occur to me you didn't know. We're in Hawaii. Our boy won a golf tournament back home – got us ten days here while he plays to win a bit of beachfront property."

"Wow, that's fabulous! I love Hawaii. That's where I first met Harlan.

Hey, are you catching up with him if he's there? Say 'hi' for me if you do. I gather he's got himself someone special – I hope he's happy."

"We have, I will, he has and he is," said John B., pleased but not surprised by the English girl's attitude.

"You guys have got to be warmer than I am! I'm freezing my bum off here!"

Stewart had a mental picture that was thoroughly disconcerting. "That's a terrible thought! Where in the world are you?"

"A little island off Scotland. I don't know if you've heard of it. Islay."

"Of course I've heard of it! Some of the world's best single malts come from Islay."

"Oh, of course – you would know that wouldn't you?" Jazz laughed. "That's why I'm here – doing some redesign work in one of the distill-eries."

"My kind of workplace! Sorry about the weather, though."

"Yeah, the wind's cold. So are some of the people. Some are okay, but I guess I'm just a bit scratchy. I haven't slept well since I got here. I keep having these weird dreams."

John B. frowned. "You too? I've been having the same problem. May-be it's the moon. Do we get the same phases of the moon in Hawaii and Scotland?"

"Beats me. That's as good a theory as any, but. It's late here and I guess I was just trying to put off going to sleep. Let him know I rang, please?"

"With pleasure. Has he got your number? Hey – hang on. I thought you and I were the last people in the Western world who didn't have a mobile phone? You travelled too much and the different networks didn't work well enough for you, I thought you said."

On the other side of the planet, the English girl laughed. "Too bloody right for too bloody long!" she said. "But I've found one of these global SIM things that seems to be okay. I figured that it'd actually be nice to be able to keep up with some people around the world that matter to me. Like Wilko."

The wizard grinned as he scribbled down the number Jazz recited. "You want him to call you back in the morning, your time?" he asked.

"That'd be nice. Or just whenever he can. I won't mind if the phone wakes me, although I must admit, I usually sleep through it."

'You can sleep through his snoring, I'm not surprised you don't hear the phone,' thought John B., but didn't say it. "I'll let him know. Good to hear your voice, mate."

"Yours too. I miss you guys. Thanks John B. – hope we catch up soon!"

The wizard put the phone down. He smiled down at the hawk. "That was an unexpected treat," he said. "I reckon Wilko will think so too – if he has any brains. Thinking of missing people, I should make a call of my own, eh?"

Hawthorn gave a quiet "*Ee-uhh*," in apparent reply, making Stewart's smile even wider as he reached for his own phone and called Q.

She answered after a few rings. "Hey babe! It must be your magic. How did you know I was going to call you when I got up?"

"When you…? Aw, jeez, the time difference! I'm sorry, pretty lady – how early have I rung you?"

"About six. It's okay, I was awake anyway."

"You're not having bad dreams, are you?" John B. asked worriedly.

"No, just woke up early."

There was an odd note in her voice, like there was something she was desperate to say but was suppressing it. Instead she asked, "How's Glexie?"

John B. momentarily wondered if Elizabeth really was showing signs of jealousy. He knew that there was nothing for her to be envious of, but he also knew she was a very long way away.

"Good – golfing well. Outplaying poor old Wilko, though between you and me, I don't think he minds too much."

"Taken a shine to her, has he?"

"Interested, at least. But I suspect he may have at least one other interest, too."

"Our Wilko? Tell me more!"

"Not much to tell, pretty lady. Call it a hunch. I think there may be someone interested in him. What news in your world?"

"Funny you should ask. That's why I was going to call you. My soon-to-be ex has gone back to live with his widowed mother."

That explains her voice, he thought. "The same Mrs. Dance who named her boy Sonny and her daughter Moon?"

"The very one. She's found religion. Or it's found her. They're on some communal farm out on the Darling Downs somewhere.

"Maybe the peaceful country life will be good for him."

"Or maybe he'll get bored with that too, and start giving some poor sheep a hard time. Frankly my dear, I don't give a damn. For now, he's right into it. And get this – they renounce all their worldly goods. He's letting me have the lot. No contest. Signed everything over to me before it could go to court."

"Wow! That's – er – good, I take it?"

"Well, I'm not mega-rich, but it is good. All up, it's better and easier than I could have wished for myself."

"Religion does interesting things to some people's minds."

"Mm. I'll just settle for the results. Hey! Talking of wishes, did you have anything to do with this?"

John B. was silent for a moment, before quietly answering, "I wished for the best for you. Same as I always will."

It was Q's turn to be silent for a short time. "Thank you," she said. "Come home soon, will you?"

"Funny – Wilko and I were just talking to an old local bloke here the other day about what 'home' means. I'm not so sure any more."

Q's voice was quiet. "Come back to me, please."

There was another silence before John B. replied, "That's a promise, pretty lady."

"I think I'd like to jump on a plane and come to you, but I've got this hearing coming up and I'd better be there to make sure Sonny doesn't change his mind."

"It's okay – I won't be long. A week or thereabouts. I'd better go – this phone's beeping at me. I've got to get into the habit of charging the silly thing, I suppose. I'll plug it in at the new place, fire it back up and call you soon, okay?"

Q sighed to herself. For a bloke who'd worked with computers for a living, sometimes John B. seemed completely hopeless with technology.

"Keep yourself safe, okay?" she settled for saying. "I'll talk to you soon."

"Can't wait…" was the last thing she heard him say before the battery at the Hawaiian end expired.

*

"Good morning, Professor. This will have to be only a quick call, I'm afraid, but I thought I should let you know of my progress."

"Ah, good. So progress *is* being made."

"Yes, sir. I've done a little – testing – and I'm satisfied with the results."

"All that you expected, then?"

  There was a sound like a short laugh. "That and more. Some people died." The voice was casual. "Casualties of war."

"Indeed," said Ritter. His voice was cautious, non-committal. "Take care, my friend. You have embarked upon a dangerous path."

"The cause is just. I cleaned up after myself. I'll be safe. I'm protected."

"I admire your confidence. Nonetheless, tread warily. As much as your faith in your protection is laudable, you must take your own measures to safeguard your own interests. You know I can do nothing more than offer a quiet suggestion or two if necessary."

"Oh, Professor – you're underestimating yourself. Your advice, your support, your inspiration – without your guidance…"

"You would still achieve remarkable things. Of that I am confident."

.oOo.

20 MISSING

Shortly before ten the golfers and their companions had assembled as directed, and their luggage was loaded onto the bus. As predicted, Harry's 'assistance' was confined to checking names off on his clipboard. Namakaeha had done the work handling the bags of those travellers who didn't look after their own.

The group milled around the foyer, waiting for the last two of their number. Hiro walked in from the elevator, looking concerned. He'd been asked to go and check on the missing men as he 'spoke the language'.

"There is no answer when I knock. I think you should ask someone on the staff to check their room, Mister Barber."

The tour organizer gave one of his irritated sighs, but conceded, "You're right, Mister Tanabe," before stalking away to harass someone at the reception desk.

A short time later Harry reappeared, trailing a duty manager who returned hurriedly to his office. Barber looked both irritated and puzzled.

"I don't get it. Their room is clean, and their bags are gone. The swipe card for their door is sitting on the kitchen bench. Apparently they booked a cab after dinner last night – didn't tell Reception where they were going. They've taken off - just like that damned Texan!"

That was another two of his wealthiest prospects gone.

"That doesn't make sense," said Wilko. "Takafumi was playing well. He won yesterday, and was right in contention to win the whole thing."

"Perhaps Mister Makkuro objected to being behind two women on the leaderboard," suggested Hoadley with a nod toward Shareta and Glexie. "He did strike me as a man of, let us say, old-fashioned thinking."

"It is not just the women he trails."

"Indeed, Mister Fernandez. I did not wish to impugn your performance. I merely wished to consider whether our missing golfer is of that particular class of men in his country who have very rigid ideas about the rightful place of women," replied Hoadley with more diplomacy than the Spaniard deserved.

Hiro Tanabe looked uncomfortable. "Sadly, such men are all too common in Japan," he admitted.

"But not universal," his wife reminded him, with a fond squeeze of his hand.

With an effort, Hands On Harry soothed his ruffled temper. There were still prospects left. Better to impress them with how well he coped with adversity.

"Okay, we might as well get going," he said.

"Um, should we perhaps tell the police?" asked Glexie.

Barber was disconcerted again. "What? Why?"

John B. looked at him, puzzled. "Two men vanish, without telling anyone they're leaving. No note, no clues. Sounds like a missing persons report to me."

"Yes, well, um…"

"He's right, Harry. Especially when they're not the first ones to disappear without a word," said Wilko.

For a few moments Barber ground his teeth, trying to work out his best response. He really didn't want to attract the attention of the law. He didn't like awkward questions.

Eventually he replied, "You're quite right Roger, sorry, Robert. The local sheriff is an old friend of mine. I'll get in touch with Barrett Lawson and let him know what's happened."

"Whatever it is that's happened…" muttered John B.

*

Their new accommodation, the *Kawaihae Harbor Inn*, appeared to be of rather more robust construction than the *Resolution Inn*, which augured well for those whose rooms adjoined Wilko's.

It didn't help John B.'s prospects of a restful night – this was the other venue where he hadn't been able to arrange a separate room. But he still had his earplugs, and plenty of good whisky in the bottle securely nestled among his swag of purple t-shirts.

As he knelt, fussing over Hawthorn's 'nest', the wizard looked up over his shoulder and said, "So, when are you going to ring Jazz?"

He'd quietly passed on the English girl's message during the bus ride to Spencer Beach. The Tasmanian tried not to look irritated. He had to have a long talk with himself. He hadn't really expected to hear from Jazz – oh sure, he'd hoped, daydreamed or fantasized a little even, but not expected. Now faced with the reality of her contact he was unsure of how he felt. No, not quite – he was sure he felt uncomfortable. Pleased – delighted, even. But he had no experience of long-distance relationships, and precious little of closer ones.

"Later," he said.

His roommate looked at him, puzzled, for a few moments then shrugged. "As you like it," he said quietly. "I think I'll spend a good part of the day lazing on the beach. What about you?"

Wilko considered briefly, then picked up his camera and said, "Yeah. Good idea. A good place to start, anyway. I might see if I can get out on the putting green for some practice later."

Relaxing on Spencer Beach seemed to be an idea that appealed to several of the group. John B. and Hawthorn were the first to arrive, settling into a shady spot under one of the trees fringing the beach. The wizard hung

169

his old bush hat on a low stub of broken branch. Well masked by foliage, the *'io* perched beside it, as if guarding the battered headwear. That image was quickly dispelled when the bird's head dropped in sleep.

John B. watched what would politically-incorrectly be called 'the talent' on the beach. He cast the same approving eye that he normally would, but was surprised by the path that his mind kept taking.

'Mm, she looks good,' or 'I like that outfit,' would have been expected to be his first thought.

But he found himself musing 'I wonder how Q would look in that?' Or 'Q would look so much better in that.'

"It must have been last night's conversation," he said to himself. "Wow – where's this going?"

Probably he already knew the answer, but he'd been a loner for a long time and asking the question was a self-defence mechanism.

His ponderings were interrupted by Wilko turning up.

"How's the view?" asked the Tasmanian.

Stewart waved a lazy hand. "See for yourself. Beautiful. You made that phone call yet?"

"I'll get around to it later. Wanted to enjoy the beach first."

"Uh-huh." The wizard decided that pushing the point would only make his friend dig his heels in harder, so he closed his eyes and just enjoyed the ambience.

Wilko's arrival was followed in fairly short order by those of Shareta and Hiro, Keeaumoku and Kahekili.

Glexie and Ariane were next, accompanied (rather to their chagrin) by Shanks, with no sign of the diplomatic influence of Hoadley. The valet had been sent on a shopping expedition, probably a spurious exercise to allow the estate owner to exercise his charm without feeling chaperoned by the older man. The Englishman was not best pleased when the girls made a beeline for the two Australians.

Even Hector Fernandez appeared, acknowledging the others with a vague wave before settling himself on a black rock on the far side of the beach. He appeared to gaze out to sea, but behind his dark sunglasses the Spaniard's eyes were closed. He was mentally replaying every hole he'd played in Hawaii, searching for remedies for mistakes he'd made.

"Where's Carlos, I wonder," said John B., watching the meditating figure in the distance.

Ariane had made a definite move to sit herself on the other side of Stewart from Shanks, just as Glexie had positioned herself beside Wilko. The legal officer put an unexpected hand on the wizard's knee and replied, "He's gone off looking for local bars again."

John B. was alert enough to realise that the gesture of affection was mainly intended to deflect the unwanted interest of Armitage, and happily played along by resting his hand on hers before saying, "Again? Wow – people reckon I'm a heavy drinker but I've got nothing on him!"

"The funny thing is," said Glexie, an arm linked in Wilko's, "I've never seen him look any worse for wear after his visits to all these bars and clubs."

"Some chaps are just resilient, you know," said Shanks. He seemed to have decided to not be put off by the girls' resistance.

"And our happy host and hostess?" asked John B.

Glexie looked puzzled for a moment. "Who…? Oh! Harry and our delightful driver! He's got a phone stuck to his ear, as usual. 'Making things happen' he calls it."

"I wonder if he's hooked up to a phone sex line?" said Stewart with a wicked grin.

That provoked laughter all round, although Shanks was a moment or two late joining in, as if perhaps the jibe struck a little close to home.

Glexie continued her answer. "The last I saw of Namakaeha she was in the dining room, drinking coffee and keeping her nose buried in a book."

"*Ancient Hawaiian Civilization*, by someone named Tuttle, I think it was," added Ariane.

"My word! I'd have thought she'd have grown up just… well, knowing that sort of thing," said Armitage.

"I don't think it can ever hurt to know more of your own history," said John B.

It was an ironic remark from a man who knew or remembered nothing of his own past before being found wandering the streets as a child. The matron of the D'Oliviera Orphanage had guessed his age at about ten. The Orphanage was where his memories began, although there had been some strange dreams since the blow to the head that had awoken the magic. None of his companions noticed the distant look on his face.

Ariane was still thinking about the bus driver. "I think there's more to that woman than meets the eye," she said.

"What – more than a sour-faced Amazon?" asked Glexie.

"Yep. A sour-faced Amazon who's actually a pretty decent driver," suggested Wilko.

John B. stood up and flexed his legs. "I might hit the water," he said. "Anyone else interested? It certainly isn't rough!"

That was true. The Pacific arrived at Spencer's Beach in gentle lapping rolls, not crashing surf.

"In a while," said Wilko lazily.

"I'm not really dressed for it," said Shanks, who'd come to the beach in the canvas pants and striped t-shirt he'd worn on the bus. He'd been too busy trying to find the girls and attach himself to them to think about changing clothes, and had shooed Hoadley away before his faithful valet could make the suggestion.

"Well I soon will be!" laughed Glexie, standing up and shrugging off the loose cotton shift she'd worn over her floral bikini.

Ariane stood and unwrapped the sarong she'd worn over her own swim-suit – another black and white print. "Count me in, too!"

The wizard gave Hawthorn a quick scratch on top of the head that got a blink and a soundless opening of the beak in response.

Both girls gave bemused smiles, then the three of them headed for the water at something close to a run.

Shanks sat with chin on hands, disappointment tempered slightly by enjoying the view. He genuinely didn't understand why women failed to find him attractive, no matter how glowingly he explained his own virtues.

The three in the water were soon joined by Shareta and Hiro – a little less exuberant but laughing and enjoying the break from competition. Keeaumoku and Kahekili even managed friendly waves, although they were too comfortable lazing in the sun to join in the aquatic frolics. Or perhaps Keeaumoku shared at least some of Hector's preference to keep the opposition at a distance.

Suddenly Shareta, who'd been looking out to the horizon, grabbed her husband's arm. "I think I saw something!" she said excitedly.

"It wasn't a shark, was it?" Glexie had meant the question as a joke, but suddenly realised that it might well have been what the Korean had seen, and that might not be funny at all.

"No, no! I think it was… yes, look! There it is again! A spray!"

All the group looked towards where she indicated. All but Hiro, who shrewdly looked a little to one side. He was right. "There," he said, pointing.

A large fin broke the surface, and a length of dark back.

"If the sharks here are that big, I'm never getting in the water again!" said Glexie.

John B. was grinning broadly. "That's no shark. That, fair lady, is a whale." He called out to his roommate on the beach. "Wilko! Grab your camera!"

Roused from a comfortable doze, the Tasmanian opened his eyes and blinked towards his old friend's voice. "Eh?"

"Your camera! Whale sighting!" Stewart called, pointing out to sea.

"I think I should use a long lens," muttered Wilko. He opened his camera bag and started to rummage around in it, looking for a lens and a selection of filters.

He was facing away from the ocean and looking down into the bag when the whale breached, rising magnificently up and out of the water like a great cetacean skyscraper before crashing back into the sea.

Wilko looked up at the sounds of the splash and much cheering from the others on the beach and in the water. "Wha…?" he managed. He was evidently the only one who'd missed the moment.

"I say – that was bloody marvelous!" said Shanks.

With considerable muttering and cursing Wilko assembled the components of his camera and trotted to the ocean's edge. But the whale didn't repeat its acrobatic effort. Perhaps there was only one spot where the seabed fell and the water was deep enough to allow such an effort.

The Tasmanian was still standing, looking regretfully out to sea, when

John B. emerged from the water, a little ahead of Glexie and Ariane. The wizard patted his friend's shoulder sympathetically, but quietly said, "There's a lesson there, old pal. Life doesn't come with a 'rewind' button. You might get replays, inside your head at least, but a moment missed is gone for good. Return the girl's call!"

"Mm," was the only reply, some disappointment and perhaps conceded agreement. Wilko shook himself and put on a cheerful face as the New England girls ran up the beach. Some serious thinking would be required.

.o0o.

21 LINES IN THE SAND

Much as feared, John B. and Hawthorn did not enjoy a particularly restful night at the *Kawaihae Harbor Inn*. Wilko's usual nocturnal sound effects show was supplemented by an unusual amount of muttering from the small man as he slept. At first the wizard had thought he was being spoken to, but when his replies got no coherent response he realised it was a dream conversation that he was not quite hearing one side of.

'Well, at least his dreams seem more peaceful than mine have been lately. Or Jazz's for that matter,' mused Stewart.

The light of the clock radio dimly picked out the wings of the *'io* extended in what looked like a stretching yawn. The bird made no sound, but was clearly disturbed by the strange noises Wilko made as he slept.

The wizard rose early, and with Hawthorn perched on his shoulder made his way down to the *Harbour Inn*'s dining room. As expected, the All You Can Eat Buffet Breakfast hadn't yet been laid out, but he wandered into the kitchen and prevailed upon the cook to part with one of the breakfast steaks (a thin sad thing that made John B. think of a meat pikelet) before it was fried. The cook was nervously happy to oblige, mostly to get the steely-eyed gaze of the *'io* out of his workspace as quickly as possible.

John B. poured himself a coffee and browsed the bookshelf in the foyer. With a smile he selected what looked like a good book about the local petroglyphs. He settled at an outside table and began to read while Hawthorn happily tore into the steak.

Engrossed, he was still there as the others in the group made their way to breakfast, then assembled for the day's golfing.

"So that's where you're hiding!" chided a pleasantly husky feminine voice.

"Oh! Morning, Ariane!" exclaimed John B., looking up. The hawk, now perched on the back of an adjoining chair, also gave a welcoming peep.

The dark-haired girl gave a little bow to the bird and said, "Sorry Hawthorn – good morning to you, too. You two must have breakfasted early."

"Ah – sort of. All that we wanted, anyway. How late is it?"

"The golfers are about to head off."

"Jeez, I'd better make a move – go and wish Wilko well for the day," he said, getting up from his chair.

Hawthorn half jumped, half fluttered onto his shoulder.

"Looks like the wing is healing," observed Ariane as they made their way out to the car park where Namakaeha already had the bus motor idling.

John B. turned his head to look at his feathered passenger. "I reckon you're right. You could take to the air any time you wanted to, couldn't you? You're gonna have to eventually, y'know. I can't very well take you back to Oz with me."

"I'd love to see the look on the flight attendant's face if you tried!" laughed Ariane.

The golfers were clambering onto the bus. Wilko and Glexie hadn't yet boarded and were standing laughing together as their respective room-mates approached to wish them well. Hugs were exchanged all round – well, not between Wilko and John B. – the Tasmanian didn't often go in for public displays of affection, especially between blokes.

Wilko was second-last to board, while the two girls shared a final whispered exchange. Namakaeha leaned on the horn, and Glexie quickly got on the bus before the door was closed. She was wearing a pale blue pair of shorts that might just have been a size too small and John B. couldn't help but admire the view as she climbed on board.

Ariane linked her arm through the wizard's and, looking in the same direction said, "Yep. Nice, hey?"

"Oh, sorry – was I being that obvious?"

"No, not especially. And anyway, like I said, it sure is a nice view."

John B. turned and gazed at her thoughtfully. A little light flickered on in his head. Cautiously he said, "So you two are…?"

"Just good friends. In weak moments I might sometimes wish otherwise, but I don't want to spoil things."

The wizard nodded. "Someone once told me that nothing ruins a good friendship like sex. I'm not so sure about 'ruin' but it certainly changes things."

Ariane hugged his arm close to her. "You got that, pal." She looked up at him. "Thanks," she said.

"For what?"

"Being a friend, and being happy with that."

John B. slipped his arm around her waist and returned the hug. "You're very welcome – my friend. So, what have you got planned for the day?"

"I thought you had a good idea writing postcards. Figured I'd do the same – maybe go back down to the beach and write them there. Do you want to come?"

"Mm. Tempting. My other idea, after reading this," he said brandishing the book he still carried, "I thought I'd see if I could get a lift up to the Pu'ukohola Heiau site. It's got quite a history."

"Kamehameha's temple?"

"You know about it?"

"Only a little. Keeaumoku was talking about it over breakfast - apparently it's got links to the sharks that are his family's totem as well as the old King's."

"Hmm – that's interesting," said John B. thoughtfully. "So, does that appeal?"

"Not a lot, I'm afraid. I'm not keen on sharks, and the way the two K's described it, well, it sounds a bit bare. Tell you what – why don't you go check it out and I'll meet you at the beach in a couple of hours. Something Hiro said over breakfast has got me thinking, so I want to do a bit of, um, research."

Stewart gave her a quizzical look.

Ariane smiled. "We were talking about Harry's 'Royal Green', and wondering what he spends so much time on the phone about. I think I'll do a little digging."

"Mm. I reckon you might see if you can talk to Nikki Martin."

"The girl in Harry's office? Yeah – I was thinking she might be a good source of information."

Stewart had a sly smile. He could see the legal officer's mind working. "Whoever wins this tournament, I'd like to be sure they're looked after properly." He put an arm around Ariane's shoulders and squeezed. "I wish you success in your research."

"Thanks. See you on the beach?"

"Definitely."

As the pair turned to go back into the motel Carlos ambled out into the car park.

"*Hola*!" he said. "A beautiful day, *si*?"

"Sure is," agreed Ariane.

"Yep," added John B. "What are you up to today, mate?"

"Up to? Nothing, nothing, *senor*. I am a good man!" the Spaniard said earnestly.

"Eh? No, no mate – I didn't mean 'up to no good'. I just meant what have you got planned for the day? The beach here is a good place to laze about."

Carlos relaxed. "Ah, *si*. No beach for me, I think. I found yesterday a very nice bar – a *caballeros* bar, where I feel very welcome."

"That makes sense," said John B. "I've been reading about the 'cowboy culture' in the grasslands of the Big Island. The old cattle country - very Argentinian, apparently."

"*Si, amigo*. I think the cattle, they are mostly gone, but there is still the tradition."

"Well, you enjoy yourself Carlos. Have a good day!" said Ariane warmly.

"Oh, I will! *Gracias, muchacha bonita*." With a wave, the Spaniard went off to meet the cab he'd arranged.

'He's right,' mused the wizard. 'She is a pretty girl. I hope she does find someone who makes her happy.' Aloud he said, "See you at the beach."

"Yep. Enjoy the temple, or whatever's left of it. Watch out for sharks!"

"It's well in shore," he laughed. "They'd have to be land sharks."

"They're the worst kind," Ariane grinned as she set off to investigate the Royal Green Estate.

*

The beaches of Hawaii are noted for sand and water. The Hapuna golf course seemed to have an abundance of both.

The first threesome to tee off – Shareta, Keeaumoku and Hector – soon found themselves getting better acquainted with both than they'd have liked. Even though the three players were all managing to negotiate the challenges to some extent, there was no doubt that the hazards were having a psychological impact.

Take the sixth hole. It was a dogleg, with trees on the right and a water hazard that ran along the left of the fairway then crossed just in front of the green. A small rise in the landscape was such that the narrow sliver of water fringing the green was almost invisible from where the second shot was to be played. Invisible to the eye, but not to the mind. Seen through the imagination it was a treacherous torrent.

"Where attention goes, energy follows," say the sages. Negative thoughts lead to negative outcomes. Self-fulfilling prophecy. Keep thinking about that water over the rise and that's where your shot will land. Three shots out of three.

Keeaumoku knew it wasn't going to be his day when, having already taken one drop he watched his ball roll teasingly into the water with a delicate little splash after his next shot found *another* such hazard. Hiro clicked his tongue sympathetically, but Hector didn't quite suppress a momentary chuckle.

The gods of golf rewarded the Spaniard's gracelessness in very short order. His own drop didn't find its way back into the water, but it did land with a loud plop in a soft patch of damp earth. He then underestimated just how deeply the ball had embedded itself in the soggy ground. He might have retaken the drop if he had. Instead, between the thinning of his shot and the stickiness of the surface he achieved neither height nor distance. The ball made the edge of the green, just, but didn't stay there, rolling back to rest in more soft ground on the other side of the water hazard.

The other two players and the caddy bit their tongues and said nothing.

Like the men, Shareta had also found the water, but at the edge of the hazard. To her husband's surprise, she asked for her pitching wedge.

"I can see enough of it," she reassured him.

Her judgement was sound. She took a short backswing and pulled the club down hard right behind the ball. The sharp leading edge of the pitching wedge cut through the water and chopped the ball up onto the green. At least two putts would still be required, but it was a good result.

The bunkers continued to be found with distressing regularity by all three players. A couple of slightly better recovery shots, like that on the sixth, were enough to give Shareta a two stroke victory over both her competitors.

The second grouping – Glexie, Wilko and Shanks – also faced similar trials with the Hapuna course layout. All three of them repeatedly buried, drilled or lobbed shots into the bunkers.

Glexie was the least troubled by this, not because she found the sand any less often than the men but because she was proving more effective at getting out of it.

Despite Hoadley's quiet advice and encouragement, the Rutland golfer resolutely failed to fully follow through on his bunker shots. On more than one occasion the ball popped up but didn't clear the sand trap, twice actually rolling back to the bemused Englishman's feet.

The problem for Wilko was with his stance. For whatever reason, he simply couldn't find the right angle between his feet and the line of his shots. So unlike Shanks, while he struck the ball well enough he consistently sent the ball away to the right of where he wanted.

The American girl couldn't get ahead on the scorecard today, though, as her previously reliable short game appeared to desert her.

After watching yet another of her putts skate past the cup by a greater margin than looked good, Wilko bit his lip and decided to have a quiet word with Glexie.

"Coming down with the yips? I hope not – you've been better than that so far," he said with genuine concern.

"Thanks. I hope not, too! But I can't figure what's gone wrong."

"Well, you know the rules say we can't give each other advice on the course. But, um... think of this as an aesthetic observation instead of golf-related… I've been watching you, and, er, I noticed… um…" The Tasmanian had gone bright red.

"Noticed what?"

"Your, um… the lower part of your body. It kind of – sways, just as you connect with the putter."

"The lower… oh! You mean my butt jiggles! Damn! Gotta keep still from the waist down, every golfer knows that. Was I doing that before?"

"Not that I noticed," the Tasmanian replied. 'And I would have noticed,' he thought to himself.

"Thanks man, I really appreciate the tip. Armitage has got ol' Hoads to look out for him – nice if we can keep an eye out for each other, hey?"

"My pleasure," he said, and meant it.

It wasn't collusion, just mutual regard, and it seemed to make a difference to both their games. Wilko played the best golf he'd managed since arriving on the Big Island, and Glexie rediscovered some of her putting confidence.

The positive supportive attitude even rubbed off on Armitage Shanks III, whose game improved markedly on the back nine.

"*That*'s more like the champion of the Lakeside Club!" Hoadley enthused after a neat medium length putt. "Sir," he added as an afterthought.

Although he still finished a shot behind the tied Wilko and Glexie, Armitage was sufficiently enthused with his game to pay generously for drinks all round in the Hapuna clubhouse.

Those drinks were still in the process of being consumed when Nama-kaeha arrived.

"Okay, everyone out. Bus is ready to go," she ordered.

Shanks protested, "Hang on, old girl! We haven't finished these drinks yet!"

The driver loomed over the smaller Englishman and said, "I don't care. I'm not going to hang around here for the afternoon watching you drink. Get in the bus."

Hoadley took a step forward to defend his employer but Keeaumoku was there first, grabbing Namakaeha's arm and turning her.

"You don't give orders. You're staff, remember? And your boss wants all of his potential customers kept happy," he said.

She sneered. "Only those with money. Don't kid yourself Barber has any interest in a 'mere native' like you."

"Just because that's all you think of yourself as, don't presume to tell me what I am!"

It looked like Keeaumoku's sharp retort would start a full-scale fight. Hoadley stepped in between them smoothly. The Hawaiian man's bellig-erent response had given the valet time to compose himself and resume his usual calm.

He leaned towards the driver and said quietly, "Regardless of Mister Papipi's unfortunate tone, he does have a valid point. Mister Barber sets high store by the wealth of his clients, and I am aware that he regards my Mister Shanks as a 'prospect'. May I suggest that it would be in your interest to indulge Mister Shanks' bonhomie for a short while?"

"I don't care how rich he is. His money doesn't mean anything to me."

"And yet here you are, employed by Harry Barber – a man you clearly don't work for out of loyalty."

"Why I do what I do is none of your business!" Namakaeha snapped.

The valet looked unruffled. Keeaumoku seemed about to make another barbed observation, but Hoadley shifted slightly to cut him off. "No, it is not. However Mister Shanks is my business. He has seen fit to show some generosity to his golfing companions. He has every right to do so. They are not constrained by any timetable that has been advised to any-one…"

Namakaeha opened her mouth to speak but Hoadley continued, not giving her the chance. "…I have not been made aware by Mister Barber, nor indeed by you prior to this point that there is in any way a 'time limit' by which the competitors must finish their play, or their social activities post-game. I understand that you may feel inconvenienced, but unfortunately that is sometimes the lot of those of us who are *employed* to *serve* in some capacity." He weighted his words carefully. "I appreciate that as driver you are not in a position to imbibe, even if you were of a mind to do so, but your very employment as driver is not least to ensure that Mister Barber's clients are free to do so as they please."

The driver again tried to interrupt the valet but he wasn't about to let that happen. He went on, "You have given sterling service thus far, madam, and I believe everyone has been impressed by your ability and reliability as a driver. It would seem to me to be most unfortunate for the esteem in which you are presently held to be compromised by an intransigent attitude to the group's quite reasonable desire to enjoy a small libation to round off an enjoyable day's sport."

Even Namakaeha couldn't help but be mollified somewhat by Hoadley's smooth flattery, despite her innate irritability.

With a deep intake of breath she finally replied, "Alright. A couple of minutes."

Hoadley gave a small gracious nod. "Thank you. Most reasonable. And look – as we've had our little chat it seems most everyone has finished his or her drink. When Mister Wilkes has consumed his last mouthful of the excellent local lager, it would appear we can depart."

Wilko raised his glass in salute to the valet's diplomatic skills, and drained its contents in a satisfied gulp.

"Thanks for the drink, Shanksy," said the Australian. "I guess we *should* get going, eh? Don't want to make life tough for you, Namakaeha – you've got a job to do."

If the driver had been about to respond positively to Hoadley's and Wilko's supportive words, the effect was undone by the smirk Keeaumoku gave her as he sauntered past. With a characteristic angry grunt she strode out to the bus, jammed the book she'd been reading into a pocket in the door, and gunned the motor.

Kahekili rolled his eyes as the man he caddied for continued to smirk.

.oOo.

22 TRACKS IN THE SAND

It was to be a fifteen mile drive to the course at Waimea. The group hadn't changed accommodation overnight because Harry hadn't managed to do a better deal than the one he had at the *Harbour Inn*. (Barber's explanation to the group had been, "The view here is so great, isn't it?" and there was, admittedly, some truth in that.) The longer travel time had meant a quite early breakfast call, which most of the golfers and their companions had gone along with.

Indeed, the Spanish pair had made a particularly early start, eaten lightly and quickly, and then adjourned to a small gym within walking range. Kahekili had also absented himself from the dining table early, announcing that he wanted to go for a walk. He'd strode briskly out of the motel, fitting his actions to his stated intent.

The only golfer not to partake of the morning buffet was Armitage Shanks III. Hoadley had come to the table briefly to announce that, "Mister Shanks is somewhat indisposed this morning, and wishes to rest a little more before facing the rigors of a drive and a day on the greens. I shall, of course, also remain in the room to attend to him as required."

The valet had received plenty of sympathetic smiles as he took a cup of tea for himself back to the room he shared with his employer.

"Oh well – we did have a few more drinks last night, and Shanksy more than most of us," observed Glexie, with an eye on the purple-shirted Australian at the word 'most'.

The wizard was unfazed as he fed a strip of bacon to the hawk perched on his shoulder. The *Harbour Inn* had a stock of a particularly good Islay single malt, and he was quite happy to acknowledge he'd reduced that stock considerably. He was an experienced Scotch drinker though, and (as long as he didn't mix drinks too carelessly) rarely suffered very much on the morning after. He probably still couldn't drive legally, but he didn't seem at all drunk.

Keeaumoku finished off the last of his steak, and looking around said, "I haven't seen our host yet. It's a bit rich when the early start was his idea."

"Hardly out of character, though, for our dear Harry," said Ariane.

As if mystically drawn to the mention of his name, at that moment 'Hands On' Harry Barber walked into the room. He looked around, apparently perplexed, before jauntily making his way to the table where his 'prospects' were seated.

"Hi everyone! It's another great morning, isn't it? I hope everyone's looking forward to a great day on the course at Waimea – it's just one more place to love on this great island! Remember, even if you don't win the tournament there's still the opportunity for you to own your own piece of this paradise. Hey, that breakfast smells great, doesn't it? Say, has anyone seen Namakaeha this morning? I've been trying to find her, but there's no sign of her anywhere." Barber really did seem to be able to speak without inhaling sometimes.

"You're not your driver's keeper, then?" quipped John B.

Harry missed the attempt at humour, as he tended to when the would-be comedian was anyone but himself.

"I wanted to go over lunch arrangements with her, but she's not in her room. I know she don't usually do breakfast with the punters, but when she wasn't in I thought, well, maybe…"

"Sorry Harry, not sighted here," said Wilko.

"Not heard either, which is how you'd usually know she's around," added Keeaumoku.

'Usually when she's arguing with you,' mused John B. to himself.

Hiro was perhaps having similar thoughts as he remarked, "Uncharitable."

His wife looked thoughtful. "I went out for a run after I got up this morning and I noticed that distinctive hat of hers, or one very like it, on a beach a little way from here. Could she have gone for an early swim?"

Harry gave an exaggerated frown and said, "Doubt it. Never known her to do any exercise."

Glexie gave Barber a hard look. "You don't get shoulders like Namakae-ha's without putting work into them. It wouldn't surprise me if she was a swimmer."

In the absence of any other suggestions, Harry decided to check the beach that Shareta had mentioned. Breakfast over, the others accompanied him. The events of recent days had left everyone uneasy about anything even faintly mysterious. Namakaeha's apparent absence certainly fitted into that category.

Her employer 'Hands On' Harry seemed the least concerned of any of them. His over-riding reaction seemed to be irritation at the potential inconvenience.

There was a beach only a few minutes from the dining room, but that wasn't where Shareta led them.

They passed a little cluster of homeless people gathered under a tree. Neither group made overt eye contact with the other, although it did occur to John B. that it might yet be useful to ask if any of them had seen their driver.

That thought was forestalled when the wizard noticed the surly ex-soldier known as Big Easy. The veteran was shouting his customary incomprehensible abuse, but it didn't appear to be directed specifically at Harry's group.

'I wonder how he travels,' John B. mused. 'Is it just him, or do a bunch of them move around?'

His attention was hauled back to the present by Shareta's voice.

"I was running along this path," she explained. "There's a little cove around this bend that I thought looked nice. I didn't stop though. There's an unpleasant smell in the air."

The Korean golfer's appraisal was soon proved correct. The little cove was quite pretty and quite deserted. That might have been due to a subtle pong. Not overwhelming, and if it hadn't been mentioned certainly some of the group may have missed it as a 'normal' beach smell.

"There's the hat," said Ariane, pointing to the distinctive striped woolen beanie.

"Hang on a minute," said John B. sharply, holding up an arm to stop any-one walking from the path to the beach. "The sand's not much disturbed. Let's not scuff it up with a bunch of footprints."

"We ought to look for Namakaeha," observed Glexie.

  Stewart replied, "Doesn't need all of us to do that – it's a small cove. Keeaumoku, you're a local…"

"Never been here before. Not my part of the island." The Hawaiian's body language made it clear that he was in no hurry to check the water or even the rocks fringing the beach.

  The wizard scratched his chin. "I'll take a look, if you're all happy to wait here."

  Wilko almost spoke but thought better of it. His old mate wasn't usually one for 'taking charge' like this, but the Tasmanian decided to trust his instinct. Not that he'd have said that in Stewart's earshot of course.

  With nods and shrugs in response, John B. stepped gently onto the sand. The overnight tide had been high and the beach was mostly pristine. It looked like only one set of tracks led down from the path.

  John B. walked carefully parallel to the impressions. He squatted beside the hat that lay quite near the trail, then stood and continued on to the wa-ter's edge. Shading his eyes from the morning sun with his own battered bush hat he looked out to sea.

"Namakaeha!" he shouted, more for show than from optimism. Shaking his head for the benefit of the watchers on the path, he skirted the small cove. He mostly avoided the water that was seldom more than shin deep as a gentle swell lapped in. He clambered onto a rock that rose to slightly higher than his knee.

"Namakaeha!" he called again.

  The slapping sound of the small rolling surf was his only reply. With his back to the path, the others couldn't see the troubled look on the wizard's face. After some moments of thought he carefully adopted as neutral an expression as he could muster.

"Well?" called Glexie, the tension audible in her voice.

"No sign," John B. called back as he got down from the rock and retraced his steps. He resisted the urge to pick up the woolen hat as he made his way back to the path.

"What did you see?" demanded Harry.

"One set of footprints leading down to the water. Hat looks like it was dropped on the way."

"None coming back out?" asked Wilko, conscious of the implications of his question.

"Nope. Harry, I think you should get onto your mate Sheriff Lawson again."

  Barber looked uncomfortable.

"Nothing else to be seen?" asked Glexie.

"Not anywhere near shore," John B. replied, but he pointed out to sea, just beyond the line of the breakers.

"What's out there?" asked the tour manager.

"Fins," said Ariane, staring in the direction John B. indicated. "Pity we don't have a set of field glasses, we might be able to identify them."

"*Mano*. Sharks," Keeaumoku said simply.

Kahekili gave his countryman a small thoughtful glance and elaborated, "Those are *niu'hi*. Dangerous ones."

"That could explain the absence of any locals on such a pretty beach," said Glexie.

Wilko nodded. "It might explain the smell, too, if they've killed something recently…"

He stopped, mouth still open, as he realised the possibility he had inadvertently raised.

John B. rested a hand on his friend's shoulder. "No sign of anything washed up," he said before turning to Harry and continuing, "I really do think you should talk to your friend Lawson."

Keeaumoku was looking along the waterline. "Sharks are efficient, especially in numbers."

Shareta was watching the dark fins, her husband discreetly holding her arm. "What could have possessed her to go out into the ocean when sharks were around?" she asked.

'Interesting choice of words,' thought the wizard. He wasn't the only one to cast a sidelong glance at the Big Island native. The man had identified himself as a "traditional Hawaiian" – just what traditions might he have really meant?

Wilko didn't think that way. "If she decided to go for a moonlight swim she wouldn't even know they were there, would she? She did say she's not from round this part of Hawaii. Isn't that right, Harry?"

"Um… er…"

Glexie snorted. "You don't imagine Mr. Barber troubles himself to remember details about the hired help, do you?"

His attention seemed to be fixed mostly on the ocean now, but John B. quietly remarked, "Oahu, she said."

Ariane nodded agreement and looked squarely at Harry Barber, but it was Glexie who spoke. "John B.'s right. You should call the Sheriff."

The tour manager shifted his weight from foot to foot, hoping for some support from some quarter. Some of the group were staring out to sea, some were staring at him. He wasn't sure which was worse.

"We don't really know she's missing yet, do we?" he said hesitantly.

"How long do you want to wait, Mr. Barber? Or perhaps, how many of our number must disappear?" asked Hiro.

*

Promising faithfully that he would contact Barrett Lawson as soon as he was finished, 'Hands On' Harry actually laid his hands on the steering wheel of the bus and drove the players out to the Waimea course.

If the disappearance of their usual driver caused some concern amongst the group, the motoring skills of her replacement amplified their tension tenfold. Barber talked incessantly – to himself if nobody else was listening – and seemingly paid little or no attention to the road or anyone else on it.

There was a feeling of relief all round as the six golfers and their caddies stood at the Clubhouse and watched the eighteen seater head away back down the road to Kawaihae, the sound of crunching gears ringing off the bitumen.

"Do you think we'll see him again?" mused Keeaumoku.

"Are you referring to Mister Barber's rather erratic driving style, or have you something else in mind?" asked Hiro, earning a curious sidelong look from his wife.

"A bit of column A, a bit of Column B, maybe," said Wilko.

They broke into their two playing groups. Wilko, Hector and Kee-aumoku teed off first.

The site of the Waimea course had long ago been a sandalwood forest. That had been cleared to make way for cattle grazing, but as the dairy industry in Hawaii declined someone had realised that there was better money to be made from tourists playing golf.

The course itself mostly comprised lots of rolling inclines. It was almost devoid of water hazards (one small pond was it), but made up for that with plenty of sand traps, craftily placed to make the most or perhaps the worst of the deceptively hard fairways and fast greens.

It might have been expected to favour Keeaumoku due to its resemblance to his 'home' course. But the Hawaiian seemed out of sorts, as though his mind was elsewhere. His short game was especially off, as he consistently underestimated the pace of the greens.

On the 12th hole, as he faced yet another third putt Kahekili approached him and said, "What's with you, man? Are you over-thinking them? Just relax and trust your judgement."

His friend frowned and grunted, seeming to imply, "That's easy for you to say."

Compounding his frustration, Wilko and Hector both had good days. The Spaniard was putting better, but the Australian's approach shots were far less wayward than they'd been the day before, and that gave him the comfort of easier finishes. They both seemed to have learned from recent experience playing out of sand.

The same couldn't be said for Armitage Shanks III in the following group. Just as he had at Hapuna, the Englishman didn't follow through sufficiently on his bunker shots despite Hoadley's quiet coaching and encouragement. The Rutland heir was unperturbed, though. He'd clearly resigned himself to not winning the competition and was happy to enjoy a nice day out in the company of two attractive women.

Shareta was happily married to her attentive caddy, and quite a bit older than would normally attract Shanks' interest, but there was no denying she was still glamorous. And while Glexie continued to inexplicably resist his charms, the American girl was still worth watching as she made her way around the course. At least the ever-diplomatic Hoadley managed to impose some restraint on his employer's tendency to make his observations out loud.

For their part, both ladies seemed mildly flattered or at least amused by Armitage's attentions. By now they both knew not to take him seriously, and were far too focused on their golf to be distracted. The New England golfer was developing enough confidence in her own game to no longer feel intimidated by the Korean woman's height advantage. Her putting game, in particular, was almost the exact opposite in character to that of Keeaumoku ahead.

She would read the green, make a decision, and play her shot without giving herself time for second-guessing. Neither Glexie nor Shareta allowed any distractions to their concentration.

When everyone gathered in the clubhouse after play, Shareta had nudged a stroke ahead of her American opponent. Wilko and Hector were two shots further in arrears. Three shots back, Keeaumoku's scant consolation was that he'd finished three shots better than the Englishman.

The group sat at the bar enjoying another round of drinks at Shanks' expense – he really had enjoyed his day now that he felt no pressure to be competitive.

Kahekili had one eye on the door. "I wonder when our bus is going to turn up? Not that I'm in any hurry to trust my life to Barber's driving again."

"Perhaps Namakaeha will have returned from… wherever she went," suggested Hiro.

"I doubt it!" said Keeaumoku.

"Certainly if she had, I'd expect her to be here by now. Whatever her faults she was always punctual," observed Shanks.

Glexie looked uncomfortable. "Maybe not talk about her in the past tense just yet, eh?" she said.

Wilko put a hesitant hand on her beautifully tattooed arm. "That's a good, positive thought," he said sympathetically.

Hiro and Shareta nodded in agreement, as did Hoadley.

"*Si*. A good thought," echoed Hector, albeit with little conviction in his voice.

The two Hawaiians exchanged looks that the others either didn't notice or couldn't read.

Just as Armitage was considering buying one more round there came a regrettably recognizable crunching of gears from the car park.

"Our chariot awaits," said Wilko.

"Didn't that mad guy Nero drive a chariot?" asked Glexie.

"*Si*, after he had had the original driver killed, I think," observed Hector.

That little reflection on European history earned him several thoughtful looks as the golfers and their caddies headed out to the bus before Harry could come into the clubhouse.

.o0o.

23 CALL OF THE WILD

It was done with a certain amount of reluctance, but after delivering the golfers to the Waimea course 'Hands On' Harry had called Barrett Lawson. The Sheriff wasn't delighted to hear from the property developer. They had a History – one that the policeman didn't care to be reminded of.

Barber briefly outlined the reason for his call – the apparent disappearance of his hired bus driver. He didn't expect Lawson's response.

"What? Another missing person? That's all I need! I've got enough other bull going down all of a sudden as it is," snapped the Sheriff.

Harry was startled. "Another one?" His mind raced – had someone else mentioned the Wilmingtons, or the two Japanese men? He was sure *he* hadn't.

"Still can't find the owner of that store that burned down. Got a bad feeling he must have been in it at the time, but the fire was so intense I don't know for sure. Could be an insurance job and he's lying low waiting to claim the money."

Trying not to let the relief show in his voice Harry replied, "Yeah, yeah – I've heard of people doing that sort of thing."

The policeman's brow creased. "You don't know anything about it, do you Harry? You're a man who knows a thing or two about the dark side of business."

"That's no way to talk to someone who bankrolled your election!"

"You helped, Harry. You weren't the only one."

"Maybe not, but you know I've been a great supporter of yours. And I'll continue to be, as long as…"

"Okay, okay. I get the message. Now, tell me about this missing driver of yours."

There wasn't much 'Hands On' Harry could tell. He'd advertised the job in the local newspaper. She'd applied, had a licence, was willing and able to be available for the duration of the golf competition, and was prepared to work for less pay than he might have offered a male driver. He knew nothing of her background, except that he "thought she'd studied something".

Barrett Lawson rolled his eyes. With Harry Barber as a boss, he could understand why the woman might get sick of her situation and simply walk out without telling anyone.

"Alright Harry," he said. "I'll have my team keep their eyes and ears open for her. Don't expect much though – we've got enough on our hands. Seems like there's some bad drugs turning up around the district, and we're trying to get a line on them."

The property developer shrugged and replied, "No expectations, Sheriff. You concentrate on the important business – that's great. I'm only telling you about Namakaeha because it's my civic duty."

'And because my damned prospects will keep nagging me about it - I've got to be the Good Guy if I want any of them to part with their dough,' was his unspoken thought.

*

John B. had not long finished two glasses of lunch and a Hawaiian culinary specialty he was developing a taste for – a Spam sushi roll. Apparently the unlikely delicacy was a throwback to postwar days when tinned meat was the only kind available on the island. With a generous lashing of soy sauce he found it an ideal snack to go with a cold local lager and a shot of decent Scotch.

He wiped a trace of sauce from his chin. What had usually been stubble was now starting to resemble a genuine beard, although his facial hair was clearly going to grow in the same random untidy way as that on his scalp. Stewart had long ago decided that he couldn't look anything but unkempt even if he really tried. Still, it seemed that didn't bother some people.

Smiling at that thought, he got out his mobile phone.

"Should be mid-morning," he observed to Hawthorn. The bird was perched on the back of the chair opposite him. In another unlikely piece of gustatory adventure, the hawk seemed to be developing a taste for the peanuts that were provided as free bar snacks. The wizard wasn't sure if this was a good idea, but wasn't going to risk a finger trying to stop his feathered friend.

Within moments, he was chatting with Elizabeth. She'd taken a day off work and was treating herself to a day of shopping.

"I'm checking out all the clothes stores, just because now I can," she explained with a laugh.

"What? Sonny wouldn't let you buy your own clothes with your own money?"

"Oh, it's not that he wouldn't *let* me, I suppose. But he made his likes and dislikes very clear, and for the sake of a quiet life I went along with it."

John B. shook his head, puzzled. An acquiescent Elizabeth didn't fit in his experience or imagination.

"Take satin for instance," Q continued, unaware of John B.'s bemusement. "I love the feel of it, but Sonny would always disapprove of my buying any. His mother convinced him it was only worn by 'cheap women' as she put it."

"She sounds like a real charmer."

"Oh, you don't know the half of it!"

"More fool him for going along with it. Still, at least she's taken herself out of your hair now, and him along with her.”

That raised another laugh from Q. “Speaking of hair, I’ve decided to let mine grow. See if it’ll look a bit more interesting than the boring and proper look everyone’s gotten used to at work.”

“Pretty lady, you have never, ever looked boring! Whatever you do, though, please don’t let Kaiser Ron’s wife get her hands on you – you’ve seen some of the things she’s done to *his* head!”

Several shoppers started in surprise at the sudden loud laugh from the pretty brunette in the dress store. “You’re right. You should see this week’s effort – I think the top of it has been styled with an iron. It’s flat enough to land a very small plane on!”

“Not a good look on him, far less you, I reckon! Seriously though Q, your hair, your clothes, should be your choice. Nobody else’s opinion should matter.” John B. chuckled. “Anyway, you know I’ll reckon you’ll look fabulous whatever you’re wearing.”

“Thank you, kind sir, for that unbiased opinion.”

“I do but speak the truth.”

The call ended soon after. Elizabeth walked around the store with a spring in her step and a smile on her face. Smiling every bit as broadly, John B. settled Hawthorn on his shoulder and set off for a stroll to the beach.

*

Professor Ritter had almost not answered his phone. He had examination papers to finish marking before his pending departure from the University. Nobody knew he would be departing, and in the grander scheme of things these academic results would not be of much importance. Probably. It never hurt to keep contingencies in mind. The future was not entirely predictable, however much he and his colleagues endeavored to steer it.

But an instinct made him change his mind. Ritter had instincts finely honed over a very long time, and he knew to trust them. He answered the phone.

"Professor, you *are* there. For a moment I was… concerned," said a familiar voice.

"Yes, I'm here. Temporarily distracted by the demands of academia."

"Oh, I'm sorry sir. I don't mean to keep you from your work…"

"Not at all. I appreciate the importance of your project. Is there something I can assist you with, in my own small way?"

There was a brief pause.

"Advice, please, Professor. I've encountered a problem. Two, possibly."

"Problems? Surely by now you know how to overcome problems?"

"In the ordinary way, yes. And one of them is less than ordinary. But the other one…"

There was another thoughtful pause. "There's something different – something special, about one of the problems."

Ritter smiled as he answered, "I would hope you remember one of my maxims I teach all my students. 'A special problem requires a special solution.' You're one of my best and brightest – I'm sure you can devise something special."

There was silence for some seconds while the former student pondered. The Professor wasn't impatient – he knew the person he was dealing with, how they thought and what they were capable of.

Eventually the reply came. "I do know a special place. But I've got other plans for it you know."

"I know your own particular beliefs are strong, but I'd counsel you to remember that there *are* other strong beliefs that have been held in the islands – and still are."

"But the strongest is…" The initial sharp response stopped. The voice continued in more thoughtful measured tones. "Mmm… yes, yes, an appropriate sacrifice to ensure the important sacrifice to come. Thank you, Professor. As usual, you've illuminated a path for me."

"I merely hold up a lantern, my friend. It is you who find your own way to your chosen destination."

  As he ended the call the professor mused that he would be pleased to be well away from that intended destination.

.o0o.

24 THINGS GO BUMP IN THE NIGHT

'Hands On' Harry hadn't organized much in the way of evening entertainment for his group. He'd pretty much assumed that after the rigors of the daily competition the golfers and caddies would be either too tired, or too focused on the next day's play, to want to go out.

The one thing he had organized was a nighttime visit to the Mauna Kea observatory. And having paid for it, even at the greatly reduced rate he'd negotiated, he was reluctant to cancel the excursion just because his driver was missing. He'd just have to drive the bus himself again.

Several of the contingent declined the invitation. The most vocal of that number were Keeaumoku and Kahekili. They knew the road to the observatory.

"I've seen you drive! No damn way I'm getting in that bus to go up that mountain!" swore the tattooed caddy.

Keeaumoku was just as emphatic, adding that, "If, or when, you don't make it back down, I'll win the tournament by default."

That provoked a startled look from Hector, who promptly announced that he would be guided by the locals' advice and likewise not be going on the excursion. Carlos jumped at the opportunity to make another trip to a local bar. He'd spent most of the day there, although he appeared little the worse for it. A little more jovial than usual perhaps, but he seemed a chatty gregarious character anyway so it was hard to be sure.

Ariane turned to Hiro and asked, "Is the road really that bad, or are these guys exaggerating?"

Tanabe-*san* looked thoughtful. "It is steep in parts, and winding, but well sealed. It is safe, provided one is suitably cautious…"

"Hey, that's a great description," said Harry. "And don't you worry – I'll be cautious. I've got to protect my investment in you all, hey?"

Neither the Hawaiians nor the Spaniards were swayed by Barber's reassurances. In truth, the others weren't much comforted either, but the opportunity to see snow in Hawaii was too appealing to resist, and Hiro was not about to leave his beloved wife's side.

The unwillingness of the locals to make the journey extended even to Hawthorn, who at the time of departure hunkered down in the box on the floor beside John B.'s bed.

"Hmmph. You're probably smarter than I am, mate," observed the wizard as he scratched the top of the bird's head. The raptor called a soft *"Ee-oh"* as Stewart closed the door and made for the car park.

"Everyone better rug up. It can get a bit chilly up at the top," warned Harry, just as they were about to set off.

Glexie cursed softly. It was Hawaii, not New England. She'd taken great pleasure in packing absolutely nothing in the way of warm clothing. It was Wilko who gallantly came to the rescue, fetching from his room one of the two weatherproof jackets he'd brought 'just in case it rained for more than one day'.

The drive up Mauna Kea before sunset proved only a little harrowing. Harry was certainly a bit more attentive behind the wheel than he had been to and from the golf course, which wasn't difficult. But the narrow, steep and winding stretches had Wilko in particular looking out of the window nervously as he contemplated the return journey in darkness. It was a road that wouldn't have been out of place in parts of rural Tasmania, with blind corners and no lighting.

By the time they reached the Visitors Centre the daylight was almost gone. Everyone piled out of the bus to line up for the toilets and/or buy souvenirs. The snowline was visible not far above, a white drapery around the foot of the observatory itself. At other times of the year, the spot where they'd parked would itself be under a blanket of snow.

"Don't be long everyone!" called the substitute driver. "We've still got a bit to go to get to the summit. It's a really great tour – you'll see!"

Before getting back on the bus Ariane stood in front of a large warning sign. "Beware of Invisible Cows," she read.

In smaller letters the sign went on to explain that the road they'd just travelled up was subject to sudden and heavy fog in places, and that those places often coincided with unfenced cattle pastures. Unwary drivers had collected large bovine hood ornaments, and if that happened at speed the results could be catastrophic.

"Have you seen that, Harry?" asked Ariane as she climbed on board.

Barber glanced at the warning in big letters and waved his hand airily. "Urban legend," he said. "Great tale for tourists – nothing to worry about. Okay everyone – let's get going!"

Although it was similar in steepness, width and lack of illumination, the road up from the Visitors Centre differed from the road up *to* it in two important respects: it was unsealed, and at the going down of the sun it was already getting a thin film of ice forming on the small stone shingles that comprised its surface.

They hadn't gone far when they reached the first tight corner. 'Hands On' Harry made a complete hash of changing gears and the motor stalled in the cold night air. Suddenly they were sliding backwards down the slope. Barber swung ineffectually on the steering wheel, doing more harm than good. Luckily there was nobody coming up behind them.

"Pull the bloody handbrake on!" barked Wilko.

Startled by the command, the driver instinctively obeyed. The bus stopped sharply, just as the rear bumper thudded into the rocky face of Mauna Kea. Fortunately they hadn't reached much of a speed.

Harry babbled a sort of apology. "Sorry, roads a bit slippery. Bit dark out there…"

"Hey Harry, I don't know about everyone else, but I don't reckon I'll lose any sleep if I don't see the observatory," said John B. as evenly as he could.

"Abso-bally-lutely!" agreed Armitage.

"But the tour is paid for!" exclaimed Barber.

"Not by us, mate. And I'm not keen to risk paying for it with my life, or anyone else's." Stewart's voice was losing its veneer of calmness. It wasn't fear, but anger at Barber's attitude.

It was Shareta who came forward and laid a hand on the driver's shoulder. "I really do think, Mister Barber, that the conditions are turning against us. Look, there are flurries of snow starting to fall. We would not hold it against you if our visit to the summit was abandoned, I think?"

She looked questioningly at the other passengers, who gave various signs of agreement.

"Ah… well, um… er…" Barber stammered in consternation.

"Come sit beside me while you gather yourself." Shareta's voice was almost a purr as she used the hand on his shoulder to guide Harry out of the driver's seat and into a seat several rows back.

Wilko slipped into the vacated seat. He looked out the back window into the darkness. "No room to turn around, and bloody dark to reverse into," he said unhappily.

"A-hem, Mister Wilkes?" Hoadley politely got the Tasmanian's attention. "As a matter of course I carry a small but bright torch in the evenings. Might that be of some assistance?"

"Well, yeah, if you wouldn't mind standing behind the bus so I've got something to aim at."

Hoadley winced at the choice of words but made his way to the door of the vehicle.

John B. Stewart accompanied him and said, "Wilko, check under the seat and in the pocket of the door. This thing should have a torch of its own."

Wilko did as suggested, and after a moment of groping awkwardly extracted a large flashlight from beneath where he sat. He flicked the switch and was pleased to find that the batteries weren't flat. His natural inclination to pessimism had led him to expect that they would be. Stewart took the torch from him.

Giving the switch an experimental click, John B. explained, "Here's the plan. Hoadley and I will light ourselves up a few feet behind you – Hoads on the rock face side, me on the side with the drop. We'll track down nice and easy. You aim to pass between us. Keep it slow so we can stay ahead of you. Behind you."

"I know what you mean," said Wilko.

"Cool. That way, if the bus does slip again you should miss both of us if it takes you a moment to pull the brake back on. One of us in the middle would be hard to dodge."

"Makes sense. Thanks mate." The Tasmanian gave his old friend and the gentleman's gentleman a grateful smile as they got off the bus.

As they took their positions behind the bus the valet said, "A good plan sir, and thank you for taking the dangerous position on the precipice."

"I told you before mate – don't call me 'sir'. Only my bank manager gets away with that," said John B. with a grin. "Anyway, your spot could be dodgy too if that thing gets away from Wilko. Getting squished between the bus and the mountain would be no fun."

Hoadley did not look cheered by that thought, but he continued backing slowly along the road. The beams of the torches played up under their chins, illuminating their faces in a manner befitting an old horror movie. An urbane Doctor Frankenstein and a shaggy Igor, perhaps. They weren't being playful. The idea was to be clearly visible but not risk shining a bright beam into Wilko's eyes. Driving blind would not be a good idea.

They'd commenced their gradual descent, with Wilko easing the vehicle down as directed. Most of the passengers determinedly looked ahead, or down, unwilling to watch the drama playing out at the rear of the bus.

Glexie was one of the few gazing in the same direction as the driver, whom she'd chosen to sit near.

"The snow's getting heavier," she observed. "Hoadley's well rugged up but poor John must be freezing! All he's wearing is that purple t-shirt over his jeans."

Wilko grunted. "That's just about all he ever wears, whatever the weather. I've seen him in the same get-up in the middle of a Canberra winter."

"He doesn't feel the cold?" asked Ariane.

"Too dense, I reckon," said the Tasmanian.

Armitage Shanks looked up from the close study of his fingernails he'd been using as a distraction. "That's a rather unkind thing to say about a chap who's out there trying to keep us all safe," he said.

"Especially when he's supposed to be your best friend," added Ariane.

Concentrating on his driving, Wilko didn't immediately say anything in his own defence. Hiro however spoke up.

"I think that it is a peculiarly Australian thing, this 'mateship' where friends can say terrible things about each other, call each others names that would elsewhere start terrible fights, but such things are like terms of endearment," the businessman observed.

"Suppose so," said Wilko. "I'd probably get pretty dirty if someone I didn't know said that about him.

The bus was moving slowly enough for Ariane to quickly dismount and run back to John B. She took the black beanie off her own head and pulled it onto his, without a word. She further surprised him (and the watching Glexie) by planting a kiss on his cheek before quickly turning and running back to remount the bus.

Wilko closed the door behind her and turned the heater up another couple of notches. 'How does he do it?' he thought to himself but wisely didn't say anything. Neither John B. nor Ariane had shared their conversations with anyone, even the close friends they were travelling with, protecting each other's privacy.

Fortunately for everyone's nerves, it wasn't long before they were back within the glow of the Visitors Centre's well-lit car park. The Centre itself was already closed, but the lights were left on as an aid to those driving back down the mountain.

Wilko opened the door. Hoadley and John B. brushed as much snow off themselves as they could before getting aboard.

"Thanks, guys," the driver said. "That made things a helluva lot easier."

"You're welcome, Mister Wilko. I won't say it was a pleasure, but it certainly could have been much worse," replied Hoadley with a smile.

John B. and the Tasmanian exchanged a quick clasp of hands. "Well driven, mate," said the wizard quietly.

"I'll say!" said Glexie warmly. "Thank you, Wilko!" It was his turn to receive an unexpected kiss, followed by a round of applause from the other passengers.

Blushing, Wilko tried to wave away the acclamation. "Thanks guys, but we've still got to get back down the hill…"

"Ah, yes," said Harry. He was the last to join in the clapping, and the first to stop. "That was great driving, Ro… er… Wilko, but I'd better take over now."

John B. looked at him dumbfounded and said what everyone else was thinking, "You can't be serious!"

"It's the insurance. Only Namakaeha and I are listed drivers. If anything was to happen, we wouldn't be covered by the policy."

"Listen mate, it's a bloody sight more likely that 'something' will happen if you're driving than if Wilko is!" snapped John B.

The Tasmanian, however, held up a placatory hand. "No," he said. "Harry's right. If we do run into anything on the way down and I'm driving, the insurance company lawyers will be all over me like a rash."

That earned a wry laugh from Ariane, the legal officer. "That's absolutely true," she confirmed.

"Anyway, I've done my shift. As long as you're up to it, Harry, the command chair is all yours," said Wilko.

Like the others, he had plenty of reservations about Barber's driving skills, but he understood the insurance situation and was willing to sound as diplomatic as possible to relieve the tension. He switched off the engine and vacated the seat.

The property developer, calmer at the prospect of being back on a properly sealed road, strode to the front of the bus and got behind the wheel.

"Thanks again, Wilko. Don't worry about the conditions, everyone," he called back to the passengers. "I can keep my nerve in a crisis."

Looks were exchanged among the passengers who'd just observed first hand the fallacy of that claim.

"Well, if we do run into anything may we do so very gently!" said Glexie.

"That'd be my wish, too," said John B.

"No worries, *moyt*," replied 'Hands On' Harry, attempting to be jovial.

It was evident though that he was still nervous, as his driving speed was much slower than it had been on the way up, even with the assistance of the downhill slope. The snow stopped very shortly after they left the car park, as it was usually confined to the upper reaches of Mauna Kea.

The respite from the weather was only brief though, as they moved into the first of several banks of fog. Harry had the bus in low gear and was letting it roll slowly around the curves of the road.

Seated beside Ariane, John B. went to return the beanie. The young woman shook her head.

"You keep it," she said. "I've got plenty, and you might need it again somewhere sometime."

"Thank you. Any time I wear it I'll think of you and smile, my friend."

She patted his leg fondly. "That's a nice thing to say. I could almost wish…" she said softly, then wiped a melting snowflake from the purple shoulder. "But no, that's your department, not mine. Like we said before, friends."

"Good ones."

The Australian's voice wasn't wistful, but they both had a sense of a 'what if' moment. Stewart was thinking of a green eyed brunette on the distant end of a telephone connection. Whatever or whoever Ariane was thinking of, she kept to herself. They smiled at each other and watched carefully out the front window as their gradual descent continued.

The first two fogbanks were passed through without incident. The passengers and driver began to relax a little. Barber had sped up by the time they passed through what looked like another curtain into a space packed full of grey cotton wool.

"Better ease off, Harry," warned Wilko.

Barber flashed his Public Relations smile. "Nothing to worry about. It's just fog," he replied airily, although he did change down a gear.

"Stop!" John B. demanded sharply.

"What? Why?" asked the man at the wheel.

"That bit of fog's not moving!"

Startled, Harry managed to stall the bus again, but braked successfully and the bus rolled to a stop. The front of the vehicle was pressing gently against the side of what had looked like a darker section of fog, but was now revealed at very close range to be a large cow.

The beast stood placidly, evidently unconcerned, even when Harry leaned on the horn button.

"Urban myth?" asked Ariane.

"If it is meant to frighten the tourists, it has done a successful job on me," said Shareta, who received an immediate comforting hug from her husband.

"Ah… er…" 'Hands On' Harry was again at a loss for words until he managed to croakily say, "I can't get it to move."

John B. sighed. "Open the door a minute, Harry."

The driver complied. The wizard stepped out into the fog. Several other cattle were sedately crossing the road, but the one they'd bumped into appeared to be appreciating the warmth of the vehicle. Standing alongside the cow, Stewart laid a hand on the top of the animal's head.

"You're a big lass, aren't you?" he said quietly. He called to the bus driver, "Back up mate, real slow and easy, please."

Harry was able to restart the engine and avoid stalling again as he put it in reverse and pulled the bus back from the cow. She started to move after the bus for a moment, but Stewart's hand never left her skull.

"No you don't. You belong with your herd," he said, stepping back and giving a gentle push behind the ears.

The cow shook her head, flapping her ears as if insects had flown into them. She trotted off the road, trailing after the last of the cattle that had just passed.

Harry was still sitting open mouthed as John B. got back on the bus.

"Let's go," said the Australian, brushing animal hair from his purple t-shirt. "And Harry – beware of invisible cows. The things you can't see are often the most dangerous."

*

The fog didn't get as far as Kawaihae. The warm sea air seemed to put up too formidable a resistance to the mantle of the mountain.

It was almost balmy in the concrete courtyard where the itinerant trolley people were making their temporary home. Some of the little band had already dossed down in a derelict shipping container that offered protection from any overnight change in the weather.

The rest sat around, singly or in small groups. Some chatted, some sat in silence – companionable or surly.

Occasionally new arrivals would turn up. Some came on foot, and some had managed to hitch a ride on one of the trucks that ran to and from the port town until late in the night.

Some arrived in their own battered vehicles. Sometimes these were stolen. Stealing shiny new cars attracted attention, but much less interest was taken in old decrepit ones. Much like people themselves, really. The more generous spirited would convey other homeless folk as they travelled. They would run the vehicles until they ran out of fuel, then abandon them rather than meet the expense of gas. There were better things to spend money on.

One of the recent arrivals was sitting alone by a small fire in a corner of

213

the compound. Huddled in a black hoodie and track pants, they were little more than a shapeless dark blob to the other trolley people, which seemed to suit everyone admirably.

Big Easy was in a rare convivial mood, though. He hadn't been drinking, it was just a quirk of his damaged psyche that sometimes the dark clouds would part and he became the sociable fellow he had been before going to war.

He circulated among the various individuals sitting alone, checking on their well-being and state of mind, offering companionship or an encouraging word where required and welcome.

Ese sat beside the hooded figure. "Nice night," he said to no reply.

"Everything okay with you?" the big man continued. "I seen you round last day or two, on your own. Anything I can do for you?"

"You can go away," said the figure.

"Yeah, I can do that. But I just wanna make sure you alright. Us folk gotta look out for each other, 'cos nobody else will."

"I said go away! I don't need help from you, or anybody!"

The speaker made the mistake of looking up in their irritation, and the small flickering flames lit up their face for a moment. Ese looked into the eyes and turned cold. He'd seen eyes like that before, and it wasn't a good memory. But there was more. He knew that face.

"You... I remember you from before," he said quietly. "You..."

Big Easy said nothing more. Ever. A hunting knife had been slid between his ribs and into his heart.

The two figures stayed huddled together long into the night until everyone else had fallen asleep. They looked to be in quiet intimate conversation although the reality was that the big man's body was simply being propped up to avoid drawing attention.

When the area was silent and still, the murderer stood and hoisted the corpse upright. Ese was a dead weight with plenty of weight, but was lifted so his feet didn't drag as he was carried.

There was a particularly rusty ruined shipping container not far away. Rain had poured through holes in the top, so the floor was a pool of water that even the most desperate of the trolley people wouldn't sleep in. Ese was past caring though, and was laid soundlessly in a corner. His body was curled up to look as though he was asleep, just in case anyone happened to glance in and notice him.

Soon though it wouldn't matter if they did. Soon they would all be dead.

.o0o.

The sixth day of play lay ahead of them. After breakfast they were all to move to their new accommodation adjoining the course at the Waikoloa Village Resort. Breakfast at Kawaihae was cheaper, evidently.

Wilko was up and active early the following morning, availing himself of the Internet Kiosk of the *Kawaihae Harbour Inn*. He was wearing a satisfied smile as his travelling companion strolled into the small room.

"I thought I heard typing," said the wizard.

He'd just gone for his pre-buffet visit to the kitchen. Hawthorn was perched on his shoulder, waiting patiently for the piece of breakfast steak that would soon be handed over to her.

"You look pleased with yourself. What've you been up to?" John B. asked.

"Well, much as I hate to admit it, the Wilmingtons had a point. I've had enough of that bloody bus."

"I can understand that, although fair's fair – we had a real driver back when the Terror from Texas was still around."

"Mmph. Yeah. But last night was the final straw, so I've gone on-line. We're playing at Waikoloa Village this morning. I've found a rental company that'll deliver to me here before we leave."

John B. looked suitably impressed. "That's good service! What are you hiring – a Rolls Royce?"

"Nah – never fancied them much. I thought, seeing as we're in the States I should get something appropriate. A Mustang GT convertible."

"Cool! But mate, we're only here for another couple of days, and based at the Village for the whole time – is it worth it?" Stewart knew that Wilko was not a man to spend money without a lot of consideration.

"Honestly, that was part of the reason. I've always wanted to drive one, and I can afford a couple of days rental. And like I said, I really am sick of that damn bus, whoever is driving it, me included!"

"All sounds fair to me, mate. And if tooling down the road in a Mustang inspires your game, so much the better!"

Wilko grinned a little ruefully. "Probably a bit late now, I'm afraid. This is supposed to be the last round, remember. Day off tomorrow, which is when I really want to take the 'Stang for a good outing, then the top two play off while the rest make up the gallery. I reckon Glexie and Shareta have got that sewn up."

Hawthorn gave a little cry of "*Ee-oh!*"

"See," said John B. "She thinks you're still a chance. You're tied with Hector and a shot up on that misery 'Moku. This is golf, man. All it takes is for one or both of the girls to have a bad day, and you to have a good one. You never know what can happen on a golf course."

"Yeah, well – that's certainly true. You never know what's gonna happen next anywhere in Hawaii, as far as I can tell," said Wilko. "Let's go get breakfast, if you and that bird of yours have left anything in the kitchen."

Wisely, the Tasmanian avoided looking the *'io* in the eye when he said that. Hawthorn settled for glaring at his back as he led the way to the buffet.

Sitting at the large group table John B. announced that he'd join Wilko on the course today, not to caddy but to offer moral support.

"You? Moral?" Wilko had asked in mock surprise.

"This is the 'mateship' thing of which you spoke last night, isn't it?" Shareta asked her husband.

Hiro smiled. "Almost certainly. I think B-*san* is a most moral individual."

"Depends on how you define 'moral' I suppose," replied Wilko, shoving a forkful of chilli-sauced steak into his mouth to hopefully avoid leaving room for his foot.

Spotting his mild discomfort, Glexie spoke up. "B-*san* – for John B. That's kinda nice. What *does* the B stand for, John?"

The wizard shrugged (as best he could with a hawk perched on one shoulder). "Beats me," he replied.

"Is it like FDR?" asked the New England accountant. "Franklin Roosevelt didn't have a middle name. He just thought the middle initial sounded more… serious, I think."

"Can't imagine you wanting to be taken more seriously," observed Kahekili. The tattooed man was smiling, but there was a sharp edge underlying his voice.

It was Ariane's turn to steer the conversation in another direction, away from the prospect of tension. "That's a good idea, John. I think I'll join you out on the course and cheer on my girl!"

Glexie grinned warmly in response.

"You know, I think I do the same!" said Carlos.

Keeaumoku looked surprised, and failed to keep the sneer out of his voice as he said, "What? You've run out of bars to spend your day in? Or run out of money?"

The Spaniard laughed, a little too heartily, and said, "No, no! I think I too, should support my *compadre* as the final round draws near."

His *compadre* gave him a look of surprise with a side order of suspicion, but said nothing. There was a definite sense that a conversation would be being held privately very soon, though.

'Hands On' Harry was, as usual, the last to appear in the dining room.

"Great morning, isn't it everybody?" he said, rubbing his hands together and not waiting for a reply. "If everyone's packed and ready we can be on our way in about half an hour, okay? I'll have the bus out front of the Inn and we can head for the Village. Unpack, look around the resort, a light lunch, walk over to the course and tee off about one o'clock."

Again he didn't wait for a response from anyone. He just beamed his Public Relations Smile around the room and walked out, phone jammed to his ear as usual.

Just outside the doorway Barber had to do what looked like a small dance with two young men in matching green polo shirts who were trying to go into the dining room.

Having got past Harry the two men stood in the room and looked about. The taller of the pair was a young Polynesian man who gave a moment's troubled stare at the tattoos of Kahekili Mehameha then quickly looked elsewhere.

"Excuse me – is there a Mister Wilkes in the room?" he said.

"That'd be me. Thanks mate!" said the Tasmanian, who got up from his chair and shook hands with the young man. They sat down together at a vacant table and set about completing the paperwork the Polynesian car-ried in a clip folder.

"Do I need to drive you back to your office now?" asked Wilko.

"No, thank you sir. That's what Clifford is here for – he'll take me back in the company Focus. Much less exciting than your vehicle, but at least I got to deliver it."

Clifford gave a wistful grin. Clearly he'd have liked to drive the Mus-tang but was outranked.

"Right," said Wilko. "Let's go give her a once-over before I sign my life away, eh?"

The three left the dining room. John B. grinned at the others around the table.

"Let's give him a couple of minutes then go and admire his new toy, eh?" suggested the wizard.

The two Polynesian Hawaiians weren't interested. Armitage Shanks was far more interested in his breakfast, and the loyal Hoadley stayed to provide such service as was required – buttering toast, slicing the top off boiled eggs.

So it was Glexie and Ariane, Shareta and Hiro, and the Spanish pair who accompanied John B. and Hawthorn out to the car park. The little green Focus was just pulling out. Wilko was slowly walking around a ruby red convertible with a slightly glazed expression on his face.

"Nice!" exclaimed Glexie.

"It's certainly a fine vehicle," agreed Hiro who admired good cars although he didn't collect them as many men of his wealth did.

"*Si senor.* I would like one of these one day," said Carlos warmly, earning a sly half-smile from his countryman.

Hawthorn gave an small peep and flexed her wings. The *'io* seemed a little uncertain.

"Good colour," said John B. "Red ones go faster."

Glexie looked surprised. "Really?"

Ariane put an arm around her friend's shoulders. "No honey. He's kidding. It's just that guys who own red cars tend to drive faster."

Wilko at last looked up. "Fast should be no problem. She tops at 155 miles per hour, they reckon."

"Don't try testing that out in front of Harry's pal the Sheriff," advised Ariane, only half teasingly.

"Okay, John, let's get our stuff and get on the road," said Wilko, not rising to the bait. He turned to the others. "Thanks everyone – we'll see who wants to come for a spin after the game, okay?"

Even Hector managed a genuine smile at the prospect. *"Gracias."*

"Si, si, amigo. That would be *bueno!"* enthused his travelling companion.

With Wilko clutching his car keys like a poor man's last dollar, they all headed to their rooms to pack. John B. looked especially happy. He was pleased for his friend's obvious delight, but was also looking forward to not sharing a room in the Village resort. There was only so much that earplugs and single malt could filter out, after all.

*

If 'Hands On' Harry was miffed at Wilko and John B. not travelling in the bus he didn't say so. Perhaps it was only coincidence that Wilko's threesome had the first tee-off after lunch so there was no time for him to enjoy the quick pre-game spin he'd hoped for.

"Better for your concentration anyway, Mister Wilkes," counseled Hoadley out of earshot of Shanks, who was playing alongside the Tasmanian, together with Hector Fernandez.

Given the garrulous natures of some of them, the six men – the golfers and their companions – were surprisingly quiet as they made their way around the course. Hector and Wilko were concentrating intently on their play, the latter taking to heart Stewart's encouragement of that morning. (Not that he would be likely to say so publicly.) Shanks was seemingly intimidated by his two playing partners, saying little to either, or even to Hoadley who hovered as helpfully as ever, but kept his own counsel unless asked a specific question by Armitage.

Carlos seemed ill at ease. John B. presumed that the two Spaniards

221

must have Had Words before play started. It was noticeable that Hector's game was below his usual standard. Wilko was gradually building a clear advantage.

The Waikoloa Village course was a genuine links course, generously sprinkled with traps and hazards, but also one of the most beautiful courses John B. had ever seen. Many of the fairways were fringed with palms. In several places these showed the effects of years of strong sea winds, growing not straight up, but at a sharp angle to the ground.

Winding its way through the course was a ribbon of the hard volcanic rock that made up so much of the Big Island's western coast. A wayward drive that clipped the black stone could fly in any direction – even straight back at the man who played the shot, as Hector found out to his dismay. Carlos' observation that it might have been worse – at least he could see where the ball landed – was little consolation.

Determined to give Wilko plenty of space, John B. progressively hung further behind the playing contingent. Wilko would signal in the unlikely event of wanting anything from him. The wizard was content to watch from a distance and admire the surroundings. He would have liked to have Hawthorn for company. The bird seemed to have known they were heading for a golf course, however. It was an environment she wasn't keen to revisit apparently. She sat in her box in Stewart's new room and refused his invitation to her usual perch on his shoulder.

His casual perambulation was so casual, in fact, that the following group caught up with him.

The scores between Glexie, Shareta and Keeaumoku were much closer than those of the three men in front. The atmosphere was no less competitive though, and Ariane, like John B., had decided to give her old friend plenty of space.

When she saw the familiar purple shirt not far ahead, she gave Glexie a nod and went to join the wizard where he was kneeling, studying an outcrop of old lava.

"Find something interesting?" she asked as she approached.

"Eh? Oh! Hi mate! I didn't hear you come up. Yeah – some more of the old petroglyphs." He smiled as the young legal officer knelt beside him.

"The stone carvings? Anything you recognise?"

"Funnily enough, yes. Some I recognise from that book I was reading the other day." He tapped a finger on one particular engraving. "This is a *niu'hi*. A shark – one of the dangerous ones. I know they were the totems for one or more of the families along the coast. Looks like this was a meeting place for them."

Ariane studied the symbol Stewart had indicated. "The shark was Papipi's family critter, wasn't it? I don't know that it's blessing his golf. I mean, he's playing okay, but he's not making up any ground on Shareta or my girl."

"Can't say I'm concerned," was the blunt reply.

At that point, a loud cry of "Fore!" from the Hawaiian golfer under discussion prompted them to turn and watch his tee shot. It wasn't a bad one: low enough to avoid the worst of the wind off the Pacific, although he'd deliberately aimed left to counteract that influence. The ball bounced twice and rolled into the shade of one of the palms on the left of the fairway. Luckily for Keeaumoku it wasn't directly under the tree as it was one of those that stuck out at a wind-borne 45 degrees from the turf.

The next shot was Glexie's. Watching Keeaumoku's result, she avoided the temptation to compensate for the crosswind, so of course the fickle air carried her ball to the right. Watching its flight, Ariane and John B. suddenly realised they were in some small peril. Dodging across the lava was a tricky prospect but they both tensed, ready to try to move in whatever direction was safest.

That turned out to be down. Ariane ducked low, the shaggy Galahad bent across to protect her. The ball shot over the back of his purple t-shirt, smacked into a conveniently shaped piece of black stone and ricocheted onto the fairway. The impact off the rock gave the ball considerably more carry than if it had hit the turf. It bounced a few more times before coming to rest in a perfect lie, well in advance of either of her opponents.

They all walked down the fairway. Ariane and John B. stood up and waited to join them. She surreptitiously squeezed his hand and said quietly, "Thanks, mate."

"No worries," was the equally quiet reply.

Approaching his own ball, Keeaumoku looked ahead to Glexie's and grumbled, "Hmmph. That was lucky."

Shareta and Hiro winced as they offered polite applause. Glexie just grinned and said, "Gary Player used to say, 'it's amazing. The harder I practice, the luckier I get.' I've been practicing."

"It shows," said Hiro.

The Hawaiian caddy was unconvinced. "How the hell do you practice a shot like that?" he asked.

"You don't. You practice until you are confident," replied the Japanese Hawaiian.

"And the positive energy creates positive results," expanded John B. "That's part of the Hawaiian shaman theory Harlan taught me a little while ago."

Hiro nodded. "He spoke well, then. I look forward to renewing our acquaintance tomorrow."

Stewart grinned at the older man. "Well remembered! He and Haveta are joining us for the rest day!"

Looking back down the course the way they'd all just come, Ariane pointed and said, "Speaking of people joining us, it looks like we've got company coming."

Trundling along the green at the best speed it could muster was a golf buggy. It carried an unhappy-looking Harry Barber and a dark-skinned man in uniform.

"Could this be news of Namakaeha?" wondered Shareta.

The buggy pulled up sharply beside the little group. The coffee-colored man leapt from it.

"Someone here is in serious trouble!" he barked.

Kahekili bunched his fists and squared his broad shoulders. "You better not be talking to me," he snarled.

"I'll talk to whoever I damn well please!" replied the uniform, just as belligerently.

'Hands On' Harry held those hands up in between the two men and hurriedly said, "No! No, Sheriff – this isn't the guy you're looking for…"

"I already figured that," snapped the lawman, " but I ain't gonna take no lip from some guy in them throwback gang colours!"

The diplomatic skills of Hiro Tanabe once again came to the fore.

"Excuse me please gentlemen," he said evenly. "Your arrival has come at a tense moment of play. Mister Barber, might we have some explanation please?"

Barber indicated the uniformed man beside him. "This is my – ah – great friend, Sheriff Barrett Lawson…"

Shareta stepped up to the officer, deftly inserting herself between him and Kahekili, and said, "Excellent! So you have found our lost driver?"

"What? Who? No!" Lawson gave Barber an angry glare. "I'm looking for the Spanish guy. I got a dead body I want to talk to him about!"

.o0o.

26 SPAIN KILLERS?

Barrett Lawson's statement dropped like a bombshell in a millpond. Shareta grabbed her husband's arm, looking for a moment as though she'd faint. The two Polynesians stood speechless – Keeaumoku's eyes darting about in apparent confusion, and Kahekili paling behind the black ink on his face. Glexie and Ariane instinctively grabbed each other's hand. The dark-haired girl's other hand clutched John B.'s hand in a similarly reflex action that he didn't resist.

It was the wizard who spoke in a steady voice. "You want to explain that, please, Sheriff? Who's dead?"

Lawson frowned at the Australian. "Local boy," he said. "Found in a club down in Keauhou. Now where's the Spanish son of a…"

"Should be just over that rise, on the next hole," answered Stewart sharply, letting go of Ariane's hand and jumping onto the back of the golf buggy as the Sheriff got back into the driving seat.

"What do you think you're doing?" snapped the lawman.

"My best mate is over there with the bloke you're looking for. If things turn nasty I want to make sure he's alright."

Harry started to protest but Lawson just nodded and gunned the throttle.

"Be careful!" Ariane shouted after them.

The players in the leading group were at the tee two holes ahead. The golf buggy caught up with them just as Armitage was in the downswing of his drive. The distraction actually improved his shot, which made the best safe yardage he'd managed all day.

Lawson had quickly glanced at a pocketbook as he drove, and now jumped from the cart and made for Hector, evidently working off a description.

For a moment the Spanish golfer looked set to flee, but then he jutted out his jaw and stood his ground as the Sheriff grabbed his arm.

"What is this?" he asked defiantly.

The other men in the group kept a wary distance, Carlos in particular starting to edge quietly away. John B. laid a protective hand on Wilko's shoulder, to the smaller man's puzzlement.

"You Hector Alvarez Hernandez?" barked Lawson.

The golfer shrugged. "*Si.* What of it?"

The Sheriff didn't relax his grip. "You got quite a rap sheet in Barcelona, didn't you?"

Hector looked blank. "Rap sheet? *Que?*"

"Criminal record. A series of drug convictions. Possession, mostly. The Spanish police tell me they could never make a big trafficking charge stick but they were pretty sure…"

Fernandez stood his ground. "Barcelona was bad for me, *si*. But that is why I left – I moved to the *Costa*, to start new. I plan eventually to play golf to make living."

Standing nearby Stewart, whose own history made him innately distrustful of policemen thought to himself, 'Plausible – a good thing even, if it's true. I wonder what this Lawson character has got on our *amigo*?'

"Not your only source of income though, hey?" continued the Sheriff. "And you've brought your filth over here with you. Big mistake. Bigger mistake – you've killed a kid on my patch, and I will see you go down for that!"

Though colour drained from his face, Hector tried to remain defiant. "*No comprende*. I do not know what you are talking about."

"I'm talking about a kid – not even eighteen – found in the men's room of a little club in Keauhou. Dead from a heroin overdose. Some of the drug still on the floor beside him – high-grade stuff. Together with the cracked open fake golf ball it had been packed in."

Fernandez swung a punch that connected with the side of Lawson's face, knocking the Sheriff to the ground. The Spaniard made for the golf buggy, but Hoadley's outstretched leg sent him sprawling at Harry Barber's feet. Harry sprang back, as if not wanting to be contaminated by Hector's guilt. The golfer started to struggle to his feet, but the valet grabbed him from behind, locking him into a wrestling hold known as a 'full nelson', immobilizing his arms and neck.

Hoadley and Hector were of similar heights, but the Englishman had the advantage of having braced himself first, and it was quickly apparent that he was considerably stronger than his captive. Fernandez squirmed and twisted but could not free himself.

"It was not me! It was not me!" the Spaniard shouted. "I know nothing of this!"

Struggling to his feet Lawson growled, "Bull! I got a witness at the club telling me the dead kid was seen handing money over to a Mexican. Ain't no Mexicans round that part of the Kohala Coast that I know of. I did some digging, and found that dear old Harry here had a Spaniard among his guests – did some more digging and found your record with the Spanish police."

"It was *not me*!" Hector shouted as he continued to struggle in Hoadley's grip.

Suddenly Carlos' nerve broke and he took off at a run. At first he went in the direction of the two Australians but veered when he saw the expression on John B.'s face. He wasn't to know that Stewart had lost more than one close friend, including his best mate at high school, to drug abuse – but he could read the look in the shaggy man's eyes.

Wilko looked up at his old friend and grabbed his arm. Some recent events in Australia were prominent in his mind. He really didn't like violence, and had been shocked to learn how good John was at it.

"Could we do this without a fight, please?" he asked.

"Always my preference, old buddy," the wizard answered.

"Mm," was the uncertain reply. The Tasmanian's grip on John B.'s arm didn't weaken.

Seizing the moment when they were looking at each other and not him, Carlos accelerated. Lawson was torn in indecision between handcuffing Fernandez and pursuing the caddy, which was giving the fleeing Caldera the opportunity to open up distance.

"I wish you'd bloody stop, you *hibrido!*" shouted Stewart.

Carlos looked back, startled at being insulted in his own language. So he completely failed to notice the big palm tree that years of coastal winds had caused to grow at an angle out over the path. Carlos' head smacked into the trunk and he landed like a sack of salsa.

The wizard didn't even break into a run. He strode up to the fallen Spaniard and hoisted the man up in the same hold that Hoadley was still using on Fernandez. It wouldn't have taken much effort to snap Caldera's neck. Perhaps that was even a temptation, as an unbidden memory of finding his friend Ferret's body crossed his mind. But he resisted, and hauled the unconscious caddy to the golf buggy.

"This is the joker that's been spending his time in every bar and club he could find," said Stewart. "Flogging golf balls, presumably." He dumped Carlos' still form across the back of the buggy. When the caddy woke he would find his wrists cuffed behind his back.

Hector had stopped wriggling and hung almost limply in Hoadley's grip. The nature of the full-nelson, properly applied, is that it reduces blood flow to the brain and gradually disables the victim while they're immobilized. When Barrett Lawson approached the valet released one arm at a time so the handcuffs could be applied.

"Wasn't me… was Calvera's idea…" the golfer mumbled as he dropped to his knees.

The Sheriff looked ready to plant a big kick in Hector's ribs, but refrained. No telling how the witnesses would react. Instead he jerked the Spaniard to his feet, and propelled him onto the back of the buggy.

"Come on, Harry. Get on. You're coming with me," ordered Lawson.

Barber looked hesitant. "Ah… Barrett… um, you don't really need me any more, do you? I found Fernandez for you. Ah… you *will* keep this quiet, won't you…?"

"Hey – do you reckon that Namakaeha found out about this, and these guys got to her somehow?" suggested Wilko on a sudden thought.

The uniformed officer gave that a moment's thought. "Reckon you're right," he said. Giving a gesture over his shoulder at the two captives he said, "I'm sure gonna ask these two some hard questions about it. Come on Barber, I said get on board. You're going to tell me all about these characters you brought into my district."

Disconsolately the property developer obeyed.

The trailing group were just catching up, game forgotten, as the golf buggy, motor wheezing under the weight of four men, trundled away towards the Sheriff's car.

"What was that all about?" asked Shareta.

"Case closed," replied Wilko. "I vote we abandon play for the day. I don't know about anyone else, but I don't reckon I could concentrate!"

"But what *happened*?" pleaded Glexie.

Hoadley was stretching and flexing his fingers as he replied, "Nothing good, Miss Hill."

"We'll tell you about it in the Clubhouse," offered Armitage.

John B. leaned close to Wilko to say quietly, "I hope you're right about this being 'case closed', old buddy. I've still got a bad feeling about it."

"You're just miffed because we didn't need your bloody 'magic' to sort things out. Relax, mate," replied the Tasmanian with a good-natured grin.

The wizard smiled back, but it lacked conviction.

.o0o.

27 FEELING LOW, LAID LOW

One of the Sheriff's team turned up at the resort later in the afternoon to search the Spaniards' room. Fernandez' golf bag had been impounded at the clubhouse but neither it, nor anything else among their collective belongings, would yield any useful forensic evidence. Carlos Caldera was thorough, careful, and experienced.

Hector had legitimately tried to 'go straight' when he moved from Barcelona to Malaga. He'd managed to stay on top of his own drug use but money was tight, and he was drawn into working as a distributor in Caldera's small operation. They'd crossed some bigger fish on the Costa del Sol, however. The opportunity to flit to Hawaii had been well timed.

In truth, Fernandez had been sincere about wanting a new chance to establish himself as a golfer, leaving his old life behind and eventually turning professional. The Royal Green tournament was a step on the road to the required credibility. But his surly nature masked a deep insecurity – one that Carlos subtly played upon to bend the aspiring golf pro to his needs. He saw an opportunity in Hawaii too, and he had been quick to try to seize on a new market.

Late in the afternoon 'Hands On' Harry Barber returned to the Village. His 'prospective customers' expected him to be a chastened man, but if anything he seemed more ebullient than ever. He almost bounced into the bar where his eight remaining guests were ensconced.

Standing by their table he threw his arms wide. "Hey everyone! Don't be down! Look, I know the news about the two amigos is tough, but at least it's all over now. Sheriff Lawson will deal with them, or they'll be sent back to Spain, or whatever, but they're *not our problem*, okay? There's still the opportunity to have one last round where all the surv… all the remaining players get a game together. Whoever tops the table at the end of that wins the prize!"

John B. looked up from a Scotch that was a long way from his first. "You're serious, aren't you?"

"Sure I am! Gotta keep moving, onward and upward. Barrett Lawson has realised that I had nothing to do with what the Spanish guys were doing, and none of you did either. He'll keep it discreet. We can all just get on with things – that's great, isn't it?"

"And Namakaeha? And that poor kid they found dead in the club?"

Hiro laid a gentle hand on the wizard's arm and said softly, "Your concern does you much credit, Stewart-*san*, but our withdrawal from the turning of the world cannot help them."

"The boy, definitely not, I suppose. But I wish I knew what happened to Namakaeha. Villains they may be, and callous about the damage their drugs do, but I can't actually picture either of them as hands-on murderers – pardon the expression, Harry."

Keeaumoku waved an expansive arm. "Either way, it's not our business. But if all of you are too distressed to play on, I'll accept your forfeit and claim the prize."

The normal cheerful expression on Glexie's face was conspicuously absent as she replied, "That's *not* gonna happen, pal."

"Indeed not," agreed Shareta with finality.

The Tasmanian golfer was torn. He sympathized with John B.'s feelings, knowing a little of what lay behind them, but he'd played well enough earlier in the day to think he was a realistic, if outside, chance to pinch the tournament on a final day's play. His gaze went between Stewart and Papipi.

"Listen John," he said. "Harry may have the sensitivity of a house brick…"

Barber was about to protest but even he wilted before the combined stares he got from around the table.

"… but Hiro has a point, too. We've got tomorrow off to enjoy the resort.

We can raise a glass in honour of the departed if you like, but it's a chance for everyone to do whatever they have to in order to get their head together, okay?"

Stewart didn't meet anyone's eyes but stared into his empty glass. "Whatever you reckon," he said quietly.

He stood, looked around the table without making eye contact. "I'm not much company right now, folks. I'm gonna go for a walk." With that, the wizard strode out of the room without a backward glance.

"So – everyone is good to play on Friday? That's great!" Harry rubbed his hands together, beamed his smile around the table, and jauntily walked off, already tapping his mobile phone.

Ariane was watching the direction John B. had gone in.

"Will he be okay?" she asked Wilko.

"Yeah. Give him time. I know he had a good mate at school who died of a heroin overdose so I think the news of that kid just opened up an old wound. You don't often see John down, but I think he just prefers to be by himself when it happens."

The Tasmanian looked to the New England pair seated beside him and asked, "Now, can I get you ladies a drink?"

Ariane gave a quiet, "Yeah, thanks," while Glexie nodded enthusiastically and squeezed his hand.

For all his concern about his friend's demeanor, there was a noticeable spring in Wilko's step as he went to the bar.

*

Hands buried in the pockets of his jeans, John B. had wandered out of the resort and out onto the nearby beach. The daylight was fading but it was still sufficiently bright for him to make his way along the sands of the foreshore.

He'd been strolling for some time, gradually pulling himself up out of his funk. 'What I *should* be doing is calling Q,' he told himself. 'I'll do that as soon as I get back to the room.'

He'd reached a narrow strip of beach, fringed by trees. As he turned to retrace his steps he noticed a small cluster of trolley people under a tall pine. He waved an acknowledgment, and was mildly surprised to receive a couple of answering waves. 'Maybe I look homeless,' he reflected, and in truth his attire of faded jeans and purple t-shirt wouldn't have been out of place among the group under the tree.

"Nice evening for a stroll, man," called one man – a grizzled fellow sitting on the ground. He was missing part of one leg below the knee, but he wore an amiable smile.

John B. wandered over. In part it was politeness, but he also realised that a genial word with a stranger would help lift his spirits.

Squatting alongside the fellow who'd called him, Stewart got into a casual but friendly conversation with a few of the trolley pushers.

"I don't see Big Easy. He's not with you folks?" asked the Australian casually. He'd hoped he might 'bury the hatchet' with the big man, if the vet even remembered him.

"Ain't been around for a day or two," answered one of the women in the group.

The crippled man gave a wry smile. "I reckon him and the new chick had a row and he took off. Reckon she's too much for him," he said.

"New chick?" asked John B., politely interested.

"Just hooked up with us a few days back. Don't say much, just hangs around… hey, speak of the devil…"

Stewart was suddenly aware of someone behind him. He looked up, and before his surprise had time to fully register he was stretched out on the ground, laid low by a cosh to his head.

"You didn't see anything, you didn't hear anything, and you don't know anything. Clear?" said the 'new chick' to the rest of the trolley people.

None of them were foolish enough to argue.

*

When John B. came to, his first sensation was of uncontrolled movement. He realised that his ankles were bound and his hands tied behind his back, and that he was bouncing around in the back of a moving vehicle. As best he could, he shook his head to clear it and looked around.

A white van that had seen better days. Bare walls and floor, a bit dented, and some stains that looked like rust. He moved to look at the driver. All he could see was the back of a head, but he recognised it, even without the striped woolen cap.

"I had a hunch the shark business was a furphy," he said.

"Eh?" Namakaeha was mildly surprised to hear his voice.

"A diversion. A hoax, even. Did you get off the beach walking backwards in your own footsteps? You'd be more nimble than I gave you credit for."

"I swam."

"Through the sharks? I thought they were Keeaumoku's totem, not yours."

There was a snort from the direction of the driver's seat. "I do not worship fish. No animals. Sharks are drawn to blood, but they won't go near the smell of dead shark flesh."

"That explains the smell on the beach. A convenient corpse, or did you

236

buy some shark meat beforehand? Clever either way," Stewart conceded. "So where do your loyalties lie? To yourself?"

"To the land! To the ancient living spirit of the land!"

John B. nodded. "Same concept happens in Australia. A much older land of course."

"Not for your people!"

The captive squirmed about in the back of the van and stared into the eyes of his assailant, framed in her rear view mirror. "My people, you say? What makes you think you know anything about me?" he said quietly.

Namakaeha was about to snap a short reply, but she caught his gaze in the mirror and the words died on her lips. She paused and thought for a moment.

"You're different. I get that. I was actually going to go quietly looking for you tomorrow, and then you go and conveniently deliver yourself to me. Don't know quite how it is that you're special, but I know you are. That's why you're here, and still alive."

"Uh-huh. Should I be thanking you?"

"No. You won't be alive much longer. I may not know quite what it is that's different about you but I'll give that to the spirit of the land. I do know the others weren't worthy."

"Others? The Japanese guys? The firebomb was yours?"

"The Japs were collateral damage. I wanted to try out some equipment, and that store was the perfect test site. The dirtbag Fitzwilliam has profaned this country as long as I've known him. He deserved to die. The loud Americans were no better. So much disrespect needed punishment."

"Americans? Ah. Buck and Wilma. I can see how they'd have gotten up your nose. Killing them seems a bit extreme though."

"They were going to die anyway. You're all going to die."

"Yep. Everyone does. You too."

"If it turns out that I die with the others that'll be my honour. But I don't expect that to happen. Pele will protect me."

John B. rolled uncomfortably as the van was swung around a tight corner, but he was determined to keep Namakaeha talking. Anything he could glean might prove useful. Somewhere. Sometime. Somehow.

He replied, "I presume we're not talking about Pele the footballer but Pele the volcano goddess. She's your 'spirit of the land' then, is she?"

The driver nodded. "Mm. Maybe that's what I noticed about you. You know a bit more about this place than most visitors. More than some that live here."

John B. was trying to position himself to see out the front windscreen. All he could see was the rapidly darkening sky. "It doesn't feel like we're going up the volcano," he observed.

"Got other plans for you."

"Other spirits to get on the right side of?"

"Yeah."

The wizard allowed himself a few moments of thoughtful silence. Namakaeha didn't initiate any further conversation – he didn't expect her to.

Unfortunately, just as he formulated a sentence in his mind and began to say, "I wi…" the van was driven off the road onto a rough forest track. The vehicle bounced and Stewart was flung into the un-upholstered side panel. His head slammed into a metal stanchion. Truth to tell, he probably wasn't fully recovered from Namakaeha's earlier attack for he lost consciousness immediately.

Hearing the thud the Hawaiian woman glanced back over her shoulder. Seeing her intended victim rolling helplessly her only reaction was to shrug.

A short time later – or maybe it wasn't, time means nothing when you're unconscious – John B. was woken by the smell of salt sea air. 'Woken' is too strong a word. His eyes opened and he got a sudden rush of impressions. The salt air, yes, and wind, and a realization of movement he had no control over.

By the time he'd figured out that he was still bound and that Namakaeha was holding him up in the air, suddenly she wasn't.

He heard the words, "The ancestors can have you!" just as he felt wind rushing past him.

A favourite book leapt incongruously into his mind. He thought, 'Here comes oblivion. I wonder if it will be my friend?'

.oOo.

28 LIFTING SPIRITS

John B. felt the sudden impact of something hard against his shoulder, and as he bounced rolled instinctively in the air back towards the cliff face. He landed face and belly-down on a narrow ledge.

Holding his breath, he listened for any sound from above. Nothing. Then footsteps, receding. Evidently Namakaeha hadn't seen him land sooner (and less fatally) than she'd expected.

With great caution the wizard wriggled and rolled onto his back. It became obvious why his assailant had missed seeing his lucky escape. The moon was a slender silver crescent barely visible through the thin high clouds that masked most of the stars. In the meagre light she wouldn't have been able to distinguish anything below – surf breaking on rocks a long way down, judging by what Stewart could hear.

'Okay, if I wait for daylight I can see where I'm at and what I'm doing. Of course, there's a very good chance I won't like what I see and it'll only make me feel worse.' "I wish some helpful soul would come along and give me a hand," he said quietly, just in case the former bus driver was still within earshot.

He lay on the ledge, watching the moon slowly make its way across the sky. He drowsed on and off. At one point he caught himself just in time from rolling over in his sleep. The realization of what that would have meant was enough to jolt him right back into wakefulness. Gingerly he sat up, keeping his back firmly pressed against the cliff face.

The idea that changing positions might help him stay awake was more hopeful than accurate, and his head soon started to drop again.

It was the third or fourth time his chin hit his chest. This time, though, he started to topple forward and forward would mean a long way down.

A sudden voice beside him snapped him back to wakefulness. *"A'la!"* it said sharply.

"Yes! Okay, I'm awake!" John B. replied just as sharply, before properly realizing he'd been addressed.

Blinking in surprise, he turned his head. The clouds had parted, allowing some faint illumination from the stars. In the dim light he could make out the figure of a tall native man, apparently in ceremonial dress including a cape of feathers, sitting beside him.

"Um… *aloha*," ventured the wizard.

"*Aloha*," might have been the figure's reply, although the sound was so soft it might have been the echo of Stewart's own voice. Then it – he – seemed to say something else. Too quiet for John B. to clearly hear, far less understand. But the wizard realized that the words weren't directed at him.

He turned his head. There was another figure sitting on the other side of him. That was quite an achievement, John B. realised, as that was where the ledge ran out.

This man, he could just make out, was tattooed in the same style that Kahekili wore. But unlike the caddy his eyelid wasn't tattooed, it was pinned open with a sliver of bone. Another peculiar thing occurred to Stewart. Even in the meagre light he realised he could see through the man. He looked back at the first figure and found that was the case with him, too.

The tattooed man spoke, a rapid tumble of soft syllables that might almost have been the reverberations of the waves breaking below.

"Sorry – I missed that. My Hawaiian is pretty limited, I'm afraid," John B. apologized.

The lips on the half-black face moved again, more slowly this time.

"*'Oe mea kaumaha ia*," the wizard repeated, concentrating hard. "Yes, I'm meant to be a sacrifice, it seems."

The whispered sound of the other man spoke, if 'spoke' is the word. "*Wahine hewa*," was what was heard.

"The woman is wrong. Well, I'm glad to hear you think so."

The spectral warrior sidled closer and said, "*Hio imua*."

"Umm… okay. I'll do as I'm told… with all due caution," said Stewart and, as directed, leaned forward.

The tattooed man produced a sharp stone knife – John B. couldn't tell where from – and sawed through the bindings on the wizard's wrists.

"Of course, Wilko would suggest I'm dreaming, and that I've actually cut the ropes on a sharp rock without noticing."

The transparent figure tilted his head to one side, and then grinned.

"The expression, the 'ghost of a smile' takes on new meaning, my friend," said John B. warmly.

Again following instruction, he stood up carefully and turned to face the cliff. Feeling a tug at his ankles he looked down, and then quickly looked back up again. It wasn't the sight of a spectral hand sawing through cords with an equally transparent dagger that bothered him. It was the faint reflection of starlight on breaking surf, and just how far below him it was breaking.

"Okay – great. Thank you. *Mahalo*. Now what?"

"*Pi'i kakou*." The one in the feathered cape seemed to be the senior of the two, or at least have some measure of authority.

"We climb. We. That's encouraging – I'm assuming you can see what you're doing, because I sure can't!"

Stewart carefully eased off his canvas shoes and jammed them into the back pockets of his jeans. "Better off without these, I reckon," he said.

Wordless now, the two figures each grasped one of John B.'s wrists. They began to scale the face of the cliff, guiding the Australian's hands to projections, fissures, small clefts and irregularities he could grasp and haul himself up on, then wedge and cling to with his toes. He didn't bother to look at how his guides were managing their own ascent. If they were what he suspected them to be, then a fall wouldn't harm them. For him though, the consequences would be… well, let's say he figured he'd be occupying something like the same space as his new companions.

The wizard lost all track of time. The climb was laborious and painful. The rocks of the cliff face were sharp. Stewart's hands and feet were sliced open and bruised, as were his chest and belly as his t-shirt was torn into purple ribbons. The denim of his jeans ripped too, the skin scraping off his knees. But stopping wasn't an option. One shoe popped from a back pocket. With an effort he didn't imagine its descent to the rocks and sea below.

Suddenly he reached up for another handhold and encountered empty air. He'd made it to the top! Getting up and over was equal parts climb, clamber and crawl, after which John B. lay face down on the ground sucking in deep breaths for what felt like ten minutes but was probably less than two. Eventually he sat up and looked around.

If anything, the light was worse here than it had been on the life-saving ledge, as overhanging trees blocked much of what little starlight was on offer. Still, the wizard could see that around the edge of the small clearing from which Namakaeha had hurled him were a dozen or more spectral figures like the two who still stood by his side.

Getting to his feet, he gave a respectful bow to each of the pair in turn. "*Mahalo*," he said.

Both returned his bow – a gesture that frankly surprised him. Something about it seemed to imply he was accepted as an equal. Was he dead too? He didn't feel dead – did that count? Again his thoughts turned to what Wilko's reaction would be.

'He'd reckon I've banged my head, I'm imagining things, and I must have climbed up the cliff in a daze. I admit that last bit isn't completely un-true,' he mused.

Thinking of the terrible climb suddenly brought to mind the pain of where the rocks had torn his flesh.

"I can't be dead – I hurt too much!" he said and sat down to take the weight off his battered feet.

Doing so, he landed uncomfortably on the remaining shoe in his back pocket. He pulled it out, looked at it and said, "One of you isn't going to do me a lot of good. Thanks for carrying me around as long as you have – now go join your mate."

With that, he flung the soft shoe far out over the cliff edge. It landed in the rolling water, sank, bumped off the head of a passing shark, and even-tually settled on the seabed to begin the steady process of disintegration.

John B. looked again at the figures standing near him. They glowed softly.

"I can't sit here indefinitely, can I? Would you mind showing me the way out of here please? Wherever 'here' is."

"*Hahai*." The word came from the man in the feathered cape, again as a sound that was barely more than a sigh of the wind.

Stewart bowed as he stood. "Follow? Certainly, as well as I can any-way."

Wincing as his steps opened up the cuts on his feet further, the wizard followed as the apparitions formed themselves into a line and marched down a trail through the trees. If the light had been better (and his brain a bit less addled) he would have found the trail for himself. It was the same path that Namakaeha had taken when carrying his unconscious form to the cliff top. He may well have collided with a tree though, as amongst the forest it was almost totally dark. The only illumination was the dim glow of the night walkers.

Stewart studied the ghostly figures ahead of him. Several had the right sides of their bodies (or the substance where their bodies had been) tattooed black. *Pahupu*, Harlan had called them. Others were dressed or adorned quite differently. There were a number of women, as fiercely equipped as any male warrior, among the group. Not all the same tribe, it seemed.

"I remember wondering if the old rivalries survived after death - it seems I have my answer," he mused aloud.

"Unite for the common good! A pity it's not a lesson learned on the other side of the veil!" boomed a familiar voice from the darkness ahead.

John B. stared into the gloom. "Courtesy?"

The big Polynesian stepped forward and became visible, lit by the glow of the line of marchers. The night walkers stopped, and Courtesy stood amongst them. There was a brief conversation, none of which was audible to the Australian, before the newcomer strode up and grasped him by the shoulder.

"You've had a rough time of it, my friend," he said in a low rumble.

"I've felt better," admitted Stewart.

"Have my jacket," offered Courtesy, starting to peel off the black windbreaker that had helped render him invisible among the trees.

John B. waved the offer away. "No. Thanks – but I'm not cold. Now if you were carrying a spare pair of shoes…"

Courtesy looked down at Stewart's feet and clicked his tongue sympathetically. "I can carry you back to my car."

"Too much to hope that you're a healer, then," said John B., smiling regretfully.

The Hawaiian gave him an odd look. "I know a little, but that's not my job. You would know more of healing than I do.”

“Only what I picked up from an old guy in Central Australia.” Stewart was looking down at his feet and missed the expression that flashed across the big dark face. “I appreciate the offer, but I’d prefer to walk if I can manage it.”

“As you wish. I’ll lead the way. Our friends will not be with us much longer – the sun will be up soon.”

The figure in the feathered cape approached and laid a translucent hand on the big man’s shoulder. “*Mahalo, ho’okele*,” he uttered softly.

Courtesy bowed his head respectfully in reply. The night walkers resumed their march, followed by the two corporeal figures. The Polynesian allowed his smaller companion to walk unaided as much as possible, but discreetly put out a hand or arm for support when needed.

“*Ho’okele…*? Paddler? No – steersman, navigator. Is that how you found me?” asked John B.

The man beside him shrugged. “It’s what I do – what I am. The ‘*aumakua* and I have known each other for a long time.”

“Kindred spirits?” Stewart enquired politely.

Courtesy laughed his bellowing laugh. “Ha! No! I’m no fighter!” He saw John B.’s skeptical look. “Oh, I’ve fought when I’ve had to, but that’s really a role best left to others more expert at it. And as honourable as all these are, they were first and foremost warriors.”

The walkers stopped, forming an ordered rank allowing Courtesy and John B. to pass. Their glow was fading fast – presumably the sun was just below the horizon.

The tall spectre in the feathered cape extended an arm and laid his fading hand on John B.’s shoulder. “*Aloha, kupua.*”

The Australian thought for a moment. "That's 'Good-bye, wizard.' Hmm, nice to be recognised – most folks in this world don't believe me when I tell them! Not that I remember telling you…" His voice trailed off for a moment, before he pulled his thoughts together and bowed to the caped figure, and the ghostly phalanx behind him.

"*Mahalo, 'aumakua ho'ohanohano*," he said sincerely. "Did I get that right?" he quietly asked his companion.

"Thanking the honoured spirits? Your pronunciation is a little strange, but the sentiment is entirely correct, my friend."

The two living men were just about to resume their walk. The *'aumakua* had almost faded from view when the caped figure suddenly stepped toward them, a look of concern, no – fear – on his face.

"*Akahele wahine ke'oke'o! Po'ino!*"

As urgently as he'd 'said' the words, both John B. and Courtesy still strained to make out the sound.

"Danger?" repeated the wizard. "What…"

"*Pahu'*…" the whisper faded like a sigh, just as the spectre who uttered it disappeared from sight.

John B. looked at his companion in puzzlement. "Something exploding? And what was that about 'beware of the white woman'? The Amazon that tried to kill me here was no more white than you are."

He explained as well as he could what had happened to him – accidentally meeting the bus driver who'd been presumed dead, the journey in the battered white van, the conversation he'd tried to have with his captor before being knocked out and waking up on his way over a cliff.

"A mystery for which I have no more answers than you. The *'aumakua* see things on a plane beyond even you and I. We have to trust that whatever we need to know will reveal itself. They've at least told us to beware."

"Namakaeha's killed at least five people, and had a red hot go at adding me to her list. I know to beware, believe me. I've got to get back to Wilko and the others in Waikoloa and make sure they're okay – bugger!" Stewart cursed as he stumbled, his bloodied foot slipping on a large smooth stone.

Ignoring his protests, Courtesy picked the Australian up in a fireman's carry and started to move in big loping strides. "My car isn't far, but we'll make much better time this way. And our first stop is to see a doctor I know. He has a little place at the other end of the Waipi'o Valley, so he's on our way to Waikoloa."

"I haven't got time for…"

"Don't argue with me!" the big man roared. "You can barely stand, let alone walk. You've lost more blood than I think you realise, and you've a lump on the back of your head the size of a *nene* goose egg. If I don't get you seen to you'll be no use to anybody!" He lowered his voice to a rumble, but it was more concerned than threatening. "Doctor Khoo isn't in the same class as your friend in the desert but he's far more skilled than I am. Plenty good enough to patch you up to move about without collapsing."

John B. was exhausted, and knew it. Courtesy made sense. He would have said as much if he'd stayed conscious. He passed out in the big Polynesian's arms and didn't even stir when he was gently laid in the back of a station wagon emblazoned with a 'Surfboards For Hire' sign.

.o0o.

29 COMINGS AND GOINGS

It wasn't a good morning for Wilko.

Probably driven by the day's stresses, the whole group had stayed on at the bar well after dinner. Harry had bought several rounds of drinks for his remaining 'prospective buyers' ("Probably feeling guilty," Ariane had observed) and was actually quite reasonable company as the night wore on.

Keeaumoku had retired early, intending to spend much of the Rest Day on the practice green. His caddy however had stayed on, conversing with Hiro Tanabe about Hawaiian history. The two men seemed genuinely interested in the different perspectives the other offered.

Wilko had spent an enjoyable evening at the bar with Glexie Hill. Flirting came as naturally to him as bicycle riding did to a mackerel, but they'd laughed and chatted over plenty of self-indulgent drinks. He'd woken with a certain queasiness and fuzziness of head. It wasn't quite a hangover but certainly a signpost on the direction to one.

He'd gone to breakfast expecting to find John B. already there, but there was no sign of his travelling companion. 'Must still be getting over his mood,' thought the Tasmanian. 'Most likely retired with a bottle of good Scotch.'

Then Glexie had walked into the dining room on her own and made straight for Wilko. She took his arm as he stood at the self-serve coffee machine. "Can we talk?" she said – a question never known to set the mind of any man at ease.

They sat at a small table in a quiet corner of the room. None of the others in their group had appeared yet, but there were many other guests in the resort. Grasping Wilko's hand earnestly Glexie said, "I don't know if I said or did anything… um… out of line last night…"

"No, no, you were fine. You were really good company."

"Thanks. Wilko – I really like you. I mean *really* like you. But just as a friend, you know?"

"Sure. I… er…"

"I just didn't want you to have the wrong idea."

"No, it's okay. I didn't have any ideas," said Wilko, not entirely truthfully.

"Like I said, I like you a lot. I want us to be friends, but that's all. Not one of those quick and dirty little holiday romances you read about, or anything like that. Just good friends, corny as that sounds. Is that okay?"

"Sure. Of course it is. Maybe not on the golf course tomorrow…"

She laughed. "Before and after the game though, okay?" she suggested.

"Sounds good."

"Thank you. You're a good guy, Wilko. I'm sorry if I…"

"No, no, it's fine. 'Friends' is fine." He shook his head. "I'm really not looking for – anything else."

The Tasmanian kept his reserve as Glexie reached to squeeze his hand. "Thanks, man. You're gonna make someone very happy someday, y'know."

"Yeah… well… um, thanks."

The girl went to order some breakfast. Wilko took his phone from his pocket, intending to call John B. and see if he was awake. He was irked to realise that he'd turned the mobile off while at the bar the previous night. After he turned it back on he was even more unhappy to realise that he'd missed a call from Jazz. That upset him more than he'd expected, too.

Finding he'd lost his appetite, he made his way back upstairs. He wanted to talk to John. Not a Deep And Meaningful conversation as such. They didn't have that sort of conversation. Didn't need to. But he could do with venting a bit, and John's was a safe and sympathetic ear.

He rapped on Stewart's door. No reply. He called his friend's name. The only answer was an agitated *"Ee-oh!"* Now worried, Wilko tried the door and was disturbed to find it unlocked. Cautiously he entered the room. A duffle bag, still closed, lay at the end of a bed that clearly hadn't been slept in. Hawthorn's box was in a corner, but the bird was perched on the edge of the bedside table. She flapped her wings and gave another little cry.

Worried that the hawk might dive at him, the Tasmanian backed out of the room, shut the door and dashed back down to alert the others.

It was to Wilko's benefit that the first people he encountered were Hiro and Shareta Tanabe. The unflappable couple was able to bring him back from the edge of panic. But even in their calm conversation, Wilko's disquiet was obvious from across the room to the only other members of the golfing party to have arrived for breakfast.

Glexie bit her lip anxiously, afraid that she'd upset the Australian far more than he'd let on earlier.

Her roommate tried to reassure her. "You can't be responsible for other people's reactions, hon," said Ariane. "I know you – you'd have been really, really gentle about letting him down." 'I have first-hand experience remember,' is what she didn't add out loud.

"I tried to be," confirmed the accountant. "But look, you can see from here how distressed he is!"

Thoughtfully Ariane watched the exchange on the far side of the room. Eventually she said, "No offense, hon, but I don't think that this is all about you. Come on – I think we'd better go be part of the conversation."

Glexie looked uncertain as she followed her friend, but her manner changed once they'd heard Wilko's report of what he'd found, or rather, hadn't found. She stood beside the Australian and put what she hoped was a supportive hand on his arm, and was pleased to get a grateful if cautious nod from him in response.

The two Hawaiians strolled into the dining room.

"Hey!" called Wilko. "Have either of you seen John?"

"Not me," replied Keeaumoku.

"Not since he took off before dinner last night," expanded Kahekili.

Hiro spared Wilko the necessity of repeating his story by outlining the details to the new arrivals.

"He hasn't just taken off, like the Texan and the two Japs?" suggested Kahekili.

Wilko shook his head. He didn't believe Stewart would do that. Besides, his minimal luggage was still in the room, as was Hawthorn. He wouldn't just abandon the bird.

"Speaking of which, I suppose I'd better try to feed the poor critter. It won't have eaten since yesterday morning," said the Tasmanian.

"I'll take care of that for you in a bit. She's pretty good with me," offered Ariane. "I think we need to get a search organized first."

"You're over-reacting," said Keeaumoku with a casual gesture. "He's probably gone over to one of the other resorts, settled into a bar there – had too much to drink and spent the night."

It sounded plausible, but Wilko recalled how he'd been led to believe a similar scenario in Melbourne recently, when John B. had turned out to have been abducted. But there couldn't be another mad Russian scientist on the loose, could there?

The pensive Glexie said, "I wish Hoadley was part of this conversation. I reckon he's good in a crisis."

"Crisis? What crisis? I told you – you're all over-reacting," Keeaumoku repeated. "I'm going to have breakfast. He'll turn up sooner or later."

His caddy didn't follow him as he left for the serving counter. "I don't think you'll see the butler for a while yet, anyway," observed Kahekili. "He doesn't go anywhere without his boss, and when we came past their room it was obvious the *menehune* was still asleep."

That was true – Shanks' snoring was clearly audible out in the corridor. Hoadley was unlikely to be asleep, but as Kahekili had suggested, he was equally unlikely to leave his employer's room. Shanks probably wouldn't know what to dress himself in when he got up.

"You don't have to help look for him, mate, but I'm going to," Wilko told Kahekili.

The tattooed man shook his head. "No, I'll help. I think Keeaumoku may be right, but your pal is a good guy, and after yesterday, well, I'd like to be sure he's okay."

He held out a tattooed hand, which Wilko shook gratefully.

"Let's get organized, then," said Ariane, and proceeded to do so.

'She's not quite in the class of Elizabeth Dance – sorry, McKew – but she is good,' mused Wilko. He'd been on the receiving end of Elizabeth's people management skills before, and remained in awe of them. But Ariane was briskly efficient too, quickly devising a plan of who would check around the resort and the nearby beaches.

"Wilko, if you take the Mustang we can check around the neighbouring resorts. Maybe Papipi is right, much as I hate to admit it. Glexie and I can come with you, assuming you're okay with that, hon?"

The accountant and the Australian looked at each other for a moment, then both smiled.

"Sure," said Glexie.

"Okay, sounds like a plan," agreed Wilko. "How about we meet in the foyer about ten and compare notes?"

"Make sure everyone has your cell phone number in case there's any news," said the dark-eyed legal officer.

With that accomplished, the group went their separate ways, some stopping briefly to snatch a coffee or something to eat. From his table Kee-aumoku watched and shrugged.

*

By the time the appointed hour rolled around, Wilko was becoming seriously worried. There had been no word from the others, nor had he and the girls had any success at the surrounding resorts.

Shareta had checked the beach. But even if any of the trolley people might have been prepared to risk Namakaeha's wrath they'd already moved on by the time the tall Korean woman got to the tree they'd been under.

The Mustang had just pulled into the car park of the resort. Wilko was getting out of the car, looking in irritation at the phone that hadn't rung.

A silver sedan pulled into the space beside him, the passenger door opened and a cheerful voice called out, "Hi Wilko! Hey, what's the matter? You look worried!"

"Oh! Harlan! Good to see you…" said Wilko as he shook the archaeologist's proffered hand.

Haveta got out of the driver's seat of the sedan and came to join the New England girls now standing by the convertible.

"What's wrong?" she asked. "You all look like you've lost your best friend."

With a wry smile at the choice of words, Wilko explained as they all walked to the foyer what they'd been doing and why.

The rest of the group had already gathered there, now joined by Shanks and Hoadley. Hiro had apprised them of the situation when he'd met them finally arriving for the English heir's breakfast. To Armitage's credit he'd insisted that they help, although Hoadley would certainly have chafed at doing anything else.

At the valet's suggestion they all relocated to the bar to sit and discuss what to do next.

"While checking this building I called into Stewart-*san*'s room a few times, in hope he may have returned quietly. But all I found was the *'io*, I'm afraid," reported Hiro.

"I put some raw steak down for her before we went out," said Ariane, "but she was pretty distressed."

Hiro raised an eyebrow. "Really? She seemed quite docile the last time I checked the room, sitting in the box that seems to be her nest."

Wilko shook his head and said, "I reckon if she could fly that bird would head straight for him. Dunno how he does it with animals."

"Some people just seem to have that kind of rapport," observed Haveta. "I've an idea," she continued. "I'll drive over to Kawaihae – I think there's a little police station there, and fill out the proper Missing Persons form."

"There's a special form for it? I shouldn't be surprised – there's paperwork for every damned thing! I should do that," said Wilko.

"No, I know all of the basic information they'll require – the who, where and when. I think you better stay here in case he does turn up," the blonde replied.

Harlan nodded agreement. "I'll stay here too, and call you if he turns up, dear one," he said.

The marine biologist wasn't the type to waste time. Having settled on a course of action she was up and away immediately.

"Has anyone contacted Mister Barber?" asked Shareta.

Kahekili snorted, "Why? You don't think *he*'d be any use, do you?"

"Perhaps not, but it would be polite to inform him that yet another of his charges has disappeared," said Hiro, instinctively supporting his wife. "He might then inform the Sheriff, who may actually be of some assistance."

"It's a funny thing," said Wilko. "I reckon I know who *might* be able to help." He turned to Ariane and Glexie. "Do you remember the big dark guy we met on the beach? Courtesy?"

"Sure do! He was pretty unforgettable," said Glexie with a grin. "Why him, though?"

Wilko looked puzzled and answered, "I dunno – instinct, maybe. He reminds me a bit of someone I met in outback Australia. An old black guy. They both have a kind of an air about them."

And it was at precisely that moment that the bar room door swung open and a voice boomed, "There you are – just as predicted! Waiting for you in the bar!"

Heads turned and eyes popped. Wilko's mouth opened and shut in the goldfish impression he lapsed into when taken by surprise.

Looking like a broody hen with a chick under its wing, Courtesy had a large arm draped around John B.'s shoulders.

Dr. Khoo had cleaned up the wizard as adroitly as the big Polynesian had promised, but bandages and Mercurochrome stains were clearly visible. It was hard to know which was more disturbing for the group assembled in the bar – the dressings swathed around Stewart's head, hands and feet, or the severely torn state of his shirt and jeans.

"John B.! You're okay!" exclaimed Glexie.

The Australian grinned a little wryly. "Not sure that's the word I'd use, but I'll live."

"What the hell happened to you?" asked Wilko.

"Namakaeha. Sorry, give me a few minutes to change, please, and I'll come back down and explain."

Of course there were a welter of questions that started to pour from the assemblage, but Courtesy held up an imperious hand as the wizard gingerly left the room unescorted.

"Best he tells you his story himself," rumbled the man who was called by some 'the Navigator'. "I will go and advise Barrett Lawson of what's been going on and tell him to search for the miscreant."

Making no further reply to anyone's questions, Courtesy strode from the room. Two thoughts flitted across Wilko's mind: the use of the word 'tell' rather than 'ask', and how did the big guy automatically seem to know where to find the Sheriff?

It was a mix of concern, astonishment, shock and plain curiosity that the folks in the bar were trying to contain. Fortunately for everyone's peace of mind, John B. was as good as his word regarding his haste in changing clothes, even allowing for the awkwardness of using his damaged hands. It was a scant few minutes before he reappeared in fresh jeans and another purple t-shirt, with Hawthorn perched placidly on one shoulder. He'd managed to fit his bandaged feet into an oversized pair of sandals that Courtesy had provided.

The barman came on duty early, intending to clean some glasses, and was swiftly prevailed upon to serve drinks. It was just coincidence, surely, that on sitting down John B. had said, "I wish I had a Scotch right now."

Fortified by a double shot of single malt held delicately between bandaged fingers, Stewart proceeded to explain to everyone what had happened to him.

As expected, his description of the nightwalkers' role in events didn't sit well with everyone.

"But… they're *legends*," said a nonplussed Kahekili, one whole belief system thrown into chaos while another more visceral one seemed to be confirmed.

"No wonder there's a bandage on your head," said Wilko. "I'm glad you're safe, mate, but you're obviously concussed." He rolled his eyes. "First magic, now ghosts!" With a sigh the Tasmanian turned to Hiro Tanabe and said, "I'm sorry mate. That was a good story you told the other night, but John, you're not even Hawaiian…"

Hiro gave Wilko a sympathetic smile and replied, "Neither was the German officer."

There was a similar smile of Harlan's face as he said, "You know, Wilko, there are tribes in parts of South America and the Pacific who don't believe that such things as aeroplanes and railroads are real. Just stories that their visitors have made up."

"That's only because they've never seen them…" Wilko stopped and shut his jaw with a snap. He could see Harlan's point, but wasn't keen to admit it, especially in front of John B. Stewart.

It was Glexie who rescued him by changing the subject.

"So what are we going to do about Namakaeha?" she asked.

"We?" repeated Kahekili. "*We* don't have to do anything except be glad she didn't manage to kill any of us."

"She's quite emphatic that we're all going to die, and she *is* still out there," John B. said quietly.

The tattooed Hawaiian spread his hands. "So? She's Sheriff Lawson's problem now."

That prompted Harlan to look at his watch. "Speaking of the law, I expected Haveta to be back by now, or at least to have heard from her if there was a problem at the station. Kawaihae isn't a long drive." He frowned. "I wonder what's holding her up?"

*

Haveta drove into the little car park behind the shops adjoining the small police shopfront. There were a few other cars there, and an old white van, but no people. No, not quite – there was one of the scruffy homeless coming out of the public toilet block, hunched in the typical shapeless coat and trousers.

It was inevitable their paths would cross, which didn't bother Haveta. She had no particular dislike for the luckless disadvantaged, not that she'd had much to do with any of them. But as they neared each other she was surprised to realise that she knew the other's face.

"Hey – you're the driver from the golf tournament, aren't you? Well, I can see you don't have any dress regulations in your job!"

Namakaeha caught Haveta completely off guard by jumping at her and planting a fist in her solar plexus. If the blonde could have caught her breath she might have apologized for her being thought rude, but she was in no condition to do that. The big Hawaiian woman darted round behind her and seized both of her arms.

"The last person to inconveniently recognise me was that loser Ese. His bad luck. Yours too, lady," she growled, locking her hands behind Haveta's head in the full nelson grip that Hoadley had used on Hector.

One good flex and she'd snap the Scandinavian woman's neck. But a split second before that thought became deed, Namakaeha realised who she held. She remembered the dinner, and the conversations exchanged.

Inspiration struck the Polynesian like a lightning bolt, and it was with a look of almost delight that she released her grip and spun her smaller victim around to face her.

"I remember you! You're that mouthy fish scientist. Oh, this couldn't be better!" said the bus driver.

Before Haveta could even attempt to frame a question, the big fist lashed out again. This time it landed flush on the jaw. Haveta hit the ground hard and blacked out.

Namakaeha looked around quickly. Pele be thanked, there was nobody in sight. Perfect. Clearly she was under the protection of the goddess! She doffed the large overcoat that made up such an effective proportion of her disguise, and then forced the unconscious Haveta's arms into the sleeves.

The garment was so oversized on the blonde that Namakaeha was able to secure her in the manner of a strait jacket by tying the cuffs tightly together behind her back.

She wore a broad smile as she deposited her trussed victim in the back of the van.

She hummed to herself as she drove out of the car park. She'd intended to make do with the American – the one with the waves tattooed on her arm. But not now. At just the right time, this one had appeared. One who'd boasted of her name as meaning 'daughter of the sea'. How per-fect!

.oOo.

30 LAST CALL

After a little while John B. absented himself from the group and went outside to call Elizabeth.

"Hey, Q! Sorry to call you at work, pretty lady, but I thought I'd better ring you to set your mind at ease."

"What? Why? What's happened?"

'Ah,' he thought, 'Wilko didn't tell her I was missing. Oops.'

Thinking quickly he said, "I didn't want to freak you out when I see you in a couple of days. I'm a bit, er, rougher round the edges than usual."

He proceeded to give an abbreviated account of the night's events.

"How do you find these people?" asked Elizabeth, recalling the Russians who she'd helped rescue him from.

"Or how do they find me? I wish I knew! I suppose one day I'll find out."

"Please, please, take care of yourself," said the brunette, not disguising her concern at all.

"I promise I'll try. I'm okay, just some scrapes and dents in the panel work."

"Hmm, maybe I can kiss them better," said Q trying to lighten her own mood.

"That's a good idea! Hey, maybe I should get a few more…"

"That isn't funny!"

John B. was immediately contrite. The distress in her voice was clear.

“I’m sorry, pretty lady. I *will* be careful, I promise, as much as possible.”

“Okay then… wait. As much as possible? What’s going on over there?”

“Sweetheart, I’m really not sure. That crazy woman’s still out there, with some sort of plan.”

“Is that really your problem?” asked Elizabeth sternly, and immediately thought better of the question. “No, wait, I understand. I know you better than that.”

The wizard smiled a little ruefully. “Thanks for that, pretty lady. There’s also the fact that whatever Namakaeha’s got planned threatens Wilko, and some other people here who I’ve gotten to be friends with. If my magic can help keep them safe, then I’ve got a responsibility.”

“You’re not a superhero, babe. Don’t go putting your life on the line.”

“I don’t aim to. But even without knowing exactly what she’s up to, if I read Namakaeha right then not doing anything is at least as risky as trying to stop her.”

“Mm, alright. So how are you going to do that?”

“I haven’t got a clue. I wish I did.”

Q gave a light laugh and said, “Well, that should do the trick. Just try not to do anything too dangerous please.”

“I’ll try. I’ll see you soon,” John B. replied sincerely.

“At the airport, babe. I know what flight you’re due in on. You are *not* getting a cab home, okay?”

“Understood. Thank you.”

She smiled down the phone. “Thank you, for caring enough to tell me what’s going on.”

As he approached her desk with a file full of problems Kaiser Ron wondered at the smile on Elizabeth's face as she put down the phone.

*

Namakaeha had pulled the van into a storage shed on the outskirts of Kona. After ensuring that her captive was still unconscious, she called a familiar cell phone number.

It rang at the airport. Max Ritter was watching his suitcases being loaded on a baggage cart. He recognised the number and offered a short but polite greeting.

Namakaeha scarcely acknowledged it. Her words tumbled out excitedly. "I know you said to take things cautiously. Climb the mountain one stage at a time. But I've known all along that this was an incredible chance, Professor. All the elements combined to make my reaching the summit more spectacular than I could have hoped."

The Professor looked at the airport clock. He had a few minutes.

Calmly he replied, "It is a remarkable thing how momentum can build after a period of inertia. I am, of course, no scientist, but it does appear to me to be an important principle in science. This is Newton's law of inertia, yes? A body remains in its state of rest or linear motion until it is compelled to change that state by a force impressed on it. We see this demonstrated routinely in things like chemical reactions."

"I suppose that's how catalysts work, eh Professor? Accelerating the rate of change."

"Certainly, yes. Catalysts, you say?"

His former pupil grinned – an expression few people had seen. "I thought I had everything worked out. Everything from the traditions you taught us, ready to set things off to wipe the slate clean and start fresh. And now something – some*one* – even better has been given to me. Oh,

263

Professor, if there was ever any doubt that this is Pele's will, my finding the daughter of the sea has wiped that away. She *is* the perfect catalyst!"

Musing, Namakaeha continued, "If one element can accelerate a reaction, then I suppose there can be others that could change it in other ways. Limit it, maybe. Contaminate the result. That's what that damn Australian could have been. But as you suggested, the ancestors took care of him."

Ritter gave a polite cough. "Not quite my suggestion, I should point out."

"Certainly your guidance, sir. Credit where it's due – you reminded me of the other spirits of the land who should be considered, at least until Pele's dominance is reasserted. You are taking care of your own safety?"

"Even as we speak. I am about to embark on a small sabbatical from the University. I should shortly be in Los Angeles. In fact, I think I must be going now," he said.

Namakaeha smiled. "Of course. That should be safe, sir. Enjoy your travels, and thank you again for all your support. Remember, whatever happens tonight may be by my efforts, but the great outcome will be due in no small part to you. *Mahalo.*"

"You're welcome. I am proud of you," Ritter said with a cryptic smile as he ended the call.

Patience would be rewarded, it seemed.

.o0o.

31 STREAMS RUN TOGETHER, FORMING A FLOOD

It would be an exaggeration to say that Haveta felt awake. Her head throbbed too much to be asleep, but her grasp on reality wasn't strong enough to be called consciousness.

Her stomach hurt where it had been punched. Her arms were numb and for some reason she couldn't move them. Vaguely she realised that she was sitting up, but being pushed and pulled around. She started to squirm.

The squirming stopped when Namakaeha backhanded her across the face. The Polynesian didn't say anything. She continued with her work, wrapping wires around Haveta's pinioned arms and torso.

As well as securing the Scandinavian woman from any useful movement above the waist, the wires also served to bind a dozen lunchbox-sized packages against her body.

Each of the packages was connected to one of the wires.

Satisfied that her 'parcel' was secure, Namakaeha twisted the ends of the wires together and attached them to a large crocodile clip. She looked around the shed she was in, tut-tutting at the detritus of wire, paper and spilled chemicals littering the floor.

"Ah well, soon it won't matter," she said to herself.

Haveta surprised her by answering, albeit groggily, "What won't matter?"

"None of it. There'll be nothing to find. No you. No one who'll care to look. This whole island will be wiped clean."

*

Harry had finally turned up at the resort, doubtless to the relief of Nikki

Martin who had been enduring his presence in the Royal Green office since mid-morning.

He'd noticed Keeaumoku out practicing on the resort's putting green and given an obligatory wave. He was neither surprised nor disappointed not to have it returned, but was a little puzzled that the Hawaiian wasn't in the company of anyone else from the tournament. 'Guess he's being hard to get along with again,' he thought with a mental shrug.

It was with genuine puzzlement that Barber greeted the subdued group still assembled in the bar. Someone at Reception (who had reassured him that nobody was trying to put any drinks on his company's tab) had directed him there.

"Hey gang – it's a great Big Island day out there! I'm surprised there aren't more of you out practicing for tomorrow. You don't want to give our islander friend too big an advantage," he chortled, adjusting the language of the last sentence just in time when he spotted the tattooed caddy in the group.

Shareta looked up at the developer through tired eyes and asked, "Are you sure that it would be appropriate to complete the tournament under the circumstances, Mister Barber?"

"Huh? Pardon?" Harry's look was as blank as a new page in a drawing pad.

Before anyone could reply Harlan returned from a quiet corner where he'd been on his phone. The archaeologist's brow was furrowed, as he said, "She's still not answering. I think this isn't good. I've called the police in Kawaihae and explained the situation."

"Good move, mate," said Wilko. "Harlan, you've met 'Hands On' Harry Barber before."

Barber stuck out an oblivious hand. "Sure! Good to see you again! Blonde wife, you both work in the University, right?" said Harry who never forgot a prospective buyer.

"That's right," replied Harlan, distractedly.

"Jeez, Harry, wake up! We've got another missing person – this time it's Haveta!" snapped John B.

"Another missing… what…? What on earth happened to you?" Harry had only just actually looked at the Australian and seen the wound dressings on his head and hands.

"Seriously? You haven't been told?" said Glexie, astonished. "The Sheriff hasn't contacted you?"

Actually, that was a major reason the developer had left the Estate office. He'd missed several attempts from Barrett Lawson on his cell phone while on other calls. When the Sheriff had tried the office number and demanded to speak to him, Nikki had been ordered in sign language to say he was out somewhere, no idea where, or when he'd be back.

He'd had a hunch that if Lawson wanted to speak to him urgently it wouldn't be good news. Probably trying to blame him for something about the crooked Spaniards, he'd guessed, and vacated the premises before he was looked for there in person.

It was the calm voices of Hiro and Hoadley that recounted for his benefit the news of what Namakaeha had done, and the prospect that she had more devilment in mind.

Now he stood slack-jawed, staring at the group, and particularly at the battered man who still sat with a hawk perched on his shoulder.

"Close your mouth, Harry. You look like a fish," said Wilko with some satisfaction.

Barber stammered, "But that's… that's… it's all too…"

"Incredible? Outlandish? Hard to believe?" asked Ariane. "I'd love to agree with you just this once, Harry. But look at John B."

"Well, yes… but… I… he…"

In a stern voice Hoadley said, "Come now, sir! Mister Stewart is hardly likely to have inflicted the injuries on himself. Even if attempting to craft an alibi, it would be profoundly difficult to do such damage to one's own hands."

"I didn't mean…! But… it's…"

"Pull yourself together, man," snapped Ariane. "Try to contribute something useful. Can you at least think of where Namakaeha might be?"

"No! No, I don't know anything except that she could drive a bus! I said that when she disappeared. I just hired her – I don't know anything about her!"

"Now that is a damn shame," came a voice from the doorway of the bar.

Barrett Lawson strode across the room and dropped a large hand on Barber's shoulder.

"I've been trying to get in touch with you for a while, Harry," he said ominously.

"Oh! Ah… really? Sorry – lots of calls this morning, then I – ah – turned the cell phone off. Needed a bit of a break."

Lawson nodded. "Sure. That's alright. When I called in to your office and your phone still wasn't answering your business partner was kind enough to tell me you might be visiting your golfers on their day off."

"Miss Martin's not my partner! She's the office manager!"

The Sheriff shrugged. "Yeah? Sure that's not what I saw on some of the legal papers that came through my office. No matter. I knew where you folks were staying, thanks to Courtesy."

"Courtesy?" asked the bemused Barber.

"Big local guy. Been around a long time. Don't know a lot about him, but he carries a lot of weight around here, in more ways than one," said the lawman with a wink to those at the table. "He came to see me this morning with a very interesting story." He looked at John B.'s bandages. "I guess you're the guy she attacked last night?"

"That's one way of putting it, yeah," agreed the wizard.

"We're gonna have to have a long talk, you and I. I wanted to see you and get some verification of what Courtesy told me. One look at you is a good start. I'll need more, but right now I've got enough to want to haul this man in first." Barrett's hand had never left Harry's shoulder and now he squeezed.

Barber wriggled under the grip. "I don't know anything! None of this is my fault!"

"The bus driver's on your payroll, she's your responsibility," said Lawson.

Some looks of surprise and satisfaction rippled around the watchers at the table.

Harry tried one last stand of defiance. "She's not the only one on the payroll…"

The Sheriff was implacable. "No you don't. Not this time. This has gone too far. You're coming back to the station to help me with my enquiries, starting with how I find this mystery woman you hired. The rest of you – later. Clear?"

"Indeed, very much so," answered Hiro before any of the more intemperate members of the party could say anything contrary.

A careful silence was maintained while 'Hands On' Harry was steered from the room, at which point a babble erupted. The gist of it remained, however, uncertainty about what to do next.

*

Shortly after the white Firebird took off towards Kona Lawson had an impulse to pull over to the side of the road. Glaring at Barber sweating in the passenger seat the Sheriff was on the radio describing the battered white van that Courtesy had mentioned when recounting Stewart's story.

To his surprise, the desk sergeant remarked that coincidentally, just such a vehicle had been reported running a red light at the airport intersection, causing a nose-to-tail collision between cars going in the crossways direction. The driver seemed to have been distracted by something in the back of the van, and had taken off at speed according to the witnesses.

The desk sergeant was a laconic man, used to Barrett Lawson's preference to avoid trouble. He'd calculated that by the time he could rustle up pursuit down Highway 19 the offending vehicle would be out of their District and not their problem any more. A description would be posted and if it happened to be spotted by someone in their team, well, it could be dealt with then.

"That was right, wasn't it Sheriff? It's not our problem?" asked the now worried voice down the radio.

Barrett drummed his fingers on the dashboard. He wasn't a superstitious man, but there had been a small cold trickle down his spine since his interview with Courtesy. He didn't quite believe in the *'aumakua*, but living in the District for a long time, and knowing some of the people, especially the old-timers… Well, you didn't discount anything.

Finally realizing he'd left the radio channel open, Lawson said, "I've got a bad feeling this could be a problem for a lot of people. I'm already on the highway. I'll take care of this myself."

He snapped off the radio. Ignoring Harry's protests the Sheriff stuck the removable flashing light on the roof of the Firebird and stomped the 310 horsepower of the V8 into life. He was officially In Pursuit of a felon.

*

Discussions around the table in the bar seemed to be going in a circle.

A few rounds of drinks bankrolled by Armitage Shanks and the Tanabes were appreciated but didn't help. In the absence of a clear plan of doing anything, the group kept coming back to doing nothing.

Then Harlan received a call from the Kawaihae police. They'd found his wife's car, rather embarrassingly, parked two minute's walk from the little station. "No sign of the lady, but no sign of foul play either," said a policewoman reassuringly, or so she thought.

The news brought more tension, but no fresh ideas. Then Shanks surprisingly broke the impasse. "I've just realised. The Sheriff never mentioned checking Namakaeha's room. We could break into it and check…"

Hoadley sighed. "A worthy thought sir," he said, "I must point out though that the woman was not with us when we arrived at this establishment. I suggest Mister Barber would have wasted no time in cancelling her accommodation."

"And working real hard to get a refund on it," agreed Wilko. "But hang on, Shanksy, you've given me an idea. Where has Namakaeha spent most of her time while she was with us?"

"Arguing with people," suggested Kahekili.

"On her own at a table, reading a book," answered Ariane, more kindly.

Glexie snapped her fingers. "On the bus!" she exclaimed.

"Bingo! We should check in there. At least it gives us *somewhere* to look," said Wilko.

After a moment of looking pleased at the breakthrough, Shareta shook her head. "I cannot think that Mister Barber would have left the bus unlocked after delivering us here yesterday."

"And the blighter's probably got the key in his pocket. Perhaps we could call that Sheriff fellow and ask him to deliver it?" suggested Shanks.

"No need for that," said John B. said. "I reckon I can... oh, wait... maybe not." He looked unhappily at his bandaged fingers. Whatever chicanery from his past he had in mind was evidently beyond him at present.

There was a discreet but slightly smug smile on Hoadley's face, though. "I believe I may be of some assistance," he said smoothly.

"Well, we're not all going to fit. You might as well all wait here while Hoadley and I have a look," said Wilko.

"If you reckon I'm going to sit here like a ham sandwich at a Jewish wedding while you're scavenging for a lead on this nutcase, you must have had a bigger knock to the head than I did," replied John B., getting to his feet.

When the wizard swayed slightly – it was his injured feet, not the Scotch, honestly – Harlan took his arm and supported him. "I'll come with you. I'd appreciate the distraction."

"And the rest of us just sit here and fret," said Ariane with some acid.

"Well, that's been the pattern for much of the day," admitted Glexie.

With a note of apology in her voice Shareta said to Kahekili, "I almost hate to admit it, but perhaps your friend has the right idea immersing himself in some practice shots. Mister Barber seemed determined that the tournament was to continue, and perhaps the diversion would be good for us?"

The New England golfer shrugged. "The putting green's as good an idea as any I guess. I suppose there is only so much room on the bus for a detective operation."

Shanks nodded. "Quite right. I can certainly do with working on my short game." Nobody rose to the inadvertent tempting line. "Hoadley old man, will you...?"

"As soon as I have assisted Mister Wilko and John B., sir. I shall bring your clubs to the putting surface."

"The driving range for me, I think," said Shareta. Her opponents were surprised – that element of her game seemed to need no great work – but Hiro recognised that the stress of the last day or two was telling on his wife. Realising that the other golfers would be elsewhere she'd nominated a spot where she could regain her equilibrium with only her doting husband and caddy to converse with.

The only ones to not make a move were Kahekili and Ariane.

"I think I'll stay right here," said the man from Maui. "Seems like there's nothing useful I can do for anyone, so 'nothing' is just what I'm gonna do."

Ariane was frustrated. "Golf's not going to do anything for me," she said. She looked at Wilko with some irritation. "I'm going to help you guys. I really don't take up that much room, you know."

John B. extended a battered hand of friendship. "Thanks mate," he said. "I'd appreciate your help."

With an exchange of nods, Harlan stepped away and let the legal officer take his steadying place beside the wounded wizard, the *'io* still sitting placidly on his shoulder. They made their way out to the car park where Wilko was already assiduously looking anywhere but at Hoadley.

Moments later, the pneumatic door of the bus hissed open.

"Lady, gentlemen, I wish you success. I shall go and attend to my employer," the valet said with a bow.

John B. grinned. "Thanks Hoads. It'd be… handy - if the rest of the crew could be kept occupied. I've got a feeling things may get hectic, and unpleasant, pretty soon."

"Indeed sir? I'm sorry – John B. I shall take that under advisement and keep a wary eye open."

'You do that anyway, don't you?' thought the wizard with a wave to the departing Englishman. He looked at Ariane, gently helping support his weight. She met his gaze.

"I can look after myself, you know," she said quietly, responding to his unvoiced concern. "Probably better than you, by the looks of you."

Stewart tightened the arm around her shoulders into a genuine hug, and then turned to face her square on.

"Ariane, I don't doubt your toughness for one moment. I would not wish what I've just gone through onto anyone, and especially not onto someone I care as much for as you." He was acutely aware of how close to death he'd come. "Call me a chivalrous old bugger, but if I can't absolutely spare you whatever danger that Namakaeha's got planned, I'd like to at least keep you as far away from the immediate threat as I can. Would you accept that, please?"

Her dark eyes bored into his for a moment. Not many people stood up to the intensity of that gaze, she knew, but this man did. He was serious. She could respect that.

"Okay," she said.

Wilko and Harlan had been scouring the bus while the other two talked. The archaeologist checked the passenger seats and luggage racks while the Tasmanian got back into the driver's seat and looked in every nook and cranny he could find. He'd pulled out the single textbook he'd located, wedged under the seat behind where he'd found the torch two nights earlier. He flicked through the pages.

In the whole book, one passage had been highlighted, with notes scribbled on the page around it. Unfortunately for Wilko, the book wasn't written in English. He sat on the front seat and called the others over to examine his find.

Pointing to the highlighted paragraph, he asked, "What do you reckon this means?"

It was John B. who answered, while Harlan was still concentrating. "When Hina closes her eyes and Pele swallows the water those who belong to the land will flourish. Otherwise is death. Burning and death."

Hawthorn piped keenly and flapped her wings.

Wilko looked bemusedly at Stewart. "For cryin' out loud! How many languages do you speak?"

"Fluently? Aah… if you count how I normally talk as fluent English, one. I know bits and pieces of others, and when I hear them, well, it's like some memory of the language comes back to me."

"Weird," was the Tasmanian's only comment.

Harlan shrugged. "Well, the passage seems innocuous enough. When it rains the land thrives, when the rains fail then things parch and die. It's a statement of fact, that's all. I suppose it relates back to a period of drought. They've happened, at least in certain parts of the islands at certain times."

Ariane looked skeptical. She was good at that. "So why highlight it? Was Namakaeha, or someone else, worried about the weather?"

John B. was looking intently at the page. He said, "That word there – *wai* – it means 'water', doesn't it?"

"Well, yes," replied Harlan. "Technically rain would be *ua*, but there's a bit of – um, variation in the translation in some words."

"Could it mean sea?" the wizard asked.

"Not normally, that'd be *kai*. But I suppose, if you just read it as 'liquid' then maybe. Why?" The academic in Harlan was momentarily overcoming even his concern for Haveta. He was intrigued.

John B. answered excitedly, "Do you remember Namakaeha's reaction when Haveta explained that her name meant Daughter of the Sea? Let's try a less benign translation. 'When the volcano – Pele – swallows the sea...' I reckon that Haveta is the 'white woman' that the *'aumakua* were warning me about."

"Really? Why?" asked Ariane.

Harlan looked doubtful. He said, "John B., I love my dear one, and respect her, but I don't think she's a danger to you."

"Not just me. A greater danger, I think. Pele swallows the sea. A tidal wave, or more likely an eruption that opens a seaward fissure? How might you cause that? A blast on the seaward side where there's a known fault line."

"Hold on," said the girl from New England. "Where did you get *that* from?"

Stewart shrugged. "A hunch? Instinct? An annoying little voice inside my head?"

Wilko gave that his usual dubious reaction and snorted. "A blast like that could wipe out the whole Big Island. Where's the sense in that?" he asked.

His travelling companion shrugged. "Whoever said we were talking sense? Namakaeha is from Oahu, isn't she? And more than a bit proud of it. She may not give a stuff about the Big Island."

"I do remember her getting stuck into Keeaumoku about it. That was the night Kahekili blew up as well, about being from Maui. I never realised the old island rivalries still went so deep," said Ariane thoughtfully.

Harlan looked uncomfortable as he replied, "Publicly, or officially, they don't. And honestly, that's true of the great majority of us who live here. But you can never tell with some people, I suppose."

A recent memory played across John B.'s mind.

Cautiously he said, "The *pahupu* – the real *pahupu* – had their origins on Maui, but I think anything cataclysmic that threatened the islands as a whole would invoke their protection. They were amongst the *'aumakua* and they all seem to work together."

There was a silence as all of them in their own way pondered Stewart's statement.

Eventually Harlan asked, "Where does Haveta fit into that scenario?"

Stewart was hesitant in his answer. He didn't want to upset his friend, but realised that there was no gentle way of explaining his fears. "Well, based on my experience, Namakaeha's big on the idea of sacrifices. I was meant for the old spirits, she said. What if your dear one is next on her list? A final sacrifice to trigger something bigger?"

'Maybe a good moment to change the subject a bit,' thought Ariane. "Does the bit about someone closing their eyes mean anything?" she asked.

The distraction worked on Harlan, momentarily at least. He explained, "Hina is the goddess of the moon. I'd assume it means clouds covering the moon – a rainstorm at night, I suppose."

Staring at the open book, John B. said slowly, "Or else… Think of the waxing and waning phases as an eyelid opening and closing. Have you been watching the night sky lately?"

The dark haired girl looked at him. "You really don't think in straight lines, do you?"

Wilko almost laughed. "Him? He makes a corkscrew look like a rail-road spike. But sometimes he makes a kind of sense."

John B. looked pleasantly surprised by Wilko's observation as his old friend prodded at his mobile phone.

They all watched for a few puzzled moments before the Tasmanian looked up and announced, "According to this app I downloaded, it's a new moon tonight.”

Stewart nodded, recollecting what he’d seen less than twenty-four hours earlier. Could it have been that recent? He was lucky to be alive - how the hell was he even awake? ‘Must be a reason. Must be something I have to do.’

“That makes sense,” he said. “There was only a sliver visible last night. Tonight it is, then. Okay, where? A volcano, presumably, but there are options on the Island, aren’t there?” The question was directed at Harlan.

The Hawaiian took a deep breath. He made an effort to be calm. All that he’d learned studying shamanism was called to mind. With patience came clarity. After only a few moments that to him, seemed longer, he answered, “Across the island there are a small number of active places. But I’m afraid there are more that might be made active if someone was determined enough.”

“If this line of reasoning is correct, and based on past performance, I think we can assume Namakaeha is pretty determined,” said Ariane grimacing.

Wilko had been turning the page to different angles. The text itself might as well have been in Greek as far as he was concerned, but he hoped to glean something from the handwritten notes.

“Does this scribble mean anything?” he asked, indicating a rough scrawl in the margin of the book.

John B. read over his old friend’s shoulder. “*Halemaumau.* House of… something.”

Harlan was also peering over the Tasmanian’s shoulder. Frowning he said, “The handwriting doesn’t make it easy. It could be ‘house of eternal fire’, or ‘house of the *ama’uma’u* fern’. Either way, though, I think I know where it refers to. Both names get used for an area around Kilauea. It’s noted for a lot of steam vents that have opened up in the ground around the crater.”

“Gentlemen, it sounds like we have a destination,” observed Ariane with some satisfaction.

The wizard smiled in agreement. "Yep. All we've got to do is get to the volcano before that final faint outline of the moon is up."

Harlan looked at his watch. He was worried. "Um… here to Kilauea is about 140 miles." He consulted his watch again, and looked at the sky. "Can your magic help, John B.?"

Wilko almost growled. "Sod magic!" he said, pulling a set of keys from his pocket.   "I've got the 'Stang! I'll get us there!"

"I wish you would," said Stewart evenly. He looked at his hands. "It's not like I could drive," he added.

As they clambered off the bus, John B. took Ariane aside.

"We're not all going to fit in the convertible. That back seat's built for children, or midgets…"

"Or *menehune*," Ariane said with a wry smile. "I get it. You have your wish – I'll stay here. You go do what you can, and you know, I reckon that'll be enough."

"Thanks," the wizard replied, scarcely noticing that they were holding hands. "I hope you're right."

"I'm sure of it. So sure I'm going to go and do some work ready for to-morrow," she said with a smile.

That got a puzzled expression in response. "I thought you were staying away from golf," he said.

With a last quick kiss to John B.'s cheek she answered, "I've got other skills, remember. Never underestimate a woman."

"Never!"

.oOo.

As they'd climbed into the convertible, Keeaumoku had approached.

"Taking it for a spin? You got yourself a plan, have you?" he asked. Evidently some of the others had at least tried to engage him in conversation.

"We're busy," said John B. with something less than a smile.

The Hawaiian gave a mirthless laugh. "I hope you're not planning on catching up with the local sheriff. You know he's got a new Pontiac Firebird? That thing can go from naught to sixty in 5.6 seconds!"

From the driver's seat Wilko looked up and raised an eyebrow. "Really? Did *you* know that the '68 Mustang could do that in 5.4? This bruiser will do it in 4.7."

He released the handbrake, turned the ignition, and worked the pedals perfectly. His exit from the car park may have been fractionally behind the figure he'd just cited, but it was enough to leave the Hawaiian golfer standing with his mouth hanging foolishly open.

That was scarcely a comfort to his passengers, hurled back into their seats. It was just as well that Hawthorn had, moments before, been settled in one of the rear footwells while John B. stretched his legs across the back seats.

As the Mustang tore down Highway 19 the hawk huddled down behind the driver's seat, glaring balefully at Wilko's back. Consciously or otherwise the *'io* was reflecting John B.'s unease. It wasn't a lack of faith in Wilko's driving. Not really. It was just that prior experience with less capable, or at least less confident, drivers had left him deeply uncomfortable in a car travelling at over a hundred miles per hour. Call it a quirk.

Stewart leaned to where he could shout around the passenger headrest into Harlan's ear. "Distract me – tell me about the *ama'uma'u* ferns, please," he asked.

In truth, Harlan Hunter was scarcely more comfortable than the wizard. A mostly quiet life of archaeology had taken him to many corners of the world but they were typically tranquil corners. High speed driving along a highway liberally sprinkled with other vehicles was a new experience for him. He wasn't enjoying it much, so the suggested distraction was welcome.

Harlan racked his memory for all he could recall of the *ama'uma'u* legend.

"The story goes that back in the ancient times, when the land of Hawaii was still being formed, it was populated by both gods and men."

"Much like the Dreamtime," shouted John B.

"Yes," Harlan shouted back. "Well, one of these gods was called Kamapua'a. He gets variously described in different stories as a deity of cloud, rain, or forest. Certainly, he was able to change the form of his body at will."

Wilko, who was listening as he drove, laughed. "That'd be a handy talent to have!"

Everyone lurched forward as Wilko suddenly stopped for a red light as they passed through the little town of Captain Cook. It was a good effort by the brakes – the car went from over the ton to a dead stop in about two hundred feet. Hawthorn, the only one not wearing a seatbelt of course, fell awkwardly and shrieked a loud protest. Disconcerted by the shrill noise right behind him, the driver apologised.

"Sorry, thought I better not risk attracting police attention," he said.

"Um, Wilko – we do have speed limits on the island, you know. And you've been quite a bit over them," Harlan pointed out.

"Oh. Yeah. Didn't think of that."

John B. looked over the back of the Mustang and reported, "It doesn't look like anyone's following us yet."

The driver patted the black leather trim. "Not much chance of them catching us if they do."

The light changed and the Mustang sped away again. This time the hawk had settled down as close to the floor as she could, and only slid slightly with the acceleration.

"It's a pity we can't just up and fly due east from here – it's only about forty miles to the crater," said Harlan as he was pushed back into his seat. "Unfortunately Mauna Loa and the Southwest Rift are in the way."

"There you go, Wilko," said the wizard from the back seat. "You should have hired a helicopter."

"Not as much fun to drive," was the Tasmanian's reply as he watched the Ground Speed Indicator – no mere 'speedometer' for the Mustang.

"Yes, I'm sure this is a very lovely drive under other – *oof* – circumstances." Bracing himself as the car whipped round a bend, John B. called, "You were saying about the forest god?"

Harlan swallowed and took a deep breath. "Yes. Kamapua'a is said to have stood on a cliff top and offered his love to Pele."

"Goddess of the volcano, and beloved of our dear Namakaeha. Yeah – know about her," responded Stewart.

"Pele answered Kamapua'a by insulting him. He was so enraged they fought. She fought with fire, he fought with wind and storm and rain. The battle lasted for a long time until the two deities were weakened."

"So it was a draw?" asked Wilko.

"Not exactly. Sort of, I guess. Both of them were exhausted. Pele, though, had a small bit of fire left. When she hurled it at him, from where we now call Kilauea, Kamapua'a saved himself by using the last of his strength to change shape one final time. He turned himself into the *ama'uma'u* fern, and surrounded her exhausted body. He couldn't hurt her, but she couldn't harm him, either."

The hawk raised her head and keened, seemingly approving of the story.

"So these ferns don't burn?" asked Wilko, looking to rationalize the legend.

Harlan shook his head and replied, "I'm not a botanist, but I think most plants burn if the temperature is high enough. They're quite heat resistant though, I think, because they grow well on old lava flows that get pretty hot with the sun on them." He caught his breath as the Mustang sideslipped slightly rounding a bend. "The other thing that contributes to the story is that the new growth on the ferns is always red, symbolizing the burns on Kamapua'a before he changed shape that final time."

"The name 'house of the fern' means they're still growing there, I assume," shouted John B.

"Correct. Lots of them, all around the crater and the surrounding area. They're especially common in an area noted for steam vents, which adds to the thought that they're very heat-hardy."

"What do you mean, 'steam vents'?" asked Wilko as they flashed past a Volcanoes National Park sign.

"Mauna Loa is still active. There's an active lava flow from a spot near to where we've already passed, and there's a monitoring station right by the main old crater. The steam vents are cracks in the ground where air heated by the underground lava escapes."

"Sounds delightful," muttered the driver ruefully. "And you reckon this is where Namakaeha has gone?"

The archaeologist scratched his chin thoughtfully and replied, "If John B.'s reasoning is sound, then yes. And I must admit, the more I think about it the more plausible it seems. Unpleasant, but plausible."

Some men would have been fretting wildly about a missing wife, Wilko reflected as he drove. Harlan Hunter wasn't. There were a number of reasons for this.

The Hawaiian academic was ordinarily calm to the point of being phlegmatic. If it wasn't his nature, then he'd certainly nurtured the attitude through meditation. Secondly, John B.s distraction had worked effectively. Recalling and recounting the legend of Kamapua'a had diverted his attention from considering Haveta's fate. The archaeologist's attention was also diverted to a large extent by the drive itself. Not all of the stretches of the big ring road that looped around the bottom of the Big Island and up into the National Park were necessarily suited to the speed that Wilko was maintaining.

Finally, and this was the bit that would have most had the Tasmanian shaking his head, Harlan had an implacable faith in John B. Stewart's magic or whatever it was.

He couldn't have cogently explained why, but the experience they'd shared in Central Australia was enough. However the purple-shirted Australian did it, he bent events. The ability to do that was a central tenet of Hawaiian shamanism and Hunter accepted that Stewart had that talent.

They'd been on the road for over an hour. The Mustang was winding up the slopes of Mauna Loa, through an area of low vegetation. Here and there white plumes of steam arose from the ground on either side of them.

"This is Halemaumau," said Harlan over the roar of the rushing air.

Wilko eased his foot off the accelerator and they all began to scan their surroundings. They passed a small sign. Had they stopped to examine it they'd have read: "To show respect for the land and your host culture, please speak in soft tones during your visit. Do not disturb the land or intrude upon native practitioners who may be paying homage to Pele. Your courteous regard of their feelings and respect for their privacy will be noticed and greatly appreciated."

The three men were however determined to very emphatically intrude upon one particular native practitioner's homage to Pele.

As the convertible slowed down they could see that many of the plants around them were the ferns described earlier. They grew in tangled mass es, leathery fronds interlaced. Nominally some were tree ferns, but the trunks were short and thick. With the decrease in speed, the *'io* hopped up onto John B.'s lap and looked ahead between the two front seats. She gave a loud "*Eee-oh!*" as they crested a rise. Two white shapes were visible in undulating land amongst the ferns away to their left.

"That way," directed Stewart, pointing to the two patches of paleness.

Wilko might have been about to argue but then noticed tyre tracks going the way he'd indicated. "Well, somebody's driven this way, so I guess I can too," the Tasmanian said.

It quickly became clear who had preceded them. As they approached, the white shapes were revealed as a battered van and a Pontiac Firebird.

"Looks like the Sheriff has beaten us to her. Hmmph – he had a head start," said Wilko.

"I hope he can handle the situation," said Harlan, concern in his voice for the first time in a while.

As the Mustang pulled up behind the Firebird John B. clambered out of the back, Hawthorn clinging to his shoulder. Even with the sun dropping the ground underfoot was very hot, and he said a silent 'Thank you' for Courtesy's generous sandals. A trail of crushed ferns led away from the parked vehicles, across some small mounds towards another ridge. Here and there steam belched up from fissures in the earth.

The wizard stood at the start of the trail waiting for the other two men to join him. They all looked out to the east, where the line of crushed *ama'uma'u* ferns led. The hawk stretched her wings and threw out her chest, as if responding to a challenge. John B. reached up and rubbed a bandaged finger on the head of the *'io*. "One way to find out," he said, and led the way.

.o0o.

33 THE MOUTH AND THE HEART OF THE VOL-CANO

Lawson had followed a trail of reports of the white van all the way along the highway. Technically, by the time it changed from Highway 19 to Highway 11 he was out of the Wiwo'ole district and thus out of his jurisdiction. He'd made it very clear on the radio, though, that this was *his* case thank you very much, and he'd call for back-up if he needed it. He was held in enough regard for this to be conceded.

It wasn't just stubbornness. It was the presence of Harry Barber. The property developer had made contributions that had done much to help the Sheriff's election. He'd never asked for any favours that were actually criminal, as such, but there was a tacit understanding that Barber's business activities not be too closely examined.

That had rankled with Barrett Lawson, who was fundamentally an honest man. It may well be that Harry couldn't be held responsible for his driver's actions, but the Sheriff would make him as uncomfortable as possible while at last asserting his authority.

Having followed his quarry's trail into the National Park, he was surprised to see the van parked, apparently randomly, off road not far from the Kilauea crater.

Getting cautiously out of the Firebird Lawson looked around warily. A flash of movement caught his eye. The top of a dark head disappearing over a ridge some distance away. He yanked open the passenger door.

"Come on, Harry. I don't know where she's going or what she's up to, but you're coming with me!"

"But I..." Barber's protest died on his lips as the lawman grabbed his arm and hauled him from the Firebird.

"It wasn't a request!"

Dodging the occasional plume of steam the two men hurried towards the ridge, trampling ferns as they ran.

Namakaeha had no idea she was being pursued and so wasn't hurrying to her destination. She had Haveta slung over a shoulder, but the blonde's weight seemed of little consequence, even with the packages and wire. With her free hand she patted the pocket of her hoodie and the comforting weight it held.

Suddenly a voice from behind her pulled her up short.

"Hold it you! No further! I want to have words with you!"

The big woman spun. A brown man in uniform – yeah, the Sheriff – seen him before, and Harry damn Barber. She snarled and crouched slightly as they approached.

Lawson moved cautiously, revolver drawn. "What do you know about an incident at the Kealakekua Store?"

"Damn place shouldn't be missed by any true Hawaiian," she growled.

"And the men who were in it?"

"Same goes for them."

"I see. Who's your friend?"

"Eh?" Namakaeha realised who the lawman was talking about. "None of your business. She's a means to an end, that's all."

The Sheriff had his gun aimed uncertainly at the former bus driver. Uncertainly, because the white woman was draped over her shoulder, hanging in a way that made her an effective shield. He didn't know of the fate intended for Haveta, or that her captor needed her alive to be an effective sacrifice.

Harry hung back as Lawson cautiously approached the big woman.

Keeping well away, and using the Sheriff between them as a shield, he shouted, "Come on Namakaeha – give this up. It can all be sorted. I've got influence you know. Come on – remember, you're my employee - you answer to me!"

Namakaeha's eyes blazed. Her expression turned from contempt to rage in a heartbeat. "I answer only to Pele!" she roared.

Lawson flinched as she flung out an arm in an angry gesture towards Barber. From behind the Sheriff came a loud cracking sound. A fissure opened in the ground directly under 'Hands On' Harry and he was engulfed in a geyser of superheated volcanic steam.

Barber's scream would haunt Barrett Lawson for the rest of his nights. He ran back to where the driver's erstwhile employer lay, flung by the blast of steam and the reaction of his own muscles. The developer wasn't a pretty sight. The pain must have been terrible, and far beyond anything the lawman's basic first aid training could help with. If the man had been a horse or a dog Lawson would have shot him immediately.

Any thought the Sheriff had along that line was quickly moot. Harry's system couldn't stand the shock and with a bubbling sound on his lips he breathed his last.

Kneeling beside the body, Barrett turned his head slowly to look at Namakaeha. He expected that at any moment the earth would split beneath him, too. The woman was gone, striding purposefully away with her intended sacrifice still flung over her shoulder.

A noise in the direction he'd just come from caused him to turn back. Three men were crunching through the ferns. He recognised one of them immediately – the bandaged one carrying the bird. He was the Australian that Courtesy had come to see him about. The smaller guy behind him, yeah, he'd been at the resort too – so had the other one, he remembered the beard.

The three rushed up to where he knelt, but the smaller Australian recoiled at the sight of Barber's body.

"What the hell happened to Harry?" gasped Wilko.

Barrett waved his hand in the direction of a nearby column of hissing steam. "The woman. She… she made the earth open up under him. He didn't stand a chance." Vaguely he added, "I don't know how she did that…"

The new arrivals saw that he'd dropped his gun, and hadn't even appeared to notice.

"Have you seen my wife?" demanded Harlan.

The Sheriff looked at him blankly.

"Blonde woman," John B. said, about to launch into a description.

"Oh. Oh, yeah. She's with the other one." His brow creased. "Tied up, I think. She was over the big one's shoulder."

Stewart grimaced and said, "He's in shock. Wilko, you better stay with him and make sure he doesn't wander off or pass out and fall into a geyser or something."

The Tasmanian winced, but he could see the sense of the suggestion.

"Harlan, I assume you're coming with me," continued the wizard.

His reply was a short nod.

John B. squatted beside Lawson, who gazed in fascination at the *'io*. "Which way did they go?" he asked.

After a moment the lawman pointed towards a spot on the ridge. Stewart and Hunter took off in the direction indicated. Gently Wilko took Lawson's arm and helped him stand. Then he cautiously steered him away from both the vent and the damp, blistered body beside it.

Meanwhile, the others had gone over the ridge. The ferns thinned out considerably here – much of the ground was bare.

Some distance ahead they spotted Namakaeha squatting on the ground beside Haveta's still form. They couldn't make out what she was doing, but the sight was enough to make them increase their speed.

John B. was hampered by the damage to his feet, so Harlan was quickly ahead of him.

The archaeologist leapt at Namakaeha, catching her off guard, grabbing her and knocking her over. It was only as they rolled that he realised how near they were to the edge of a considerable drop. Startled, he instinctively pulled back. That was all the opening Namakaeha needed to land a crashing right cross to his jaw. Harlan fell back stunned - fortunately for him, away from the precipice.

They were at the edge of a jagged spur of the caldera. A steady cloud of steam rising from the depths somewhere behind where Haveta lay was evidence of a deep fissure or fissures somewhere below.

John B. didn't try to repeat his friend's headlong charge. Instead he slowed to a walk.

"We have unfinished business, madam," he called.

Namakaeha's eyes widened in recognition. She half dived, half crawled over to Haveta and fumbled with the object she'd already pulled from her pocket.

"How the hell are you still alive? I threw you to the ancestors at Waipi'o!"

"Like the song says, I get by with a little help from my friends. Seems you didn't think to ask the ancestors if they approve of your plan."

"It doesn't matter! Damn the *'aumakua*! It is Pele who rules! I will wipe away the shame and the indignities that have been heaped on her land and Pele shall reign again!"

John B. nodded, his walk now slow but implacable, never taking his eyes off the woman. "Figured it was something like that. But why now? What was so important about Harry Barber's golf tournament that it triggered all this?"

"Barber was a fool!"

"Granted, yes. But being an idiot doesn't justify being scalded to death. That was a nasty piece of work."

She snarled. "It doesn't matter. You're all going to die anyway. He deserved to go first though!"

"You still haven't said why."

"When he advertised the job, boasted about his damn tournament and its 'grand prize'… That was the final straw – *giving away* our land for a stupid game."

"I thought you said you played golf yourself? Was that a lie?"

"No! Yes! I mean, yes, I do play. That's how I know it's a stupid game!"

"Ah well, I can't argue with you there. A good walk wasted, someone once said."

"The waste is the land – sacred land wasted, for a stupid American game…"

"Hang on, hang on. Credit where it's due please. Scotland's actually the home of golf."

"Alright – an invaders' game!"

"Ah, Space Invaders – there's a game I remember. You'd be too young, wouldn't you?"

"Stop trying to distract me!"

Now John B. was perhaps fifteen feet away from her. Still not close enough to actually *do* anything, even if he'd had any idea of what to do. Close enough to see Harlan lying several feet away, and to see with some relief that Haveta was still breathing.

Namakaeha saw the direction of his glance, and quickly got to her feet. She seized the unconscious woman and lifted her with one hand. With the other she pointed to the device clipped to the wires swathing Haveta.

"This is an impact detonator. You know what happened to Fitzwilliam's store. She's wearing six times as much explosive – when she hits the wall of the crater down there Pele's reign of fire will be reborn! *Pele swallows the sea!*" she screamed and before Stewart could make another move flung the blonde like a rag doll into the air.

"I wish you a safe landing, Haveta!" John B. yelled, even as she disappeared from view.

Time seemed to stand still for a moment as, in their different ways, they braced themselves.

The steam still rose from the caldera but that was all. Baffled, Namakaeha peered over the rim.

"Damn you, Kamapua'a! Damn you – after all this time!"

The wizard couldn't see it, but he figured correctly that Haveta's falling form had been caught in a tangled mass of ferns and the detonator hadn't actually hit anything.

"Pele will not be cheated! I will not be cheated!" Namakaeha pried a large stone from the ground and raised it above her head with both hands, aiming to hurl it down to dislodge her deadly intended sacrifice.

John B. knew he couldn't cover the distance in time to stop her. But a small, feathered nightmare launched from his shoulder. With a keening cry, Hawthorn raked her talons across the woman's face.

Shrieking and still clutching the rock, Namakaeha staggered back a few paces – back over the edge. Her shriek didn't last long.

The *'io* soared aloft on outstretched wings that beat once, twice. She circled over John B. who was looking up, grinning at her. The hawk swooped once, passing just over his head. Then, with a final "*Ee-oh,*" she was gone, heading towards an area of forest her sharp eyes had already spotted.

Stewart got to the precipice and looked over. Haveta lay on a dense cluster of brown and green ferns that projected from the volcano wall, looking as though she was sleeping in an oversized nest. Close by her an area of broken fronds indicated where the descent of the much larger, heavier woman hadn't been stopped.

"Haveta…?" came Harlan's groggy but desperate voice.

"She's okay," said the wizard gently. "She's over here. Don't panic."

Hunter appeared at his side. "When you said 'over' here, you weren't kidding, were you?"

"Between the three cars back over the rise, there must be a length of rope. You go grab it and bring it back. I'll stay here, talk to her and keep her calm if she wakes up. Make sure she doesn't wriggle or roll over."

"I should…"

Stewart cut him off. "You should do exactly what I just said. You can be at the cars and back before I'd hobbled a third of the way in one direction. Now go, mate. Your dear one will be fine!"

And so she was.

.o0o.

34 COLD CALLING

Elizabeth could hear the shiver in John B.'s voice. It wasn't the cool of the Waikoloa night. It was shock. It had kicked in during the (much more sedate) drive back from the Volcanoes National Park, while Stewart sat in the front seat of the Mustang.

Sheriff Lawson had regained his composure, and agreed to take the Hunters in his Firebird to collect their car in Kawaihae. Once rescued, 'defused' and unbound, Haveta had regained consciousness quickly.

"It was a weird thing," said John B. down the phone. "It was as though she'd switched herself off as a protective mechanism, and when she was safe she just turned back on. A bit bruised and battered, but otherwise her usual self."

"Which is more than you sound, babe," replied Elizabeth. "Does all this mean you'll have to stay there for a while longer?"

Stewart almost chuckled. "Funnily enough, I don't think so…"

"I've got a lot of questions I'm going to want answers to!" Barrett Lawson had said.

After settling his dear one in the back of the Pontiac, Harlan had turned to the Sheriff and quietly said, "Yes. I think for a start there are a number of questions you'll be asking yourself."

That prompted a worried look from Lawson as he started his car. Even as the archaeologist was getting into the front passenger seat, his wife had started detailing exactly what she believed had to be done next.

An ambulance had been summoned to collect Harry Barber's body. A Park ranger had been detailed to watch over it in the meantime, with another stationed at the taped off area near the crater's edge. The messy job of cleaning up where Namakaeha had landed would wait until morning.

The two Australians had exchanged looks as the white sedan pulled away.

"There goes a lawman that is about to have the law laid down to him by those two," was Wilko's observation that Stewart recounted.

"But surely, even in Hawaii, there's got to be a legal process," protested Q.

"Oh sure, but Namakaeha is beyond the reach of any earthly court. So too is Harry Barber. Let's say I'm confident that Harlan and Haveta will have made it clear that it wouldn't add anything of value to the Sheriff's final report if Wilko or I were retained for questioning." The wizard yawned expansively. "Sorry sweetheart. Eyelids are slamming shut. It'll feel funny not having Hawthorn nearby. I've gotten used to sharing my bedroom with a bird."

"I'm going to excuse that because you're tired, sir. Otherwise it would count as the worst pick-up line I've ever heard."

"Eh? What? Oh, jeez... Q, sorry, I didn't mean..."

Elizabeth laughed. "I'm teasing! Good night, Sir Galahad. You've rescued the maiden. Now get some sleep. I'll see you soon."

"Really looking forward to that. Good night, pretty lady," was the drowsy reply.

*

Max Ritter sat in the lounge of a comfortable Los Angeles hotel, watching the television. The late news broadcast had just finished.

With a sigh, he took out his mobile phone. He dialed a number few people in the world were privy to.

"Ma'am? Ritter. There is no news of significance from Hawaii. It would seem that everything remains *intact*, I'm afraid. A pity – I had entertained hopes…"

The voice on the other end of the line was cold. Not lifeless, not even emotionless. But devoid of sympathy. "So, this gambit failed?"

"It was always an outside chance," said the Professor, as sanguine as he dared be.

"Many of our most spectacular successes have been what you call an 'outside chance', you know."

"Indeed, ma'am. And that is an important part of what has made those successes spectacular. Where is the glory in the mundane and predictable?" asked Ritter.

"Glory? Is that your ambition? Have you forgotten our ultimate objectives?" The inflection of the voice didn't waver, but the rebuke was obvious.

"Of course not! I seek… alternative approaches."

"That is your nature, and it has ever been thus. Remember, knight, our truest strength."

"Patience."

*

It had taken a while. It had also taken a close encounter with the dead body of Harry Barber. On a positive note, it had also taken the sheer bloody excitement of driving an open top convertible down the Big Island highway at a hundred plus miles per hour.

Wilko was calling Jazz. It was a balmy evening in Hawaii, but a rather less balmy five o'clock in the morning off the Scottish coast on Islay.

Of course, the time differential hadn't occurred to him. Well, it had, but he'd miscalculated somewhat.

The engineer was, nonetheless, wide awake when the phone rang.

"Hey. Hi! It's my favourite little guy! I am *so* glad to hear from you."

"Heh – ah – that's good. Um… sorry it's taken me so long to call you back…"

"It's okay, mate – I figured you were busy winning the golf. So – how's that going?"

Wilko paused. There had been a lot happen in the last few days. Where to begin?

"Last day of play tomorrow. I'm probably… an outside chance. I wouldn't bet on me."

Jazz smiled, "You never would back yourself, would you mate? That's probably one of the things I love about you."

It was said utterly casually – and it landed in the conversation like a hand grenade in a fishpond. There were several seconds of silence while both of them digested the sentence. Then, as if by unspoken agreement, it was like both had failed to hear the moment.

Wilko spoke first. "I'm playing okay, but I'm trailing and the two women leading have both been consistently strong. More than I'm likely to compete with, anyway."

"Oh, come on, you can handle any woman you want… oops… sorry, I could have phrased that better, eh?"

"Just a lot, yeah… So, how are things in Scotland?"

Jazz looked around the bedroom of the cottage she was renting. "Honest answer? I'm not sleeping well. It's weird. It's cold. I'm lonely."

"I'm sorry things are so grim. I wish I could do something to help."

"Thanks. Sorry, sunshine – I didn't mean to bring you down. I've just got a touch of the early morning glums. You've got a big game to get yourself ready for! I want you to get out there and be bloody brilliant!"

The Tasmanian laughed self-consciously. "I'll do my best," he said.

"Seriously, that's all you can ask of yourself, eh?" Quietly she added, "I wish you were here." Then with a little laugh of her own Jazz added, "Hey – get John B. to wish it for us – that should work!"

"I wouldn't encourage him. No, but… I wish I was there, too."

Later that evening it dawned on Wilko just how much he really meant that, but at the time of the call he left it at, "I'll talk to you soon, okay?"

.o0o.

35 WINNERS

After all that had gone before, the last day of golf was perhaps anticlimactic.

Nikki Martin had arrived at the resort at breakfast time to advise that she'd be at the Clubhouse at the end of the game, ready, willing and able to present the prize to the winner.

If she held any remorse for 'Hands On' Harry there was no indication of it. She'd been made director of Royal Green to give Barber someone to deflect trouble onto if required. Now she was sole proprietress, and there was frankly a good deal less likelihood of trouble.

Prior to the start of play some of the group had a quiet conversation, concerned about any prospect of gamesmanship from the Hawaiian golfer or his caddy.

"Please do not concern yourself with Mister Mehameha," said Hoadley. "I will *guarantee* he will not affect the outcome of the game."

Ariane smiled. "I'll help you with that." She gave Glexie an encouraging hug and said, "I won't caddy, but I'll be there, every hole, cheering you on."

"I'll just bet you will," laughed John B. "Wilko, I'd love to be out there with you, but there's no way my feet can sustain eighteen holes."

"It's okay mate, I understand."

It was Hiro who suggested the use of a golf buggy just for the non-participants. The golfers, even Shanks, all preferred to walk.

"It's possible that the term 'to use Shanks' pony', meaning to walk – comes from my family, you know," he said at the first tee.

"Oh yeah?" said Wilko, trying to focus on his game and not in the mood for the Englishman's self-importance.

"Indeed. The family has a history of breeding racehorses. Unfortunately the great majority of them seem to have galloped at little more than walking pace."

Keeaumoku waited for the laughter (which included his own) to die down before taking his tee shot. Perhaps he didn't wait long enough, because it was a disappointing mishit. The Englishman apologised profusely – and to everyone's surprise the apology was accepted gracefully.

The previous night's explanation by the Australians of Namakaeha's plan, and her motivations, seemed to have given real weight to the expression, "It's only a game".

The game progressed in good spirits. In their 'spectators buggy' John B. and Ariane raised a quiet toast to this, sharing from the thermos of bourbon and soda she'd discreetly brought along.

"I must admit, I'm a little surprised that Royal Green is going ahead with the prize, all things considered," remarked John B. idly at one point.

There was a trace of wickedness in Ariane's smile as she replied, "Ms. Martin really didn't have a choice. Harry's commitments were too well documented to be reneged on."

"Uh-huh. A good legal person would have checked and made sure of that."

"And reminded Ms. Martin of the facts yesterday after her business principal was hauled off by the local Sheriff."

The wizard grinned. "So this good legal person is satisfied that the prize is legit?"

"Well, reasonably so. The winner won't actually *own* the property. That's not how things work on Hawaii. It's all leasehold. It turns out Harry had managed to snap up that big parcel of land from a deceased estate at a very good price, not least because there's only ten years to run on the lease before it has to be renegotiated with the State government. There was probably something underhanded about it, but the deal was done before Nikki joined the company and Mr. Barber is past asking, even if you could have gotten a straight answer from him."

"One more thing for Lawson to sort out, if he didn't already know about it."

Stewart looked thoughtful before continuing, "You mean, Harry was never actually 'giving away' a piece of Hawaii. It's really just a piece of paper? Albeit with some rights of tenancy or something I presume. So Namakaeha really was wrong in every sense – that's ironic!"

"I guess she didn't know much about property law. It seems that in more ways than one she was misguided. And I'll drink to that!" said Ariane, pouring more bourbon into their plastic cups.

The question of who had been doing the guiding crossed John B.'s mind, but he didn't mention it. He just raised his cup and replied, "Cheers!"

*

The new sole proprieter of Royal Green Estate proved to be as good as her word, waiting at the Clubhouse when the golfers and their entourage came in from the eighteenth hole.

She'd been watching from the patio, and had joined in the generous applause when Glexie had rolled in an excellent twenty-foot putt to finish the tournament on a note of quality.

Glexie's excited leap into the arms of her roommate said all that was needed to know who had won. The final putt was a bonus – a wayward approach shot two holes earlier had done for Shareta and the New England girl had enjoyed a two shot lead going into the last anyway.

Soon after, Nikki was carrying out the formality of checking the cards.

301

"Looks like everyone had a good game today," she said.

Keeaumoku shrugged. "It was probably the best any of us have played since we started," he conceded.

"That's surprising, given the amount of golf you've all played over the past fortnight. I'd have thought you would have been tired."

"A little, perhaps," said Shareta, who had been the first to congratulate Glexie. "But I think that today we all played feeling, hmm, how to say it – free. As though a malign spirit riding with us had been removed."

If Nikki speculated on whether the Korean was referring to Namakaeha or 'Hands On' Harry, or both, she didn't say. She simply got on with her job.

The small ceremony of handing over the Prize Certificate was conducted to a sincere ovation. Afterwards, Ariane kept a careful eye on proceedings as the paperwork was completed to transfer the possession of a good parcel of beachfront property to Miss Glexandria Hill of Ogunquit, Maine.

*

The final celebratory dinner was a low-key affair. Keeaumoku had already departed, having evidently used up his store of politeness. Glasses were raised, friendships toasted and cemented.

John B. made a point of sharing a couple of drinks with the gentleman's gentleman while Armitage was deep in conversation with Nikki Martin. If she felt so inclined, she was far more likely to secure the Englishman's investment in a piece of property than Harry ever would have been.

"Alas, a fluttering of the eyelashes may be sufficient. Still, if I conduct due diligence on my employer's behalf, it may actually prove to be a worthwhile investment."

"Talk to Ariane…" The wizard saw a gleam in the manservant's eye. "You already have, haven't you?" He laughed. "Hoadley, if I'm ever in the market for a valet come caddy, you're the bloke I want!"

"A generous offer, sir – sorry, John B. However if, as Mister Wilkes has seemed to indicate, the last several days have been not untypical of your life – par for the course, one might say, then I'm afraid I would have to decline. The difficulties and frustrations of service with Mister Shanks shall, for some little while now I think, seem *refreshingly* dull."

Soon after, Glexie surprised everyone by announcing, rather sadly, that she was 'over' her fascination for Hawaii.

"It's a great place to visit, but not to live. Hiro, I've thought about what you said - how 'you don't have to be born here to be Hawaiian' and realised that that's just not me." She gave Ariane an affectionate hug and said, "But hey, we have ten years of visits ahead, if we want."

Kahekili kept his eyes on his beer as he said, "I don't want to sound critical. I truly don't. But that seems to me like a waste, especially when there's a lot of people out there who don't even have a home."

Glexie sighed and said, "I suppose it is, really. But it's not like I've got the money to do anything about it. I've got the land for ten years, and with a bit of luck I could maybe park a trailer on it to stay in when I visit."

A little later in the evening, after a quiet conversation with each other, the Tanabes approached Glexie.

They had a proposition, if Miss Hill was serious? Assured that she was, Hiro explained that they wished to leave Japan and settle in the land of his birth. He would fund the construction of a shelter for the homeless on Glexie's property, and buy an adjoining allotment for himself and his wife to occupy.

"We could perhaps arrange for a small beach house to be kept for your exclusive use when you visit?" suggested Shareta.

"That… that would be nice," said Glexie, a little overwhelmed.

John B. and Ariane exchanged looks that were not so much suspicious as cautious.

"Would you run this place, Hiro?" asked the legal officer. "I mean, with respect, you're not a young man…" She was thinking of the likes of the belligerent Big Ese, unaware that the body of that unfortunate would finally be found in another few days.

Hiro gave a small bow of acknowledgement. "Indeed. I offer to oversee the administration of the enterprise only. I have some experience in business."

"Maybe Courtesy could help?" suggested John B.

Kahekili gave a surprisingly nervous cough. "Um… I'm at a bit of a loose end, employment-wise. I could help? Maintenance, maybe security if it's ever needed."

The wizard gave him a long look. Certainly, the man with the *pahupu* markings could look intimidating. Then he recalled the moment when the tattooed man had stepped in between Namakaeha and Ese outside Fitzwilliam's store.

"That'd be a good thing, if you do go ahead with the idea, Glexie," Stewart observed.

"The more I think about it, the more I think I will. What about you, John B.? Could I talk you into staying on? Using that magic of yours to help protect the new hostel?"

Wilko rolled his eyes. "I keep telling you all, don't encourage him!"

The wizard gave his old friend an indulgent smile. "In this case I reckon the land protected itself," he said, thinking of the *'io* and the *ama'uma'u* ferns, and then the *'aumakua* who had saved his life.

Hiro carefully patted the wizard's bandaged hand and said, "It had help."

"Thanks. No Glexie, I won't stay. Thank you for the thought, but I've got other places to be and other things to do – even if I don't know quite what they are yet. No, the best I can do for you is to wish you all success."

"That should be a big help, my friend," said Ariane.

She put her arms around him. They hugged and shared a tender kiss that would have set tongues wagging back in Kaiser Ron's office. The gossip would have gotten it wrong, of course. Even Wilko, now enjoying his own affectionate hug from Glexie, had figured that out.

*

The flight back to Australia was, as far as John B. and Wilko were concerned, blissfully uneventful. No uncomfortable turbulence, no difficult passengers nearby, no wailing children within earshot. The wizard couldn't have wished for better.

Both of them slept for a substantial part of the journey, and John B.'s rest wasn't disturbed by the strange dreams that had started to plague him.

Even the transition to the connecting flight from Sydney to Canberra went smoothly.

As their plane taxied into Canberra Stewart stretched and said to Wilko, "At least neither of us have to get a cab home, mate. I got a text from Q - sorry, Elizabeth, while we were in Sydney. She's hired a decent sized car to take both of us and our luggage."

"That was nice of her!"

"She reckoned it sounded like we'd both been through quite enough dramas on our 'vacation' to want to face the dubious delights of a Canberra cabbie."

Wilko grinned. "No arguments there. Most of them are okay, but there's some weird ones amongst them, and it'd be just my luck…"

The Tasmanian gave his companion a sidelong look. Being met by Elizabeth was clearly important to him – no surprise there – but it was the first time he could remember seeing Stewart wear anything other than a purple t-shirt. In its place was a bright new button down shirt – a Hawaiian print that was, of course, in purple and white. Still, it was as close as he'd ever seen his pal come to 'dressing well'.

Collecting the baggage and passing through Customs proved as simple as the rest of the trip home.

As they walked out into the terminal John B.'s eyes lit up.

Q was standing waiting for them. She wasn't wearing the conservative, smart attire she normally wore to work, or the nice but non-descript casual clothes they were used to seeing outside office hours.

A shoestring-strapped clingy sea green satin top emphasized her figure in a way the usual loose blouses and shirts never had. Glossy black tights and calf length leather boots enhanced the effect, creating the impression that a fair proportion of the lady's height was made up of legs.

She and John B. greeted each other with enthusiastic hugs. If she was at all perturbed by the dressings on his feet, hands and head she gave no sign of it. Wilko stood back diplomatically.

"Are you okay, Wilko?" Elizabeth asked over Stewart's shoulder. "You're looking like a goldfish."

"I just… haven't seen this side of you before," said Wilko, changing his expression to a smile.

'I haven't seen this *much* of you before' was his unspoken thought. Not disapproving, just surprised. Elizabeth had always seemed so, well, business-like.

If John B. harboured any similar surprise he didn't show it. What he did show was approval.

"You look fabulous, pretty lady."

"You did warn me you'd say that whatever I wore."

"That's true. But it doesn't make it any less sincere."

"The divorce has come through. No more dressing to please anyone else. I'm officially on my own now!"

"If that's what you want," said John B. quietly, taking a small step away.

Elizabeth strode up to him and took his arm. "What do you reckon, babe?" she said, and they exchanged broad smiles.

Wilko smiled to himself. 'Nah, she's not on her own. Neither of them are.'

If there was any wistfulness in the Tasmanian's thought, then he didn't betray it, even to himself. He had a long distance phone call to make when he got home.

.oXXo.

-ALOHA-

The *Dubious Magic* Books:

THE WIZARD OF WARAMANGA

THE CARVINGS OF COBBEMARMOO

THE MAD MACHINES OF MUNDARA

Visit **www.renoirwords.com**

Next: If you die in a dream, do you die for real? It seems like it. John B. and company are in Scotland – home of strong spirits of more than one kind – where someone is using a remarkable power to gain a different sort of power. And what secrets do the three old sisters know?

THE SPIRITS OF SRON DUBH – The Fifth Book of Dubious Magic